I0574398

THE
APOTHECARY'S
APPRENTICE

C.S. Doraga

Dragon's Nest Books

THE APOTHECARY'S APPRENTICE

Copyright © 2025 by C. S. Doraga

All rights reserved. Printed in the United States of America. No part of this book may be used or reproduced in any manner whatsoever without written permission except in the case of brief quotations embodied in critical articles or reviews.

This book is a work of fiction. Names, characters, businesses, organizations, places, events, and incidents either are the product of the author's imagination or are used fictitiously. Any resemblance to actual persons, living or dead, events, or locales is entirely coincidental.

No Generative AI Training Use.

For avoidance of doubt, Author reserves the rights, and [Publisher/Platform] has no rights to, reproduce and/or otherwise use the Work in any manner for purposes of training artificial intelligence technologies to generate text, including without limitation, technologies that are capable of generating works in the same style or genre as the Work, unless [Publisher/Platform] obtains Author's specific and express permission to do so. Nor does [Publisher/Platform] have the right to sublicense others to reproduce and/or otherwise use the Work in any manner for purposes of training artificial intelligence technologies to generate text without Author's specific and express permission.

First Edition: 2025

Cover Design by 100 Covers

ISBN (paperback): 979-8-9985869-0-3
ISBN (hardback): 979-8-9866198-9-7
ISBN (ebook): 979-8-9985869-1-0

Also By C.S. Doraga

WOLVES OF HIGHFELL SAGA
(can be read in any order)
The Apothecary's Apprentice

RISE OF THE EMPRESS
Defy
Shatter
Ignite
Storm (Coming Soon)

To the crew at Legacy,
who ensured I high fived the roof

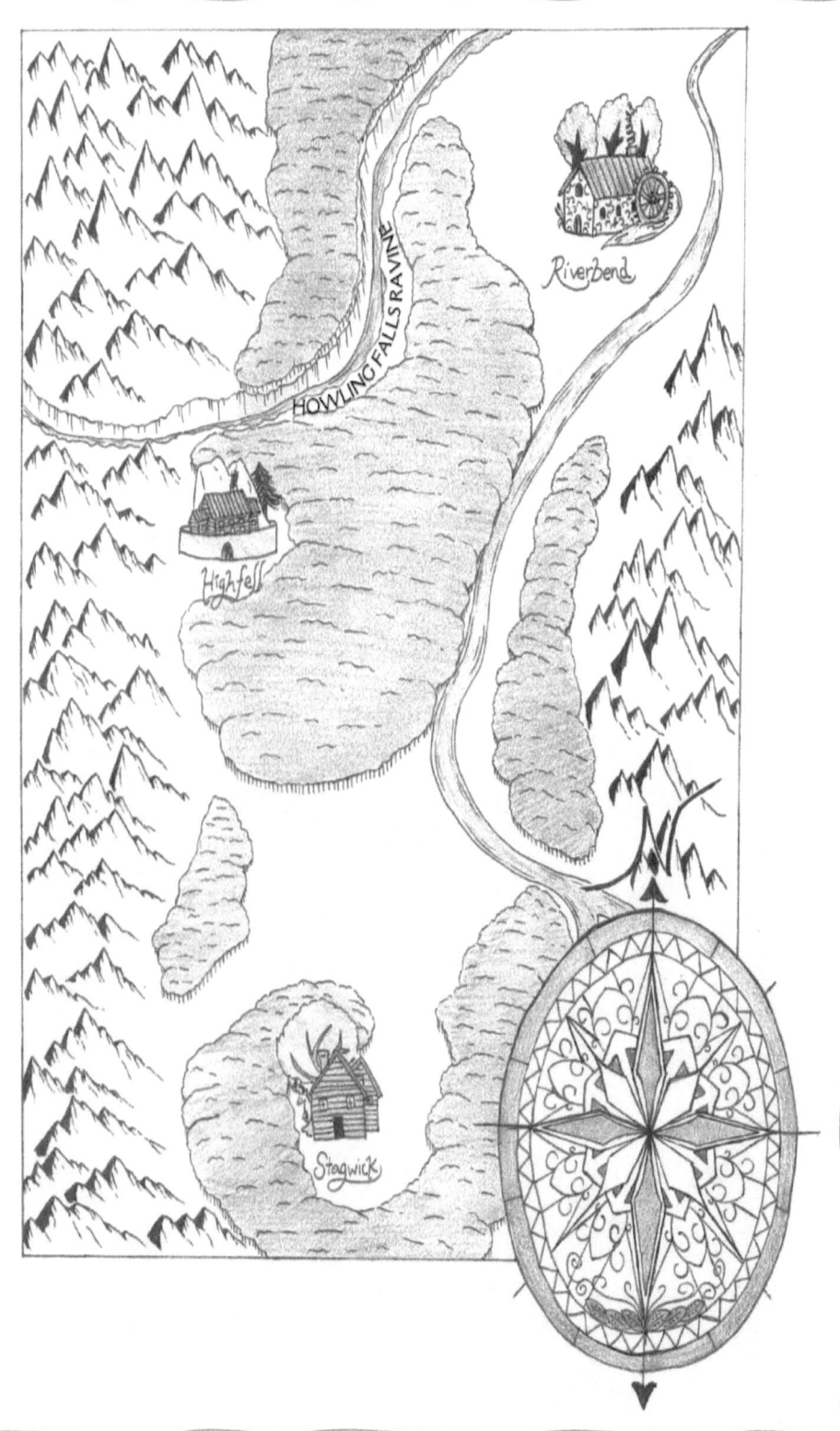

Pronunciation Guide

Cast (in order of appearance):

Daciana:	DAH-see-ah-nah
Florin:	FLOH-rin
Sorin:	SOH-rin
Calin:	KA-lin
Ionel:	AI-nehl
Radu:	RAH-doo
Aurel:	OR-ehl
Fen:	fehn
Petre:	PEH-treh
Gavril:	GAV-ril
Mitica:	mi-TI-cah
Ecaterina:	eh-KAH-tah-ree-nah
Liviu:	LEE-vioo
Andrei:	AHN-drey
Nelu:	NEH-loo
Marian:	MAIR-ee-an
Narcisa:	nahr-SIS-sa
Bogdan:	BAHG-dan
Eusiebiu:	YOO-see-boo
Raluca:	RAH-loo-kah
Tania:	TAH-nee-ah
Sabina:	SAH-bee-nah
Lucia:	LOO-shah
Crina:	KREE-nah
Violeta:	VAI-oh-leh-tah
Cornel:	KOR-nehl

Silviu:	SIL-vio
Dragos:	DRAH-gohs
Sebastian:	seh-BAS-chan
Mihai:	MEE-hai
Reanu:	REE-noo
Xandru:	ZAN-droo
Felicia:	feh-LEE-shah
Boian:	BOY-ahn
Nicolae:	NI-koh-lay
Razvan:	RAZ-van

THE
APOTHECARY'S
APPRENTICE

1

Plants brought both life and death, healing and hurting. The right plant could save. The wrong would kill. Daciana had known this for as long as she could remember, the words so deeply ingrained, they might as well have been inscribed on her heart and written in her blood.

A gentle hush lay over the forest as she worked, the golden light of the early morning filtering between the branches of the towering oaks and pines. A few hesitant birds let out cascading notes of song, filling the air around Daciana with a hum of life that didn't quite exist anywhere else. This was another one of the reasons why she loved being an apothecary.

She smiled as she snipped tall, dew-laced feverfew stalks, adding each one to her basket with care. Tomorrow morning, before heading into the workshop, she'd have to hunt for more chamomile. Her favorite gathering spot wasn't quite ready, so she'd have to rise before the sun in order to trek out to the next best patch and return in time to help Master Florin prepare to open for the day.

As her thoughts turned to her master, she remembered the day he'd come to her home and requested the right to take her as his apprentice, even though she'd been a mere eight years of age. Because her dad had chosen to marry a woman from a nomadic tribe, she, their child, hadn't been accepted in the village, but that hadn't stopped Master Florin from arriving on their stoop and asking her dad to let him take her on as his apprentice.

'A natural gift, she has,' he'd said, his warm, rich tones, making Daciana take an immediate liking to him despite the fact she'd hidden behind her dad's legs. 'And I want to help her make the most of it.'

In the end, her mom had talked her dad into it, and since that day, Daciana had walked the path of an apothecary.

Once she'd gathered a few more stalks, Daciana rose and stretched the stiffness out of her back and legs. Then, once she'd covered her basket, she turned and began the walk towards home, admiring the sky as she went. The rising sun crested the eastern mountains, washing the heavens with gentle pinks and golds, the deep velvet purple of night giving way to the soft blue of morning.

The shadows of the mountains receded as she walked back to the village of Highfell—towards home—listening to the lingering strains of a few brave crickets as the songs of the birds filled the air. It wasn't a long walk, but she always enjoyed it all the same.

Before long, the large stone wall ringing the village came into sight, the iron-wrought lanterns already extinguished for the day.

As she neared the gate, the watchmen on duty didn't turn to greet her, but that was because they were deep in conversation with the notorious watch leader, Sorin.

At least, people whispered he was notorious. She hadn't spoken with him all that often; they'd only crossed paths a handful of times and only when they had reason to. In truth, Daciana didn't think notorious was a good word for him—stoic was. Then again, she supposed that was the demeanor required of one who'd been given the responsibility of the entire village's safety when he was only twenty.

When she drew level with the gate, one of the watchmen noticed her and waved her in, but unexpectedly, Sorin halted his conversation and whirled to face her.

Daciana paused, almost startled by his abruptness.

"Why are you out of the village so early?"

In response, she lifted the cloth covering the basket. "It's my job to gather the herbs for medicine. I'm Master Florin's apprentice, you know?"

He studied her basket with an unusual level of scrutiny. Granted, every time Daciana saw Sorin study something, it seemed as though he was searching for its soul. "I see. Feverfew, isn't it?"

"That's right," she replied, a small part of her pleased he'd figured out what it was. Beyond her and Master Florin, few people could recognize any herbs on sight.

"Do you have to travel far for these?" he asked, lifting his deep brown gaze from the basket to her face.

She shook her head. "Not usually. Most everything we use grows close by. However, I will have to go a bit far tomorrow for the next herb I need."

He frowned. "Wolves have been spotted in the area. You shouldn't go out alone."

She frowned in response. "There's plenty of game in the forest right now, so I doubt they'd waste their energy going after me. They only attack humans when they're desperate, right?"

"Yes, but," he began, brow furrowing, "they might take the chance if you're alone. It's not unheard of."

"Don't worry about me," she said, shifting her basket from one arm to the other. "I know how to handle myself with wolves around. But thank you anyway." Dipping her head his way, she turned and entered the village, heading up the main road towards Master Florin's workshop.

Yep, if anything, Daciana thought Sorin leaned more towards

obstinate and reserved than notorious. After all, while she could, in all likelihood, handle herself in the event of wolves, it would've been difficult—perhaps impossible—if he hadn't thought to warn her. Sometimes, it was hard for her to believe he was only twenty when he seemed so mature. After all, she was the same age, and compared to him, she felt like a child.

Maybe that was just what happened when she was from a small family of little to no consequence to the village while he was from the magical head family; he'd probably been born with more maturity than she had.

Shaking those thoughts away, Daciana opened the rickety wooden gate that led to her master's well-maintained herb garden. He'd spent a great deal of time in his youth cultivating rarer and more difficult to obtain herbs so that they could be grown here, always on hand when needed. Many different shades of green peeked out from between stands of small flowers, some pale white while others bore deep purples and blues. The wind stirring the plants carried faint hints of both mint and cinnamon, and the breeze made the fluffy heads of the chives bob. Bees were already busy at work amongst the plants, and once the gate was closed, it was as though Daciana had stepped into the realm of a peaceful fantasy land, completely detached from her village and the problems that came with it. The garden was one of her favorite things about the workshop.

She knocked on the large wooden door of the workshop before letting herself in.

Master Florin sat at the worktable in the center of the room, extracting tiny leaves from a fragile, dried plant with a look of intense focus on his face. Without looking up, he said, "Welcome, Daciana."

"Good morning, Master," she called as she walked into the back. They didn't speak again while she dismantled the plants, setting both the flowers and the leaves out to dry, while placing the stems aside.

When she finished and returned to the main room, Master Florin still hunched over his project, concentrating so hard, the tip of his tongue protruded from between his teeth. She shook her head, unable to help smiling a little.

A few shrieks of laughter carried to them through the open window, getting Master Florin to glance up. "I guess the wedding is going to start soon."

"Were you invited, Master?" she asked. Her master was a favorite amongst the villagers. He seemed to be invited to every wedding, every birthday party—everything.

Because of Daciana's heritage, she was...less welcome to such things.

"I was, yes," he said, and, with a dejected air, he set down his project. "I suppose we'd better go."

"Thank you, Master, but I wasn't invited," she said, glancing towards the back room again. "We have lots to do here, so I'll be all right."

Slowly, Master Florin rose to his feet, glancing at her as he did so, and she had a pretty good idea of what he was about to say. "Daci, as my apprentice, the invitation extends to you as well. No one will be bothered if you come with me."

She smiled, though under his stern gaze, it was a strain to keep it fixed in place. "It's okay, Master. I'm fine."

"Daci," he said, his voice soft but still scolding, "You can't keep yourself shut up forever. Our little village would love you if you'd just let them get to know you."

She dug her nails into her palms, doing her best to keep a smile on her face. "Master, really, it's okay. You should go have fun."

He held her gaze for a minute longer before sighing. He didn't say it, but the disappointment in his blue eyes was evident. "If that's what you wish, Daciana." With a parting nod, he stepped outside.

After a moment's hesitation, she wandered over to the little window, watching her master join the others making their way to the main square.

There were a lot of people, so she supposed whoever was getting married must be from one of the more influential families in town. Daciana wasn't offended; her family was never invited to such things, and the resulting sting had faded a long time ago.

Even still, a part of her wondered what it would be like to go with her master, to walk out there and pretend she fit in. More than likely, no one except her master would talk to her, the other village girls would sit and gossip behind their hands while taking surreptitious looks at her before bursting into giggles, and it wouldn't be long before the head family chased her off like she was no more than a stray cat.

Tucking those feelings away, Daciana abandoned the window and returned to her work in the back. There was plenty for her to do here, so she was fine.

After a while, the distant peals of laughter and strains of music faded, and she supposed the wedding must have started. She wasn't sure who was getting married, but she thought she'd heard it was one of the watchmen. Either way, she remained focused on her work, but she found herself glancing up when a loud cheer rose from the distant crowd. Perhaps that meant the ceremony was over.

A few minutes later, it grew loud enough outside that Daciana took her mortar and pestle with her as she went and checked the window, just in time to glimpse a handful of the watchmen rush towards the gate. She hoped it wasn't anything too serious calling them away. Even still, after a moment more of thought, she set aside her grinding and laid out a few strips of bandages, just in case.

The morning wore on, and around noon, there came an urgent knock at the door. Daciana glanced up before hurrying to the door. Her eyes went wide at the sight of Sorin, but a split second later, she spotted the man he supported, a significant amount of blood dripping from the fellow's hand.

"My men are fetching Master Florin," Sorin said.

"We don't have to wait for him," she said, shoving the door open wide. She pointed to the couch under the window. "Put him there." Then she raced to gather the bandages she'd laid out and a couple of the herb jars from the cabinets along the back wall, setting them on the nearby table before running to fetch water. By the time she returned, Sorin had cut away the man's tunic to expose a rather nasty wound to his shoulder, and Daciana got to work straight away.

It needed to be cleaned first, and then slowing the bleeding was her next priority. There were a handful of herbs she could use, but in her opinion, yarrow was the best.

Once most of the grime was flushed out, she sprinkled yarrow powder over his wound before clamping a clean towel over the wound and pressing hard. Given the fact the poor man had been stabbed, this would take a few minutes.

She glanced to the side, noting Sorin hovering nearby, almost appearing a little lost.

"What happened?" she asked, hoping it might distract the young man from the situation a little.

"Thornwood Fell Bandits," was all Sorin answered, however.

It was all the explanation she needed though. Little skirmishes like these broke out often between them and the Thornwood Fell Bandits— a rogue bunch of men who seemed to take delight in murder and plunder. There'd been many attempts to pluck them out, but as of yet, none had been successful. Daciana didn't much fear threats like wolves or bears, but the bandits did make her uneasy. She knew her father often worried about her excursions into the woods alone, but, fortunately, the bandits had never been very active in the early mornings.

A few minutes later, she gently lifted the towel to check the bleeding. It'd slowed to a trickle, which was good. So long as the man rested, he would recover fine.

As she wrapped the wound, Master Florin arrived. "Ah, see? With my apprentice here, you didn't need me, as I said."

Despite the situation, a smile tugged at the corner of her mouth. "On the contrary, Master, a second pair of hands is always welcome." She glanced at him as he approached.

He waggled his aging hands. "Aye, two sets are nice, but perhaps not if one of them look like mine."

"Master, your hands are fine, and I'm sure they will be for many years to come."

He laughed, the sound warm and rich. "Don't listen to my apprentice, Sorin. She would have me working long past my season."

Sorin watched their exchange in silence, his gaze bouncing back and forth between the two of them. However, to her surprise, there was the slightest, just detectable upturn of the corners of his mouth and a hint of an amused light shining in his eyes. "We would miss you if you were to retire."

Master Florin threw up his hands. "All my dreams of being a gardener—ruined by hooligans!"

Daciana laughed, and to her surprise, even Sorin's smile became more noticeable. If she'd given room to the rumors, she would've believed him incapable of smiling at all.

Shaking those thoughts away, Daciana glanced at Sorin. "Your fellow will be fine so long as he gets some rest. If you tell us where he lives, we'll bring by some medicine to help with the pain as soon as it's ready."

Sorin gave them the information and in short order, his fellow watchman was on his way, with Sorin close by his side.

Master Florin watched them walk up the lane. "I feel a bit foolish having come up here. Do forgive me, Daciana."

"You haven't offended me, Master," she said as she cleaned up after their patient. "I appreciated you coming."

"No, you're just being kind," he said approaching her and tapping the silver, leaf-shaped necklace she wore. "I am very eager for the day—

the fast-approaching day, mind you—for when you get to trade your silver leaf for your gold one."

She fingered her leaf. A gold leaf would mean she was a Master Apothecary, a true apothecary in her own right. Once she had it, she could move out on her own and run her own shop, she could earn more money for her family... In fact, there was a chance she could earn enough to move her family out of the village altogether. They could go somewhere where they didn't have to hide from the rest of town and have real jobs, real means of support instead of just getting by. After all, while the idea of her own shop held some allure, she didn't want to be in competition with her master.

"I'm only earning it because I have a good teacher," she said.

For some reason, instead of the smile and laugh she'd expected, he paused, staring at her. "Daciana, you are a thoughtful young woman, but your compassion is wasted on a withered old man like me."

She caught the hint there but simply smiled. "It's not a waste."

A smile tugged on the corner of his mouth. "Don't be like that. You're a wonderful, smart young woman, and you deserve someone who'll devote themselves to you and make you happy. It's better than drying out like a pathetic old plant, believe you me. At least plants are useful when they age."

That made her laugh.

"Daciana, are you sure you don't want to come to the wedding? It'll be more enjoyable with you there. Plus there are many wonderful young men there; you might meet someone special."

"As if," she said with a bit of a laugh. "Go on, Master. You'll have more fun if you don't linger here with me."

He let out a sad little sigh before slipping out the door and leaving Daciana alone once more. Even still, she smiled a little. Master Florin was a sweet man, and not for the first time, she wondered why he'd never married. It wasn't any of her business, but even still, a part of her appreciated his sentiment that she should seek that out for herself, though she wasn't sure marriage would ever be in her future. She had too much responsibility to her family to consider tossing them aside for the sake of such desires, plus she didn't plan on living in this village for the rest of her life.

That said, what would be the point while she was still trapped in a village where the men never gave her more of a passing glance anyway? Most important of all, Daciana wasn't alone nor was she lonely. The path of an apothecary may have been a solitary one, but she had her family and Master Florin. She was happy—truly happy—with her life as it stood. She didn't need anybody else.

2

Sorin debated the meager list of places he could go to hide from the hubbub of his friend's wedding and the men and women attempting to introduce him to their daughters. Even his friend—the star of the wedding, Calin—kept trying to get him to dance with his cousin. He didn't want to, plus he was a bit sore from their impromptu skirmish earlier; though he was grateful Radu would be all right.

After a few minutes of wandering and ducking out of sight, he stumbled across Master Florin and his uncle, Ionel, tucked away in a quieter corner of the village square, talking and laughing.

Sorin blinked. "Sorry."

"Don't worry about it, Sorin," Master Florin said. "On the contrary, why don't you sit with us?"

"I imagine you're hard pressed for company," his uncle joked, almost making Sorin crack a smile.

"Thanks," he said, slipping onto the bench next to his uncle.

"So how's being the village watch leader?" Master Florin asked, leaning forward. "I'm sure it's been an adjustment."

"I'm doing my best." In truth, he was inadequate. For example, just today, if he'd been more prepared or faster, Radu wouldn't have gotten hurt. If it hadn't been for his second-in-command, he doubted they would've gotten through that fight with no further injuries or no casualties. However, nobody wanted to hear him say those things, so he kept quiet.

"It is a big job," Ionel said, thoughtfully swirling the drink in his cup. "I was a bit surprised when Elder Aurel assigned it to you, but now that I've seen you at it, I'm not sure he couldn't chosen someone better suited."

Sorin's insides squirmed with discomfort, but he stayed still.

"I wasn't surprised at all," Master Florin said with a grin. "Especially since he has you to guide him, Ionel. I don't think he could ask for a better teacher than one of the best watch members we've ever had."

Ionel laughed.

"I think the village is in good hands. After all, he handled today's skirmish well enough." Master Florin said, shooting Sorin a sly grin.

"That's true," Ionel said, clapping him on the back. "You did a good job taking care of that. Is Radu doing well? I heard he was a bit bad off."

Sorin nodded. "Master Florin's apprentice put him on the mend without delay." In truth, he'd been a bit surprised by her efficiency. However, he supposed it made sense. Just a couple days ago, he'd overheard Master Florin discussing elevating his apprentice to the rank of master with Elder Aurel, the village elder. Without a doubt, she was skilled if her master deemed her ready to set out on her own. He'd never realized it since he rarely saw her; while he'd heard rumors and speculations about her, she'd always kept to Master Florin's workshop and to herself.

"Speaking of," Ionel said, "I see you couldn't manage to convince her to come with you once again, Florin. Is she still shy?"

"A bit, but she has...other reasons for not coming." Master Florin smiled in apology.

Sorin sensed something else behind those words, but he couldn't figure out what. Even still, it made him wonder.

"Sorin!" Calin called, and Sorin flinched a little. He supposed there wouldn't be a chance for such ruminations now.

Getting to his feet, Sorin excused himself. "I'm going to find somewhere else to hide."

"Good luck!" Ionel called with a bit of a grin.

Sorin hurried away, just managing to evade Calin by ducking behind a house. Some part of him appreciated his friend's efforts—he meant well by them—but even still, there wasn't any point. Sorin's life had never been his own; while he appreciated Master Florin's compliment about his ability as watch leader, it would've been nicer if it had been a career he'd wanted. It would've been nicer if it'd been something he'd gotten to choose.

But he hadn't. He doubted Elder Aurel, his grandfather, would even let him choose who he wanted to marry, and the idea of that made him shudder. Dread filled him at the thought of marriage, and as his twenty-first birthday marched closer, he wasn't sure how much longer he could escape it.

All his life, he'd been kept on a short leash, but now he couldn't help thinking the end of his tether lay only inches away. How many more days like today could he survive before something he couldn't handle came? What would Elder Aurel do if he failed? Worse still, what else would the elder dictate about his life?

By the time the wedding finished, Daciana had completed most of the projects she and Master Florin had and was exhausted. Her heart skipped at the prospect of going home. Master Florin had returned to the workshop, toiling away at his earlier project, when she left the back room.

"Don't stay too late," she called as she headed out.

"Good night, Daci," he replied without looking up from his project.

Leaving the workshop, she turned down the lane and walked to the little cottage at the end, near the edge of the tall stone wall surrounding the entire village. Home.

Before she'd even stepped in the door, the warm scents of dinner reached her nose, making her aware of how hungry she was. Hastening her step, she hurried inside, the warm, aromatic smell of her mom's cooking enveloping her in a comforting embrace. She grinned as her dad gave her an enormous hug, and they both chuckled at her two younger brothers squabbling over the finer details of a building they'd sketched in the earthen floor. As they settled down for supper, she did her best to tuck her exhaustion out of sight, spending most of the meal listening to her brothers chatter about the bits of the wedding they'd managed to sneak peeks of.

While her work as an apothecary was solitary, the long hours never bothered her because she always came home to this. All her happiness was right here, more than enough to sustain her through the monotony of her career's isolation. While some part of her did want to get married, she was okay if it never happened. She'd long been reconciled to the reality that because of circumstances beyond her control, she'd live the rest of her days alone. However, so long as she had her family, she'd be all right.

Later, full and sleepy, Daciana headed to bed, curling up on her little cot in the attic. The window was propped open, letting the cool summer breeze blow through, bringing with it the occasional lilt of wolf song. Her last thought before she drifted to sleep was that Sorin had been telling the truth after all.

When Daciana reached the village gate early the next morning, she pulled up short, nearly tripping over her own feet. Sorin already waited there, leaning against the stone wall near the smaller guard's door, eyes closed and arms folded. In truth, there was such a serene air about him, she couldn't help wondering if he'd slept there.

Doing her best to stay quiet, Daciana crept past him. She didn't want to attract any untoward attention, and having Sorin, of all people, escorting her to gather herbs was a sure way to do that.

However, as she lifted the latch, he said, "Sneaking out?"

She jumped, banging the latch against the wood. Covering it with both hands to keep it still and quiet, she looked askance at him. "What was that for?"

He stared back with a blank expression, though, after a moment, she couldn't help noting the subtle turning up of his mouth at the corners. "I didn't do anything."

Choosing to ignore that, she finished unlatching the side door and said, "Don't you know how early it is?"

He lifted an eyebrow. "Wolves are the most active around this time."

She stared, and he stared back, arms still folded. A full minute passed with neither of them yielding.

Since she needed to get to work, she relented. "Suit yourself."

"I will." He followed her out the guard's door. "Thank you."

She risked a peek over her shoulder at him before fixing her gaze straight ahead. Two more words to describe him struck her: stubborn and determined. It was a rare person who would get up this early in order to escort someone they barely knew.

On the other hand, he was the watch leader, so perhaps rising at the crack of dawn was something he regularly did without much thought.

Her gaze lifted to the sky as they walked, taking in the faintest smear of pale blue and wheat-yellow light brushing along the horizon. It was early enough only a handful of people were awake, and while she was used to it, she imagined there was a good chance Sorin was not. Hopefully he wouldn't pass out before the day was over.

After a while of walking with her new shadow only a pace behind, Daciana glanced back. "You truly think wolves would come after us?"

He shrugged a shoulder. "Like you said, the chances are slim. However, a lot of males leave their packs and strike out on their own, and some even get chased out, so a desperate one could try it." No expression passed over his face as he spoke, which she wasn't sure how to take. Regardless, he made a fair point.

They walked the rest of the way to the chamomile patch in silence, and once they arrived, Daciana gathered her herbs with Sorin trailing behind her, his gaze roving the nearby fell and surrounding forest the entire time. He took his job seriously indeed.

Once her basket was full of chamomile fronds with their cheery, daisy-like flowers, the sun itself peeked over the eastern horizon, washing a few lingering clouds with pale gold light.

Rising, she hefted her basket onto her arm, using her hip to help counterbalance the weight. Sorin moved as though he was about to offer to help, but all at once, a howl split the quiet of the meadow, making a chill settle over the forest. Daciana glanced at Sorin, who stared towards the fell, so she turned to it as well. There really were wolves, and that one had sounded close.

"It's nothing serious," Sorin said at last. "Wolves howl to talk to each other, and that one wasn't as close as it sounded."

She nodded, and they left. Like they had pretty much the entire time, they walked in silence, and the absence of conversation allowed Daciana's mind to wander. Her thoughts returned to her master's words from yesterday.

'You deserve someone who'll devote themselves to you and make you happy.' In truth, she wasn't sure she'd ever find someone like that—at least, not so long as she lived in this village.

Even still, remembering that brought yesterday's wedding to mind. If she remembered right, Sorin was one of the oldest bachelors in the village, and Daciana herself only had a couple unmarried young women older ahead of her. There were other young men besides Sorin close to his age, but even still, among the ladies, he was the one they talked about the most, which (when she snuck a peek at him and allowed herself to admit it) was because with his dark brown eyes and hair, strong jaw-line, and well-built frame, he was quite handsome. Plus, he was a member of the head family. Marrying into his family would elevate anyone in the village, and there was always the chance you'd bear a child who could wield magic, something unique to his family. That too would grant you a considerable amount of prestige.

She shook her head. All of that was a mess, and to be frank, she found the idea of marrying someone just so you'd wouldn't have to do as much hard labor around the village such a wanton use of something like marriage. Though perhaps, since she'd been taken on as the apothecary's apprentice as a child and enjoyed her work, she couldn't relate to the women who toiled in the shops and the fields.

Those thoughts kept her occupied for the rest of the walk back to the village, and before long, they were within the safety of its large stone wall. Even still, Sorin tagged along behind her.

She glanced back over her shoulder. "I appreciated you following me out there, but it's a little weird in here."

"I'm not following you," he explained. He pointed a few blocks up the street, towards a wood building a bit longer and taller than most the others. "That's the main watchhouse and it's where I'm going."

"Ah, forgive my assumption." She eyed the stern expression on his face. "Are you going to insist someone tags along with me the next time I go out?"

"When is the next time you go out?"

"The next time an herb is low, so...in a couple days, I imagine."

All he said in response was: "The wolves will still be around."

So...she supposed that meant yes? Another word: laconic. In an okay way, though, she supposed.

Shaking that thought away as she reached the workshop gate, Daciana dipped her head to Sorin, who'd stopped when she had. "Thank you for coming with me today."

He dipped his head in acknowledgement of her gratitude. And remained where he was. Was he going to wait until she'd gone inside? She supposed that was just polite, but still...

"M-make sure you eat breakfast," she said in a rush before hurrying through the gate. She didn't hear footsteps, so he must really be waiting there. Her cheeks flushed, but she took a deep, calming breath. If she was quick, no one would see and harass her about it later.

Daciana hurried to the porch, knocking on the door before grabbing the latch and pushing. To her surprise, the door didn't open. After a moment's hesitation, she tried again, having to push with all her strength. The door moved a little, accompanied by a harsh grating that vibrated the wooden porch, but it still didn't open.

Sweat trickled down her back. This was abnormal. Strange enough to set her heart pounding against her ribs.

"Master Florin?" she called. He was always here before her, so maybe he was in the middle of a strange project. "Are you in?"

There was no answer.

"Master Florin?"

"Is something wrong?" Sorin called from behind her, her nerves jangled enough she actually jumped.

Slowly, she glanced back, and the second their gazes met, Sorin let himself through the gate. Daciana had never been skilled at hiding her emotions, and the panic zipping through her veins must've been showing through.

"The door's not locked, but I can't get it open. And there was no answer when I called," she said once Sorin reached the porch, her voice hushed because of the tightness of her throat. "Master Florin never does anything like this."

With a frown, Sorin gave the door an experimental push before putting his weight into it. The door gave way at a begrudging pace that made her agitation fester, whatever blocked the way grating against the floor as it moved, the rattling of the floorboards making her teeth grind against each other.

Daciana's heart pounded a frantic rhythm in her chest like a caged bird. She prayed nothing was wrong and she was simply overreacting to an abnormal situation.

It was nearly a full, agonizing minute before Sorin forced the door open enough to allow him to slip through. However, once he was inside, he didn't say a word.

Hands shaking, Daciana set down her basket before worming her way in after him.

Master Florin's overturned worktable had been blocking the door, but even more shocking was the state of complete and utter upheaval the rest of the room was in. The cabinets in the back wall were thrown open, one of the doors only hanging on by a single hinge, plants and glass scattered across the floor. The overturned worktable lay against the door, and Master Florin's stool lay on the other side of the room with one leg missing. The large rug in front of the hearth twisted like it was in pain, and even the couch under the window had been upended, cushions strewn haphazardly nearby.

However, where her gaze fell was the center of the mess, where Master Florin lay lifeless in a pool of his own blood.

3

Sorin had seen a few crimes scenes since he'd taken over as watch leader a few months ago, but this was the first time he'd encountered a murder. Master Florin, of all people, was dead. Killed by someone.

Almost as if in a daze, Daciana took halting steps towards the body and crouched next to it, hand trembling as she touched two fingers to the man's neck. From the way she lifted her hand before clenching it and pressing it tight to her chest, he knew she hadn't felt a pulse.

He was really dead. Even though just yesterday, they'd had a laugh in his workshop and he'd given Sorin a place to hide during Calin's wedding.

Though it took significant effort, Sorin fought off the shock. He didn't have time to stand here gawking. Stepping forward, he put his hands on Daciana's shoulders, aiming to steer her towards the door.

She didn't budge, instead staring back at him with wide, glistening eyes that made his chest ache a little. "He's dead," she whispered.

"I know," he said, doing his best to be gentle. "And it's my job to figure out who did it. You should go sit outside."

She didn't respond, but she did let him guide her out the door and set her down on the front steps.

"Stay here, understand?" he said.

She nodded.

He then walked to the gate at a brisk pace, scanning the street for one of his fellow watchmen. At this time of day, someone ought to be on their way to the guardhouse—

"Fen!" he called, getting the older fellow's attention.

The man spun on his heel and hurried over.

"Get a few of the others and get back here as fast as possible."

"What's wrong?" Fen asked, brow knitting.

Sorin hesitated before he sighed. "There's been a murder."

The older man paled, but Sorin strode back to the workshop after no more than a glimpse. Murder. A murder had never happened in the village as long as he'd been alive. The last murder had taken place fifty years ago, in a time distant enough, few people remembered it or even knew of it. So why had one happened now?

As his mind caught hold of that thought, Sorin shook off the shock constricting his mind, his thoughts clearing. The question he needed to be asking is why Master Florin was killed. That was what he needed to focus on.

He ventured back inside the house, took a deep breath, and stepped over to the body. His nose curled at the sight, the urge to vomit following close behind, but after a minute of staring, he was certain it was safe to conclude the cause of death was the man's partially smashed-in skull. Apart from that, he couldn't find another wound on the man's body. It was strange to think, but he was glad the man's suffering had been brief—perhaps only a few seconds, no more than a few minutes.

After a moment of thought, that made Sorin frown. The room was in such a state of upheaval, he'd suspected a struggle, but the man's knuckles were neither bloody or blemished. No mark beyond the wound that had killed him marred his body. Odd.

Sorin turned his attention to the rest of the room. The heavy worktable lay behind the door while its accompanying stool rested on the other side of the room, a leg absent. He frowned, eyeing the remaining legs.

"Perhaps big enough to have been the murder weapon, especially since..." He trailed off as he studied the room once more. The missing leg was absent from the space.

He didn't pay much attention to the twisted rug as he inspected the hearth. His eyes narrowed. In the hearth's smoldering belly lay the fire-eaten remnants of a smooth and polished piece of wood, unlike the rest of the half-burnt logs. That and its shape was similar to the rest of the stool legs. Most likely the murder weapon then.

The door behind him creaked open, making Sorin turn. Fen stood there with a few of the others, their faces paling as they took in the scene. Each of them made a hand gesture of respect before dipping their heads in prayers.

Sorin waited until they'd finished before speaking. "I want two of you to stand guard at the gate. No one is to come in or out of this place without my say so."

Two men nodded and went out.

"Next I need someone to send the watch out on extra patrols and someone else to inform Master Florin's sister before telling the head family. Lastly, I need someone to go for the carpenter."

The remaining three of them left, leaving Sorin to his thoughts again.

A minute later, he sensed more than heard someone else enter and glanced back to find Master Florin's apprentice standing in the doorway, her hand on the doorknob.

"You should stay outside," he said.

"I'm fine," she said, though her voice was quiet and subdued. "I figured you'd have questions, and I'm the only one who can answer them."

He hesitated at first, but if she felt up to it, now was as good a time as any. He stepped over to her, not entirely realizing it when he placed himself between her and her master's body.

"There was no sign of a forced entry," he said, "and the door wasn't locked. Is that normal?"

Daciana nodded, making the ends of the blue scarf wrapped around her dark hair bob a little. "Whenever Master Florin was here, he'd leave the door unlocked in case someone needed him. He always stayed late and came in early."

"When was the last time you saw Master Florin?"

"Last night, as I was leaving."

His gaze shifted to her basket, but before he could ask his question, she said:

"The basket was my master's, but since gathering the herbs is my responsibility, I take it home with me at night. Then I go gather what we need before I come in."

"Have there been any threats? Anyone hanging around or coming by more often than they should?"

She shook her head.

He frowned. A few more pieces, but they didn't help him yet. If Master Florin left the door unlocked, anyone could've come and gone without leaving a trace. Plus, no one had been behaving in a way to make his apprentice suspicious.

Daciana stepped past him, arms wrapped around her waist like she was cold as she gazed at the room, studying the epitome of chaos. Sorin watched, waiting to see what she would notice since she was familiar with this room.

Slowly, she approached her master's body once more, but she wasn't focused on him. After a couple minutes of staring, her gaze made its way to the shelves taking up the better part of the back wall. Some of them still held their jars, and, all at once, he recalled that there'd been a dozens more jars on those shelves yesterday.

Daciana moved closer to the shelves, standing with one hand extended towards them.

"Miss Daciana," he called.

She'd jumped twice today when he'd spoken to her, but this time, she did not. "I'm not going to touch it. I know better." She stood that way for a minute more before turning back to her master's body, a frown twisting her mouth.

In a near whisper, like she spoke to herself, Daciana said, "Why does he have glass on him?"

Folding his arms, Sorin joined her, studying Master Florin's body again. "The glass might've gotten on him as his killer moved around the room. Or it could've been from when he fell."

The frown didn't leave.

"Is there anything missing?' he asked.

Raising an eyebrow, she glanced at him. "Missing?"

"It might've just been a robbery and Master Florin caught whoever it was in the act." The room's chaos could've been a result of that.

She studied the room again. "It doesn't seem like anything is missing except most of the jars, though I think most of those are broken. It's hard to tell. The only thing of value here are the tonics and salves."

"Then, if it wasn't a robbery, there's a good chance whoever did this came here with the intent to kill Master Florin." He turned to face her, looking her right in the eye in hopes of getting across to her how serious this was. "Until we have a better grasp on the situation, I want you to go home and stay there. I'll send someone to guard you for the time being."

"But I—"

He shook his head, cutting her off. "Is there any urgent case you have to address at this moment?"

"No, but—"

"Miss Daciana." He stressed her name, getting her to stop. "I need you to understand that whoever did this could very well want to do the same to you, and our village would lose the only apothecary it has left. If that's what they want, then you have to do your part to make sure they don't succeed. If something urgent comes up, I'll send for you. Otherwise, you need to stay where you won't be easy to target, understand?"

Fight was still in her eyes, but when she glanced at her master once more, it vanished. "All right."

He led her back out to the front gate and called to one of the nearby guards. Once she was sent on her way with the guard he trusted most to keep her safe, Sorin took a deep breath. It was time to get to work.

Heavy footsteps sounded up the dirt path leading to the apothecary workshop, getting Sorin to glance to the side.

"Watchmaster Sorin." Heading up the way at a rapid pace was a man of small stature, though he sported salt and pepper gray hair and hard muscles, visible despite the distance. The carpenter, Petre.

"I'm glad you came quickly," Sorin said, opening the gate for the man.

"I can't quite believe it, if I'm honest. Florin wouldn't hurt a fly—heck, we couldn't even get him to go after the spiders."

When they entered the house, Petre paused for a moment, a long moment, his gaze sweeping across the complete and utter chaos of the workshop. Then he bowed his head. "Poor Florin."

Sorin didn't speak, silently echoing the sentiment.

"Well, it'd be wrong to leave him like this for much longer. Florin would hate to be the reason for his workshop staying like this. I want to take him to my shop, if that's fine."

"It is." He leaned out the door and beckoned the couple watchmen lingering by the gate inside.

"Who found the body?" Petre asked while they waited.

"His apprentice and I," Sorin explained.

A pained expression crossed the man's face. "Poor lass. An apprentice should never have to find their master like this."

When the men arrived, they wrapped Master Florin in a cloth before lifting him and taking him from the workshop, working under a strange kind of silence.

Remaining where he was, Sorin glanced around the workshop again before he closed his eyes. Dozens of puzzle pieces lay strewn around him, waiting for him to pick them out and fit them into a picture he couldn't see. There were a hundred things to do, but at the same time, it was almost so daunting he didn't know where to start.

He needed to comb the workshop in greater detail now that Master Florin was gone. He needed to hunt for any possible witnesses who might have seen or heard something. And he needed to keep the village calm and from going haywire.

4

Moving slow, Daciana adjusted her pan in the fire, taking care so that none of the chamomile oil would drip onto the embers and be lost. Now that she would have to work alone, the time she had to make her oils and balms was reduced by a drastic amount, and she couldn't afford to waste resources she no longer had as much free time to track down. Once things were cleared up and her status as Master Apothecary became finalized, finding an apprentice of her own would become her top priority. It unsettled her more than she cared to admit that in such a short span of time, all her dreams of moving her family away from the village had vanished like seeds in the wind, snatched off to some unknown place they wouldn't return from.

Her oath as an apothecary—even though she was just an apprentice—demanded she care for all in need. Abandoning the village now that Master Florin was gone was out of the question.

Once the pan was better positioned, she sat back in her chair by the hearth, drinking in the familiar scent of chamomile, her mind feeling like it was spinning like a top and standing stock still at the same time. Master Florin was dead. Killed. By a human.

Her dad sat in a nearby chair, and she had to admit: even though there was a watchman standing outside her house, her dad brought with him a special kind of peace and safety she hadn't been able to find all day. Word of Master Florin's fate had spread like wildfire, and the second the news had reached her father in the fields he'd been helping tend, he'd abandoned his work and come straight home, despite the fact it was the first job he'd been able to take up in nearly a month.

Fortunately, his friends in the village who snuck him odd jobs whenever they could had understood his predicament.

"Daci," he said after a few minutes, getting her to glance back. "Are you sure it wasn't wolves? They do wreak havoc in the village once every blue moon, though not as much as they used to before we had our wall."

She considered that before shaking her head. "If it'd been wolves, they would've eaten him. They hunt for food, not sport."

"Aye, that's true," he murmured, sitting back in his chair. "But it still makes more sense than someone wanting to go after Master Florin of all people."

Her master's death made no sense to her, but there wasn't a doubt in her mind whether his killer was human. A person. Most likely someone in the village. Someone who might even turn their murderous gaze to her. Yet, at the same time, she couldn't even begin to imagine who in the village would benefit from the death of the apothecaries. They were the only ones in the village who knew how to use the local herbs for medicine, and they, like most apothecaries, charged little if anything for their work. No one would benefit physically nor financially from their deaths, which made Daciana unwilling to believe whoever had killed Master Florin would be coming after her too.

That said, she was sure if she tried to go about her regular business, Sorin the stoic, stubborn, determined, laconic watch leader would make sure she was returned home before she'd even taken two steps beyond the door. So for the time being, it was best to sit and wait.

Footsteps against the earthen floor made her glance up. Her mom came and sat in the chair between her and her dad, tightening her blue shawl with the most intricate embroidery dancing in graceful patterns across the fabric around her thin shoulders. Daciana distracted herself from her troubles by studying the patterns and colors weaving through the shawl.

Then, her mom said, "Are you well?" The familiarity of her mom's lilting accent helped put Daciana a little more at ease.

She frowned at her little pot, unsure how to vocalize her feelings for a while. "Somewhat," she eventually said.

Staying quiet, her mom reached over and took her hand, and for several minutes, that was how they stayed. The moment only broke when Daciana rose to check the progress of the chamomile. The fronds she'd been working on were nearly steamed out, but there was some life left in them still.

As the evening wore on, they didn't speak anymore, and Daciana continued working on her extraction while her mom sat near, embroidering a red shawl in a similar fashion to the one she wore. Her dad stayed too, a shadow appearing in his eyes every time he glanced at the door or windows. Her brothers returned from their explorations near dusk, neither of them speaking. However, the instant they crossed the threshold, they both came and wrapped Daciana in tight hugs. She understood that behavior from her younger brother, Mitica, who was barely twelve, but her other brother, Gavril, caught her off-guard. He was sixteen and had long since stopped tolerating hugs or most kinds of affection from her and their parents. Even still, Daciana hugged the two of them back without hesitation, overwhelmed with gratitude that while she was heartbroken, at least she still had her family. Even if Master Florin was gone, at least she wasn't alone.

Dinner was a silent affair, and while everyone else gradually went to bed, Daciana kept working, her mind still gnawing at her, hunting for answers she didn't have.

Investigating a murder didn't leave Sorin with much of an appetite, but since it was their usual day to eat dinner with the entire head family, the elder had insisted they maintain their regular schedule. Half-hiding in the shadows of his parents, he slinked into the dining room, doing his utmost to remain as small and inconspicuous as possible, his younger siblings trailing in his wake. The two youngest in particular seemed to be making a game of trying to avoid being seen at all, which made his parents smile.

His parents led them to the far end of the table, opposite where his grandpa, Elder Aurel, would be sitting, which alleviated some of his stress. It wouldn't help him avoid the man, but it would lessen the abuse.

The rest of the family trickled in, and the only topic of conversation that cropped up was Master Florin's murder, which he did his best to tune out.

However, when Elder Aurel took his seat at the head of the table, the family hushed. Elder Aurel was an old man—the multitude of wrinkles and white hair standing as a testament of that fact—but today, the man seemed ancient, like a relic from a distant age.

With a heavy sigh, he said, "Let's not discuss today's events. The watch," he paused, his gaze flicking up and finding Sorin's face, "is taking care of it, correct?"

Sorin nodded.

The elder seemed to relax, and the side doors opened, allowing Sorin's aunt, Ecaterina, and her kids in. Each one of them carried trays of food and accompanying scowls. Sorin's gaze flicked to his cousin, Liviu, as the young man made his way around the table, his blue eyes cold when he glanced at Sorin. Liviu stopped at the end of the table, depositing petite loaves of bread in front of each person.

As he set one in front of Sorin, Liviu hissed out of the corner of his mouth, "Don't worry, Sorin. Just use your magic and you'll solve the murder in no time—won't you, golden boy?"

Sorin shot a glare at him but said nothing. He didn't want to fight with his cousin today, especially since they'd once gotten along.

Every one of his cousins shot Sorin a pretty nasty scowl as they served him a portion of dinner, and even though he was used to it, he wanted to disappear.

Once all the food was served, Ecaterina and her kids joined them at the table and Elder Aurel motioned for them to eat. Sorin did his best, but he had no appetite. Plus, his aunt, the head of the kitchens, had been experimenting with herb heavy recipes lately, which brought to mind Master Florin's destroyed workshop, making Sorin's stomach churn in an alarming way.

The usual chatter filled the silence—discussions of magical repairs needed on the wall, who would be sent to fix a washed-out road or repair a broken well or windmill, who could be spared to teach the handful of younger children who'd begun displaying magical talent—but it was strained, constantly broken by brief, but tense spats of silence.

About halfway through the meal, Elder Aurel finally spoke, making the stilted conversations die off. "I have an announcement to make."

"You do?" one of Sorin's uncles asked.

"I've found a match for Liviu."

Up the table, Liviu dropped his fork, ears reddening as he scooped it back up. Without lifting his head, he mumbled, "I don't want—"

"Spare me your protests," the elder said, ripping a piece off his bread and dipping it in his soup. "You know that as the only family in the village with magic, it's our duty and privilege to ensure the next generation will have the protection of that magic as well. The entire village is counting on us to continue to provide a safe way of life."

"I don't even have magic," Liviu spat, tossing a glare at the elder. Then he mumbled something to his younger brother, Andrei, who sat next to him, before shooting a searing glare Sorin's way.

"No, but there's always a chance your children will, which is why you must marry as soon as possible. Magic runs in all of our blood, even if it runs its course in silence. Our family carved our mighty wall out of the earth, changed the course of the river in the Howling Falls Ravine to ensure our crops would grow, and, most importantly, defended the village with their abilities, even when it cost them their lives. You would do well to remember that legacy, Liviu, even if your only part in it is raising the next generation."

Liviu glared at the table, his mouth pressed into a thin line.

Andrei rolled his eyes, moodily stabbing at his food.

Elder Aurel eyed the two of them with a bit of a haughty air before turning his gaze to Sorin, who averted his gaze. "And I'm in the process of finding a match for you."

Sorin's insides curdled and he nearly dropped his cup, but he tightened his grip.

"I will make sure whoever she is, she'll be well-suited to you. As someone who bears strong magic themselves, your children are more likely to express the same talent, and it is essential you have as many as possible."

Remaining quiet, Sorin set his cup down before he could drop it. As the elder continued to harp on and on about the duties of their family—and Sorin in particular seemed to be his target—what little there'd been of Sorin's appetite vanished.

Master Florin was buried the next morning to save his body from the summer heat. For a burial, it was customary for there to be more of a celebration, almost—festivities, of sorts, to celebrate a life returning to the heavens. However, it was hard to be in the mood when that life was taken too early, sent back by human hands rather than God's.

Daciana was allowed to go (Sorin and his watchmen wouldn't have been able to stop her) and take one final look at the face of the man who'd spent a little more than a decade teaching her everything he knew. Dozens of memories twisted through her mind like ribbons in the wind, days spent listening to his voice and instructions while in his sunny garden, times when he'd lectured her for choosing the wrong herb, times when he'd praised her for choosing the correct one. She'd even recalled going home to her family in tears a handful of times after being scolded for making a mistake.

However, as she stood near the open earth that would soon be her master's grave, one of his most familiar mantras came back to her: a negligent apothecary wasn't fit to hold a person's life in their hands. She hadn't appreciated his lectures or sternness before, but at that moment, gratitude rushed through her for all those instances where he'd taken the time to pause and explain why she had to be certain and accurate. There was no longer anyone here to glance over her shoulder and prevent her from making a mistake.

The wound on the back of her master's head was hidden from view, his eyes closed like he'd simply fallen asleep. However, his skin had a waxy appearance to it, almost blotchy, different from the faces of people who'd left this world in a more peaceful way.

Deep in Daciana's chest, anger stirred.

Someone had taken him from them. Whoever it was, they were facing no repercussions; they still walked free somewhere.

The burial in and of itself was a somber affair with most the village gathered around, silent observers as Master Florin's close family each tossed a handful of dirt into the grave. Then they stepped back as Master Florin's brother-in-law scooped up a shovel and filled the grave nearly to the top.

Master Florin's sister, an older, haggard woman with her head and shoulders drooping from the weight of her grief, then stepped up to the grave, a little brown paper bag in her hands. It took a few seconds before Daciana realized what she held: Lady's Bedstraw seeds. The flower

Master Florin had always requested to have laid over his grave.

With a gentle sadness, the woman strewed the seeds over the grave before her husband eased a layer of earth over the top.

When that was finished, the crowd dispersed, everyone continuing on about their days, but Daciana remained where she was, unable to forget the poignant fact that someone had caused this. This was someone's fault instead of life's natural order.

Someone had taken a brother from his sister. They'd taken an apothecary from his patients. They'd taken Daciana's master away from her—they'd stolen the sunny afternoons she and him would spend working with the herbs and the evenings by the fireside reviewing plants and patient notes. The entire village had been robbed of one of the kindest men to grace the earth because of someone.

Daciana had never been big on revenge; revenge wasn't what she wanted. What she wanted was to ensure that whoever had done this never got the chance to do it again. Furthermore, she wanted to put a face on the mysterious enigma who'd stooped low enough to take a human life. She wanted that answer even if she had to subject herself to the ridicule of the village in order to get it.

"Miss Daciana?" Sorin said, calling her from her thoughts. He didn't say anything else, but there was a question in his eyes.

She glanced over her shoulder for the watchman who'd escorted her here, and he was still hovering nearby. Then she returned her gaze to Sorin. "I was just thinking."

He still didn't speak, but he didn't move either. That almost felt like an invitation.

"I know it's only been a day, but have you discovered anything yet?"

For a long moment, she didn't think he would answer her, but then a hint of sympathy passed over his face. "No."

Wordlessly, she stared at him. They'd never worked in close quarters before, but from the rumors she'd heard, no one was as clever at solving crimes as Sorin was proving to be, yet even he hadn't made any progress.

"Nothing?"

"No one saw or heard anything out of the ordinary." He shook his head. "That said, the workshop has been cleaned a bit, so if you're up to it, I'd like for you to come and check if anything was taken again."

"All right," she said without hesitation. "Let's go."

"Now?" he asked, his tone mild but the arch of his eyebrow a bit severe.

"The trail is going cold, so we don't have time to waste, do we?"

Turning on her heel, Daciana marched down the grassy slope overlooking the town, her gaze fixed straight ahead. She sidestepped a couple people who must've been from the head family who were busy repairing cracked sections of the massive wall around their village. Their hands glowed with light as they worked, the light flowing through the cracks in the stones like water. The glow lingered for the briefest of moments before vanishing, diffusing into the rock, leaving them whole and intact.

Since she spent most of her time indoors, she almost never got to see the head family's magic, even though it fascinated her. The way they were able to repair the stones was nothing short of beautiful.

They passed the blacksmith's on the way, and she noticed a young woman inside laughing and inciting the flames in the forge to burn hotter and higher, the crackles and pops in the smithy intensifying at her urging. There was a gaggle of people gathered there, some young men and some young women as well, oo-ing and ah-ing as they watched the flames dance.

As Daciana passed, she noted a couple of the young women pinching their noses when they glanced at her, but she ignored it and them.

A few minutes later, she was back at the workshop with Sorin and her escort on her heels. A shiver of fear raced down her spine as she stared at the familiar building, but she shook that away. Master Florin wasn't there. While the space had been violated, it was still hers, and no one would chase her out of it. So, taking a deep breath, she let herself through the gate and into the workshop.

Most of the chaos had been erased: Master Florin's worktable was in its correct place, and one of the stools from the backroom sat beside it. The rug had been straightened, and the scattered herbs had been tidied. The only thing out of place was the dark smear in the middle of the room, the mark most likely a permanent stain.

"We saved the herbs as best we could," Sorin explained as he stepped past her, indicating the collection on the worktable. "There's still glass mixed in, so I don't think they're usable anymore, but it'd be helpful if you'd check them as well."

She nodded and set to work, making her way around the room, searching for anything absent. Master Florin hadn't been the type to keep anything not useful in the workshop, so it was only tools, and all of them remained. In almost no time at all, she turned her attention to the herbs she and Master Florin had spent countless hours working to preserve, so much of it ruined, the damage irreversible. She made a mental note to send letters to the apothecaries from the nearby villages to ask for anything they could offer to hold her over until the harvests.

Then, she tugged out the ledger from the lone bookshelf in the room and set to work assessing the damages, her complete focus on her task, causing her to tune out the rest of the room. After calculating the losses of the herbs that'd been gathered from the floor, she inspected the shelves. A frown twisted her mouth as she worked, growing more severe as she went.

When she finished a few minutes later, she slammed the book shut, anger roiling in her chest like a thunderstorm.

"Is it that bad?" Sorin asked, reminding her he was there.

"Disregarding the ruined herbs, at least two jars of every herb are unaccounted for—and I don't know if they were shattered or snatched," she snarled, her nails digging into the book's leather cover. "Whoever did this stole or ruined nearly everything we had."

Some of those loses wouldn't be impactful—she'd gathered feverfew and chamomile just the other day. However, for herbs like lavender and hyssop, it would almost be an entire year before she could gather more. Worst of all, they were nearly out of lovage, and since their plant had died, Daciana had no way to gather more of it unless she as lucky enough to find another plant or get a start from another apothecary. At this rate, her remaining stores would only last a matter of weeks, if that.

"Maybe it really was a robbery gone wrong," the other watchman offered.

"Robbing an apothecary doesn't make much sense," Sorin pointed out, a tired note in his voice like he'd argued this point many times. "The majority of the herbs can be gathered by anyone, and the valuable ones are the ones in the garden—all of which went untouched. The things of greatest value are the salves and tinctures because only trained apothecaries can make them." He turned to her, almost like he was asking for confirmation.

She nodded. "That's why Master Florin kept those separate from the normal herbs. Even still, whoever did this didn't take any of them."

Sorin's brow furrowed.

The other watchman frowned. "Then maybe they wanted to make it look like a robbery while Master Florin was the real target."

Closing her eyes, Daciana fought to tame the roiling rage in her chest. Who would do this? It seemed so stupid and senseless, but whoever it was must've had a reason. There was an explanation, always. The trick was finding it. Those were the words Master Florin had sworn by.

With a sigh, Sorin said, "Well, thank you for your time, Miss Daciana. Now, you should—"

"No," she cut in as she returned the ledger to its shelf. "I'm not interested in sitting at home. If someone is going to come after me, then being at home will put the rest of my family in danger. Our house is away from the village's main thoroughfare, and it would be a lot easier to kill me there than it would've been to kill Master Florin here."

He didn't interrupt her, but the downturn of Sorin's mouth suggested he wasn't pleased.

"Besides, I was Master Florin's apprentice. This was personal, and I'm going to help you catch whoever killed him, got it?" Daciana met his gaze, resolved that nothing would stop her. Not even their stubborn, terse watchleader.

5

Sorin didn't know how to feel about the fire burning in Daciana's brown eyes as she stared him down, clearing daring him to tell her no. For someone who'd spent most of her days as a recluse, this was odd behavior he didn't know what to do with. Not to mention sticking her nose into a murder investigation could get her hurt, or worse, cost her life.

"How will you be able to do that and fulfill your duties as an apothecary?"

Her expression remained unchanged. "I'll manage."

His frown deepened.

His fellow watchman, Nelu, leaned closer to him. "If she was with us, it would be easier to protect her. No one would ever be far away."

That was a fair point though. Besides, he supposed Daciana might be able to provide them with a few insights into the apothecary business that could prove useful.

"Fine," Sorin said, turning towards the door. "You may for the time being, but if it gets dangerous, you're done."

"Perfect," she said, adjusting the black headscarf holding her dark braid out of her face. "Where are we going first?"

"Headquarters," he said as he turned on his heel and marched out of the workshop, Nelu right behind him. Daciana grabbed something from behind the door before hurrying after.

The watch headquarters were only a few buildings down the lane from the workshop, and this morning, its yard bustled with activity like a beehive. Despite the short distance, he noted some villagers crossing to the other side of the street instead of walking past them, shooting dark glowers at Daciana as they went. That was the second time today alone he'd noted such behavior.

However, as they arrived at the door of headquarters, he set those thoughts aside. Shoving his way through the door, he greeted a nearby group of watchmen, who appeared to be discussing the night watch schedule, their tones terse. Master Florin's murder had everyone on edge.

Sorin led Nelu and Daciana to his table at the back of the room, his heart sinking a little at the lack of paper on the desk. He'd told his men to leave reports if they'd found anything interesting; no paper meant they'd still found nothing.

With a bit of a huff, he sat on the edge of it, mind whirling. How could there be no clues outside of the workshop? How could Master Florin's killer have simply disappeared?

At that moment, the door opened, and someone Sorin hadn't expected to see stood there, looking like he'd raced out the door in the middle of getting dressed. His belt and sword were in one hand, his jacket and one boot in the other.

"Calin, what on earth are you doing?" he called as the guy came in, breathing hard like he'd been running. "You're not back on duty until tomorrow."

"I know that," Calin snapped as he made his way towards them. "And don't give me that crap. Once Mirabela and I heard about it, she all but kicked me out the door."

He made no response. Calin and his wife had only been married for a little more than a day, and in truth, he was impressed to see them apart.

"Give me a job, boss. Though, I'm sure there aren't any good ones left," Calin said as his bare foot found its way into its boot and his jacket made it onto his shoulders.

"You can be my second brain while we review what we've got. And my extra set of eyes. To keep track of her." He motioned towards Daciana, who'd helped herself to a chair and was busy scrawling something across a piece of paper.

She didn't pause in her task as Calin glanced over. In a barely audible whisper, the man asked, "What, is she suspect number one?"

"Not even close," Sorin said. "She didn't benefit at all."

"You sure? If we're talking motive, I'm sure taking over as the village apothecary would be a pretty good one."

"That's only because you don't use your brain. Her killing Master Florin makes no sense because she's a Master Apprentice. I also know for a fact Master Florin sent in all the official paperwork to the head family, and come this autumn, she'll be a full-fledged apothecary in her own right. They were equals in everything but name. If you keep pulling out comments like that, you're going to be fired from being my second brain."

While Daciana still didn't lift her head from her work, the corner of her mouth quirked upwards.

"Oh, when you put it that way, I suppose you're right. She wouldn't benefit at all."

No, Daciana did not. On the contrary, she'd come out of this affair with a losing hand. So far, they all seemed to have come out of this at a disadvantage, but somehow, someone had benefited from the death.

"Okay, but while you stew on that, can we talk about something lighter for a minute?"

"Absolutely not. This is a murder investigation, Calin."

"You have to tell me what you thought of my cousin—the one I introduced you to at my wedding."

"I said we're not having this conversation. I'm working."

His friend laughed, the sound a little out of place given the situation. "You're never not working, and you and I both know it's on purpose. However, now that I'm married—"

"Shut your mouth before I shut it for you," Sorin snapped.

A bit to his annoyance, Daciana's smile broadened. Even still, she remained focused on her work.

"All right, fine," Calin said with a long, drawn-out sigh. "So what do we know?"

"Someone entered the workshop, killed Master Florin, and made off with a significant amount of dried herbs. No forced entry, no footsteps leading in or out, and nothing outside of the main room was touched. No one saw or heard a thing."

His friend frowned. "We can rule out it being a spur of the moment thing then, right? Like a client getting out of hand or something?"

Sorin raised an eyebrow.

"I mean, otherwise they would've left some sort of clue; they wouldn't have been planning to hide."

"That may be true. In which case, whether or not whoever went there intended to kill our apothecary, they must've gone there for a suspicious reason since they left no trail whatsoever." Sorin closed his eyes, picturing the apothecary workshop in his mind once more, conjuring to life the mess of the scene.

There had to have been something he'd missed. Something he hadn't seen at the time. The weapon had been tossed in the fire, the room in upheaval like there'd been a fight—though Master Florin's body had shown no signs of such a struggle—and the shattered jars.

He frowned. Daciana had said most of the jars were either missing or broken, and there'd been a lot of glass on the floor. The cupboards had been broken as well; he distinctly remembered a door hanging off its hinges.

All at once, something Daciana had said resurfaced in his mind: 'why does he have glass on him?'

He'd explained it away before, but since their investigation hadn't yielded results, he returned to it now. The glass could've been stirred up when the man fell, but if that had been the case, there would've been shards stuck to the man's back and side. While they could've accidentally kicked more shards onto the body as they'd moved around the house, they hadn't.

"Which means the glass must've been broken *after* he'd been killed," he murmured.

Daciana lifted her head. "The glass on Master Florin's body?"

He nodded.

"Then that means someone broke in and killed him and then wreaked havoc on the workshop and the herbs, right?" she asked, meeting his gaze.

Once again, he nodded. "That is most likely the case."

"Then perhaps whoever it was only killed Master Florin because he'd stayed late, and the herbs were their real goal."

"So we're back to the robbery gone wrong theory," Sorin said, frowning at the ground.

"In that case, we need to focus on why someone would go through the trouble of taking herbs," Calin pointed out. "If some of the jars were tossed to the floor and broke, do you think the thief was searching for specific herbs?"

"Almost every herb was snatched, so that helps us little."

"Maybe they didn't know what to grab, and just grabbed some of everything," Daciana offered after a minute of silence. "Maybe the jars were broken because they were in a hurry."

"That could be. Panicking makes people clumsy," Calin mused. "Still, this one is baffling me. Especially when I try to think of people who might stand to gain something."

Sorin turned to Daciana. "Is there anyone you know of who had an interest in herbs or anything?"

She shook her head. "Not enough to steal them."

That made him frown more. Every time he thought he was getting somewhere, the clues led him to nothing.

Calin had apparently grown bored of being Sorin's second brain because he wandered over to Daciana, frowning at the papers in her lap. "What are you working on, Master Apprentice?"

"I'm writing letters to the apothecaries in the nearby villages to ask for some of their herbs. I need to restock, but most of them aren't in season now, so I can't go out and get them."

"Will they do that?"

"Us apothecaries tend to stay in touch with each other—in the event of outbreaks and that kind of thing," she said in response to Sorin's raised eyebrow, "and Master Florin was on good terms with them. I'm sure when I explain the circumstances, they'll lend a hand. After all, during the floods last year, Master Florin helped them replenish their stocks too."

"I didn't realize you apothecaries were so close knit," Sorin said slowly.

"It's unlikely for it to have been another apothecary," she said. "In case that's what you're thinking. The less of us there are, the more ground we have to cover."

"That's true," he murmured, frowning at the floor again.

"But you would get more business," Calin pointed out.

The glare she turned on Calin made Sorin lift an eyebrow. "No, I'd ultimately loose business because both me and my resources would be spread too thin."

Calin leaned back a little, looking rather chastised. "That is a fair point."

Then her glare softened as a little sigh slipped out of her. "Though I imagine there might be some people who would try that if they thought it'd make them a little extra money."

Sorin closed his eyes, his thoughts darting in circles like yappy dogs.

"All this thinking is going to give you a headache, Sorin," Calin called. "And it's not like thinking hard is going to give you your answer. Let's go do something productive instead."

Sorin just stared at him.

"If that's what you want, you can follow me over to the post office. A walk might generate some thoughts." Daciana got to her feet, her letters in her hand.

Sorin hesitated before he relented, dismissing Nelu with a nod. Then he followed Daciana and Calin back out of the guard house. It wasn't like any of his men had found something newsworthy anyway.

The walk to the post office did not grant him an epiphany, and a part of him decided it was Calin and Daciana's faults, since they chatted the entire way there. Within a few minutes, she had her letters posted and they were back on the streets.

She stopped in the middle of the road, bringing him and Calin to a stop as well. "So if there aren't any more clues we can glean from the workshop, where should we search instead?"

He scowled, still not interested in having her follow him around on what could be a dangerous investigation.

"If you keep frowning like that, Sorin, you're going to end up looking like a gross old man by the time you're thirty."

Sorin's glare shifted from Daciana to Calin in the blink of an eye. "You're starting to annoy."

That just made Calin laugh, as he feared it might.

All at once, someone shouted, "Miss Apothecary!"

Daciana spun on her heel as Sorin glanced over.

His uncle, Ionel, raced up the way. The man appeared frantic, his normally neat, dark ponytail and tunic a little askew.

"Ionel?" Sorin asked as the man arrived, panting hard. "Is something wrong?"

Ionel waved a hand while fighting for his breath. "Miss Apothecary, you must come at once. The elder is ill."

Sorin stiffened. "Grandpa?"

"He was fine this morning, but now he can't even get out of bed."

"Take me to him," Daciana said, straightening what Sorin now realized was her satchel.

Ionel raced back up the lane with the three of them on his heels, heading for the large, gated building at the end of town. Sorin's family's compound.

6

Daciana hurried inside the large bedroom, surprised by the simple furnishings inside. Besides the massive, four poster bed, there was a wardrobe, a handful of matching chairs, and a nightstand with a couple books resting on it. Considering this was the bedroom of the head family's elder, Daciana had always imagined the main house would be a bit...more.

Shaking those thoughts away, she approached the bed and the older gentleman lying on it.

Despite his obvious age, he didn't have the thin, withered frame many of her other elderly patients did. That said, his cheeks were flushed but at the same time, the general pallor of his skin sent a jolt of alarm through her.

"Elder Aurel?" she called softly.

His eyelids fluttered, but an unfocused, feverish light lurked in his eyes. Whatever was wrong seemed serious.

Glancing up, she spied Ionel and Sorin entering the room, and she held up a hand, making them halt. "Until I know what this is, get out."

They both hesitated, glancing at each other. Then, Ionel eased himself out of the room. However, Sorin remained where he was.

"This would be a perfect opportunity to attack you, so I will remain here," he said.

She could tell from the tilt of his head that nothing she said would get him to change his mind. Forget stubborn; he was muleheaded.

"Fine," she said, "but take two steps back."

He did.

After pausing to calm herself, she set to work examining her patient, noting all his symptoms: fever, chills, tenderness in his abdomen, clammy hands, mild wheezing, and his disoriented state. She frowned at her treatment log. This was the first time she'd encountered an illness quite like this before, and the realization she was on her own to figure it out hit her hard.

"Do you know what's wrong?" Sorin asked, cutting into her thoughts.

"No," she replied, turning and digging through her bag. Since she didn't know what was going on, she didn't want to overload Elder Aurel with herbs, but she thought a little bit of chamomile and feverfew might help alleviate his discomfort.

"I need some water," she called as she pulled out her mortar and pestle.

A moment later, she heard Sorin speaking with someone outside of the room.

In short order, she had the herbs ground up, and as she finished, Sorin crossed the room with a small pitcher of water and a cup.

She eyed him in exasperation.

He stared back with a blank expression. "How else would I get it to you in an efficient manner?"

"All right," she said, deciding it was better not to waste her energy arguing a moot point. "I just hope it isn't contagious."

He gave no visible reaction. Instead, he poured some water into the cup and held it out to her.

She added the herbs with care and—whether she approved or not—had Sorin's help administering them to his grandfather.

"Now what?" he asked. If she stared at Sorin really hard, she could almost detect a hint of concern in his eyes.

"We wait," she said, dragging over one of the chairs. Then she sat and studied her treatment log again, thinking through the peculiar symptoms.

Sorin pulled over one of the other chairs and sat next to her.

She glanced his way before returning her attention to her log.

"He is my grandfather, you know," he said, almost as if he was explaining himself. "And I don't care about getting sick."

"Are you close?" she asked.

He was quiet long enough she glanced at him. "Not really. But he's still family."

She nodded, mulling over that as they returned to silence. A few minutes later, she rose and checked the elder. His fever had dropped slightly and his breathing did seem to be less labored, which, while minor, was still an improvement.

Even still, any improvement was a good sign.

Sorin didn't speak, but she still felt the need to say, "He responded to the herbs, which is good. Now we have to watch him and see how he does."

Sorin didn't respond, but she didn't get the chance to think about it before the door of the room swung open to admit a tall woman Daciana had seen in the workshop a handful of times. Her dark brown hair flowed around her shoulders and her dress seemed kind of...tight. There was a certain air the woman carried about her, perhaps something about the way she stared around the room with a satisfied tilt to her head, that made Daciana wary.

Her mother would've used some colorful terms to describe her, she was sure.

"I heard Elder Auler is ill. Is that true?"

To Daciana's annoyance, the woman didn't look at her; she turned to Sorin.

To Sorin's credit, he didn't respond.

The woman put a dainty hand on her hip, her lips puckering in a pout. "Sorin, don't ignore your aunt."

"I'm not the apothecary, Ecaterina," he said in a cool tone. "So I'm not the one you should be asking."

The woman turned her eyes from him to Daciana with near comical slowness. "Oh, I didn't even see you there, muffin."

It took all of Daciana's willpower not to scowl at the nickname.

The woman turned back to Sorin anyway. "So is he ill or not?"

"Yes," he said with a hint of a bite.

"Is he going to die?" Sorin's aunt didn't sound like she cared much.

"Not yet," Daciana said, not bothering to keep the irritation out of her tone.

An irksome simper twisted the woman's lips. "Easy, muffin. There's no need to snap at me. It was just a question."

"You've asked your question," Sorin snapped. "Now get out. Elder Aurel needs quiet."

With a scoff, his aunt left, slamming the door hard enough both of them winced.

Daciana stared at the door for a moment before glancing back at Sorin. "Not to be rude, but you're really related to that?"

He snorted, the closest she'd ever seen to a smile touching his face. However, when he met her gaze, it was gone. "Sorry about her. I'd say she means well, but she doesn't. And yes, I am...unfortunately...related to her."

Closing her book with a soft snap, Daciana tapped the spine against her chin. She knew family members weren't all duplicates of each other, but even still, while Sorin was obstinate and frank, at least he wasn't rude like his aunt.

"Actually," Sorin began, pulling her attention back to him. "Since you've already been exposed to it—you're our only apothecary now, so you're going to get the brunt of it—I should tell you about...my family."

That got her attention. The head family was a reserved group, and while Master Florin had been alive, only he had been allowed to treat them. Daciana was sure she'd only been permitted this time because she was their only option. Either way, the only thing she knew about the family—beyond the fact most of the village fantasized about marrying into it—was that they were the only people in the village who had magic of some kind. That was the reason they'd been the head family since the birth of their village.

"My grandfather has seven children, one of whom is my mother. Of the seven of them, two were born without any magic: my uncle, Ionel, and my aunt, Ecaterina. Two of my uncles have strong magic, but the rest don't. Their magic is mostly useful for keeping fires at a good temperature or purifying water and things like that. Only about half of my cousins have magic, and most of it isn't strong either—and none of Ecaterina and Ionel's children have it. The people who are given positions of power in my family and the village at large are the ones with magic."

"I see," she said. She'd never realized there were members of the head family born without magic before or that it came in varying degrees of strength.

"It's the head family's job to protect the village from outside threats, which is why those of us born without magic play smaller roles. Some people don't care, but there are some that do—a lot. Hence Ecaterina is the way she is. She's making up for her lack of magic in...other ways."

Daciana nodded, stewing on that. In a way, she understood the mentality. Their village was small, and they had two bigger neighbors who could do them in—not to mention the persistent plague of the Thornwood Fell Bandits. If the people in charge of protecting them failed, the village would be wiped out.

"I can understand why," she ventured. "Though it's unfair to have your opportunities in life dictated by something you can't control."

Sorin dipped his head a little, but he didn't respond.

"But I also think that's a part of life."

He glanced at her.

"I mean, every person is born with different talents and abilities. You can develop other ones, but there are some things that will come more naturally to you than it would to someone else. That said, I think what you choose to do with your gifts, or lack thereof, is a much better reveal of your character than what your gifts are."

Sorin's mouth opened like he wanted to say something, but after a few moments, closed it and remained quiet. Even still, she detected some kind of emotion in his eyes, something he probably didn't want her to witness, so she looked away.

"But I guess because you were made the watch leader, you have magic too, don't you?"

"That's right," he said, his voice a bit soft, almost like he was embarrassed. He extended a hand towards the pitcher on the table, making the water inside rise and bloom like a rose. The water caught bits of the sunlight streaming through the window, making it glitter and shine like it was a myriad of jewels. Then, the water slipped back into the pitcher without spilling a single drop.

Daciana refused to gasp, but she couldn't help her wide-eyed stare. Sorin's magic was incredible, even if he'd merely been performing a trick.

"They're the same powers my mom has, but mine are stronger than hers. I'm...the strongest one in the whole family. So far."

Daciana thought having magic at your disposal would be phenomenal, but the expression on Sorin's face—just there, and she could only see it if she really scrutinized him—said otherwise.

Actually, now that she thought about it, the only times she'd ever seen anyone from the head family in the village were the times she saw them working with the elements throughout the village. Never had she considered they were unhappy doing the work. She hadn't even realized there were members born without it until Sorin had told her as much.

They lapsed into silence, and after another hour, since Elder Aurel's condition remained stable, Daciana gave strict instructions to his attending servant before taking her leave, Sorin dogging her shadow. She didn't know what to make of the head family or the things he'd told her about them, but for now, she decided not to make anything of it. It may be one of those things she would only figure out how to address once she had more time.

Heading to the workshop, she fell into the calming, almost ritualistic routine of tending the herb garden. It'd been neglected yesterday, so she'd have to make up for that today. Sorin remained outside the gate, watching her work for a few minutes before speaking. "I need to check the guard house again, in case anything's been discovered."

Daciana caught the hint, but she looked him in the eye. "It'll only take you a few minutes, right? I need to tend the garden—there are several priceless herbs here, and I can't let them die. So you go, and I'll stay right here, in plain sight of everyone on the street."

That was met with a scowl.

"Sorin, I don't think whoever killed Master Florin will attack me in broad daylight on the main street like this. I'll make sure not to duck out of sight. Promise."

He glared for a solid minute before relenting. "Fine. But don't leave the front yard."

She agreed, and he hurried up the way. Even though she knew the attention was solely because he was concerned there might be an attempt on her life, a small part of her wanted to believe that perhaps it was because he was concerned about her too—concerned about her as a person, not just as an apothecary—but that was asinine. They'd known of each other for a while, but the first time they'd spoken to each other had only been a couple days ago.

Shaking her head at her antics, she bent, inspecting the aloe plant Master Florin had worked his tail off in order to grow. It was a desert plant, and they didn't live in a desert by any stretch of the imagination. However, it was the most useful plant for dealing with burns, so helping it thrive was worth the effort, even if summer was the only season of the year in which it could be outdoors.

Out of the corner of her eye, she spied movement and glanced in its direction. To her surprise, it was Sorin's uncle, Ionel, setting a barrel of what appeared to be grain in an already well-loaded cart. He was neither tall nor stocky, but somewhere in between. However, despite his lack of intimidating size, it was apparent he was a strong man.

As he gathered his horse's reins and checked its ties to the cart, he noticed her. With a hint of a smile, he dipped his head in her direction, the warmth in his deep brown eyes catching her attention. She returned the gesture and he headed up the street, back towards the head family's compound.

It occurred to her that she'd seen him in town several times before with his horse and cart and had never made the connection he was one of Elder Aurel's children. However, she supposed in a society where their lives depended on the people with magical gifts, those without it, even those from the head family, lived much more mundane lives than the others.

With a sigh, she forced her attention back to her work and a much greater problem: Master Florin's murder. Closing her eyes, Daciana stewed on that for a long time, but her thoughts led to no answers, so instead, she shifted her attention to Elder Aurel's strange illness.

None of his symptoms were unusual, per se, but all of them together were. She'd seen each one in a separate illness, and a handful of them together, but it was the wrong time of year for any of those illnesses. Unless it'd been brought in from outside the village, in which case she might hear something from another apothecary in a day or two, warning the rest of them.

Desperately, she wished Master Florin were here. He would've been able to get to the heart of the illness soon, if not have the answer already. But it was just her. On her own. For one of the first times in her life, the sensation of being utterly alone, like she stood in the middle of the forest, surrounded by dark trees and silence, descended hard enough she couldn't breathe. Whether Elder Aurel lived or died was up to her and her alone. If someone else fell ill or was injured, saving their life rested solely in her hands. An almost unbearable weight settled on her shoulders, the reality of her situation looming in front of her like a beast.

"Miss Daciana?" Sorin suddenly called, making her jump and drop her shears. She jumped again, just avoiding skewering her toes.

Her heart racing, she looked back to find Sorin standing inside the gate, staring at her with wide eyes.

"Are you...okay?" he asked.

Her cheeks flamed as she retrieved her shears. "Yes, sorry. I was...thinking."

He nodded, but there was a hint of an emotion dancing in his eyes, one she couldn't see clearly enough to decipher.

"Did you finish your errand?" she asked, since he didn't say anything.

He nodded again.

"So what do we do next?"

"I need to talk to some of the people in town," he replied. "My watchmen have started, but so far there's nothing. And I'm not leaving you here for that long."

"Oh," she said, discomfort wedging into her spine at the thought. She'd never gone into anyone's house without Master Florin before, and even his presence hadn't spared her from the nasty stares people liked to give her.

"I..." She cleared her throat. She couldn't very well expect to help solve the murder if she hid in her master's garden, could she?

Even still, the idea of going out amongst the village without being called on to do so as an apothecary made her hesitate, her heart stuttering and her hands turning clammy and cold.

Sorin raised an eyebrow. "I thought you said you were going to help solve Master Florin's murder."

He said that in a straightforward manner, but she detected a challenge in the words, which made her draw up straight. He'd been hesitant to allow her to help at all, and if she balked because of something as contrary as discomfort, that would be enough justification for him to send her back to her house.

So, taking a deep breath, she set her tools on the porch and dusted off her hands before following Sorin into the village. She kept to his shadow, but if he noticed he didn't seem to mind, and she was grateful for that.

7

Dawn came early the next morning, earlier than Sorin was ready for it to. However, he rolled out of bed anyway, quickly getting ready and making his way to the kitchen. His family was up, as usual, his mom and younger siblings making breakfast while his dad and brother prepared for their day working in the fields. Not for the first time, pride flared to life in his chest at the thought of how hard his mom must've fought to marry a man most of the family considered 'too common.' The feeling was swiftly dampened by the reality of his own situation. Even if he'd had the courage to go toe to toe with his grandpa, he didn't have anyone to fight for. Sometimes, he wondered if his grandpa had given him the post of head watchman, despite several objections, in order to keep Sorin busy enough he wouldn't have the chance to find anyone.

As he sat down to breakfast, he shook those thoughts away so he could focus on enjoying his mom's cooking. Before he left the house, he made sure to give her his compliments.

She grinned, waving a hand at him. "Oh you— Just be careful out there, you hear?"

"Sure," he said with a hint of a smile. Then he was out the door, heading towards the center of town.

To his surprise, Daciana and her escort, Marian today, were already making their way towards the compound. Like yesterday though, he noted that while walking through the village, she tended to walk behind him or his watchmen with her head bowed, almost like she was trying to make herself smaller and less noticeable. However, like yesterday, he didn't comment on it, and once she'd reached the gate, her normal spark returned, and she took the lead. How odd.

"Early, aren't you?" Sorin asked, stopping in the middle of the path.

"Your grandpa's condition wasn't worse, but it wasn't better either last night, and he's old enough things could take a turn in the blink of an eye. Of course I've come to check on him as soon as I could."

Behind her, Marian yawned wide. From the shadows under the man's eyes, Sorin gathered he'd been her night guard and, as a result, had been up most of the night.

"Marian, you can head off. I'll keep an eye on her."

The man hesitated.

Sorin frowned.

After a moment longer, Marian conceded and said, "Thanks, Sorin."

Once Marian departed, Daciana resumed walking, heading to his grandpa's room without a hint of hesitation despite the fact she'd only been there once before. Inside, Elder Aurel was still in bed with the servant she'd left in charge the day before curled up on the floor.

She went to the servant first, giving his shoulder a gentle shake. After talking to him for a minute, she went to the elder's side where a frown twisted her mouth.

Sorin stepped past the servant who'd already fallen back asleep. His chest tightened at the sight of his grandpa's wan face and bright red cheeks. Somehow, he appeared worse than he had yesterday.

Daciana was already rifling through her bag.

"Water?" he asked.

"Yes," she said without looking up.

He checked the pitcher on the table. Empty. Picking it up, he hurried out of the room and down to the kitchen. He didn't bother wasting time getting close to the water barrel filled with fresh water. Instead, he tugged on the water inside, forming a large droplet and urging it into his pitcher. It complied, splashing a little due to his haste, and he raced back to the elder's room.

Daciana administered the herbs the instant he delivered the water, and then they waited. However, unlike yesterday, the herbs seemed to have no effect. On the contrary, Elder Aurel seemed to get worse, his breathing growing more labored, becoming an actual wheeze.

While Sorin didn't know what to do—the feeling almost overwhelming—Daciana leapt into action, examining the elder, taking notes, and reviewing other notes before giving the elder just plain water.

All at once, her gaze fixed on Sorin, a stern light in her brown eyes. "You were around him a lot yesterday. Do you feel sick at all?"

He shook his head.

Frowning, she said. "The servant doesn't either. Which means it isn't contagious, but—" Cutting herself off, she reopened her notebook, flipping through the pages at a rapid pace. Her frown deepened, and there was a stiffness to her shoulders that hadn't been there before. Closing her book, she turned to him, the sternness of her expression setting him on edge. "Do you know how many people came to visit him yesterday?"

"You said he shouldn't have visitors," he reminded her.

That stern expression didn't falter. "I did, but considering the way your aunt treated me, I'm not at all confident your family took me seriously."

She...had a point there.

"I don't know. However, my family didn't come by last night."

"Is there a way you can find out for me?" she asked.

Sorin was still hesitant to leave her alone, but lingering here could mean delaying the correct treatment for Elder Aurel, which, at the man's age, could be fatal. "Don't leave the room."

"I won't," she said, a hint of a smile in her voice.

He turned and hurried out.

The main family's compound was mostly dominated by the main house, and the rest of the space was occupied by several smaller houses fanning around it. His aunts and uncles lived in them with their respective families, though there were a few standing empty since his grandparents hadn't had as many children as some of their predecessors had.

Sorin crossed the grassy yard the houses stood in a ring around, relentlessly knocking on each door until someone answered. His half-asleep relations didn't seem to appreciate him bothering them, giving him half answers until he put on his watch leader tone. Then they gave him answers.

When he checked the last house, he headed back towards the main house, walking fast. In short, outside of his parents and his aunt Raluca's family, nearly everyone had visited the elder against Daciana's orders. He understood she wasn't Master Florin and they didn't know her the way they had him, but still, it was a slap to her face. Annoyance flared in his chest, followed swiftly by embarrassment over his family's actions, and the two emotions warred for dominion.

As he made to enter the main house, a couple of his cousins, Liviu and Narcisa, made to step out. All three of them pulled up short, staring with wide eyes. Unease scratched as Sorin's spine, but he was frozen to the spot.

Narcisa recovered first. "You certainly have a lot of free time on your hands, don't you? Unlike us *normal* people."

He scowled. "I don't have free time; I'm investigating a crime."

"Oh, do you think it was one of us?" she asked, one dark eyebrow lifting. "Is that why you're in the compound?"

"Elder Aurel is sick, and I'm guarding the apothecary," he snapped.

"So the rumors are true," Liviu said with a nonchalant stare. He huffed. "Serves the old man right." Without another word, he marched past Sorin, hitting him with his shoulder as he passed. Sorin staggered back a step, allowing Narcisa to slip past.

"Good luck, Eyesore," she chirped as she went.

"Liviu, wait," he called, getting his cousin to stop and throw an annoyed look over one shoulder. When he'd gone to the watch house yesterday, there'd been a collection of reports of where people had claimed to be the night of the murder. Liviu's had stuck out to him for a glaring reason: his cousin had refused to say where he'd been.

"Where were you the night of Master Florin's murder?"

He expected some snarky reply in return, but to his surprise, his cousin snapped, "Your watchmen already bugged me about that, and it's none of your business."

"It is if you don't want to be a suspect," Sorin returned.

"You would want me to be a suspect, wouldn't you? Wouldn't it just be so quaint for you to get rid of magicless people like us that way? You don't own us, Eyesore." Liviu huffed and stormed away.

Narcisa regarded him with a scathing expression before following her brother.

Sorin stared, uneasiness coiling around his spine, though he couldn't say whether Liviu's refusal to answer was its cause or not. Either way, he'd have to keep a close eye on his cousin. Unfortunately.

Sighing, he did his best to shake the encounter away. When he returned to the elder's room, to his surprise, the servant from before stood at the door, trembling as he stood his ground against Ecaterina herself.

"If I want to visit the elder, I can," the woman huffed, a fist on her hip. "I'm part of the head family, and a servant like you can't boss me around." She made to grab the door handle, but the servant shifted his weight so he was right in front of it.

"Miss Apothecary said no one is allowed inside. No exceptions," he maintained despite the fact he shook like he was on the verge of rattling to pieces.

"Are you deaf? I'm a privileged member of the *head family*. Some little brat of the outsider has no right to tell me where I can and can't go."

Sorin took a deep breath before intervening. "Ecaterina, a person's heritage doesn't decide their worth. Miss Daciana is the village apothecary, and her orders are to be obeyed. End of discussion."

Ecaterina spun on her heel, her eyes lighting up when she spotted him. "Oh, my sweet nephew! Be a dear and use your manly intimidation to get this boy to let me see my father. Please?" She stuck her bottom lip out in a petulant pout.

It took all his strength not to roll his eyes. "No."

She drew back, a hand on her chest. "Sorin, I didn't think your parents raised you to be so rude."

"Miss Daciana said no one could enter since the elder's gotten worse. You're not exempt from her orders; none of us are." He lifted an eyebrow. "So you see, my parents did, in fact, raise me to be respectful to those who merit it."

Her pout dissolved into a glare in the blink of an eye, but she stalked away without another word.

Sorin waited until she'd vanished before he turned to the servant.

A bit sheepishly, the young man grabbed the handle. "Miss Apothecary did say you were the exception, though I figured Lady Ecaterina wouldn't like hearing that."

"No, she wouldn't." Sorin stepped forward, before stopping and turning to the servant. "Are you busy?"

The young man shook his head with a wry smile.

"If it's all right, will you do something for me? Go to the guardhouse and show them this." Sorin tugged the watch leader insignia off his belt. "Tell them I need two of them here immediately, understand? I'll make sure no one goes in while you're gone."

With a nod, the servant rushed off.

Sorin ducked inside the room, holding the door closed behind him just in case.

Daciana regarded him, one eyebrow raised.

"My family is stupid," he said.

She snorted but quickly regained her composure. "I take it several people came by. And no one else seemed sick?"

After a moment of thought, he shook his head.

A frown twisted her mouth once more.

All at once, someone gave the handle a hesitant twist, and Sorin tightened his grip, preventing whoever it was from pulling it open. He waited until they released the handle before stepping into the hall, coming face to face with one of his uncles, Bogdan. The man stared, wide-eyed, before a sheepish expression touched his face. Of all of Elder Aurel's children, Sorin was pretty sure Bogdan looked the most like Elder Aurel.

Sorin stared at him. "What did I just tell you?"

"I-I know, Sorin," the man said, hurrying to explain, holding up a vase of pretty red, yellow, and purple flowers. He spied some clematis and salvia, but didn't know the names of the rest. "But I just wanted to bring him these since my wife cut them this morning, so..."

"I'll take them. You will scat," Sorin said, accepting the vase.

Still looking a bit sheepish, his uncle disappeared back up the hall.

Sorin waited where he was, one hand tight on the doorknob still, convinced if he went back inside, someone else would try and barge in. Lo and behold, a few minutes later, a couple of his other magicless cousins strode up. Both were younger than him, and while they'd never been close, these two had chosen to follow Liviu and Narcisa's example.

"I heard from mom no one can go in," one said, tucking a stray strand of hair behind her ear. "And yet here you are. Just because you have magic doesn't mean you can get away with anything, Eyesore."

Sorin didn't respond to her goading.

"Having magic must be so great," she continued. "It makes you get married to a stranger. I've heard grandpa talking about it—the wedding he's planning for you? Are you excited about it?"

Sorin's chest clenched, but he stayed quiet. She just wanted him to take the bait, after all. He stared at the wall, keeping his cousins within his sight while avoiding staring directly at them.

The other one scoffed. "You're such a snob, just like your mom."

Spinning on her heel, she stormed off, the other one shooting him a cold glare before following suit.

He released a sigh, forcing away the dozens of emotions crowding in on him.

Mercifully, the next pair of faces to emerge from around the corner were his watchmen. As soon as they reached him, he turned the guarding of the door over to them and ducked back inside the room.

Daciana must've been staring at the door because when he stepped in, she hurriedly turned away. Sorin set his uncle's vase on the bedside table.

All at once, Daciana shot to her feet and snatched it, studying it with a bizarre level of scrutiny. He stood frozen, watching her in alarm.

After a long minute, she set it back down with a gentle knock. "Just wildflowers," she murmured, leaning against the table while watching Elder Aurel.

Sorin stared, not sure what to make of her behavior.

After a minute, she seemed to notice him staring and straightened, sweeping her braid off her shoulder. "Sorry."

"I'm sure you had a reason," he said, hoping she'd elaborate without him having to press her further.

She glanced at him, chewing her lip a little.

He waited.

After another moment, she took a deep breath. "I don't want to sound paranoid or anything, but..."

"But?" he prompted.

She glanced over her shoulder towards the elder, whose condition still didn't seem to be improving. "I...I'm not trying to think ill of your family out of spite or anything like that, but since they're..." Her gaze flicked to the door, and he knew she'd overheard the conversations in the hall. "Do they always treat you that way?"

Sorin hesitated, but he nodded.

When she spoke again, her voice was hushed. "It's just...whatever is wrong with your grandpa is strange; I've never seen anything like it before. And after all that, I can't help wondering— It was just a passing thought, mind you— I didn't mean to think it—"

"What is it?" he said, taking a step forward.

"I'm starting to think your grandpa's illness...isn't natural."

A chill slithered down his spine. "What do you mean?"

"I think he's sick because someone *wants* him to be," she admitted at last, a wary mien settling over her.

Sorin's mind raced. First Master Florin's death, and now this. He glanced at Elder Aurel, who was worsening still, with a sickness even Daciana didn't recognize. If she was right, then there was some dark force at work in their village, and Sorin didn't have a single clue as to why.

8

Daciana left Elder Aurel around midday after ensuring a servant sat with him since Sorin insisted on following her once more. A part of her wanted to snap at him for gluing himself to her shadow instead of hunting for Master Florin's killer, but from what she understood, the investigation had reached a stand still. As it was—maybe she was paranoid after her master's death—she couldn't shake the notion the elder's illness wasn't natural.

Well, that, and given the way his family treated Sorin, she didn't want to do something to make him upset. Plus, considering the current circumstances in the village, she wasn't sure she wanted to be alone. That panic from earlier kept threatening to swallow her with all the speed and efficiency of a white-water river, but being around others did keep it at bay. It was all odd though, so she did her best not to overthink it.

Regardless, she needed to restock the herbs in her satchel. Then she wanted to go through Master Florin's old treatment logs to see if he'd ever encountered something similar to this. She couldn't let paranoia determine the diagnosis here.

They stopped at the guardhouse on the way, and Daciana's heart sank a little lower at the fact Sorin's desk still stood bare of anything pertaining to the investigation. They continued on to the workshop where she retrieved what she needed, adding the herbs and logbooks to her satchel.

On the walk back to the compound, they remained silent. Daciana's mind raced. Someone had killed Master Florin, and now, someone had set their sights on Elder Aurel. Was it the same person or were these two separate events?

She hated not knowing; it left her agitated like the surface of a lake in a rainstorm, and...if she allowed herself to be honest, not knowing opened a chasm in her chest that seemed to go on forever. One that would devour her if she wasn't careful.

Part of an apothecary's job was fighting the unknown and making it known, and Daciana had long lost her fear of that. Even still, there was an uneasiness coiling through her, tightening every muscle, at the reality that the unknown in this case was a person. This wasn't her job; she shouldn't be here, doing this. Yet what else could she do?

As they passed through the head family's front gate, a chill swept down Daciana's spine. It was undoubtedly just her imagination, but now that the idea of a murderer prowling the village had taken root in her mind, the world itself took on a harsher light. The sun sharper, the shadows deeper. The only one standing between Elder Aurel and his would-be killer was her.

"Miss Apothecary!" someone called out, almost making her jump.

A man who looked similar to Ionel raced up to her and Sorin, his face pale.

"Eusiebiu?" Sorin asked, a note of concern coloring his voice.

"Miss Apothecary," the man grabbed one of her hands in his clammy ones and dragged her forward. "It's my wife. She collapsed."

A chill raced down her spine. "Show me. Quickly."

He bolted, still gripping her hand. He ran so fast, she tripped twice but managed to keep her feet beneath her. They raced past the main house and into a ring of smaller wooden houses surrounding a grassy courtyard. Near one of the houses to the left, a woman lay on the ground, a basket next to her on its side with a couple apples tumbled out. A kid who couldn't be more than five gently cradled her head, wide-eyed and pale.

Daciana knelt next to her, taking note of the symptoms. Fever, chills, clammy hands, stiff joints, wheezing—almost a perfect match to Elder Aurel. A cold sensation took root in her chest.

Glancing up, she met Sorin's gaze. "Take her to the elder's room. It's the same thing."

He scooped up the older woman like she weighed nothing and made his way towards the main house without a word.

Daciana glanced at the man and the child who seemed to be his son, the fear roiling in her chest reflected on their faces.

"Will Mommy be okay?" the boy asked, gripping his father's pants so hard, his little knuckles were white.

Master Florin's words rang through her mind: 'Don't give our patient's family false hope, but don't leave them in despair either.'

Taking a deep breath to calm herself, Daciana said, "I think so. I've almost figured out what it is, and once I do, I'll do everything I can to help her get better, okay?"

The boy nodded, and she didn't wait another second before racing after Sorin.

By the time she arrived in the elder's room, the woman was already settled on a cot, with Sorin glancing back and forth between her two patients. For a split second, it occurred to her that the scene was almost comical, in an endearing kind of way.

Shaking that thought away, she approached the woman, reaching for her satchel, dozens of herbs running through her mind. Feverfew would help with fever, chamomile with the aches—

She froze. Herbs hadn't helped Elder Aurel's condition. On the contrary, even though it'd been slow, they'd seemed to make it worse.

Reaching for herbs was instinctive; doing otherwise felt very, very wrong. However, what if the herbs were reacting negatively with the poison? What if the poison worsened with more drugs in their systems?

While trusting herbs was a matter of instinct, her gut feeling insisted they were the wrong choice this time. So she needed to wait and see what would happen if she trusted her gut before deciding her next move.

She straightened and found Sorin already watching her with an expectant air. "I need more water. It needs to be clean, okay?"

He grabbed the pitcher and raced out.

While waiting for him to return, she got her patients as comfortable as she could before settling between them and pulling out Master Florin's first logbook, the one he'd kept when he'd become an apprentice. Perhaps he'd once encountered something that would prove useful.

Sorin returned in record time, but caring for her two patients didn't leave her with much time to study her master's notes. Then two became three by mid-afternoon. Three became four by evening.

Sorin was sent to fetch water on a regular basis, and a part of her cringed every time she did so, knowing that him serving as her errand boy kept him from the investigation—though when she tried to explain that, his stubborn insistence to remain by her side won out. To top it off, when night arrived with little change in her patients, he and his watchmen made sure her family was informed of where she was and why. Despite the situation, she was profoundly grateful for all of them and their efforts, but it did increase her anxiety to save his family.

Daciana no longer believed this illness was contagious, and yet, four people were sick. Sorin's emotions were never close to the surface, but if she inspected his features, she noticed there was a knot between his brows that hadn't been there before.

For a moment, the atmosphere strained due to the faint wheezes of her patients, Daciana stared at him, trying to figure out how to ask what was on her mind. "Sorin?"

He gave her his attention.

"Everyone here is part of your family, right?"

He nodded.

"And as far as you know, no one else from the village is sick like this, right?"

Another nod.

If it was just a sickness, it was plausible that only the head family was exhibiting any symptoms because most of them stayed in the compound, associating with the rest of the community very little. That said, some of them still did go out, like Ionel. If it was just a sickness though, surely it would spread to a few others beyond the compound at least, and yet...

Shaking her head to prevent herself from drawing a premature conclusion, she refocused on Master Florin's notes. When it got too dark to see, she lit a candle and kept reading, her ears tuned to the wheezes, and she constantly assessed whether they were getting harsher or weaker. As the night settled in, she stayed on guard for what she feared most: the breathing getting fainter.

Sometime around what she guessed to be midnight from the deepness of the night and height of the moon, Daciana rose, stretching stiff joints before checking on her patients. With simple rest and water, they hadn't grown worse, but they weren't improving much either.

As she turned back towards her studies, she found Sorin hadn't left. She'd been so engrossed in her research she hadn't realized it, but he'd curled up on one of the spare cots the servants had placed in the corner as a precaution and had fallen asleep. He wasn't an expressive person, but in his sleep, he was far less stern, and in a way, she could see him for the twenty-year old he was.

"I'm sure you bear a lot of burdens," she mused to herself. "That seems to be expected in a family that designates so many more responsibilities to you. And there seem to be many in your family who don't understand how they make those burdens worse."

Smiling a little to herself, she returned to her vigil beneath the window. The distant howl of a wolf split the quiet of the night, making her glance at the dark window. She supposed the wolves hadn't moved on yet. She returned her attention to her studies, and before long, the candle burned low, the flame dancing just above the pool of clear, melted wax. The flickers of light across the surface caught her eye, and she ended up watching it, the little bursts of orange and yellow making her drowsy. Her eyelids grew heavy, making it difficult to read her Master's untidy handwriting.

Sometime later, she awoke to someone giving her shoulder a gentle shake. Blearily, she looked up, surprised she'd fallen asleep and even more surprised to find Sorin was the one who'd roused her.

"There's a cot if you'd prefer," he said, voice hushed.

Slowly, she straightened, her brain needing a minute to register what he'd said and the fact the sun's early morning rays illuminated the room. Her hand was trapped between the pages of the logbook she'd been reading, and it tingled with pinpricks of pain. "No, I'm okay. But thank you. I should check on them."

Daciana got to her feet, stifling a yawn while hitting her hand against her thigh to wake it.

The patients were the same, but at the same time, their symptoms did appear a bit better, their fevers less severe and their breathing less labored. The urge to reach for her satchel returned, but she needed to wait a little longer. She had to be as certain as possible before making her next move.

Once she was satisfied they were all right for the time being, she returned to her window, a bit surprised Sorin was still there, having pulled a chair up next to hers. He seemed alert, but even still, an air of sleepiness hung over him that was, in a way, kind of...cute.

No. Those weren't the kind of thoughts she should be entertaining.

Settling herself back in her chair, Daciana forced her mind to think of other things by saying, "So, who is everyone?"

Sorin obliged her. Motioning to the first woman who'd been brought yesterday, he said, "She's another aunt of mine, my Aunt Raluca. And the other two are a couple of my cousins, Tania and Sabina."

"Did any of them visit your grandpa the other night?"

"Tania and Sabina, maybe, but not Raluca. Her family was the only one other than mine who listened to you."

Daciana frowned. Raluca had fallen ill sooner than Sorin's two cousins even though she hadn't visited the elder after he'd fallen ill. Of course, the illness could've been more contagious before the symptoms appeared, but if that was the case, why weren't more people sick? The idea that whatever was going on wasn't natural took further root in her mind like a noxious weed. However, before deciding whether or not it needed to be ripped out, she had one more question.

"Do any of them have magic like you?" she asked, glancing at Sorin.

He didn't answer right away, his gaze dropping to the floor. When he finally lifted his head, allowing her to see his eyes, there was something there, something she couldn't name, that made an ache blossom in her chest. "All of them do."

There was always a chance this was some kind of illness that only affected people with magical abilities—which she'd never heard of outside of fables.

The reality that this was some kind of induced illness was taking shape, which meant there was a good chance the magic-bearing members of the head family were being targeted.

They sat in silence for another hour or so, the morning sun gradually filling the room with its golden light, before their reverie was broken by the arrival of patient number five, this time one of Sorin's uncles.

She didn't ask it, but once they were alone, Sorin met her gaze and said, "Wind magic."

The odds of that being a coincidence were miniscule in Daciana's mind.

Once his uncle was settled amongst the others, she touched a hand to Sorin's arm, getting his attention. "Sorin, why do you think someone would want to attack the magical people in your family? I've seen them around the village, and they only ever seem to be helping people. So what possible reason would push someone to go after you?" They maintained their wall, helped the blacksmiths keep their fires hot enough—and she was sure they did a lot more for the village.

He looked away, and for a minute, she thought she wasn't going to get an answer.

"Probably because of the difference in how we're all treated," he explained, not meeting her gaze. "What those of us who have magic are allowed to do in both the family and the village often feels like favoritism—even to us. My uncle, Ionel, for example, was the most experienced member of the watch before his retirement. The number of cases and disputes he'd solved is extraordinary; no one in the history of our village solved as many as him. He asked my grandpa several times to make him the watch leader, but instead, my grandpa chose me."

Under Daciana's fingertips, his arm tensed.

"Ecaterina, for all her...quirks, is a talented musician. My mom said she's never heard anyone who can play like her sister can. However, she's in charge of the kitchens, which, while she's a good cook, everyone knows she hates being there. A cousin of mine, Liviu, is incredibly talented at building contraptions and working with his hands. I have a wolf he carved me once—it's incredible, and he made it when we were kids. But now he's just a delivery boy who's expected to marry whomever the elder chooses before he's tossed out of the compound. Most of my cousins born without magic were married off the compound to work on farms and such—there are some I haven't seen in years. If they happen to birth a child who has magic, that kid gets to come back, but the rest of their family doesn't."

Daciana's insides curdled at the disturbing pictures Sorin sketched for her.

"But those of us with magic have houses promised to us already, and jobs that will more than provide for any current or future family, and..."

She studied his face, sensing emotions he wasn't letting show. "Sorin, did you want to be the head watchman?" she whispered.

He still didn't meet her gaze, but at the same second, they both realized she still had her hand on his arm and took a step apart. "It's not so bad."

She studied him, once again sensing emotions he wasn't letting through. Her thoughts from last night about what burdens he bore wove through her mind again, and even though it was clear he didn't want to let her in at all, she was getting a glimpse anyway.

"I take back what I said the other day."

The slightest furrowing of his brow appeared.

"About talents," she said, wrapping her arms around herself. "What's the good of having a talent if you get no say in how it's used? Sure, maintaining the wall is significantly easier with magic, but it can be done without it. So can repairing roads, a-and diverting water from the river for irrigation. I get protecting the village is important, but why does it have to come at the expense of your happiness?"

Sorin met her gaze, and for the briefest second, what he hadn't wanted her to see before became clear: fear, anguish, even despair. Even though neither of them spoke, in an instant, something shifted between them, like the wall of acquaintanceship separating them had crumbled a little.

Then he turned away. "I have some things I need to do, but there'll be a couple watchmen right outside if you need something."

"Okay," she said.

Half-glancing back at her, he dipped his head before heading for the door.

As he touched his hand to the knob, a bone-chilling thought dropped into her mind like an anchor, making her call out, "Hey, Sorin."

He paused, glancing back, which allowed the sun to illuminate the golden hues of his brown eyes, something about it taking her breath away a bit.

"If someone is targeting those in your family who have magic, they're going to go after you too, so...be careful, okay?"

He stared before nodding. "Of course." He left without another word.

Daciana touched a hand to her chest, startled her heart was beating as fast as hummingbird's wings.

9

Despite the fact Sorin didn't know Daciana well, for some reason, her warning to be careful ignited a cheery little fire in his chest that refused to go out. Perhaps it was because he worked with men all day, every day, but hearing someone vocalize concern for his wellbeing was...nice. His watchmen didn't. Well, they were concerned about him, he was sure, they just didn't show it much, except in the occasional punch to the arm after a job.

Even still, hearing her say something like that—seeing the concern in those remarkably attractive brown eyes of hers—did something to him. For a split second, he'd been on the verge of spilling everything to her, of laying out every fear and doubt that tormented him. Instead, he'd kept himself reined in with the stern reminder that they hardly knew each other. The only reason they were in such close proximity now was because of a murder.

Even still, though she had only a hint of the tension surrounding him and his family, hearing her give voice to the thoughts and sentiments he kept to himself made him...light. Lighter than he'd been in months. Years. And for some reason, where she'd touched his arm still seem to...tingle.

Shaking his head, he left the main house, heading for home. He hadn't intended to fall asleep amongst Daciana and her patients, but since he had there were a couple things he needed to do before he could return to his self-appointed duty of being her day guard. Before yesterday, he'd been on the verge of questioning whether or not she still needed a guard; after all, in the few days since Master Florin's murder, there hadn't even been a hint of an attack on her life.

However, with someone attacking his family, by her side with all the afflicted patients was exactly where he needed to be. Plus, if Daciana was right and managed to find a cure for it, he was sure whoever was behind it wouldn't sit idle. The trick, however—if it was, in fact, poison—would be preventing the situation from repeating itself.

"Sorin!" his uncle Ionel called, startling him out of his musing.

Pulling up short, Sorin glanced over, pleased to find his uncle standing in his doorway with a steaming kettle.

"This just came off the stove, and you look like you've had a long night." Ionel smiled. "Want some tisane before you head on your way? I acquired a new flavor, and you're pretty much the only one who hasn't gotten to try it yet."

Sorin hesitated. He didn't want to be gone from Daciana and her patients for long; a clue could surface at any time. However, his watchmen were there, and he was sure Daciana would inform him if she found anything promising. Plus a steaming cup of tisane sounded perfect this early in the morning.

"All right," he called, turning and following his uncle into the house. "As long as it's quick."

Ionel laughed before setting the table, setting out two cups and sprinkling dried herbs in them.

Sorin lifted an eyebrow. There was nothing wrong with dried herbs in tisane—but fresh were more flavorful.

His uncle noticed. "I know. It's a shame they aren't fresh like I prefer, but it's a foreign herb, so there's not much I can do. Herbs transport better dry than they do fresh."

"Ah," Sorin said while his uncle poured the still steaming water in their cups. "Maybe Miss Daciana could cultivate it in Master Florin's herb garden. They have several plants there that aren't native. That way, if we like it, we could have it fresh next time."

"Now there's an idea. Master Florin did mention his apprentice has a bit of a green thumb." Ionel sat, wrapping his hands around his cup, drinking deeply of the perfumed steam. "But I'm sure she's too busy with all her new responsibilities. Honey?"

Sorin accepted the proffered bowl of honey, adding a few drips to his drink before stirring it.

It was a different kind of tisane than any his uncle had discovered before, and the smell was almost familiar, but also not.

"Oh, wait." Rising, Ionel retrieved a plate of scones from the counter. "Ecaterina sent these out to everyone—a couple new flavors they're experimenting with in the kitchen, she said. There's too many for me and Lucia, so you can have a couple if you'd like."

Sorin nodded, taking one. It had the bite of cheese combined with the flavorful burst of a fruit he couldn't place. For half a second, he wondered if Daciana might like it. Then he wondered if she'd be put off by him offering her food.

"So," Ionel began, swirling his cup a couple times before taking a hesitant sip. Recoiling, he grimaced. "Too hot."

That almost got Sorin to smile. "So?"

"How's the investigation going? Any closer to uncovering Master Florin's killer?"

He worked to restrain a sigh. If it'd been anyone else, Sorin would've dodged the question, but since it was Ionel... "No. We find a lead and it leads to a dead end, and that's where we're stuck."

Frowning, Ionel said, "Aside from the murder, obviously, the boys told me the only odd thing was the stolen herbs, right?"

He nodded.

"Maybe it was no more than a simple robbery by some passing stranger. It's weak, but that might explain the dead ends."

It was Sorin's turn to frown. He didn't think there were enough clues for that—and why would a passing stranger work so hard to conceal all traces of themselves? That said, if the killer had fled, it could be why the clues seemed to lead nowhere.

"Or," he mused, "whoever it was is clever and knew what clues not to leave behind. Or maybe they wanted to keep us searching elsewhere."

"You think they might have stolen the herbs to lead you astray?" Ionel asked, raising an eyebrow.

Sorin nodded again.

"It could be a bit of a misdirection," his uncle mused. "That would imply that someone was after Master Florin though. Have you found any evidence that would steer you that way?"

When Sorin shook his head, the man 'hmmed' and took another experimental sip of his drink. A hint of a smile touched his mouth, and he drank more deeply.

That encouraged Sorin to follow suit. Gingerly, he picked up the warm cup and took a drink. It had an odd tang to it, and he couldn't quite place the flavor. If he was honest, he didn't like it. However, not wanting to offend the uncle who continued giving him mountains of advice about Sorin's new line of work despite being retired, he forced himself to swallow.

"It's different, isn't it?" his uncle remarked once Sorin set his cup down.

"Very. I'm...not sure I like it much."

That made the man grin. "It was fun to try something new though, eh? Don't worry, you can use Ecaterina's scones to get rid of the taste."

"Sure."

Tossing his head back, Ionel laughed, a deep warm sound that always managed to make Sorin's spirits lift and bring the sunny afternoons they used to spend training together with spears to the forefront of his mind.

Growing serious once more, Ionel reached across the table and patted Sorin's shoulder. "It's a tough position you're in with this case, but I trust you'll figure it out. Just remember not to rush. I know there's that temptation to charge ahead and jump to conclusions, but it's important to take the time to find as much of the picture as you can before you put it together."

At least one of them had confidence in him.

Once he polished off the drink, Sorin said, "Thanks for the tisane," and devoured two of the scones (one a rich herby one while the other was a bizarre fruity one that was kind of doughy) to get the taste out of his mouth.

"Anytime." Ionel leaned forward, resting his elbows on the table. "And I hope you catch whoever did this. Master Florin was my best friend, you know."

Sorin got to his feet and turned to leave, but before he did, he stopped and turned back. "Would it be all right if I took a couple of the scones to Miss Daciana?"

His uncle raised an eyebrow. "I guess, but can I ask why?"

"The others are pretty sick still, and she refuses to leave their side. I'm not sure when she last ate."

"By all means," Ionel said, pushing the plate of scones forward. "I'd hate for her to suffer more than she is."

Sorin scooped up a few scones (avoiding the doughy ones) and wrapped them in a cloth his uncle provided. Then he left, making for his own house.

Once he'd tidied some and his mom had shoved a decent breakfast down his throat (and added some food to his makeshift sack for Miss Daciana), he hurried to the watchhouse.

As he'd feared, no information relevant to Master Florin's death lay on his desk, but a wrapped bundle did with Calin seated nearby, watching him with interest.

Sorin lifted it, raising an eyebrow as he did so. He'd expected it to have some heft given its thickness, but its lightness surprised him. "What is this?"

"It's for the apothecary, from one of the other village's apothecaries. We had the post leave it there since she's stuck in your family's compound, and you seem to keep buzzing around her like a horse fly."

He shot his friend a scathing look. "Any news?"

Unperturbed by the glare, Calin shook his head. "There're rumors circling, though. Apparently, someone is spreading the idea that a ghost must've committed the crime, and at this rate, given the severe lack of clues, I'm tempted to believe it."

Sorin grunted in agreement as he flipped through the rest of the papers on his desk. Nothing of consequence that couldn't wait until things calmed. With a bit of a sigh, he turned towards the door.

Calin got to his feet, making Sorin glance back.

"What?" Calin said. "I'm supposed to go take over for guard duty for the apothecary, so don't glare at me like that."

Choosing not to respond, Sorin left, leaving his friend to follow.

Calin scrambled to catch up. "You know, maybe I'm the weird one, but you're kind of putting a lot of effort into protecting this apothecary, you know?"

"She has a name."

"Fine, Daciana."

"It's more productive than sitting at a desk waiting for information," Sorin said as they passed through his front gates. "And ensuring the safety of our only apothecary is of the utmost importance."

"No— I mean, I get that. What I'm saying is that you, yourself, are putting in a lot of effort. You, Sorin. It's kind of weird. You've never worked this hard on a case before."

He stopped, staring at his friend, trying to puzzle out the

implication there. Knowing his friend, Sorin was positive Calin thought he had a crush—

"Are you trying to stay so busy no one will get the chance to tease you about being one of the oldest single men or try and set you up with one of their daughters?"

That was so far removed from what Sorin had anticipated that he just stared at his friend, completely mute.

Calin stopped too, staring, his eyes getting wider and wider the more time passed. When they were nearly the size of the moon, he asked, "Am I right?"

"No," Sorin snapped. "This is serious, Calin."

"Aw, I thought I'd finally guessed what you were thinking."

"Actually, if you want the truth," he said, voice lowered despite the fact they seemed to be alone, "Daciana thinks this sickness might not be natural."

Calin's brow furrowed. "You don't mean poison?"

"She's not sure, which is why I haven't mentioned it yet. But it's looking that way. So I think if I stay there, I might find more clues than not."

Calin frowned in a thoughtful way, but before he could speak, a voice that sounded a lot like Sorin's dad's barked, "Out of the way!"

Sorin leapt back as his dad raced past with—

Mom. His heart stuttered at the sight of her in his dad's arms, face pale and cheeks flushed—just like everyone else. For a moment, all he could do was stare before shaking himself and vaulting up the stairs after his dad, Calin hot on his heels.

When he arrived in the room, he stopped, shock rendering him immobile for nearly a solid minute, both packages in his hands forgotten.

In the brief time he'd been gone, the number of patients had *doubled*. With Sorin's mom joining the queue, the number of sick was up to nine. Dread crept through his insides like frost as he gazed around the room;

everyone who was ill had magic. All of them.

Daciana stared at Sorin's parents before her gaze shot around the room. "There's no more space in here. Is there somewhere larger where we can take everyone?" She turned to Sorin, out of breath.

"There's the hall," he suggested. "We don't use it often, so it should be all right."

She opened her mouth before pausing. "Is it closed off from the rest of the house?"

He caught her drift immediately. "Yes."

"Perfect. We need to move everyone there now."

Sorin jumped into action. This was something he could do. While he was powerless against this malady and perplexed by the murder case, this was something he could tackle.

Turning, he got Calin and the other watchmen, and the five of them moved the patients down the stairs and into the main hall. Sorin ensured at least one of them stayed with the patients at all times, and if the others thought it strange, they said nothing.

When there was only one patient left, Sorin hurried up the stairs after Calin. At the top, his foot missed the step as a dizziness swept over him, nearly throwing him to the ground. He caught himself, banging his knee in the process.

"You're not sick too, right?" Calin demanded, turning back.

"No, no," Sorin said, getting to his feet. His knee smarted, but the dizzy spell had passed. His late night must be catching up with him; he'd been fine until he'd exerted himself.

"Oh, you've been overworking yourself again. Good grief, Sorin. At this rate, you're going to die before you can get married!" his friend cried in exasperation.

"Less talk, more work," Sorin snapped as they hurried to the room.

That made Calin laugh.

Once they'd taken all the sick to the hall, Sorin stationed two guards outside the door with strict orders not to allow anyone inside, period, before crossing to the other side of the room and locking that door. It was smaller and more out of the way than the other, but he wasn't about to take any chances.

When Daciana herself arrived, she stared around the room, breathing hard with sweat glistening on her brow. At that moment, he remembered the food and package he'd brought for her, but he was fairly certain she'd ignore him if he tried to give them to her now. They may have only been in close contact for a few days, but he'd learned a great deal about her work ethic in that amount of time.

Then, with a deep breath he equated to rolling up her sleeves, Daciana went right back to it.

After a moment of hesitation, Sorin followed suit, doing his best despite his limited abilities in this situation. More than once, he found himself studying Daciana as she went about the room, never pausing to rest. It struck him that despite her having been Master Florin's apprentice for years, time in which he had seen her and they had met in passing, he felt as though he was seeing her for who she truly was for the first time.

All he could think was that it was no wonder Master Florin— respected in more than one village for his skills as an apothecary—had chosen her to continue his legacy.

Fire ignited in his chest, flaring bright and hot with his determination. For her sake, he would solve this mystery. No matter what it took.

10

Dusk arrived before Daciana was aware of it doing so. She had nine patients now, though the ones who'd been under her care for a day or two faired better than the ones who'd only arrived today. Sorin had already confirmed that everyone who was sick possessed magic. She no longer believed this was a coincidence; the symptoms were all the same and they'd all fallen ill so fast.

However, since the head family barely listened to her as it was—most of them disregarding her orders not to visit Elder Aurel—how in the world would she get them to listen to her hypothesis that someone was out for their blood?

Exhausted, Daciana sat in a chair in the corner of the room, by one of the few windows, and Sorin padded after her. She glanced his way. "I know you have a lot on your plate but thank you for helping me today."

"It's the least I can do." He met her gaze for a brief second, just long enough for her to notice the way the candlelight made his eyes shimmer.

In the distance, the haunting lilt of a wolf's song brushed her senses, making both of them glance towards the window. She wondered how long the wolves would linger so close to the village.

"Sorin," she began, tugging her attention from the window. "I'm not sure who's doing it or how, but I'm positive someone is poisoning your family."

"I agree."

"Until I figure out how they're doing it, you need to be careful and tell the rest of your family to as well. They're more likely to listen to you than to me."

He dipped his head, almost as though he would nod, but he froze instead. "Hold on."

Without explaining, he walked towards the door and retrieved a couple bundles from a chair there. When he returned, he held them out to her.

"What's this?" she asked, noting that one package was sturdy and the other appeared to be no more than a simple cloth.

"This came for you." He indicated the package. "And this..." His gaze flicked to the cloth, and for some reason, he swallowed and refuse to meet her eye. "I... You don't eat much when you're working so I...well, it was supposed to be breakfast."

She blinked, caught a little off-guard, before remembering her manners and accepting both of the bundles. For some reason, when she peeked inside the cloth, getting a glimpse of the scones and bread, her vision misted over. Her stomach churned, a poignant reminder she hadn't eaten anything all day; there simply hadn't been time.

"Do you not like it?" Sorin asked, catching her enough off-guard she glanced up.

Her heart stuttered as she fought to blink away the tears. "No, I do. I do, don't worry. Thank you."

He remained still before bringing over a nearby chair and setting it next to hers. Then he sat. Another moment passed before he said, "I don't want to pry, but if you like it...why were you crying?"

She flushed. For half a second, she debated blowing it off as being so hungry or something like that, but the fact Sorin had spilled the dark parts of his family with her made her reconsider. He hadn't had to do that, but he had. So maybe it would be okay if she trusted him with this; after all the only other person she'd ever been able to tell about it had been Master Florin, and he was gone.

"Well I..." she began, fingering her other package, "You know my mom wasn't born in the village, right?"

A bit to her surprise, Sorin said, "She's from the Inama tribe, isn't she?"

She nodded. "A nomadic tribe. But when she decided to marry my dad, she chose to leave the tribe and settle here. Because she's a foreigner, most of the village doesn't accept her. And many of them...extend that curtesy to the rest of my family. Even my dad has to rely on the generosity of his friends for work because no one will give him a steady job. If it hadn't been for Master Florin making me his apprentice, I don't think my family would've been able to..."

She risked a glance Sorin's direction, and there was an emotion there, one that softened his expression a little bit. Quickly, she returned her gaze to her gifts.

"It doesn't bother me much, but I guess I'm a little tired today." Fingering the bundle of food, she whispered, "This is one of the nicest things anyone's ever done for me, especially since Master Florin—" The tears burned at her eyes again, and she stopped speaking, afraid they would escape.

To her surprise, Sorin reached out, touching the back of her hand with his fingertips. He didn't speak, but when she met his gaze, she was met with a look that contained such kindness and understanding, one of those tears slipped past her defenses. Even still, she couldn't pull away from Sorin's gaze, something about it making a warmth blossom in her chest, a feeling she hadn't had in seemingly forever.

One of her patients made a funny noise, so she rushed to excuse herself and go to their side. She hastily scrubbed at that traitorous tear and the trail it'd left as she worked.

It may have been because of the stress dragging on her like heavy chains, but warmth still lingered in her chest, returning when she remembered the expression on Sorin's normally impassive face. She could be wrong, but she might be falling for him, which wasn't a good idea given their backgrounds and village standings. Besides, she was sure that quiet kindness was a part of his nature; she doubted it was because he harbored feelings for her. So it was better to let this go.

Even still, it was nice to imagine he cared about her as a person rather than just her as an apothecary.

By the time she returned to the corner, she had herself back together and busied with her second package. Inside were herbs wrapped in neat bundles and a note, and many of the herbs ones that were out of season, the relief that flooded her making her knees so weak she collapsed into her chair. Daciana eased the note out, smiling a little at the condolences and advice from one of the neighboring apothecaries. There was one less thing for her to worry about, the sudden absence of that burden making it feel as though she might float away.

"Good news?" Sorin asked.

She smiled. "Herbs from one of the other village's apothecaries. Thank you for bringing this to me." She gently settled the package in her bag before taking out the journal she'd been studying last.

To her surprise, Sorin opened the cloth of food and gave her a meaningful look. Once she'd eaten one of the scones (one of Ecaterina's creations, he explained), he nodded towards the treatment log. "What is that?"

"One of my master's treatment logs from his first days as a Master Apothecary."

Very subtly, he cocked his head.

A flicker of the warmth from earlier sparked in Daciana's chest at the movement. Doing her best to ignore it, she said, "I thought there might be a chance he'd encountered something similar to it before, which might give us a lead on whatever this is. That'll help me treat it better."

"Ah," he said. "Do you have another one?"

Daciana raised an eyebrow, staring mutely.

A hint of a smile touched his mouth. "Two of us will be able to search much faster. Plus, since it's most likely poison, it's my job to investigate."

She relented, fighting off those feelings once again, and they slipped into quiet companionship, accompanied by the occasional hiss of the candle, the raspy breaths of her patients, and the howls of the wolves in the fells. Night settled in while they studied and while Daciana made her rounds, doing what she could to ease her patient's discomfort. One of her younger patients mumbled something about being thirsty, making her smile.

Making requests was a good sign. Hopefully, that meant the worst of it would be behind them.

After her second set of rounds, when she returned to her seat, she was a little surprised to find Sorin asleep already, the logbook he'd been studying lying open in his lap. For some reason, that made her smile.

The rumors surrounding him hadn't done justice to how dedicated he was or how calm he remained in the face of frustration. While she'd promised herself she would help track down her master's killer, her frustration at the lack of progress was dampened because she had a massive problem demanding her attention. However, Sorin had two such problems, and he handled any frustration he may have felt far better than she could've. Clearly, he had a lot of trust in his watchmen since he allowed them to do the groundwork while he worked here.

Another way the rumors disgraced him was their failure to mention his kindness. Just the memory of that hint of a smile he'd given her made her tingle from head to toe. Moreover, for the first time since this had all started, she wasn't hungry, to his credit.

As she reopened her treatment log, she shyly glanced his way, allowing herself to admire the deep brown color of his hair, the hue reminding her of rich, freshly tiled earth.

"No wonder all those girls in town fawn over you," she murmured, forcing her attention to her logbook. "You're handsome, you know. I admit I didn't notice it until now, but even I find you attractive."

A blush burst across her face despite the fact she was alone and no one heard her.

11

Sometime later, Sorin roused himself, appearing more than a little out of sorts, which got Daciana's attention. For what seemed like an entire minute, he stared around the room like he couldn't figure out where he was.

He yawned, noticing her while in the middle of doing so. His cheeks took on a pink hue. "Sorry. I didn't mean to fall asleep."

"It's okay," she said, stifling a laugh as best as she could. "I'm used to this, unlike you."

He yawned again. "I feel like I didn't sleep at all," he muttered, rubbing his head and making a couple clumps of his short hair stick out like wings.

She smiled, thinking nothing of his comment for a split second before a chill swept through her chest. Sorin had magic too; if someone was targeting all the magic members of his family, then he, with the strongest magic out of all of them, was the largest target of them all.

"Sorin, are you feeling okay?"

There was a delay before he responded. "Huh?"

Her treatment logs forgotten, she hurried to him, pressing the back of her hand to his forehead. Warm, but not as feverish as the others. His breathing was normal, but he was a bit pale. Though, that could be because he'd just woken up.

"Sorin," she repeated, speaking slowly, "are you feeling okay?"

There was an unfocused light in his eyes, screaming something other than exhaustion was at play. She was almost positive he'd been poisoned too, her heart skipping a beat at the thought.

"I...think so?" he managed. "I feel fine. I'm just tired."

Daciana frowned, staring at him intently, picking out the beginnings of the poison taking hold. He'd been in here all night, which meant the poison had to be slow acting, something administered either hours or days before the symptoms would appear. "I need you to think: have you eaten anything strange lately? Anything different or unusual?"

A long pause. "No? Well...my uncle and I tried a new tisane, but he said he'd been giving some to everybody." Sorin's brow furrowed, making him the most expressive she'd ever seen him. "And my aunt made a bunch of new scones. She said they were experiments..."

"But I ate those too," she murmured. "And not everyone is sick." Just how was this sickness being administered? How was she supposed to stop it? Even if everyone recovered, how would she prevent it from happening again?

Sorin made to rise, but Daciana stopped him by putting her hands on his shoulders. "Sorin, I think you're poisoned too."

After the customary pause, he shook his head. "I'm just tired." Fumbling a little, he managed to close the treatment log in his lap and hold it out to her. She took it, and he took advantage of that to get to his feet. "See?"

He took a couple steps before he stumbled. She lunged to steady him but only succeeded in getting dragged to the floor with him when he fell, banging her knee against the stone floor. It seemed to take Sorin a moment to realize he'd fallen, and when he did, he put a hand to his head, looking completely bewildered.

He struggled back to his feet, staggering in his attempt to do so.

"Sorin, stop. You need to lay down," Daciana said, hurrying to her feet and fighting to keep him steady. Within a couple steps, he nearly pitched them to the ground again. She grit her teeth, just managing to keep him upright at the expense of her muscles. "Moving around is going to make it worse!"

Even still, Sorin fought to stay on his feet.

All at once, she recalled the watchmen he'd assigned to guard the doors and that it'd mostly been the same four people on rotation. Sorin's friend had been on it. What was his name again?

"C-Calin?" she called, stumbling as she fought to keep Sorin from falling while trying to drag him in the direction of one of the empty cots.

He, stubborn as ever, kept pulling her towards the door.

Then, mercifully, one of the front doors opened, and Calin poked his head in. "Did I hear my name?"

"Help," was all Daciana managed to say before Sorin stepped towards the door with enough force to yank her off balance. She fell hard, landing on her hip. Sorin stumbled one step before he collapsed.

Calin sprinted across the room, reaching Sorin just in time to keep him from getting back up. "Cut it out, mate! You're going to kill our apothecary all on your own."

"Got to go—"

"Nowhere," Calin finished firmly. "Miss Daciana says you're sick, so you've got to go to bed. Come on."

Calin manhandled his friend over to the spare cot, getting the young man to lay down at last.

Daciana climbed to her feet, rubbing her smarting hip. "He's stubborn enough when he's normal. Why does it get worse when he's sick?"

That made Calin snort with laughter. "Tell me about it. Whenever he got sick as a kid, his mom would practically have to sit on him to get him to rest. I think they legitimately had to tie him to his bed once."

Daciana frowned, her chest tightening at the sight of Sorin even paler than before, his cheeks flushed, and his breathing heavier. Whatever the poison was, it was setting in now. Though Sorin still sat upright—a defiant light in his eyes—he leaned back on his elbows and slumped, his slouch growing more pronounced with each breath.

"Quit being so stubborn and rest before you make it worse," Calin snapped.

At long last, Sorin relented and collapsed on the cot, pale and breathing hard.

"What's wrong with 'em, Miss Daciana?" Calin asked, his gaze roving around the room.

"Poison. I just can't figure out what kind."

"Poison?" Calin spluttered, eyes wide. "Isn't that...extreme?"

"It is, but it's the only explanation I have." She paused, considering keeping the most important piece of information to herself. However, Sorin trusted Calin, so it would be all right if she did the same. "Plus...Sorin said everyone who's fallen ill so far are those of his family who have magic—and only those with magic. I don't know of an illness that does that."

Calin stilled, his gaze settling on Sorin.

"I don't know much about the head family," she continued, "but from the three days I've been here, I've overheard more than one argument between someone with magic and someone without. It seems the family members without it resent their counterparts very much."

He didn't speak for a long minute. "Enough to kill?"

"Perhaps." Daciana watched Sorin too, noting his symptoms already seemed more severe than the others' had been. "After all, someone killed a person like Master Florin too."

Calin stayed quiet before turning and looking her straight in the eye. "So how can I help you?"

She stared at him in surprise. "But the door..."

That almost got him to smile. "I got here early, and besides, Miss Apothecary, you're severely outnumbered here. More importantly, if you're right, then someone is trying to kill my best friend. I'm not going to stand by and twiddle my thumbs."

"Okay, what I need is water. Fresh water that hasn't passed through the family's hands, to be safe. Can you do that?"

"Sure can!" Calin said with a wink. "You just wait here, and I'll bring you all the fresh, safe water you can handle." He all but raced out.

Tension knotted itself in Daciana's chest, but she did her best to take deep breaths and remain calm. If she panicked, it would cloud her judgement and she'd make unforgivable mistakes.

Someone groaned behind her, making her whip around. To her relief, Elder Aurel was sitting up, still pale and drawn, but his breathing had eased.

"Where on earth...?" he began, trailing off when Daciana arrived at his side. He squinted at her, accentuating the wrinkles lining his face even more. "Miss...Apothecary? What are you doing here?"

"There's been a situation," she said, indicating the rest of the room, though he didn't look. "More importantly, how are you feeling?"

He groaned. "Like I met the wrong end of a draft horse. What happened?"

There was no point in mincing words. "You were poisoned."

His eyes went wide. "Poison?"

"Something slow acting but poison all the same. That's why..." She trailed off as he took stock of the room and all the sick people around him.

When his gaze returned to her, a startled look in his eyes, she continued. "If there's anything you can tell me about the days before you became ill, it might help me narrow down what it is. I don't want to cast blame on anyone, but there are too many strange coincidences for it to not be intentional."

With a frown, Elder Aurel dipped his head, remaining that way for several minutes. "I'd love to help, but I can't seem to remember anything."

"Nothing?" Daciana leaned forward, her heart skipping a beat.

"My memories are...hazy. I don't recall anything from the last couple days."

For a long moment, she stared at him. Hazy memories surrounding the events of an illness weren't uncommon, but it was disheartening that there wasn't anything he could tell her. A part of her had held out hope he would've possessed some token of knowledge that could've steered them forward.

"More importantly," Elder Aurel continued, scrutinizing her from head to toe, and she braced herself for a bit of unpleasantness, "why are you here? You're not allowed here."

"Who else would you have had come then?" she asked.

"I don't know," he said with an indignant scoff. "Anyone but you would have been preferrable. Now your filth has contaminated my family's home."

She crossed her arms and raised an eyebrow. "Would you like me to get someone else? Master Florin's ghost, perhaps?" Wincing internally, she scolded herself for that. Even if he was being crotchety, he was recovering from being poisoned.

Elder Aurel opened his mouth to say something, but she spoke before he could.

"Look, Elder Aurel. The nearest apothecary besides me is in Riverbend, which is several hours away. If we'd gone there instead, there's a good chance you and the rest of your family would be dead. I'm sorry for trespassing, but the rest of us figured your life was more important. Now, no more talking. You need to rest." Without a backwards glance, Daciana strode away, though she was keenly aware of his glare burning against her back as she went about her work.

As she set another treatment log back in her bag that evening, Daciana couldn't help frowning. In Master Florin's early years as an apothecary, he hadn't encountered anything similar to what she currently faced. He'd run across a handful of cases that'd been similar, but nothing that fit all that well with what had been playing out before her eyes.

The third day of whatever this was had nearly come to an end, with her receiving only three more patients. Elder Aurel steadily grew more alert and complained of hunger—which was a good sign—and the patients that had arrived the second day displayed signs of improvement as well. A twinge of guilt tugged at her for keeping their diets restricted to water, but that was what worked and until they were better, she wasn't sure how brave she was willing to get. After all, overwhelming their bodies could make things worse if she wasn't careful. That said, if Elder Aurel continued to improve, she'd promised him a warm meal come morning.

"Your search not going well?" Elder Aurel asked. She noted his posture had improved since he'd first woken up.

"Is it that obvious?" she asked, doing her best to keep a good-natured smile despite the fact they'd argued last time they'd spoken.

"People only slam books shut for a couple reasons," he said.

She frowned, gazing at her patients for a moment before rising and padding over to his cot. The lack of information from the treatment logs left her drained, so perhaps a bit of a distraction would do her good.

"May I ask you some questions?" she said.

A pained look touched his face. "If you want to ask after my memories again, I've been wracking my brain all day and nothing's returned. I think they may be well and truly gone."

"That's all right. My current question is about something else." Daciana paused, trying to figure out how to be as unoffensive as possible with what she wanted to say. "I...don't want to insinuate the idea someone from your family is behind this, but I was wondering if you had any ideas why someone would want to poison the magically gifted members of your family."

The elder frowned, staring at his hands. Even still, Daciana caught the bit of a side eye he shot her way. For the first time since this illness had erupted, she wondered how many people in Sorin's family would be upset about her being in the compound.

When Master Florin had been alive, she hadn't been allowed in here at all.

Even still, the elder said, "A few people come to mind."

She raised an eyebrow.

A bit of a rueful smile touched his mouth. "Even though we are the head family, we do tend to keep to ourselves, so it doesn't surprise me that you're surprised. But every family has their issues. I'm sure yours does as well."

"We do, but not big enough to kill over." She gave him a meaningful look.

"Yes well," he said—a touch of annoyance in his voice—before letting out a sigh. "Magical gifts are highly valued in our family. After all, it's our duty to keep the peace and ensure the safety of the entire village. Magic makes that possible, and it's the reason my family was elected as the heads of the village when we first settled here. Because of that, it's easy for those without that gift to become offended when they are overlooked or bypassed for something they wanted. Perhaps it is a little unfair, but it has kept us all safe for over a century."

Daciana frowned. Sorin had explained that before, and while what the elder said made sense, now that she'd gotten to know Sorin a little better, she still didn't like it. Having your life determined for you before you were even old enough to know what you wanted to do with your life was wrong. Having your path in life dictated based off something as arbitrary as talent wasn't fair.

"There's no guarantee someone will be born with strong magic— most of our current bearers fair on the weaker side—if they're born with magic at all." There was a harsh light in the Elder's eye that clued Daciana in to the idea he wasn't telling her this willingly. "Which is why those born with it carry such responsibility."

"So more of your family is without magic than those with?" she asked.

He nodded. "Yes. All of the next generation who've awakened to their magical talent are here in this room."

Daciana glanced towards the rest of her patients. Of the thirteen here, only eight were around Sorin's age. He had several aunts and uncles and she didn't recall them having many funerals for lost children, meaning most of them lived. Eight people wasn't much for the future of the village to stand on.

"Wouldn't it be better if we found a way not to rely on magic so much?" she asked. "That way those who have it aren't stretched so thin."

The elder drew himself upright, and she was positive that if she hadn't been the only apothecary in the village, she would've been tossed out on her ear. "It's our family's duty and legacy, and those with magic are obligated to carry it on. No one who has magic objects to what's asked of them."

Daciana cocked an eyebrow before she could help it, recalling so poignantly the despair in Sorin's eyes when she'd asked him if he was even happy. However, she didn't think it was wise to press the point. Instead, she pivoted the conversation. "So, despite the risk it would pose to the village, someone is still willing to kill all of you."

"Or give us a good scare, at any rate," the Elder said with a shrug. "That said, there's no one left to poison, so I doubt you'll get any more patients if your poison theory is, in fact, correct."

Daciana had to bite her tongue. It hadn't so much been what he'd said as it'd been *how* he'd said it.

Before she could even consider how to respond to that, one of the watchmen at the door called out: "Miss Daciana? Someone's asking for you."

Confusion twisted her mind, but she fought it off, excused herself, and left the room.

A woman stood a few feet away, tall and her bearing proud. Her long, blonde hair was tied back in its signature tight braid that trailed over one shoulder, and the skin around her deep earth brown eyes crinkled with a smile when their gazes met.

"Well, aren't you a sight for sore eyes?" the woman said, hands on her hips. "How long's it been since I last saw you?"

12

"Master Crina!" Daciana cried, throwing her arms around the woman. It'd been a few years since she'd traveled to the nearby village to the south and spent six months under the tutelage of an apothecary other than her own master. Master Florin had insisted it was an old tradition to help foster good relationships between the apothecaries and villages, but it was also good to learn from more than one person.

Master Crina hadn't been as kind as her own master, but the woman had been clever and precise in all her work, something Daciana still strove to be able to emulate half as well.

"I came the second I got your letter," Crina said, voice dropping to a whisper as she cast a wary glance towards the watchmen. "And when I arrived, I heard you're already battling an outbreak. If you're doing this on your own, then I know for a fact Master Florin has passed on. He wouldn't leave you to handle such a mess on your own."

The emotions Daciana fought to keep at bay nearly got the best of her, but now wasn't the time or place for them. Not yet. "It's not an outbreak, Master Crina. It's poison, and it's deliberate; I'm sure of it."

The woman's brow furrowed. "Poison? Which kind?"

A sigh managed to slip out of her. "I haven't figured it out yet. There're too many symptoms for any illness or poison I know, but the only people falling ill are ones with magical gifts."

"Odd, indeed." Crina paused before straightening. "I brought you as many herbs as I could spare, but before we get that sorted, I think I'll stay and help you out. The more hands, the better the care, right?"

That gave her a turn. "But what about your village? Won't they need you?"

"They're all right. I've two apprentices, one nearly a full-fledged apothecary in his own right, like you. They'll be fine without me for a while."

"If you're sure," Daciana said, her heart lifting an inch.

"Come on then," Crina said, a stern tone in her voice. "Don't dawdle. Show me the patients and your treatment plan."

When Daciana had first arrived to study under Master Crina, the woman's direct nature had intimidated her. Now, however, it made her laugh. "All right, come see."

She introduced Master Crina to her patients while they discussed the one treatment she'd given that seemed to do anything: water. When the woman was satisfied, Daciana returned to her corner and pulled out another treatment log.

"Studying your master's notes for clues?" Crina asked, one eyebrow raised.

Daciana nodded. "I haven't found anything, but it might prove useful yet."

"It's a clever idea at any rate. If I'd known about your problem, I would've brought my own. As it stands, lend me one and I'll help you search."

Daciana happily complied, and they quickly fell into a comfortable routine of research and rounds, the work significantly easier with another apothecary to lend her a hand. The hours ticked away, the sun setting and forcing them to light a couple candles.

When the candles were burnt low, mostly just pools of melted wax, Crina leaned closer to her flame, studying one line for a long minute before straightening and extending the journal to Daciana.

"Here, Daci. Tell me what you think of this."

She took it. Leave it to the Master Apothecary to find, in a matter of hours, the answer Daciana had spent days hunting for. Shaking that thought away, she read the section Crina pointed to.

8th day of Fire Wolf Moon
Patient—older woman (62 summers)

Affliction—herbal overdose; claimed several ailments and took multiple herbs to treat all

Symptoms—delirium, shortness of breath, lethargy, muscle weakness, high fever

Treatment—flushing of the system with water. Condition had not yet progressed to the point of severe problem; allowing the herbs to work out of the system was the best solution. It took several days for the herbs to take effect, and several for them to be completely flushed. Good food and rest aid recovery.

A chill rolled down Daciana's spine. The symptoms were similar though not quite the same. More importantly, it made so many things make sense. In order to overdose on herbal medicine, it would take time—possibly days or weeks in order for the victim to suffer the effects of the overload to their system. Someone could easily have laced their food and drinks with herbs; it wouldn't have had to be a lot. Just consistent. At a slow but gradual pace, they would've been able to poison their victims by overwhelming their bodies with extra, unnecessary chemicals until they'd reached lethal levels.

If Daciana hadn't trusted her gut, Sorin and his family would've died. If Master Florin hadn't been as incredible a teacher as he had been, she would've failed with him gone. For one horrifying second, it hit her with alarming clarity that this might very well have been the reason her master had been murdered. Master Florin had seen something similar to this before, and he would've figured it out long before she had.

"It makes sense, kid," Crina said, her stern voice calling her back to the present.

"I know. It fits."

"Which means giving them nothing but water was the best choice you could've made," Crina said, nudging Daciana's knee in a rare show of affection. "Admittedly, recovering from this will take them time and care, but I'll help you work through the worst of it. My apprentices can hold down the fort long enough for that."

"You should send them a letter though."

Crina smiled. "Tomorrow."

Daciana frowned, her mind working. "It would be easier if we knew what herbs they'd been poisoned with. The reason the symptoms were slightly different for Master Florin's patient than for mine is most likely because the herbs were different."

"I thought the same thing. It would be easier if we knew what was used, there's still plenty we can do without that knowledge. We're going to have to make do without it anyway."

Daciana was on the brink of agreeing when a thought stopped her cold. If Master Florin's murder was related to the poisonings, then perhaps she *did* know which herbs had been used. Or, at the very least, a way to figure out.

After all, Master Florin's killer had stolen a lot of herbs. Admittedly, whoever had poisoned Sorin and the rest of his family had been doing it for some time, before the murder had happened, but it'd only been after his death that their overdoses had spiked to such a severe level. Was that a coincidence or were the person who killed her master and the person after Sorin and his family one and the same?

And if they were the same person, was this the real reason her master had been killed?

Once Daciana had a chance the next morning, she left the head family's compound and raced to the workshop. She was in such a hurry to unlock the door, she dropped the key and fumbled it trying to pick it up, almost dropping it again. Once she successfully unlocked the door, she proceeded to get the key stuck in the lock. With a huff, she worked it free before racing inside the workshop where she grabbed the massive logbook. Then she hurried out, locked the door, and sprinted back to the compound, ignoring the questioning stares she got from the other villagers.

As she hurried through the gate of the head family's compound, all at once, a heated conversation pricked her ears, enough out of earshot she couldn't make out the words. She paused, glancing over to find Ecaterina and a boy, who appeared to be about Sorin's age, squaring off face to face. She could tell from their features he was part of the head family, and since they both had angular faces and dark brown hair and eyes, Daciana thought the boy might be Ecaterina's son. Regardless, Ecaterina was red in the face, her fists bunched as she hissed something at the boy, who glared back without a word.

All at once, Ecaterina huffed, loud enough Daciana heard it. "I swear, Liviu, you're driving me crazy! Just tell me where you keep going! If you don't tell anybody where you were that night, they're going to think you killed Master Florin!"

The boy, Liviu, snapped something back, but his response wasn't loud enough for her to hear.

After a moment, they both realized she was there and promptly culled their argument. The boy turned his fox-like face her way, and after a second Daciana recognized him. He'd come to the workshop multiple times in the last few weeks, getting small batches of more uncommon herbs. Was he one of Sorin's cousins?

"What?" he snapped.

"Liviu, be kind," Ecaterina hissed, catching Daciana a little off guard.

"Why?" he asked, his sharp eyes flicking to the woman. "It's not like kindness has gotten you anywhere."

A red tinge touched Ecaterina's cheeks, her scowl deepening.

Scrambling to keep things from escalating further, Daciana hastily said, "I didn't mean to interrupt, I was just passing by—"

"Then keep walking," Liviu snapped.

She blinked. That had been straight up rude, though there was no point in arguing with him, not when he was in such a bad mood.

"Liviu!" Ecaterina snapped again.

He huffed before stomping off.

"Liviu!" Ecaterina shouted, hurrying after him. "You're not being forced to get married yet, and even still, once it happens, you won't have to live here anymore. He won't be able to control you anymore."

He stopped and whipped around. "Right, because that worked for you."

Ecaterina flinched.

Dipping her head, Daciana scurried into the house, not wanting to see any more than she already had. Once again, that pang she'd felt for Sorin and his happiness echoed through her for his snotty cousin, despite his bad manners. While Master Florin had said he'd wanted her to find someone to marry, at least he hadn't tried to force her into that kind of relationship. She couldn't even imagine the things that kind of stress might drive a person to do. A chill raced up her spine at the thought, but she shook it away.

Back in the hall with Crina, Daciana flipped open the book to the end, showing the woman the list Daciana had made detailing all the loses the workshop had suffered in the wake of Master Florin's death.

Crina studied it for a few minutes without making a sound. "That's a lot of herbs."

"I know." The pressure of having such drastically reduced stores weighed on Daciana. The herbs from her neighbors had been a tremendous help, but it would still be difficult for some time. "It's a lot to account for in everyone's recovery too."

"Yeah. If your culprit made a concoction out of all this, it's going to be days before everyone will be back to normal. With any luck, they won't have any serious, lasting injuries either." Crina clapped her hands. "The longer we stand around thinking about it, the worse it'll get. Let's get food in the ones who are well enough. I convinced the kitchen staff to give us some food, and I gave everything I could a proper wash. You're a far better cook than I, so I'm leaving that part to you."

Daciana glanced over the woman's shoulder to the far end of the room, where a fire was lit in the wide floor hearth and a table stood near with several foods, glistening with little beads of water. "You've been busy this morning."

Crina laughed. "Like I used to tell you, we apothecaries run on little sleep in times of crisis."

After she set the logbook on her chair, Daciana hurried over to the makeshift kitchen and set about preparing a hearty porridge, packed with fruits and vegetables cooked until they were as soft as they could be without being complete mush. Somehow, Crina had managed to bribe the kitchen out of some raw chicken as well, so Daciana cooked and added that to the porridge too. Chicken was easy for the body to digest and it was nutritious, making it ideal when one was ill and weak. Lastly, she found herself reaching for her satchel, a handful of herbs she could add running through her mind, but she froze. Would it be safe to add an herb to their diet so soon?

Her hands settled on a bundle of nettle, and she examined the dull green of the dried leaves while she thought. It wasn't an herb she and Master Florin had stocked a lot of, but it'd been spared in the robbery, so she doubted it'd been used in the concoction that had left everyone in this state. As such, they might help everyone get back on their feet that much faster, since nettle aided the digestion, which could help their bodies sweep out the poison sooner.

After a long minute of debate, she crushed the nettle leaves and added them as well.

Only a handful of their patients were well enough to eat the meal, mostly just the patients who'd arrived that first day, but each one of them ate the meals with gratitude.

Elder Aurel even smiled a little as he returned his empty bowl to her. "Perhaps it's because I haven't eaten in a few days, but that was one of the best meals I've had in nearly all my years."

She laughed a little. "Being hungry makes everything taste good." Then she scurried away before his mood could sour.

Her other patients weren't in as good spirits as the elder, but health returned to their cheeks once they'd eaten. Though, as Daciana returned the bowls to their makeshift kitchen, her gaze happened to come to a rest on the still prone Sorin. If he was like the rest of his family, he wouldn't wake for a while yet; however, she realized she missed him a little. At the very least, it would've been nice to tell him what she and Master Crina had discovered. And ask him about those relations of his she'd overheard arguing. Even though they hadn't known each other long, without him around, it was almost...lonely.

Hastily, she shook that away. She wasn't lonely; she was tired. She was stressed. Sorin just...helped take her mind off it. That was all.

Crina sniffed the remnants of the porridge after the patients had all eaten. "I'm not sick or ravenously hungry but that still looks delicious. May I?"

"Knock yourself out," Daciana said, her own stomach knotting with hunger. She hadn't had a chance to eat much since Sorin had brought her those snacks a couple days ago.

Crina dished both of them up the last of the porridge, and Daciana was so hungry, she was almost startled when she scraped against the bottom of the bowl, having devoured her food in what seemed like seconds. There were few things better in the world than good food when one was hungry; Master Florin had sworn good food was one of the best remedies in the entire world. The only thing better was good company. Daciana allowed herself a little smile at the memory before setting the emotion aside and returning to her work.

By nightfall, most of the patients who'd arrived on the second day had roused enough to eat a little food. It wasn't much, but they were much better for it.

One of the patients who came to her senses was Sorin's mom; Daciana still remembered the distress that had been on both his and his dad's face when she'd succumbed to the poison. The woman groggily sat up, her eyes nearly the same warm brown shade as Sorin's. Their hair was almost the exact same shade too.

"Oh...you're Master Florin's apprentice, aren't you?" Sorin's mom asked, her voice a bit raspy.

"I am," Daciana said, kneeling by her cot. "How are you feeling?"

"Not great," the woman said with a wince, putting a hand to her head. "I'm quite queasy, actually."

"Well you were poisoned, so you're going to be a bit out of sorts for a while yet." Daciana took her temperature before turning away to grab the cup of water she'd brought.

The woman gasped—almost startling Daciana out of her skin—and cried, "Sorin!" before bolting off her cot. She stumbled two steps before her legs gave out. Fortunately, Crina caught her before she could hit the ground.

"I know you're worried, but you're in no state to tear across the room," Crina said, gentle but firm.

"Please, let me see him," the woman pleaded, tears shimmering in her eyes. "Is he okay? Is he hurt?"

Daciana blinked, taking a moment to shake away her surprise. "He's doing better today than he was yesterday, so I think he'll wake tomorrow. However, you need to rest, ma'am."

Crina tried to lead the woman back to her cot, but the woman dug her heels in and refused to go. Daciana pursed her lips. So that was where Sorin got it from.

Getting to her feet, Daciana took the woman from Crina and led the woman to Sorin's cot. He was still pale and his cheeks flushed, but his breathing wasn't as labored and he didn't seem to be as uncomfortable either.

"Wait here, and I'll move your cot over," Daciana said.

The woman nodded, her gaze fixed on Sorin's face.

Daciana moved the woman's cot next to his before insisting the woman drink the water. Now that she was happy, the woman complied without a hint of resistance and even allowed herself to be led to her cot. From there, she kept an eye on her son, something about the scene making Daciana smile a bit.

All at once, as she turned to go, the woman reached out a hand, calling her back. Daciana returned, a bit surprised when the woman took her hand in her own. Since it seemed like the woman had something to say, she crouched next to the cot.

"You're very kind," Sorin's mother said, her exhaustion evident in her voice. "You must've been working hard to care for us."

Daciana shrugged. "It's my job, so I don't mind."

"I never got to meet you before, and while I'm not happy Master

Florin died, in a way, it's responsible for me meeting you, for which I'm grateful. Your name is Daciana, isn't it?"

"That's right."

"I'm Violeta. I'm Sorin's mother."

"I'd figured that," Daciana said with a bit of a smile.

"You're clever," Violeta said with a hint of a laugh. "I'm grateful for what you've done for me, but especially my son. We're in your debt." The woman released her and she left, leaving the two of them in peace.

13

As Daciana turned from Violeta's cot, she happened to catch Elder Aurel's eye, and he called her over too. Intrigued, she approached him.

"I'm sorry for calling you from your work, but I wanted to thank you for the kindness you've shown to my children and grandchildren, especially dear Violeta. She's always been protective of Sorin."

Daciana cocked her head. "She has?"

He beckoned her a bit closer, lowering his voice. "Yes. You already know how precious magic is to our family. Violeta bore six children, but so far, Sorin is the only one who bears strong magic. She was against him being appointed as watch leader and still is, though she stays quiet about it. It is a dangerous job, but since Sorin is the oldest grandchild with magic, he's the only one who could do it." He nodded a bit when he said that, something about his satisfied expression making her insides go cold.

"Did Sorin want to do it?" she asked.

Elder Aurel's gaze snapped to her so fast she knew in an instant that had been the wrong question to ask, but she didn't regret it. "Don't—" he began, his voice so loud it echoed around the room, getting the attention of everyone who was awake. He cut himself off, but she recognized the anger on his face: the red tint, the snarling of the eyebrows, the darkening of the eyes. Many people in the village had familiarized her with the expression.

Even still, Daciana remained calm and quiet.

When he spoke again, his voice was hushed, coming out in an almost hiss. "It would behoove you not to stick your nose where it shouldn't be. You are a mere apothecary, and we are the head family."

It took a lot of restraint not to sigh. "Yes, I am the one Master Florin chose to train as an apothecary, and I'm the one you've got. And so long as it is a matter that concerns the happiness of one of my patients, then that's where my nose should be." Since they had the attention of most of the room now, she didn't bother to lower her voice.

"No, you are permitted to treat Sorin's illness—his happiness is no concern of yours."

"Happiness is an important factor in a person's health and their ability to recover, so yes, it is my concern."

"Listen to me, you half-breed," he snarled, pointing a gnarled finger at her.

Despite herself, she had to fight against a flinch and straightened a little to hide the involuntary movement.

"I would not finish that sentence." Master Crina stepped up on the other side of the bed, drawn up to her full height with her fists on her hips. "At least, if I were you, that is."

Elder Aurel glowered, a harsh light in his eyes. "Who are you?"

"Master Apothecary Crina, from Stagwick. I'm here to help Master Apothecary Apprentice Daciana, of Highfell, with a string of poisonings. She was also, for six months, my apprentice, at Master Florin's behest, and is the sole reason you draw breath. So watch your tone, mister."

Daciana frantically tried to catch Master Crina's eye, but the woman's gaze was fixed on Elder Aurel.

"She's done nothing worthy of being insulted and harassed by you. Understand?"

Elder Aurel eyed her before glancing at Daciana. "I hope you'll keep a good eye on Sorin since he's putting in a considerable amount of effort to protect you." His words were clipped, and the malice in his eyes made a chill race over her skin.

Daciana said nothing. The way he'd said that made it all too clear he believed she *owed* Sorin for doing his job, while also implying that Sorin owed her nothing for Daciana doing hers. All at once, she couldn't help wondering if Sorin's silent, withdrawn nature wasn't his personality so much as it was a symptom of something else, something deeper.

After all, what would it be like to be landed with a job your own mother didn't want you to have solely because you'd been born with an inherent gift—all in the name of upholding an ancient family legacy? The memory of when she'd posed the question about the village's safety coming at the expense of Sorin's happiness and the fear that had been on his face was still vivid in her mind. Between that and Elder Aurel, she could sketch a haunting picture of how Sorin's life had played out.

Without responding to Elder Aurel's demand, Daciana turned and left his bedside, continuing about her duties despite the heavy silence hanging over her patients. Even still, the rest of the day passed in relative calm, the only other interruption being a spat out in the hall between Ecaterina and the watchmen. Crina chased her off, and before long, night fell once more.

Daciana didn't have treatment logs to search through anymore, so she just sat in her chair, tucked her knees under her chin, and thought.

What she wanted to do, more than anything, was confer with Sorin, but he had yet to wake. That said, she wasn't sure he'd be up to an in-depth conversation so soon, so the wait would probably be even longer.

So her mind returned to her earlier realization: whoever had attacked Sorin and his family was more than likely the same person who'd attacked Master Florin. They'd stolen those herbs to administer the final, lethal dose of poison. At least, that was what she now suspected, though it wasn't like she could prove it.

Her eyes narrowed. That had to mean someone had been coming in to the workshop and getting herbs before, probably several times. After all, if they'd been going out and picking their own, why would they have needed to steal from the apothecary?

Opening the logbook, she glanced through the list. After a few minutes, she scowled and closed it. There were several repeat customers, many of them from the head family. That didn't help her at all.

"Well, someone looks like she's had a long day and needs to take a rest," Crina said, making her glance up. The woman smiled. "I can stay up for a while. You lay down and stop thinking."

"I'm fine," Daciana said. "Really."

"Oh Daci, don't argue with me and go to sleep. I mean it." Crina turned away, but her gaze shot to Elder Aurel's sleeping form, and she glared, the expression fiery enough to make Daciana a bit uneasy.

She'd figured the woman would still be thinking about what he'd said, but she'd heard such things often enough they hardly fazed her for long anymore. However, instead of saying anything (because Crina would argue with her about it instead of listening), she relented and curled up on her cot.

As she lay there—attempting to get comfortable and not remain attuned to the breathing of her patients—despite the fact she wasn't fazed by the names people called her, her heart curled inward, burying itself deeper inside like a bulb retreating back underground, hiding from the lashing sting of winter's cold. For one intense moment, it set in that this was her new reality. She'd long dreamed of leaving the village, but without Master Florin, there was no way she could bring herself to abandon it, even if that left her exposed to their scorn. However, maybe once she had her gold leaf, she and her family would have to leave anyway; she couldn't do business if no one trusted her to treat them. Tears stung her eyes as she curled into a tighter ball, but she refused to let a single one fall.

There were better things to cry for than this.

The howling of the wolves in the fells brushed across her senses, distracting her from the miserable emotions bubbling up inside her, and they were the last things she heard before she fell asleep.

The wolves howling across the fells woke Daciana the next morning too. They were quite active this year, but before she could really think about it, she glanced out at her patients right as Sorin shifted, groggily sitting up. Her heart, still a bit raw from last night, danced at the sight.

Hurriedly, she rubbed the sleep out of her eyes and went to his bedside.

For a long minute, he blearily stared around the room, half-wrapped in his blanket. After a moment, he found her face, blinking a couple times before he croaked out, "Daciana?"

She did her best not to get distracted by how endearing he was with his hair askew. "Welcome back. I'm going to take a wild guess and say you feel terrible."

"Yeah," he said with a bit of a groan. His gaze flicked around the room. "How is everyone?"

"Fine. We figured out what was wrong and caught it in time to prevent it from turning lethal. In a few days, everyone will be fine."

He was still pale and haggard, but the smallest smile tugged on the corners of his mouth. "You figured it out?"

"I did," she said. "But before I tell you anything, you have to have some water." She left his side to fetch it.

Before they could talk, however, her other patients began to awaken. Instead of being able to chat with Sorin, she spent the next couple hours addressing their needs (Crina refused to let her near Elder Aurel any longer, though). Now that they were all recovering, they were much less grumpy. That said, since Daciana had seen no reason to hide the source of their ailment, there was a somber air hanging over everyone. However, what disturbed her the most was that none of them seemed surprised, not even the teenagers. It was almost as though they'd lived their whole lives in anticipation of this state of affairs.

She couldn't even imagine what it would be like to look at your family and believe someone among them would want to kill you.

Daciana wasn't able to get back to Sorin's side until after she'd made breakfast, the same thoroughfare as the day before. To her amusement, when she handed Sorin and his mom their bowls, both of them were practically drooling.

"I don't know how Daciana does it, Sorin," Violeta said, "but it's delicious and makes you worlds better after you eat it. Don't leave a single drop."

Sorin said nothing in response because his mouth was full. At least he had a hearty appetite.

Once he finished, Daciana pulled a chair over and sat by his cot. A bit of pallor still clung to his cheeks, but his eyes were alert.

"So?" he asked softly. "Did the treatment logs help?"

His mom moved to sit on the edge of his bed, watching the two of them in earnest.

Hiding a smile, Daciana said, "They did. And I'm not sure you're going to believe what we found."

His brow furrowed a touch.

"It wasn't an exact match, but the closest thing we could find was the case of a woman who'd stuffed herself full of herbal remedies trying to fix everything wrong with her at once."

His brow furrowed even more, and he made the connection just as quickly as she'd expected he would. "Herbs?"

"I believe someone was slowly administering herbs to all of you, in small doses so you wouldn't notice, but often enough the drugs built up in your systems. Then, Master Florin was killed and a ton of herbs were stolen, and I bet within a day or two, the lethal dose of herbs was administered, pushing all of you into an overdose."

"So there must have been something each of us had in the last week that was contaminated. And if you're right—" darkness clouded Sorin's face— "Master Florin's killer and our assailant are one and the same."

She nodded.

Sorin's mom frowned too, though once again, Daciana couldn't help noting the woman didn't seem shocked by the idea. "Which means your master's killer is most likely someone from the head family."

14

Sorin leaned back a little, turning Daciana's new information over and over while doing his best to ignore the nausea churning in his gut. Whoever had poisoned them had most likely killed Master Florin, which led him to believe it might have been a robbery gone wrong after all. Or, perhaps, it had been—

"Daci!" a voice he didn't recognize called out, making him look up.

A stern woman with her hair pulled back in a braid beckoned Daciana away, and with an apologetic glance his direction, Daciana went.

Sorin's mom watched her go. "I didn't know Master Florin's apprentice was so capable. And she's so sweet. Did you?"

He shook his head. His thoughts turned back to Calin's wedding, when he'd sat with Master Florin and Ionel. Ionel had called Daciana shy, but Master Florin had said there were other things that kept her away, and at the time, he hadn't been able to imagine much. Since then, she'd told him the village had shunned her because of her foreign mother. She'd brushed that away when she'd confessed it to him the other day, but he wondered if it bothered her more than she let on. After all, she hid behind the watchmen as much as possible when in the village. Sorin wasn't blind; he'd noticed the glares and scorn people shot her way whenever she'd passed. Was that why no one had gotten to know her until circumstances had forced her to leave the safety of her isolation?

Once Daciana finished speaking with the woman Sorin didn't recognize, she proceeded to rush around, attending to the needs of the others, fetching water, and speaking with the watchmen faithfully guarding the door. He'd never realized how demanding an apothecary's job could be. Now that she was the sole apothecary in town, how on earth would she keep up with all the work? How would she handle caring for people who treated her like some diseased animal?

Even still, she went about her work with an air of determination, not seeming the least bit deterred by the mountain of work marching ahead of her without pause, even with the other woman's help. After a while, Sorin found himself admiring the way a few wisps of her hair escaped from under her black headscarf, the locks resting on her forehead without her seeming to notice. Despite how busy she was, whenever she stopped at someone's bedside, it seemed like all of her attention turned to them. He'd never seen his aunts, uncles, and cousins as happy as they were when she spoke to them; they seemed to almost...glow as they basked in her kindness.

His mom nudged his arm, calling him from his thoughts. "Be honest with me: you like her, don't you?" She gave a subtle nod in Daciana's direction.

If Calin had asked him that question, he would've dodged it like it was an arrow, but since it was his mom, he said, "I'm not sure. I don't know her very well, but..."

"Oh? But what?"

"She's smart. And kind. And tenacious." It also occurred to him she was exceptionally pretty, but that was too embarrassing to say out loud.

"That's high praise from you," his mom said with a hint of a teasing smile.

For some reason, that almost got him to smile. "It's the truth

though. And when she's working, there's this sort of...glow about her."
She was far happier here, despite the situation, than she had been in the
handful of moments where he'd realized her thoughts had returned to
her master. They were subtle, moments she hid well, but for a second,
the light burning in her eyes would dim. It was clear to Sorin that
although she kept it to herself, the loss of her master had broken her
heart. The more he got to know her, the clearer it became she kept most
of her pain hidden from everyone else, even if that meant she physically
withdrew. Even if that meant she spent who knew how many days in
complete isolation and would undoubtedly return to it once she had all
of them back on their feet. And that...didn't sit well with him.

However, his mom nodded, shaking him from those thoughts. "Yes.
I can see the glow."

"Cut it out." He nudged her arm.

She chuckled, though she seemed to be fighting against it. "In all
seriousness, Sorin, we both know what your grandfather's planning for
you. However, if you realize Daciana is something a bit more than just
smart, kind, and tenacious—if she's special, I mean—then go for it. I'll
support it. Unlike the other girls your grandfather is considering, she is
a woman worth fighting for."

Sorin's gaze flicked to Elder Aurel, who was in a cot kitty-corner
from him. The man's gaze followed Daciana as she moved around the
room, and he watched her with a glare that bordered on being
contemptuous. He also realized she hadn't gone to the elder's bedside
once since Sorin had been awake. The other woman did.

"He doesn't like her at all," he said, startled by the elder's demeanor.

"Oh, there's no mistake about that," his mom said, keeping her voice
low. "You missed the argument."

"Argument?"

"It was shortly before you woke up. I won't repeat the name he called
her—let's just say it was a moment that made me ashamed of my
father—"

Sorin could only stare.

"—though not surprised." She shook her head. "Remember your grandfather didn't approve of your dad either. The elder's favor isn't a worthwhile factor in the decision of your future happiness, understand?"

Sorin opened his mouth before shutting it again. He didn't know Daciana that well, but from what he did know, the idea of marrying her didn't fill him with fear. He couldn't quite picture them together, but it wasn't an unsavory idea either. Even still, it was weird to think about.

"Of course, I'm not trying to pick for you or force you to choose someone," his mom continued after a minute. "But I want you to find someone and marry them because you love them rather than being forced into an unhappy situation. And if that someone happens to be Daciana, I'll do everything in my power to make sure it happens."

He stared at her. "It's really weird to talk about this."

His mom's cheeks went a little pink, but they both ended up laughing.

Then, since the nausea didn't subside, Sorin laid back and rested his crossed arms over his eyes and thought.

If the killer was someone from the head family, that made a long list of suspects; everyone without magic would have to be on it. Ecaterina was the first to come to mind. She had full access to the kitchen and made it clear she held nothing but disdain and resentment towards everyone with magic. However, she seemed too obvious. Though that could be intentional, as a way of diverting suspicion. On top of that, she'd been experimenting a lot with herb heavy dishes of late, which, for the time being, had to be taken into consideration.

He considered Ionel next—the man had been passed over for the position of watch guard. He knew how the minds of the watch worked, so arguably, he'd be able to create a crime impossible to solve. However, the man seemed happy in his retirement, plus he and Master Florin had been best friends for years. Sorin couldn't imagine his uncle being able to kill his friend in such a brutal manner.

Sorin supposed a jealous spouse could've done it—sort of like they'd been seeking justice for their partners. That said, Ecaterina's husband was meek and quiet, while Ionel's wife was ailing. She spent all her days in bed and had been a big part of why Ionel invested in tisanes. They weren't going to cure her, but they did ease her suffering.

Finally, he turned his thoughts to his cousins, most of whom had been born without magic. Some, he knew, weren't bitter about their fate, and when they'd married, they'd moved away from the compound and Elder Aurel's immediate influence. The others were his unmarried cousins, most too young or weak to have been able to smash someone's head in with a single blow. That said, there were a few who might've been able to pull it off. They could've even been working together for all he knew. Even though it stung, Liviu and Narcisa were the first to pop into his mind. They were angry enough, and Liviu refused to tell anyone where he'd been that night, which was dubious.

Either way, that left a decent handful of possible suspects, and he didn't relish the idea of investigating anyone. He didn't want it to be any of them, despite the fact the evidence was pointing that way. However, despite his uncertainty, it was a matter of life and death he figure out which one of them was responsible before someone else died.

"Miss Daciana," Calin called from the doorway, making her glance up from her notes. "We did as you asked."

She exchanged a glance with Master Crina before leaving the room. As she'd asked, Sorin's second-in-command had managed to gather all the rest of Sorin's family into the main hall of the house. Some looked curious and others nervous, but she noted that Ecaterina seemed annoyed, and the woman's irritation intensified when she laid eyes on Daciana.

"Is there a point to this, muffin?" Ecaterina asked.

Daciana stared at her, not saying a word.

"Well?" Ecaterina demanded.

She held her silence, not shying away from the woman's ire.

With a huff, Ecaterina glanced away.

"I did call all of you here for a reason," Daciana said, glancing around at Sorin's family. "I've identified what's making the rest of your family sick."

"It's about time," Ecaterina huffed.

A young man who was familiar to her shot the woman a withering glance. "Mother." After a second, Daciana realized he was the one she'd seen arguing with Ecaterina the other day.

"Don't give me attitude, Liviu."

"Enough," Ionel said, shooting his sister a look.

Doing her best to be unperturbed, Daciana continued. "It's poison."

The shock that rippled through the room was palpable.

Sorin's dark-haired father stared at her in alarm. "P-poison? Are you certain?"

She nodded. Her heart thudded in her ribcage, but she plowed ahead with her plan. "It behaved in a way I've never seen from any illness, and so far, the only people who've fallen ill are the magical members of your family, and a normal disease isn't picky about who it targets."

Several of them glanced at each other, and it tugged at her heart that they didn't seem surprised—not even the younger children who were present. Like the others, they also seemed like they'd been expecting it.

"That said, whoever is behind it may try coming after others, so I want you to know how it was done so you can make sure it doesn't happen to anyone else. The poison used was herbs. Whoever did this administered them by degrees, adding them to their food and drinks a little bit at a time."

"Herbs can't kill anyone," a younger boy standing beside Liviu piped up, his face a bit pale. "That's why they're medicine."

To her surprise, several people nodded, appearing confused.

She folded her arms. "Herbs are medicine—when used properly. But they can just as easily be toxic. In this case, the herbs are poisonous because they weren't needed. They were just building up unnecessary materials in their bodies, materials their bodies couldn't use. Then, in the last few days, each person was given a massive dose of herbs—I don't know how—which compounded the buildup inside. That's what made them sick. If it'd continued, they would've died."

"Too many herbs?" someone asked, brows so knitted, they were almost tangled. "Is that possible?"

"It sounds right," Sorin's father interjected. "After all, you can die from drinking too much water or getting too much sun, both of which are essential for us to live."

That summoned a few thoughtful frowns.

One woman then asked, "Miss Apothecary, how is everyone doing?"

"They've passed through the worst of it, and everyone's awake. They'll all be able to go home soon."

They burst with smiles and sighs of relief.

"Everyone is all right?" Ionel asked, leaning forward and making some of the strands of his ponytail slip off his shoulder.

She nodded. "Whoever did this to them is still out there, so you're going to have to be careful to avoid something like it happening again. Don't eat or drink anything you haven't seen being prepared, and if you begin to feel off, send for me at once. Is that clear?"

Most of them nodded.

Daciana returned to her patients, a fire burning in her chest. Since she was certain the attacker was someone from the family, then whoever it was had most likely been there and heard what she'd said. She'd spilled their plan to everyone—it would be next to impossible for them to attempt to kill their family the same way. Now that the deed was done, it was time to wait and see how the killer would respond.

Sorin was so caught up in his thoughts that when Daciana tapped him on the shoulder sometime later, he jumped. Lowering his arms a little, he blinked at her.

She held out a cup of water. "You have to drink plenty of water in order to flush the herbs out of your system."

Slowly, he sat up, realizing it was late afternoon. "Right," he said, accepting the drink.

Daciana watched him with a critical eye until he'd drained the entire cup. As she took it back, she said, "Just so you know, your watchmen wanted me to tell you they're handling everything, and your second-in-command—" an embarrassed look crossed her face, "—I can't remember his name."

"Marian," he supplied.

"Right. He said he orders you to stay on bed rest until you're fully recovered or else he'll throw you in the holding cell until you are."

One of Sorin's cousins snickered, and Sorin shot a glare at him.

"So there's been no reports or anything?" he asked.

"They said there's been nothing they couldn't handle, and they're still searching for evidence for the murder. Still nothing though."

The disappointment he felt at hearing the news was written all over her face. "I see."

Then, Daciana stepped closer, leaning down before whispering, "Just so you know, I told the rest of your family about what's going on. I didn't hide anything."

A knot of worry tied itself in his stomach. "That was a good idea," he whispered back. "but you might've made yourself a target."

"I know." A grim smile twisted her mouth. "I want whoever did this to know that we know what they did. If that makes them nervous, they might make a mistake we can catch."

He stared, unsure whether to berate her for putting her neck on the chopping block or be impressed with her courage. It was risky, but at the same time, it might be the catalyst to help them solve this mystery.

However, after a moment, something his mom had said came back to him. Keeping his voice low, he said, "Hey, my mom said Elder Aurel said something to you."

Her gaze dropped, though she didn't speak. However, given the way the light in her eyes dimmed, she didn't need to.

"I'll talk to him for you, if you want." His heart stuttered as the words came out of his mouth. Talking to Elder Aurel about his behavior was close to defying the man outright. However, he realized it was true—if she wished it, he'd brave the man's anger. "I don't know what his exact words were, but that was out of line."

She stared at him for a moment before smiling. "I appreciate the thought, Sorin, but if you lecture him, you'd have to lecture most of the town too."

That caught him a bit off-guard, and before he could come up with a response, the other apothecary called out:

"Daci! I've brought the stuff you need for dinner!"

"Coming," Daciana called as she straightened.

"Who's that?" Sorin asked, nodding towards the woman.

Daciana seemed surprised for a second before another grin lit her face. "Oh, that's Master Crina. She came while you were unconscious but she's an apothecary from Stagwick. As part of my training, Master Florin had me study under her for six months, and she brought me some herbs to help my stores. When she learned of the illness, she chose to stay and help me for a bit."

So that was it. "She had good timing."

"That's the truth," Daciana said with a smile. She stepped back. "I'm going to go cook now."

For lack of anything else to do, he watched as she went to the makeshift kitchen she and Master Crina had set up. The two of them spoke for a minute before Master Crina moved, leaving Daciana to sort through the basket of vegetables the woman had brought. She made short work of organizing what had been provided for her, but as she reached into the basket again, she suddenly jumped, retracting her hands, her eyes wide. Sorin was on his feet and moving before he even had a chance to think about it. Moving increased his queasiness, but it didn't stop him.

By the time he reached her, she had recovered from her shock and frowned as she stared into the basket.

"What is it?" he asked quietly, doing his best not to alert the others.

She tilted the basket his way. His heart skipped a beat. Coiled in the bottom was a snake.

"How'd that guy get in there?" Maybe it'd slithered in hoping for a place to sleep. That wasn't uncommon.

"That's not much of a mystery," Daciana murmured as she lifted the snake's head with a finger.

Sorin's heart nearly stopped. The snake wasn't sleeping; it was dead, its belly slit open. A dark stain lay beneath it.

"Poor thing," she whispered. "Someone chose a cruel way to let me know they're unhappy."

His jaw tensed. Daciana had been hoping to make someone nervous, and she'd succeeded. "You only told my family about the poison, right?"

She nodded.

That confirmed his fear. If it'd been someone outside the family, he doubted they could've threatened her so fast.

After another moment, Daciana eyed the vegetables she'd just removed from the basket. "I guess I'll have to wash everything again." She gave him a stern look that made him wary. "You should go back to bed."

"I'm all right," he protested.

"Only because you've been resting, not because you are all right," she said, her expression unchanged. Then, catching him more than a little off-guard, she nudged his ribs, making him stare. A hint of a smile touched her mouth. "Go on. I'll even get one of the watchmen to follow me around, just to put you at ease."

That almost made him smile a little.

In short order, Daciana gathered the vegetables back into the basket and left the room.

Sorin hesitated where he was, debating returning to his cot as the nausea intensified, before making his way to the door. By the time he got there, he was utterly exhausted and wondered if he would puke. Even still, he cracked the door open, leaning against the frame for support, the coolness of the wood easing his discomfort slightly when he rested his head against it.

He wasn't sure if he should be pleased or annoyed that Calin was the one standing there.

His friend glanced at him once before doing a double-take. "What is wrong with you? You're not supposed to be up!"

Sorin held up a hand. "I know, I know. Trust me, I can feel that I shouldn't be moving around; I just needed to tell you something. I figured our apothecary will forget with how busy she is, but you guys need to know."

Calin kept quiet, his brow furrowing.

"We have a better idea of who the killer is, but they just made it clear they aren't happy Daciana discovered the poison. She was threatened. It was subtle, but very much a threat."

His friend stared, a hard gleam appearing in his eye. "So this creep wants to play like that, huh? I can't wait until we get our hands on 'em."

Sorin nodded. She'd saved his life, so he was determined to make sure she made it through this ordeal alive. Especially since whoever was behind this seemed to have no qualms about killing her too.

15

As twilight faded into night, Daciana curled up in her chair beneath the window where she'd spent most of her nights during this ordeal. With her patients on the mend, the knot of worry that had tied itself in her chest loosened. Even still, that didn't stop her mind from returning to the snake that'd been left in the basket. It hadn't even been a poisonous one; just a common garden snake. After delivering her challenge to the killer, whoever had snuck into the kitchen to leave it must've been in a hurry and had grabbed the first snake they'd found.

A shudder trickled down her spine at the message that'd been so plainly laid out, but even still, it made a grim sense of satisfaction well up in her chest. Someone was nervous, and that made her happy. If they'd been hoping she would've been incompetent without her master, they'd been dead wrong—and so long as she was around, she wasn't about to let someone get away with more murder.

After a few minutes of sitting in the quiet, the howls of the wolves in the fells reached her ears again, but tonight, there were only a couple wolves crying, and for some reason, the cries struck her as lonely. Her gaze shifted to the dark window, and for a while, she got lost gazing at the dusting of stars, the howls of the wolves seeming to echo inside her, reverberating with a part of her soul.

Without the chaos of the poison to keep her distracted, Daciana's thoughts turned to Master Florin and the cavernous absence he'd left in his wake. When this was over—which it would be soon—Master Crina would have to return to her own village. When they caught the killer, Sorin and his watchmen would no longer need to be at her side. All too soon, she would be completely alone, and the reality of that situation settled in her chest, leaving a deep, pulsing ache. The ache wasn't new; Daciana had grown up friendless and alone. She was so used to the snide remarks, the whispers, and the stares, they practically bounced off her. However, when Master Florin had been by her side, the pain had been so easy to ignore. He'd been like a balm, and she'd never realized how much she'd relied on him until he'd been ripped away.

Without him, she was aware of just how deep her wounds ran, of how much they stung with only the faintest bit of agitation. Perhaps this agony was what kept the wolves howling night after night.

She shook her head, fighting against the intense sting of tears. Once she was home with her family, the aches and sores would ebb. They always did. Yet, for the first time in her life, fear of endless, empty days filled her, and she couldn't help imagining herself as a little withered plant in a forgotten corner of a garden. Her family might be able to soothe the raw ache, but this loneliness before her would persist for years, dragging on her like a boulder, and she couldn't possibly shoulder the weight forever. Was this really what awaited her for the rest of her life?

Hiding her face from the rest of the room as best she could, Daciana succumbed to the sorrow that had taken root in her chest and let those tears go.

Could she and would she be fine on her own? Of course she would; she'd gotten by all her life this way. Yet, all at once, the monotony of hollow and vacant hours filled her with pure terror and made the weight of every burden and sorrow so heavy, it was unbearable.

She may have lived her life like this up until now, but after getting a taste of a life filled with constant and steady companionship, going back to the life she'd had before felt like a prison.

By the next evening, everyone who'd been poisoned was well enough to leave Daciana's care. She reprimanded each and every one of them (even onery Elder Aurel) on the precautions they needed to take to avoid this happening again—watching for signs, not eating anything they hadn't seen made, and (though it stung to say) not trusting that someone wouldn't try something else.

Sorin seemed ready to insist on returning to escorting her, but his mom corralled him, forcing him to go home and rest. That made Daciana smile a little.

Then she left, with Master Crina and the watchmen following after. As they left the compound, Daciana couldn't deny that, all of the sudden, she was lost. There was so much she needed to do without her master to help, that for a moment, she was too overwhelmed to do anything at all.

When they reached the watchhouse, Marian—Sorin's second-in-command, a dark haired fellow who was somewhere in either his thirties or forties—waited outside, his attention fixing on her the second she neared.

"Miss Daciana," he called, making her stop.

Master Crina stopped too, a hint of concern etched on her face.

"Yes?" Daciana asked.

"Can we speak for a few minutes?" His gaze flicked to the watchhouse. "In private?"

Daciana shot a hesitant glance at Master Crina.

The woman shook her head. "Don't worry about me, Daci. Your mom's expecting us, so I'll head on there, all right?"

She nodded, and Master Crina departed. Wordlessly, Daciana followed Marian into the watch house. He led her into a side room illuminated by a couple candles and shut the door.

"There's no need to be alarmed," he said as he took a seat and motioned for her to do the same. "I just don't want the wrong ears to overhear."

She took the proffered seat.

"Sorin said you were threatened." Marian's dark eyes grew so serious, it almost frightened her. "I need you to tell me everything about what happened."

Daciana had forgotten to inform the watch about the snake, but at least Sorin hadn't. Making a mental note to thank him later, she described the event, and by the time she'd finished, Marian frowned at the table.

"How disturbing," he muttered. It was nearly a full minute before he met her gaze again. "Has there been anything else besides the snake?"

"Not before nor since," she replied.

After another minute's pause, he said, "Sorin also mentioned the two of you found some leads. I'll ask his thoughts later, but I want to hear yours first."

"M-mine?" she asked, unable to help herself. The watch had asked for Master Florin's advice and insights on cases before, but never hers. "Are you sure?"

A smile softened Marian's features. "Miss Daciana, anyone who can fearlessly tackle poison and prevail has thoughts worth hearing."

Feeling conspicuous, Daciana complied with his request, letting him know all her thoughts and suspicions, and how she and Sorin were certain the killer was someone within the head family. She even risked telling him her belief that Master Florin's murder and the attempted murders of Sorin and the others were connected.

Marian asked her a few more questions before sending her on her way with a guardsman glued to her heels and strict orders not to go anywhere alone.

She thought about protesting, but at the same time, the snake had been a clear sign of what someone might be willing to do if she kept pushing forward. When she thought about that, she didn't want to be alone for even a second. Plus, though it was more a façade than anything else, she could pretend for a little bit longer she wasn't lonely.

When Daciana arrived at home and was welcomed by the smell of a familiar dinner, she relaxed for the first time in nearly a week. Her family smothered her with hugs—even her obstinate brothers tackled her once more—but she lingered in her dad's embrace the longest. For the first time since the murder and the poisonings, she could forget about all the fear and panic that had taken up residence in her shadow. Having them near made the loneliness inside her recede until she could forget about it too.

As long as they were together—talking and laughing over dinner and by the hearth—her troubles remained nothing more than distant smears on the horizon. However, once she went to bed, she lay wide awake, sleep elusive, all those troubles rearing their heads once more.

She was safe at home, yet Sorin was still in the middle of a viper's nest. What if the killer tried something not so subtle next time? What if she couldn't stop them? The idea of something happening to him, to Sorin, made a dread she'd never felt before crash through her chest. She doubted she meant much of anything to him, but the idea of losing him like she'd lost Master Florin was so horrible, she couldn't bear considering it.

Guilt prodded at Daciana the next morning when she went out to fetch herbs. Since Sorin was still out of commission, one of his poor watchmen had to drag himself out with her. A few wolves serenaded them as she worked, but they were distant and the chore passed without incident. When it was finished, she returned to the village where she said goodbye to Master Crina, the watchmen traded out, and then, for the very first time, Daciana went to the workshop and began her work alone. For the first hour, she had to keep swallowing her tears, but even once she recovered from that, the day marched on in secluded silence.

Around midday, a patient came by, tentatively discussing their concern with her—something new for her. When Master Florin had been alive, it'd been a rare instance when she'd interacted with anyone; most of their customers avoided her anyway. Even still, for some strange reason, Daciana found herself disappointed it hadn't been Sorin.

After that patient had been treated and was gone, Daciana pulled out the ledger to record it. She flipped to the blank pages in the back and froze, gaze glued to the last few entries. The dates were a bit old, going back to two days before Master Florin's death, and she knew they'd had patients the day before his murder. After a minute of further investigation, Daciana found the signs of two ripped out pages. What little remained was barely noticeable; whoever had ripped the pages out had been intent on making it appear as though they'd never been there at all.

Daciana's blood went cold as she fingered the jagged stubs of the pages. Why would someone come and rip these pages out? Did that mean there'd been some kind of clue here? Would that clue have answered the question of whether or not Master Florin's murder had been intentional or an accident? There must have been. Something had been in the ledger the killer hadn't wanted her to find.

All at once, it struck Daciana that she had to tell someone. She didn't know if it would help, but it could mean something.

Almost in a daze, she walked to the front door of the workshop, barely aware of the watchman there, asking her a question she didn't hear. Should she go to Marian or Sorin? Did it matter? Or would passing the information through more hands ensure the killer realized she'd found another clue? However, it wasn't like she could just walk into the compound to visit Sorin; that would be a dead giveaway.

After giving it another minute's thought, Daciana snatched her satchel from the wall hook, apologized to her guard for the confusion, and returned to the head family's compound.

While she had been here just yesterday, as she stepped through the gate today, she was hit by a wave of dread. Her family had chased it away for a time, but it returned full force now. The reality was that when she came here, she was on the killer's territory—and whoever it was knew it.

Steeling herself, she headed to the main house. What better way to avoid arousing the killer's suspicions than by coming under the guise of a concerned apothecary? As a formality, she paid a visit to Elder Aurel first, though he was not pleased to see her and made his sentiments plain. She ignored his attitude and protests as she worked, and, once she was finished, made her way to the smaller houses flanking the back, where the rest of Sorin's family lived.

The houses sat a fair distance apart, far enough she reasoned something could happen to her when she was between them. The houses stood around an enormous grassy ring, but the houses were all separated by stands of trees, some of them thicker and more obscuring than others.

Reminding herself of what she came to do, Daciana gathered her courage and went to the first house on the right. It wasn't Sorin's house, but one of her patients ended up being there, so she checked in on them before continuing on her way. The next three houses held no magical patients or Sorin, but when she arrived at the fourth house, she paused.

A young man she somewhat recognized was in the front splitting wood, and after a moment, she recognized him from when she'd told the rest of the family about the poison. He'd been standing beside Liviu. He was young, but she imagined he was only a handful of years younger than Sorin, no younger than fourteen or fifteen. Then he spotted her and paused, wiping the sweat off his head.

"You want something, Miss Apothecary?"

It wasn't rude, per se, but she didn't consider that particularly nice, either. Even still, Daciana tucked away her indignation and said, "I'm checking on my patients, but you're the first person I've seen outside."

"None of them live here," he said.

She glanced at the house. "Who's house is this one?"

He looked askance over his shoulder at her. "Mine."

Her annoyance flared before she could stop it. "Oh, no way. I never would've imagined that."

He paused, lowering his axe with an exasperated sigh. "If you wanna know which sibling lives here, it's Ecaterina, okay? I'm just her non-magical kid."

Daciana stared at him as he turned back to his wood chopping, debating taking her leave. At the same time, in order to figure out who the killer was, she needed to know more about Sorin's family. So, instead of leaving, she ventured closer but stayed clear of his axe.

"Hey," she said, getting him to glower at her in annoyance again, "I'm not trying to be nosy or anything, but you're...one of the ones without magic?"

"You think I'd be stuck out here chopping wood if I had some magic?"

"What else would you be doing—ramming your head against it?" she snapped. Then she checked herself. "Sorry."

He hesitated, a tiny smile touching his mouth for a second. "That would be dumb, miss." Hefting his axe, he split the thick log in front of him with a single swing. "If you came to check on your patients, why are you wasting your time here with me?"

Daciana detected a bitter note in his voice. Maybe this kid was used to being overlooked, and even though she hated thinking it, he was strong enough to smash in someone's skull. Not for the first time, she wondered if there was a chance that the killer had been several of Sorin's cousins working together.

"I remember you from when I talked to your family a couple days ago," she said. "I didn't get your name. So who are you?"

He stared at her like it was the first time he'd ever been asked that question. "A–Andrei."

She almost laughed but kept herself in check. "This is kind of weird question, but do you...hate Sorin? And the others who have magic?"

The tension from earlier returned. "Why? You think I'm the one who tried to kill them?"

"No," she said. "But, from what I've heard, pretty much everyone who was born without magic hates the ones who were born with it. I was wondering how true that was."

Andrei hesitated before lowering his axe from his shoulder. He glanced around before beckoning her closer, and with a wary glance at his axe, she complied. "You want the truth?" he asked, voice low. "I don't hate anybody, least of all Sorin. He's cool."

Daciana caught a brief flash of a smile.

"It's just...hard. He's the favorite. Elder Aurel gives him everything and picks him for everything. Even my mom says she wishes Sorin was her son."

"That is frustrating," she said, lowering her head.

"That said, I know for a fact most of my cousins do hate his guts, so if you're investigating murder suspects, you've still got plenty to go through." Quirking a smile at her, he hefted his axe onto his shoulder once more.

She cringed. "Was it that obvious?"

He shrugged his free shoulder. "Nobody talks to me for fun, you know?"

That pulled her up short.

Andrei pointed towards the last three houses at the other end of the ring. "By the way, those are the last houses that'll have your patients."

"There really aren't many of you with magic, is there?" she whispered.

"Nope," Andrei said as he cut through another log. "That's why our family needs to stop prioritizing it so much. Otherwise we're all going to die to some angry neighbor because there aren't enough of us who are as strong as Sorin."

A chill seeped into Daciana's gut; not because of what he'd said, but because she knew Andrei was right. Though the head family remained aloof, even she'd heard the stories—the tale of how their first village chief had carved the large village walls out of the earth with his magic; the tale of the village chief who'd single-handedly destroyed a bandit crew intent on seizing the village; even a tale of Sorin who'd once won a nasty skirmish against the Thornwood Fell Bandits, alone. The reason their village had lived in peace for so long was because of the head family's magic, but even still, she couldn't help but wonder if it was right to depend on it so much.

Were there things only those with magic could do? Of course. However, putting so much pressure and expectation on them and them alone? Shunting aside everyone who couldn't reach a bar only a few had the potential to even hope to meet? Their village couldn't possibly survive for much longer with that mentality, whether because of not being able to protect themselves or because everyone abandoned it and its archaic ways, the end result would ultimately be the same.

Magic couldn't be the only talent worth anything.

16

Sorin was genuinely surprised when Daciana arrived at his house shortly after noon with her apothecary's satchel slung over her shoulder. He and his mom had been ordered to stay near the hearth and do absolutely nothing by his dad, and while Sorin didn't mind the break—somewhat—he was bored out of his mind. It gave his thoughts opportunity to wander, and for some reason, they kept straying to Daciana.

So, when Sorin's younger sister opened the door and toddled over to his mom saying, "It's the 'potacaree," he was immediately flustered.

She still kept her hair out of her face with a black headscarf instead of the blue one he'd first seen her with, and despite the fact she hadn't had to stay up half the night taking care of him and his family, shadows lingered under her eyes.

"Oh, Daciana!" His mom grinned from ear to ear, radiating sunshine. "I didn't think we'd get to see you again so soon."

Daciana smiled a little. "Of course I'm going to keep checking on you until I know you're all right again."

Sorin was still flustered enough he couldn't think of anything to say.

Daciana chatted with his mom while she checked her over, but when she turned to him, something about her brown eyes making the flighty, fluttering sensation intensify. He wasn't sure how he would survive being in close proximity to her when he was like this, but all at once, as she began checking him over, she said in a hushed voice,

"I found something at the workshop."

That chased the anxiety from his mind. "You did?"

She nodded. "We have a ledger where we keep track of who takes what herbs and how many."

"I remember."

"When I checked it today, the last couple pages are missing."

That struck him like a boulder dropped out of the sky. "Were they there when you checked it the other day?"

"I can't remember," she admitted, a pained expression crossing her face. "Either way, I don't think it was a robbery gone wrong. Master Florin only wrote someone's name once they'd made a purchase. That's all I needed to tell you."

After checking a couple more things, Daciana cleared both him and his mother to return to their normal routines tomorrow, provided they didn't outpace themselves. Then she left.

Sorin stared after her, his mind whirling so fast, it was hard to keep up with his thoughts. If Master Florin had written his killer's name, whoever his killer was had gone there under legitimate pretenses. Then, for some reason, things had gone sour. Either that, or Master Florin could have tried to leave them a clue, and the killer had disposed of it.

After a few minutes, he realized his mom stared at him with an unnerving intensity. Furthermore, she smiled.

"What?"

"Be honest with me and yourself, Sorin. You like her, don't you?"

"I do, but..." he began, his thoughts distracting him enough, it took him an extra few seconds to realize what he'd said. Closing his eyes, he hid his face in his hands. "Mom."

She made a sound like she cleared her throat, but he knew she was fighting to hold in a laugh. After a minute, she reined it in and grew serious. "I'm not trying to rush you, but you and I both know if you want to have a say, you're going to have to act fast. I just...want you to have the chance to choose someone *you* want instead of getting roped in with someone you don't."

"I know," he said. Elder Aurel may have been his grandfather, but Sorin didn't enjoy the idea of the man deciding any more of his life for him—he'd already dictated his career and many of his childhood relations. Though Sorin didn't want to confess it, he was miserable. If Elder Aurel was allowed to decide the rest of his life, would Sorin ever stop feeling this way? How was he supposed to stand on his own two feet with someone so determined to sweep them out from under him?

It would be one thing if the man chose with Sorin's best interest in mind, but he wouldn't. The elder didn't even consider the best future for the family or the village; he acted to preserve a bloodline they needed to learn to stop depending on. After all, the rest of the watchmen didn't have magic but they were able to do their jobs well. A large part of the village's safety was due to their efforts, their blood and sweat—not just Sorin's. Plus, with how erratic their magic gift was with its grace, there was never a guarantee the next generation would end up with anything. Then where would the village be?

Even still, despite those thoughts, he couldn't help the powerlessness inside him sapping at his resolve, the sensation of being trapped under heavy chains with no way to escape his situation almost smothering. He'd never once been able to defy his grandfather; how could he dare do so now?

The next morning, Sorin woke at his usual, early time, and while he still felt a bit drained, he was almost back to normal. After a moment of indecision, he got ready and went out to check the front gate. To his surprise, Daciana was there, a basket slung over one arm, accompanied by one of his faithful watchmen, Nelu today.

"Already getting back to it?" he called.

They both turned, their expressions lighting up. However, Daciana's smile was the one that made his heart lift. "I didn't think you'd be on the move already. Are you feeling okay?"

Nelu chuckled. "Even if he's not, I doubt he'd confess it."

Sorin shot the man a look before turning to Daciana. "I don't have much energy, but for the most part, I feel back to myself. That aside, you're going out to collect herbs?"

She nodded. "I've got to stock up whenever I get the chance since I'm alone, so..."

Sorin glanced at Nelu. "You can go. I'll take it from here."

Despite the dark circles under his eyes, Nelu hesitated. "But sir..."

"I'm fine enough I can protect her, I promise," Sorin insisted.

With a tired smile, the man left.

Daciana cocked her head at him, her honey brown eyes catching the early morning sun a little, making them seem to glow. "Are you sure you're well enough to escort me around?"

Whether or not he was actually up for it was debatable, but being in her company did seem to take the edge off. He didn't get it, but he appreciated it all the same. It called to mind his mom's words from the other day. He didn't know if Daciana would be the person he'd be happy with quite yet, but what would he regret more: giving it a shot or never even trying and succumbing to Elder Aurel's whims?

Shaking that aside, he said, "I'm really all right."

She studied him before leading the way through the gate. They went to a different grove than they had the last couple times they'd come out, and she immediately set to work, rooting through the underbrush until she found the plant she wanted.

Sorin kept his ears tuned to the wolves but couldn't resist the urge to crouch beside her as she gathered leaves from the plants with a practiced, methodical air. "What is this one?"

"Mullein." She glanced at him with a wry smile. "You can recognize feverfew on sight, but not this?"

He shrugged a shoulder. "My mom keeps some herbs in the house, including feverfew. That's why I knew it."

"Ah. I guess I thought too highly of you."

Sorin froze for a second before he caught a hint of a smirk flash across her face. She was...teasing him? For some reason, that almost made him smile. "I didn't realize you thought about me at all."

She flushed, which made him grin. "O-only sometimes, so don't flatter yourself, sir." Glancing at him, she abruptly froze when their gazes met.

He stared, a bit alarmed at the sudden shift. "What?"

"Nothing," she said quickly, cheeks reddening. Sweeping a stray lock of hair behind her ear, she returned her attention to the plants. "You've never smiled like that before."

Sorin paused. Did he not smile all that often? He supposed he didn't. He hadn't even noticed.

Before he could think of something to say, Daciana gasped and scurried deeper into the brush. "Look at this!"

Sorin hesitated before following, pushing a stray branch out of his face. She crouched next to a little plant barely older than a sprout bearing little leaves similar to poplar leaves, but not at the same time. She didn't pick any of the leaves, instead staring at it with an expression close to wonder.

"What is it?" he asked.

"Lovage," she said, not taking her eyes off it. "Master Florin had a plant, but it got a disease and died two summers ago. We've been searching for a replacement ever since because it's so hard to find."

Sorin nodded.

"Summer's not the best time for transplanting," Daciana said as she grabbed a shovel and little pot from her basket he hadn't noticed, "but if I'm careful, there's a good chance it'll survive."

Working carefully, she dug a big circle around the plant before gently wedging the shovel under it.

With a glance at him, she said, "Help me?"

He did, not sure what he was doing, but together they managed to ease the plant into the pot without exposing any of the plant's roots. Daciana smiled at it, turning the pot this way and that, not seeming to care that her hands were covered in dirt. Sorin couldn't help noting she was pretty cute when she did that.

All at once, her gaze lifted from the pot to him as her smile broadened, making her eyes sparkle.

Sorin couldn't help smiling back, an almost giddy, effervescent sensation surging through him.

All at once, he realized what these feelings were, and while fear and doubt coursed through him, another emotion took root, one he hadn't felt in so long, it took him a moment to identify it: hope. For the first time, there was a glimmer of light shimmering on a dark horizon, a brightness brought by Daciana. With her came a chance, a possibility of a brighter future than the one he'd envisioned for himself.

She admired her little plant a bit longer before glancing at the bits of pale sky peeking out from behind the leaves of the trees towering above them. "It's getting too late to pick anything else, so we'd better head back."

He rose with her before glancing around the woods where they were one last time. Then he followed her back to the path. They were both quiet.

Sorin thought back to that awful moment when Elder Aurel had said he was in the process of finding a match for him. If he didn't act now, there would be yet another aspect of his life decided for him. He didn't know if Daciana was the person he wanted, but he liked her and he wanted to find out. There was only one way to do so.

Under normal circumstances, he doubted he'd have the courage to do this, but considering the speed at which his leash was shortening, he was willing to risk it.

After they'd walked a few minutes with no sound between them but the lilting songs of the birds and their shoes against the earthen path, Sorin worked up his courage and said, "Daciana?"

She looked up from her find and met his gaze.

"When are you going out to gather herbs again?"

She frowned in thought. "Probably the day after tomorrow. Are you still planning on accompanying me until this whole debacle is over?"

"Yes," he answered. His stomach tied itself in knots, but he went for it. "Though...I'd like to keep going after it was over too."

Daciana stopped.

He did too, but it took him almost a full minute to work up the courage to meet her gaze. "I..." he began, having to take a steadying breath before he could continue, "I like you, Daciana. A lot."

She stared at him with wide eyes, but at least she didn't stare in horror or something like that. Her shock quickly faded, replaced by a soft smile and a blush. "I like you, too."

The relief that washed over him almost left him dizzy. He didn't know what to do next, but as they resumed walking, Daciana adjusted her pot—shifting it to one arm—before wiping her hand on her apron (the hem of which was quite muddy, he now realized) and slipping her hand into his. It made his heart flutter and sparks zip over his skin, but it made him smile too. He didn't know where this would lead, but for what seemed like the first time in years, he was happy. He'd forgotten what that was like.

17

When they were almost within sight of the front gates, Daciana pulled her hand free, making the little flame of happiness inside Sorin flicker.

"Sorry," she said, with an apologetic grimace. "As much as I liked that, I'm not sure things would go well if anyone saw."

He cocked his head, thinking back to not only what she'd told him about her mother, but the way Elder Aurel had treated her. "They really treat you that way because your mom is foreign?"

She dipped her head, not answering, but that in and of itself was an admission.

Sorin retook her hand, just long enough to give it a reassuring squeeze. "I think they'll change their minds in time, but you're right that it's best we keep this between us for the time being. After all, Elder Aurel won't be happy unless the woman at my side is one he chose. Keeping this secret is our best chance."

She nodded, but then her eyes narrowed like she studied him. "Hey, can I ask you a question?"

"Okay?"

"Elder Aurel..." she began before shaking her head. "I was

wondering—and you don't have to answer if you don't want to—but I need to know: are you the watch leader because you wanted to be or because he decided that you..."

As she trailed off, Sorin glanced to the side. He tried not to think about it, but when he thought back to the night the elder had come to his house and told him he would be taking on the role, a fear like he'd never known had flooded him. He'd been the watch leader for a few months, but that fear hadn't left.

"I see," she said, surprising him a little. "I've often wondered what I would've done if, after all that Master Florin did to make me his apprentice, I didn't want to be an apothecary."

He dipped his head. He'd never confessed a word of this to anyone—not even his parents—but it felt safe to tell her. "I've been in the watch for a long time, because that was what Elder Aurel wanted. And even though I accepted being promoted to the leadership role, I...I never wanted it. I still don't. But at the same time, I can help protect the village here."

"But wouldn't it be better for us to stop relying on magic so much? Wouldn't it be better for you to be free to be happy and do what you want?"

He shrugged.

"I mean, it makes no sense to rely on just one person—even a person with magic—to always be able to protect our village. Magic built our foundation, but it takes more than just a foundation for a village to stand right? Most of the watchmen don't have magic," she glanced at him for confirmation, and he nodded, "but our watch is still very capable. While we're having issues with the Thornwood Fell Bandits, it's not like they've successfully plundered us like they want."

Sorin had to give her that.

"With the magic so selective anyway, shouldn't we try to not depend on it so much that we might leave those who come after us to struggle?

What if one of the generations that comes after us has no magic at all—or at least no magic strong enough to be of any use? Shouldn't we focus on finding a way to ensure those who are born like you get to be happy too? They can still use their magic for the village, but wouldn't it be better if they could choose to do that instead of being forced to?"

At a loss for what to say, Sorin stared at her. Her words stirred something inside him, something he hadn't felt for a long time, like a fire was being stoked to life in his chest.

"If you want an example, Master Florin said apothecaries and healers used to be exclusively those with magical prowess. But not many people are born with that gift—healing magic is extremely rare. Despite that, there are a lot of people who get sick—therefore those without the obvious talent for the healing arts had to step up. I'm sure I can't do as good a job as someone who has healing magic—"

"You're still one of the finest apothecaries I've ever seen," Sorin declared, making her blush.

"See?" Daciana grinned, resuming their walk to the village, and he followed. "Relying solely on inherent talent can only get you so far. Our lives are what we make of them." A ghost of a smile touched her mouth. "Master Florin used to tell me that."

In that moment, Sorin desperately wanted to hold her hand, but considering they were within sight of the village, he refrained. Once they reached the village, they headed to the apothecary workshop.

Daciana stepped through the gate before waving Sorin on. "It's your first day back. Your men are probably looking for you."

"But—"

"I'll be right inside, and one of your watchmen will come find me in a matter of minutes. I won't shut the door, I swear."

Sorin didn't like it, but he managed to persuade her to let him ensure no one lurked in the workshop and she was safely inside before he hurried to the guardhouse and sent one of his watchmen to her. Then he could relax a little.

He made his way over to his desk (which took longer than usual because everyone stopped him so they could check on him), barely getting a minute to sift through the stack of papers on his desk before Calin appeared at his elbow.

"I heard an interesting story today," his friend said, making Sorin look askance at him. "You wanna know what it is?"

"No, but I'm sure you're going to tell me anyway."

Leaning closer, Calin whispered, "Radu said he saw you holding hands. With a woman."

Sorin glared at him.

"I'm serious!" Calin hissed, eyes wide. "And not just any woman— Miss Daciana!"

"Mind your own business."

If possible, Calin's eyes grew even wider. "Wait, it's not just a rumor?"

"Whether it's true or not," Sorin hissed, "if Elder Aurel catches wind of anything, he's going to do whatever he can to snuff it out."

His friend's eyes narrowed. "You're not denying it. Did the poison alter your brain?"

Sighing, Sorin closed his eyes. "Look...my mom reminded me the elder is working to make me a match already, and if I want any say, then I have to beat him to it. And I'm pretty sure anyone I choose would make him mad. Think about what he do if he heard the rumor; you know what he's done in the past. So, if you hear any more rumors like that one, make sure you keep them quiet. For her sake, at least. The elder hates her enough as it is."

Calin stared at him, a sly grin touching his mouth. "I see."

"The trick is not seeing," Marion murmured as he walked past the two of them, making Sorin glance at him in alarm. The man simply smiled.

Before Sorin could respond, the watch house door swung open. He turned, pleased to find Ionel standing there. After greeting a few of the watchmen, his uncle came to him, a warm grin on his face.

"You seem better than you did a few days ago."

Sorin nodded. "I feel better too."

Then the smile slipped, and Sorin could already tell this wasn't going to be pleasant. "The elder sent me as his errand boy. He wants to see you, and the fact that you're working is unimportant to him. The faster you go, the sooner it'll be over."

Sorin groaned.

Calin made a face that summed up Sorin's thoughts, but Sorin followed Ionel back to the compound anyway.

Elder Aurel waited in the main sitting room of the head house, sitting in his favorite rocking chair by the window. Sorin entered slowly, taking his time. He noted the elder was the only one in the room, but that gave him little comfort. Eventually, he stopped near the elder's chair—not close, but not too far either. If he got much closer, the thudding of his frantic heart would give away the distress he kept buried.

"Sorin, I'm glad you could come. Have a seat," the elder said, grinning at him.

Sorin sat, noting—not for the first time—that when the elder smiled like that, it didn't make him look happy or amused. It was something else, something more...sinister. As such, Sorin kept himself poised on the edge of his chair, the need to run already clawing at him.

"You're turning twenty-one come fall, and it's high time we settled the matter of your marriage. As one of the only people with strong magic, it's of the utmost importance that you have children as soon as possible. The continuation of our family legacy depends on you."

Sorin's heart thudded harder, but he kept quiet. What Daciana had told him came back to him with alarming clarity, so intense that, for a moment, he thought she'd followed him. She cared about his happiness; did Elder Aurel?

"I've picked someone I'd like you to meet," the elder said with the air that he'd made a grand and glorious proclamation.

Fear's cold hands squeezed Sorin's lungs.

"She's quiet—she won't get in your way. More importantly, she's willing to have as many children as it takes to ensure—"

"This is disgusting," Sorin said before he could stop himself.

The elder raised an eyebrow, staring at him for nearly a full minute before speaking. "Excuse me?"

Sorin hesitated. He could take it back; he could pretend he'd never said it. He'd done it before. However...all those times before, sitting quiet, taking the slag Elder Aurel incessantly dished onto his plate, had never once made Sorin anything but miserable. It had never stopped his cousins from hating him. It'd never made his mom happy either.

Taking a deep breath, Sorin said, "I said, 'this is disgusting.' I'm not interested in marrying someone just to use her like a broodmare."

Elder Aurel's brow quirked upwards, accentuating the wrinkles in his face. Sorin recognized the threat but pushed ahead anyway.

"I may have a higher chance of having a kid with powerful magic than some of my other cousins, but that doesn't mean I should make someone have baby after baby. Those of us with weaker magic or without magic are people too."

"Sorin," the elder warned but Sorin ignored him.

"I'm going to choose who I marry on my own, without your input. Just leave it and me alone," Sorin said before rising and leaving the room.

"Sorin." Elder Aurel snapped, but Sorin didn't stop, his heart on the verge of breaking his ribs from pounding so hard. "Sorin!"

Sorin rounded the hallway corner, pulling up short as he came face to face with Liviu himself. His heart skipped a beat, and for a second, he couldn't even think. His cousin stared at him with wide eyes. The two of them gaped at each other in complete silence; Sorin wasn't even sure if he was breathing. Was the fear he fought to hide on his face? He couldn't tell.

Then he realized Liviu stood next to the other door of the sitting room. Which was cracked open. Had Liviu heard...?

Unable to bear any kind of teasing, Sorin turned and ran.

Even still, once he was out of the compound and his pulse had slowed to a more life-sustaining rate, the realization that Sorin had opposed his grandfather for the first time in his life washed over him like the light of the sun. He wasn't sure if it was a good thing or not—and a part of him wondered what Liviu would do with yet another weapon—but he couldn't deny that a weight seemed to have lifted from his shoulders. For the first time in his life, he'd said what he'd wanted to—what he'd actually thought—and the only different thing in his life now compared to before was Daciana.

18

Daciana found an excuse to visit Sorin's family compound the next day, and even though there was still an ominous air hanging around the place, it couldn't pop the little bubble of happiness bobbing in her chest. She and Sorin had something special, something between just the two of them—and for some reason, it made her tremble with excitement.

As she entered the compound, Sorin attempted to walk out.

His eyebrows rose as he stopped. "What are you doing here again?"

"I came to check on some of my patients, but I thought it might be a good chance to ask some questions about the murder."

His mouth pressed into a line.

She lowered her head. "I'd rather not, since they're your family, but..."

"I understand," he said with a shake of his head. "I'll help you. I was going to the guardhouse, but there probably won't be anything there. This will be a better way to spend my time."

Daciana nodded, appreciating his company. She went to check on the elder first, though, to her surprise, Sorin remained out in the hall. Checking on the man was an unpleasant visit—she'd never been on the receiving end of such a cold glare for so long—but she did her duty and promptly took her leave. She and Sorin shared a knowing glance once they were reunited, and she had to fight hard not to grin like crazy.

When they went out to the ring of houses out back, Daciana noticed Sorin relaxed. It was subtle, just a dropping of his shoulders. Most of his emotions seemed to lurk beneath the surface where no one would see them, but she was learning how to read them. Once again, she wondered if that was a part of his personality or if...it'd been necessary for him to keep his true self hidden.

After a moment, he noticed her gaze and glanced at her. Blushing, she quickly turned away. He didn't say anything, but a teeny smile tugged at his mouth.

While she checked on her other patients, Sorin asked a few questions here and there, but they didn't learn anything they didn't already know. By the time she'd finished, they'd remained right where they'd started.

Frowning, Daciana paused at the edge of the grassy court. On a whim, she headed towards Andrei's house. He wasn't out chopping wood today, but she did find him in the back pulling weeds from a gorgeous flower garden bursting with color.

"Daciana?" Sorin asked warily.

"Trust me," she murmured, shooting him a smile before turning to Andrei. "Hello again."

He lifted his head. "Oh, hello again, Miss Daciana." Then his eyes went wide, his gaze riveted on Sorin. "A-a-and you too, Sorin."

Sorin dipped his head a little, and if she looked really close, she could detect a hint of embarrassment. Or perhaps he felt awkward?

"You're not still searching for patients, are you, Miss Daciana?" Andrei asked, pulling her attention back to him.

She almost laughed at his question. "Not this time. I wanted to ask you something. You spend a lot of time outside, don't you?"

He nodded.

"On the night Master Florin was murdered, were you outside at all?"

Andrei's face scrunched up. "Ah...I think so? My mom had me out beating a rug, I think. But I also checked the garden. Moths are eating my flowers."

"You were beating a rug at night?" Sorin asked, head cocked to the side.

"Yeah, she doesn't care what time of day it is when she gives me chores to do."

"Do you know of anyone who wasn't in the compound that night?" Daciana asked, repeating one of the questions Sorin had asked the others.

Andrei frowned. "My mom was gone—but that's normal. She's supposed to be doing stuff for the kitchens, but I know she lies sometimes. Ionel was out getting supplies, and—oh! Liviu went out, but I don't know why. He's been sneaking out a lot—he has been for over a year, actually."

Daciana frowned, thinking back to that argument she'd overheard between Ecaterina and Liviu. So Liviu had been sneaking out for some time, but nobody knew where he'd been going—nor was he willing to tell a soul, despite the fact it could end up incriminating him for something he may not have even done. Odd.

Sorin frowned. "That's it?"

"Those are the ones I know of," Andrei corrected. "I was focused on the rug and the flowers."

Daciana smiled a little as she admired the garden. "Do you tend this by yourself? It's gorgeous."

Andrei's entire face lit up. "Yeah, nobody takes care of it but me, but I like it. Especially when the bugs aren't devouring everything."

That made her laugh. "I know how that is. Actually, if you know what kind of bug is eating your plants, I might be able to help."

With a grin, Andrei explained, and in the back of Daciana's mind, it occurred to her that he knew a lot about plants—not herbs, but herbs weren't that different from flowers. Perhaps, if he was up for it, *he'd* turn out to be a good apothecary too—

Sorin sucked in a breath, almost hissing.

Daciana turned, a bit startled by the sight of Liviu, leaning against the side of the house, arms crossed, not quite glaring at her and Sorin, but steel gleamed in his eyes, convincing her he wasn't the least bit pleased to see them.

"Whether you're looking for patients or criminals, you won't find them here," he said, his words clipped.

Sorin was rigid, brow lowered, making Daciana wary. Even Andrei seemed uneasy, glancing between the two young men.

"We're looking for neither," Daciana said quickly, easing herself ahead of Sorin to take Liviu's focus off him. "I came here to talk to Andrei. Is there a problem with that?"

Liviu pushed himself off the wall with a huff. "That depends on why you're bugging my brother."

"They weren't bugging me," Andrei protested.

"Spying for Elder Aurel now, Sorin?" Liviu continued, ignoring Andrei and making him scowl. "Just being the favorite isn't enough anymore?"

Sorin said nothing, but the glare on his face more than made up for that.

Daciana, for her part, didn't appreciate such antagonism being directed at Sorin. She reached into her satchel and retrieved a small vial of a dark, purple blue mixture. "Here. I think you need this."

Liviu raised an eyebrow, glancing between it and her. "What is that?"

"Bilberry tonic," she said. "It helps your eyes. Since yours clearly don't work well."

He flushed and took an aggressive step forward, making her heart lurch, but she still held her ground.

"It's obvious to anyone whose eyes work that Sorin isn't happy, so stop insinuating he is. He didn't choose to be born with magic any more than you chose to be born without it. It's obvious you're miserable, but are you so blind that you can't see he is too? Why do you have to antagonize each other instead of the real threat?"

Liviu's glare became white-hot, but there was something else nestled there, something she couldn't read. Before she could, Sorin surprised her by tugging her back and planting himself between her and his cousin.

"Don't," was all Sorin said, and for a moment, she wasn't sure who he directed it at. However, since Liviu huffed and turned away, she supposed the order had been for him. The next second, Sorin grabbed her elbow, steering her towards the backside of the next house. She whispered a hurried 'thank you' to Andrei before they rushed out of sight.

Daciana waited until they were past the house before speaking. "I take it you and Liviu don't get on?"

Sorin hesitated before he said, "We used to. But not anymore. Now he... He's different."

She nodded, not pressing him further.

"Where are you two sneaking off to?" someone called, their voice familiar.

Daciana turned, a bit surprised to find Ionel sitting on the back porch of the next closest house. So he did rest sometimes.

The moment Sorin spotted his uncle, he relaxed before beckoning her to follow him as he stepped up to the porch. "We were investigating, but Liviu arrived."

"Ah," an easy smile came to Ionel's face, "so you're hiding from him."

"It's either that or make drama," Sorin said with the barest hint of a smile.

"I hear you already did that."

Daciana glanced at Sorin, who swallowed. Uncomfortable, she decided.

Ionel seemed to notice it too and changed the subject. "I've heard you suspect a member of the family is behind Florin's murder."

With a nod, Sorin said, "It seems that way."

"That would be a shame, but I can see it," Ionel said with a world-weary sigh. All at once, his gaze shifted to Daciana, and something about it made her nervous. "I also heard you were threatened."

"H-how did you hear that?"

He smiled. "I still have some friends in the watch, and they keep me updated from time to time. If someone's threatening you, you'd best be careful. You're our only apothecary."

She was well aware of the weight of the responsibility. "I know."

"Well, I shouldn't keep you two any longer, and I confess, I want to sit in silence," he said, leaning back a little in his chair. "You'd best get back to it, eh?"

Sorin smiled. "We'll figure it out."

They parted ways then, and even though Daciana felt bad about it, it was a relief to put some distance between her and Ionel. After all, he'd been out that night and he didn't have magic; for all they knew, he could be Master Florin's killer.

Or it could've been that cousin of Sorin's—he and Sorin had had a falling out and Liviu certainly had the threatening anger down pat. That combined with the lack of magic could've been enough motivation. Sorin had even shielded her from him, and she'd been glad for that.

The last person Daciana thought it could be was Ecaterina herself. She had the disposition—and if desperate, a woman could smash a man's head in. Plus, she had complete access to the kitchens; poisoning her own family would've been all too easy.

All three of them had been gone, and all three of them had motive. Daciana supposed that meant they needed to learn if any of them had had the opportunity.

19

The next morning, when Daciana arrived at the gate to go after another herb, Sorin already waited, his usual light restored to his eyes. She smiled, unable to help herself, and, even though it was small, he smiled back. Most of his smiles were quiet smiles, with only the corners of his mouth moving upwards, but they still managed to soften and light up his entire face.

"Shall we?" she asked.

He motioned towards the gate, and they left together. Once the gate was out of sight and lost behind the trees, Sorin intertwined his fingers with Daciana's, making her heart skip a beat and warmth flood her senses. In truth, his confession the other day had caught her a little off guard, but at the same time, it'd filled her with so much happiness, she'd nearly burst from all of it bubbling inside her. Someone liked her, and she liked him; it was surreal. Better yet, if it ended up going somewhere, perhaps Master Florin would be able to rest in peace. Plus, Daciana wouldn't be so alone.

That thought made her pause. She'd always insisted she was happy with her life the way it was, but thoughts like those kept creeping up on her. Perhaps she'd never truly been as happy as she'd thought.

By the time they made it to the woody hillside where the feverfew flourished, a sliver of sun peeked over the eastern horizon, thin rays of pale, early morning sunlight brushing along the ground beneath the trees. Songs of the birds and the occasional wolf howl split the stillness, but there was a calm air about the woods.

As Daciana set to work, Sorin crouched beside her, not speaking but watching her work with a curious expression. She did her best to hide a grin but it was a losing battle.

"Hey, Sorin?" she asked after a few minutes.

He cocked his head to the side, she was immediately distracted by how endearing his open curiosity made him. It was like she'd found the real Sorin at last, the one he kept hidden away.

Shaking off her distraction, she continued with her question. "Once I'm officially a Master Apothecary, I think I'm going to have to take on an apprentice right away. There's so much work, it would be difficult to handle it all."

Sorin seemed to consider that. "Do you have anyone in mind?"

She opened her mouth to discuss Andrei, but all at once, something occurred to her that shattered the happiness bubbling inside her like a fountain. Her gaze dropped to the feverfew leaves.

"What?" he asked.

"I just... I think Andrei would take to being an apothecary. He knows a lot about flowers—he'd take to herbs well, I think." Slowly, she turned to him. "But, even though he doesn't have magic, do you think Elder Aurel would let him?"

Sorin opened his mouth, but it was nearly a full minute before he spoke. "No. If he had magic, perhaps, but because he doesn't..."

She dipped her head. As she'd suspected. Unlike Master Florin, she didn't have the clout or the respect to fight for Andrei's sake.

"Is there nothing that man won't meddle with?" she asked in more of a hiss than she'd intended. "If it made Andrei happy, then why shouldn't he be able to train as an apothecary? What right does he have to decide that for all of you? He's already made you the head watchman; what else is he going to force on you?"

Sorin shifted, something about it getting her to look at him again. Once again, there was a hint of an expression there—mostly in his eyes— that read as uncomfortable.

"What?"

"He's trying to force me to get married," he admitted quietly.

"Force you to..." she repeated, a sickening lump curdling in her stomach. "But what if it made you unhappy? What if you don't love her or she doesn't love you?" Furthermore, she didn't want him to get married to somebody else, she realized.

"That doesn't matter to him." Sorin huffed, his emotions rising closer to the surface, close enough she could pick out the frustration and weariness. After a moment more, she found fear too. "Just so long as I make whoever it is have as many kids as possible, that's all he cares about."

She laid a hand over his, the act more instinctual than intentional. Even still, Sorin caught hold of her hand. "Is this the drama Ionel mentioned yesterday?"

Sorin sighed. "Part of it. Most of it is the fact I told him no."

"You did?" Daciana asked, eyes going wide.

"I've never told him no before. I almost couldn't sleep, I was so convinced he would burst into my room at any second." All at once, the walls Sorin had built around himself crumbled, and a rainbow of emotion spiraling through him burst to life, the panic, the distress, even longing.

Daciana stared, marveling in the change, basking in the wonder of seeing Sorin for who he actually was. He was almost a whole other person—perhaps a better way to think of it was that he was finally a real person rather than a puppet.

"I know it's stupid, but I'm scared I won't be able to get out, that he'll trap me."

There weren't any words Daciana could give him. Instead, she leaned forward and hugged him, hoping that would tell him the things she wanted to say but couldn't find the words to express.

Sorin stiffened in surprise. Her heart thudded a hundred miles per hour, but then Sorin hugged her back, making her nerves scatter like seeds in the wind.

After a minute, she pulled back, her cheeks burning. Even still, Sorin didn't let her go, and when he met her gaze, she realized their faces were close. That realization made her next words come out in a whisper. "If he tries, I'll help you escape. We'll go find Master Crina, and she'll make sure no one can force you to marry someone you don't want to."

He cracked a smile—a real, genuine smile. "I can see her doing that."

"And she doesn't like the elder much, so you'd better believe she'd help us."

All at once, another wolf howl split the forest quiet, but this time, it was close enough to make Daciana's hair leap to attention.

Sorin was on his feet in an instant.

Daciana remained in place, one hand drifting to her basket. The wolves had never come so close before.

A couple minutes of a tense, unnerving silence dragged past before another howl rang out, closer than the first. Sorin stared for only a second more before motioning for her to get up.

She did, clutching her basket tight. "Wolves?"

He shook his head and hissed, "Wolves gang up on their prey to scare them into a pursuit. They don't sneak. If wolves were as close as their howls say, we'd see them."

Her stomach clenched. There was a group of bandits who liked to pretend they were wolves.

Sorin stepped back, pulling her with him. "Into the brush," he whispered.

She obeyed, wrestling herself and her basket beneath the low branches. Sorin slipped in after and motioned for her to stay low and move.

Holding her basket in her teeth, Daciana stayed as low as possible, crawling at what must have been a snail's pace. The minutes dragged by with agonizing slowness, her heart hammering in her throat every second. Without warning, almost making her soul launch out of her body, Sorin grabbed her ankle, his grip firm. Somehow, she knew he was telling her to stop. Her heart hammered against her ribs, pounding in her ears so loud, it was almost the only thing she could hear.

Another wolf cry rang out to Daciana's left, but this time, it was close enough she could hear the human qualities in the cry. Her gaze shifted to the side, though she fought to keep her head still.

Creeping through the shadows between the trees were three men with axes whose sharp blades glinted whenever they caught the light of the sun. Cloaks that appeared to be made of wolf pelts were draped over their shoulders, the hoods designed to create the silhouette of a wolf's head. Even still, that didn't obscure the harsh black lines inked across their faces and their bare, sinewy arms, the sight of them making Daciana's mouth go dry and her limbs tremble.

The Thornwood Fell Bandits.

The men prowled around and eased aside the brush near the path with their axes. It took all of Daciana's willpower not to bolt; if it hadn't been for Sorin's grip on her ankle still, she would have.

After a few minutes, one of the men parted the bushes close to Daciana; he couldn't have been more than five feet away. There was an almost bored expression on his tattooed face as he studied the surrounding brush. All at once, his gaze slid upwards and he stopped right on Daciana's face, their eyes locking. Her breath caught in her throat. His expression didn't change. Sorin's grip on her ankle tightened.

Had the guy spotted her? Or not?

To her horror, the corner of the guy's mouth quirked upwards as he continued to stare.

Her heart stuttered.

Still staring her right in the eye, he, in a heart numbing near-whisper, hissed out, "Awoo."

With a wild cry that alerted the other bandits, he lunged, seizing Daciana by the hair and dragging her from the brush, the branches biting as she was ripped through. Sorin's grip vanished, and the next second, Daciana stood face to face with her assailant, the hungry grin on his face making tears flood her vision.

"Now that's a prize," one of the other bandits said with a laugh as he eyed her in a way that made her squirm. "Boss might even let you keep it."

Terror like she'd never known flooded her, making her shake and tremble, barely able to even breathe.

Her captor laughed, and then, all at once, Sorin launched out of the brush, spear in hand. The bandit dodged, but the spearhead still sliced through his side. Daciana's hair was released, and she spied a smear of dark blood before Sorin shoved her back. Fear rendered her limbs slow to respond, and she hit the ground on her side, a sharp burst of pain shooting through her hip. She scrambled away from the fight, turning back in time to see Sorin catch the second bandit's axe on the shaft of his spear and toss the man off balance. Before he could press the attack on that man, the third man leapt into the fray, and Sorin just dodged. His spear helped him avoid the reach of the axes, but even still, there were three of them and one of him. He flicked open a water pouch at his waist, and tugged the water free, using it and his spear in tandem.

Daciana flinched as the bandits swung at him again. One tried to race past him, but Sorin lashed out, preventing him from doing so. Then another would try it, sometimes two would try and break past in sync. Between the three of them, Sorin was stuck keeping them away from her, even with the aid of his magic.

For a second, she debated running, but she'd have to leave Sorin behind and hope she'd be able to outrun a bandit or two if they got past him. Instead, she glanced behind her, dragging a loose stick from the brush while ignoring how badly her hands shook. She rose onto her knees, watching the bandit closest to her. She and her brothers had often entertained themselves by throwing sticks inbetween the spokes of a moving wheel to try and stop it in their free time—and a man's legs were similar to wheel spokes. Plus, Daciana beat her brothers a lot.

When the bandit took a step to the right, trying to lunge past Sorin, Daciana threw her branch. Sorin swiped at the bandit, making the man step back. Right as he went to do so, the stick shot between his legs, catching him at the knees and sending him sprawling. Sorin didn't hesitate for a second before plunging his spear into the man's chest. Daciana flinched.

The remaining bandits let out roars of anger, but Sorin's attention was no longer divided by three. His spear and his magic were blurs of motion as he fought, his ferocity making the bandits seem like kittens in comparison. The competition between them was short-lived. In less than a minute, Sorin felled the last two bandits in quick succession.

Daciana's heart raced so hard and fast she was sure it would erupt; she was convinced she would throw up. Her breathing came in ragged, shaky gasps.

Sorin stared around the woods with a stern glare before turning to her. "Are you okay?" Red blood dripped from a slice across his cheek, making his mien almost terrifying to behold.

Even still, she was able to nod. Thanks to him, she was fine.

He heaved a sigh, the tension leaving his face as he turned back to the bandits.

Hesitantly, her hands still shaking like leaves in a windstorm, Daciana retrieved her basket and the herbs that had spilled before joining Sorin, a startling burst of peace and safety rushing through her the instant she reached his side. She averted her gaze from the bandits' bodies, the pools of red staining their fronts vividly calling to mind the day they'd found Master Florin's body.

Instead of gawking at them, she kept her gaze focused on Sorin's face. "These...were some of the Thornwood Fell Bandits, right?"

He nodded, brow furrowed. "Yeah, but..."

The fear roiling through her chest cracked with the intensity of lightning, and before she fully realized it, she grabbed his hand. "But what?"

He squeezed her hand, his grip tight, but it was nearly a minute before he spoke. "These guys have based their lifestyles off wolves—especially their hunting style. It's...odd there were only three. That's not how they operate. Unless..."

Her grip tightened, her heart still pounding.

Slowly, Sorin looked her directly in the eyes, that fear she'd spied before coming out in full force. "Unless they were hired. They make exceptions for that."

"Hired?" Her throat was tight enough her voice came out in a fractured rasp.

"It's not uncommon for people who don't want certain deeds traced back to them to hire bandits to do it instead. And the Thornwood Fell Bandits get hired a lot."

The dead snake in her basket flashed through her mind. That had been a threat. Yet things had escalated so fast. The pounding of her heart was wild and erratic. "Y-you think someone hired these bandits to come after me?"

"I do." He put an arm around her shoulder, pulling her tight to his side. "Let's go in case there are more."

20

The watchmen on duty at the front gate met them before they even reached it, their probing gazes zipping up and down Sorin. Fatherly concern worried both their faces; he'd known both of them since he'd been a child, after all.

However, before either of them could say a word, Sorin barked, "Bandits. Thornwood Fell. There were only three. The bodies are—" He stopped, unable to remember the place.

"I-it's near Vlandeau Grove," Daciana managed. Even though her voice was steady, it was strained, and she was visibly shaking. She'd walked herself back to the village, but she was paler than snow.

Sorin turned his attention back to the watchmen, the lingering rush from the attack making his words clipped. "One of you get a team—no less than six of you, understand? Investigate if it's safe. Otherwise get back here immediately."

"Right," the men said, and one of them hurried away. The other ushered them into the safety of the village walls, his gaze scanning the forest behind them.

Sorin led Daciana to the workshop. He'd need to take her to the guardhouse at some point, but that was crowded, and he wanted to give her a few minutes to gather herself before she had to deal with questions and an audience to her distress.

Once they were within the peaceful quiet of the workshop, Sorin led Daciana to the stool behind the worktable and sat her down. Then he finally allowed himself to examine her.

Apart from the strands of her hair that had been ripped from her braid, she appeared unhurt, which took a massive weight off his shoulders he hadn't even been fully aware of. She was still pale and shaking, but given what had happened, that was a normal reaction. Daciana had been able to go toe to toe against disease, blood, and poison without a flicker of fear—but a different kind of courage was required when someone charged at you with a weapon with the intent to harm and abuse. That kind of threat sparked a different kind of fear.

Moving slow, he sank onto one knee in front of her so he could study her face. In a near whisper, he asked, "Are you all right?"

"I—" She met his gaze, her eyes glistening with tears threatening to spill over before she hid her face in her hands. "I'm sorry. Crying is stupid, but I can't—" A sob cut her off. "S-sorry."

"Crying when you're scared isn't stupid; it's just a reaction. My mom says crying is like taking the lid off a boiling pot: it doesn't get rid of the heat, but it takes away the pressure so you can deal with it. So if you need to cry, you should."

That seemed to be what she needed to hear because the tears she'd been holding back broke free as she sobbed, the sound breaking Sorin's heart. Rising to his feet, he hugged her. She'd hugged him in the forest, and that had touched his heart with a peace he hadn't experienced in years. Perhaps he could do the same for her.

Daciana wrapped her arms around him without hesitation, and the stool was tall enough she cried against his chest. Tears of his own pricked his eyes in response to her pain, but he stayed quiet and waited. If she was anything like his mom and sister, she would eventually cry herself out.

After a couple minutes, her tears turned into sniffles, and almost self-consciously, she pulled back. "Sorry." Grabbing her apron, she wiped the tear stains off the front of his leather armor, something about it almost making him smile.

"It's nothing to apologize for," he said.

She glanced at him with the hint of a smile before it vanished and her eyes went wide, catching him off-guard. "Oh you—!"

Leaping to her feet—Sorin had to hastily dodge—she snapped, "Why didn't you remind me?" She dashed into the back room, leaving him standing in complete confusion.

A minute later, she returned with a container, a bowl of water, and a towel.

"What are you doing?" he asked as she set it all on the table.

Pointing at the stool she'd vacated, Daciana said, "Sit."

He hesitated long enough that she guided him to the stool and, standing on her tiptoes, put pressure on his shoulders, encouraging him to sit. Once he had, she dragged another stool out of the back and sat across from him. She wet her towel before turning his head and dabbing at his face. The resulting sting reminded him the bandits had almost gotten him a couple times. Daciana had saved his life when she'd knocked one to the ground.

"It's not that big of a deal," he said, embarrassment building in his chest like water behind a dam.

"Don't be like that," she said, her fear long gone now that she was in her element. "Of course it's a big deal. Why wouldn't your injuries be worth worrying about?"

She shot him a scolding look, and for the first time, he realized her eyes were almost golden-brown in color. They were striking, the sight chasing every other thought from his mind.

For the second time that day—because of something she'd done—his heart fluttered, leaving him a little breathless.

After spending most of his life burying his pain and worries and fears, the fact she didn't dismiss or ignore them left him almost speechless. No one had ever done that for him before.

Once Daciana finished cleaning his cheek, she applied one of the most abrasive smelling ointments he'd ever encountered. She smiled in sympathy when he recoiled.

Leaning back, she studied him with a critical eye. "You don't have any other injuries, do you?"

He hesitated. Between the shock of the attack and his concern for Daciana, he hadn't paid much attention to himself.

He stood, looking himself up and down. As he did so, he became aware of a sharp pain in his forearm and inspected the area.

On the back of his arm, near his elbow where his leather gauntlet didn't quite cover, the sleeve was stained red.

"Oh," he and Daciana said at the same time.

They hastily removed the gauntlet and Daciana rolled his sleeve out of the way. Sorin grimaced at the long, bloody cut. He didn't like the sight of blood, but to Daciana's credit, she didn't bat an eye as she cleaned it with surprising gentleness, scrutinizing it as she worked.

"It doesn't need stitches, does it?" he asked, the idea making his stomach clench.

She studied it for another minute before she answered. "I would like to, if that's okay. It'll ensure it heals right."

"All right," he managed.

She smiled at him, her warm smile setting him at ease. "Don't worry, I'm very good at this skill."

She retrieved a needle and thread before resting his arm on the table. Sorin was already wincing in anticipation, but she caught him off-guard by tapping the skin around the cut a few times. When she inserted the needle, Sorin hardly felt it.

"How did you do that?" he asked as she continued to tap and sew.

"It's a trick Master Florin taught me," she explained without glancing up or pausing in her work. "If you tap your skin a few times, it'll briefly render the spot a little numb. The stitches don't hurt as much this way."

Sorin fell silent as she worked, her stitching fast and neat. There was some pain, but it was minor. Within a few minutes, she finished and applied an ointment that nullified the worst of the stinging. It carried the faint scent of chamomile with it, the scent helping soothe his nerves. When she finished that, she wrapped his arm in a soft cloth.

All at once, Sorin was aware of how close they were, the realization making him forget the pain in his arm. "Will I make it, you think?" he asked softly.

"Well," she began as she glanced at him, her voice soft and cheeks turning pink, "you might. But only just."

He smiled a little, and so did she. Almost unconsciously, he caught himself leaning in and stopped. However, Daciana leaned in too, close enough he could marvel at the myriad browns and golds shimmering in her eyes, the sight of them making his heart beat faster. Had her eyes always been that beautiful?

A bit hesitant, Sorin reached up and brushed away some of the errant strands of her hair the bandit had ripped lose. Daciana relaxed into his hand, her eyes almost closing. Sparks ignited in his chest, and Sorin leaned in more. He'd never wanted to kiss someone before, but he wanted to kiss her so bad, he could hardly stand it—

The front door of the workshop banged open, and Sorin and Daciana jerked apart like they'd been burned.

"Oh... Am I...interrupting something?" Of course it was Calin.

Sorin closed his eyes to keep the frustration in check. Once he had himself a bit more together, he turned towards the door where Calin stood with wide eyes, staring at the two of them.

"What do you want?" Sorin bit out, unable to keep the annoyance out of his voice.

"Th-they said you were hurt so I..." Calin bore a striking resemblance to a kicked puppy, which made a tinge of remorse worm through Sorin's chest. But only a tinge.

"I'm fine," he said, lifting his bandaged arm.

"Great. That's so...great," Calin said, his tone deflated and defeated. After an awkward minute of the three of them staring at each other, he took a step back, pointing behind him. "So, uh, come give your report when you're, uh...ready. I'm just...gonna go..."

He scrambled to find the doorknob and hastily shut the door with a snap.

Sorin kept his attention on the door, trying to calm his racing heartbeat. It was as though one of his younger siblings had released a net full of butterflies inside him, but to his surprise, the sensation was pleasant. Almost thrilling.

However, because of Calin, that special but fragile moment he and Daciana had been swept away by had shattered, and as the flutters faded, he couldn't deny he was incredibly frustrated by it all.

21

When Sorin had the willpower to turn back to Daciana, he noted her bright pink cheeks, but when she smiled at him, he knew that special moment had passed. They both shifted a bit further apart.

"Thank you for this," Sorin said, nodding towards his arm as he retrieved his gauntlet from the table.

She smiled. "Anytime. And thank you for saving my life too."

He smiled a little. "We should go report what happened in the forest."

"Both of us?" she asked, eyes a bit wide.

"Anything you noticed will be of use," he said.

She set her basket on the table before following him towards the door.

As they stepped outside, he couldn't help saying, "From here on out, you're going to have two guards with you—always. Even still, be careful. Please."

"I will," she said, hugging her waist as they walked through the herb garden towards the front gate.

"And maybe, for a couple days, don't go near the compound. We don't want to encourage another attack like that one."

"Don't worry. I planned on keeping my distance." She paused as he held the gate open for her, some of her usual fire rekindling in her eyes. "For now."

It shouldn't have, but that made him smile. That was more like it.

Right as they arrived at the guardhouse, Calin hurried out, making all three of them pull up short.

Sorin eyed him. "What are you—"

Calin cut him off with a shake of his head. "Cornel's sheep are out again."

"Again?" Sorin sighed. He glanced at Daciana. "You can go give your report. I'll see you later?"

She nodded in response, and Sorin fell in line with Calin and several other members of the guard as they hurried out of town to the farmer's pastures. Cornel's sheep got out from time to time, and since the sheep were a large part of the town's lifeblood, it was part of their duty to protect the animals as well.

As they reached the nearby fell that Cornel used as grazing land, the scattered sheep came into sight before they were even close. Cornel and his dogs fought to round them up, but the sheep seemed agitated, almost frightened, and refused to go back in the pen.

"Wonder what's got them spooked today," Radu muttered as they hurried to work.

Even though herding sheep annoyed Sorin to no end, he kept it quiet while they helped gather the animals and guide them back to the pen. Once they could get one of them to go, the rest would follow. The problem was always getting the first one to go.

After a few minutes of fruitless attempts to herd them in, Cornel went into the pen and called the sheep. Gradually, they trickled in, cautious at first before they were reassured by the familiar presence of their shepherd and the safety of their pen.

As the last few trickled in, one of the leggy lambs spooked and bolted the opposite direction. Sorin watched it go, he and his watchmen experienced enough to know the worst thing they could do was chase it.

Once the last sheep was shut in the gate, Sorin turned, saying, "I'll go get that lamb."

He slowly walked after it as it nervously darted back and forth, its ears turning in all directions, its steps jittery and unsure. It seemed to want to run back to its pen while simultaneously get as far away as possible. As Sorin followed after it, he was filled with gratitude not to have been the son of a sheep farmer. He did not have the patience to deal with sheep.

It struck him that he didn't enjoy being watch leader either; he didn't hate it, but it wasn't something he wanted to do for the rest of his life. That made him wonder what he would want to do if he had the freedom to choose. Having the freedom to choose for himself opened the door of his life so much, the amount of options overwhelmed him, and he had to shake the thoughts away.

After a while more of walking, the little lamb stopped and bleated in a way that made him think its fear had at last given way to exhaustion, so he risked catching up. It turned and butted his knee with its soft, dainty head before he scooped it up.

"Finally ready to go home, eh?"

The lamb dropped its head on his shoulder with a weary huff in response. They had to help herd the sheep so often, Sorin no longer frightened them, and he wasn't sure if that was a good or bad thing.

Cornel plopped on the top of the pen wall once Sorin delivered the lamb and the little beast was back with its mom. He wiped the sweat from his forehead. "Thanks, Sorin. The lambs always seem to have a soft spot for you."

Sorin tried not to make a face, but he was pretty sure he grimaced because Cornel and the other watchmen laughed. Once Cornel had the sheep under control, they took their leave, the farmer thanking them and apologizing in the same breath.

For his part, Sorin was glad it was over, the sheep were safe and all accounted for, and he could get back to the mystery on his hands.

They returned to the watchhouse, and Sorin had to stretch the kink out from between his shoulder blades. The strain of his tussle that morning was already making itself known.

To his surprise, Daciana was still there, talking with Marian, and he noted she'd rebraided her hair.

Before Sorin could react, Calin shoved him forward and sat him in the chair right beside her. Marian's sharp eyes flicked to him as the other watchmen gathered around.

"All right, sir," the man said, arms folded. "Daciana's been discussing the attack with me, and I'd like to hear your account as well."

Sorin filled them in.

"Thornwood Fell Bandits," Calin murmured. "And you two are sure Daciana was the target?"

Daciana nodded, her usual fire burning in her eyes. "They talked about convincing their boss to let them keep me. I imagine even bandits don't have much use for dead bodies."

Sorin was secretly impressed with her ability to maintain her calm when he knew this had deeply unsettled her. "They only attacked once they'd found her as well, and while I was fighting them, they were determined to get past me more than actually fight. Between the threat and this, I think it's safe to say someone is getting nervous."

"Which means we're getting close," Marian said.

"So if we're too slow or lax in our duty protecting her, whoever is behind this might succeed in eliminating her," Calin murmured.

"I think they're intending to kidnap her," another watchman said. "The bandits usually kidnap women rather than kill, but the change in their attack style makes me think this wasn't a normal abduction. Especially since it seems implied their leader is invested in Daciana's capture."

"That is odd for them," someone else said.

"That's a little better than murder, I suppose."

"Hardly," Calin said, his tone dark. "Even if they're being paid to abduct her, we know full well what the bandits would do if they got the chance."

Sorin shuddered, not wanting to think about what such ruthless and wanton men like those bandits would be eager to do—what he knew full well they *did* do to the young women they snatched. Granted, he didn't know if they would do that to someone they'd been paid to abduct, but he wouldn't have put it past them.

Shaking that thought away, he said, "I think we need to have two guards on her at all times. Whoever is behind this is getting serious, and I don't want to take unnecessary chances." He met Daciana's gaze, hoping she would hear the words he couldn't risk saying. "You are our only apothecary after all, and without you, we'll all be in serious trouble. It's important to us you stay safe."

A tiny smile twitched her mouth, and he hoped she'd understood. "I'll do my best not to take unnecessary risks as well. If someone is coming after me, it would be stupid to make it easy."

Calin eyed her, a hint of a smile touching his mouth. "You know, Miss Daciana, you've got a lot more fire than I gave you credit for."

She blinked at him in surprise.

"Don't worry, miss," one of their other watchmen said with a grin. "Whoever's behind this won't have the chance to get their hands on you, we swear."

She stared at the watchmen, her eyes wide. Then she smiled, a beautiful smile that made her face seem to radiate light like the sun. "With men like all of you determined to protect me, how could I possibly be worried?"

That made them laugh.

Sorin couldn't help taking in the men around them, the determination on their faces almost catching him off guard. If Daciana hadn't had any footholds in the village's favor before, she was gaining them now. That made him happy.

22

Daciana wasn't sure what to think the next morning when the two watchmen waiting to escort her spoke to her on their way to the workshop the next morning. Instead of letting her trail behind them, they walked on either side of her, and for the first time in her life, she didn't notice if anyone gave her any untoward looks. On the contrary, a couple other watchmen greeted her on her way to the workshop, which caught her even more off guard. For half a second, she wondered if she'd woken in a completely different village.

It helped prevent her from fully noticing the seeds of disappointment sprouting in her heart that because of yesterday's attack, it would no longer be just her and Sorin, and their secret would be even harder to hide. Even still, she appreciated the change to two guards; not only did it cocoon her in a peculiar sense of security, but it made her heart flutter that the watchmen—and Sorin in particular—were so determined to protect her. It was new, but...she liked it. It wasn't like Master Florin was back, but when the watchmen were there, the workshop didn't feel empty, at least.

Dislodging those thoughts, Daciana opened the workshop for the day, though she confessed she didn't expect to be visited by anything beyond boredom. Since Master Florin's death, the only time she had patients was when an emergency reared its head.

Her day was quiet until about noon when the guards changed out. Then, to her amazement, a couple people entered the workshop for non-emergency related problems and even tried to talk with her. The first time that happened, she'd been so startled, she'd almost forgotten how to speak. It was so strange, but she supposed it was a good strange.

Later, she was even asked to make a couple house calls, something she'd never been personally asked to do before. The two guards following her everywhere she went made a sensation of peculiarity stick to her like moss to stone, but at least her patients didn't seem to mind. One of them—an elderly lady whose back and legs kept her bed bound—clasped her hand and told her to not let anyone scare her from finding Master Florin's killer. That had touched her heart so deeply, she'd nearly burst into tears.

However, all the peculiarities of the day did not prepare her for when Liviu stepped into the workshop.

Her heart stuttered, but after a moment, she realized he appeared weary, diminutive almost; it was as if he was a different person compared to the last time they'd run into each other. That said, one of the watchmen was always in the workshop with her, so she wasn't too worried to have him here.

"Good evening," she managed, eyeing him for an injury or ailment instead of allowing herself to recall their last encounter. There didn't seem to be anything wrong with him, at least. "How can I help you?"

At the sound of her voice, his eyes focused, a jolt of surprise shooting over his face before a hint of what looked astonishingly like guilt trailed behind it.

She stared, waiting, her palms sweating, and for whatever reason, he just stared back in shocked silence.

After a minute of the most uncomfortable and confusing staring contest she'd ever had, Liviu cleared his throat and took a few, hesitant steps closer, approaching her where she stood by the herb cabinets, but not in a threatening way.

In a quiet, hard to hear whisper, he said, "I'm sorry about last time we met. There's...a lot on my mind, and I keep letting it get the best of me."

"I..." was all she managed to get out, unable to think of something to say in response.

"But, Miss Apothecary, can I ask you a question?"

She was tempted to say he already had, but there was an abashed, almost flustered expression spilling across his face that kept her tongue in check. "Of course you can."

He swallowed a couple times before speaking at last. "So...I have this friend, and his wife is pregnant. S-she's due any day now."

He paused long enough she said "Uh-huh?" to encourage him to continue.

"A-and I was wondering," he gesticulated a little before he said, "if you had anything I—I-I mean, he could give her."

"Give her for what?"

He blushed to the roots of his hair, catching her by surprise. "W-well, she's...worried. Her mom had difficult labors, so she's afraid..."

"That she'll have the same problem?" Daciana finished, raising an eyebrow.

He nodded.

"I see. Is this her first time?"

He nodded again.

"Well, it'd be easiest to determine what would work best if I could examine her first—"

Liviu shook his head so fast, it almost made her jump. "Sorry, but she lives in Riverbend, so it's too far for her to travel."

Daciana was tempted to point out that while the woman in question might not be able to make the trip, Daciana herself was quite mobile.

However, it did strike her as odd that the apothecary in that village couldn't be turned to for advice. That said, she wasn't sure how honest Liviu was being about his relationship to the woman in question.

Turning back to her cabinets, Daciana grabbed a large jar of broad leaves. "These might help. Granted, if she's close enough to give birth any day, there might not be enough time for them to take effect. However, you...or rather, your friend, can make her a tea out of these. One cup a day should help things be a little easier for her."

Liviu stared at the jar of leaves in wonder.

Opening it, she took a few out and placed them into a little bag. "She'll only need about one or two leaves a day."

"So if I make her a tea with these, the birth might be okay?"

She didn't point out his slip. "Yes, but not just with these. These leaves are nasty on their own; absolutely terrible. And I'm sure she's uncomfortable enough as it is, so we should do our best not to make it worse."

Liviu watched her with wide eyes, like she'd revealed the secrets of the universe.

"So it's best to brew it with equal amounts of spearmint and rose hip. Those will make it much more palatable."

"I see," he said, some of the weariness leaving his face.

Returning the jar in her hands to its shelf, she grabbed the spearmint and rose hip next. "I don't have much of this because of the robbery, so if you need more, she'll have to go to the apothecary in her own village."

She divided the herbs into separate bags and made sure they were clearly labeled before writing out the instructions for making the tea. She handed them all to Liviu once she'd finished.

Liviu, straightening like the weight of the world had come off his shoulders, held them like they were the world's most precious treasure. "Thank you so much. How much do I owe you?"

She told him, and he paid without hesitation. As he turned to leave, she said, "Hey, do you have a midwife?"

He paused. "Not...yet."

"I have experience with it, if you can't find anyone. Unless your wife— I mean, your friend or his wife have experience, she's going to need someone's help. If something does go wrong, having someone there who can help right away will be the difference between life and death for both the mother and the baby. Keep that in mind."

"I will," he said, appearing calm for the first time since he'd arrived. He took a step back before he paused and met her gaze again. "I really am sorry for yesterday. I'm not normally so...surly."

"Sorin says otherwise," she said before she could stop it.

He huffed, but instead of annoyed, there was something different, some other complicated emotion she couldn't quite pinpoint etching across his face. It was almost exhaustion, almost confusion.

Given what he'd revealed to her, she could imagine a few reasons why. "It seems like you're under a lot of stress," she ventured. She dropped her voice to the barest whisper. "What with the baby, and all. I'm sure becoming a parent is difficult."

His gaze shot to her face, pure terror in his eyes.

She shot him a sympathetic grimace and a shrug.

Closing his eyes, he just sighed. "Yeah," he managed after a minute. "But...the only other person who knew was Master Florin. So please don't...say anything."

"Apothecaries never reveal the secrets of their patients," she said, straight-faced. "So it's safe with me."

He attempted a smile, but it was weak.

As he turned to go, she called for him to stop. He did, turning with an uneasy expression on his face.

"Here," she said, turning back to her shelf and grabbing a few sprigs of lemon balm, chamomile, and lavender. She bundled each one, wrote out the instructions for each, and held them out to him. "For you."

He eyed them. "Not bilberry this time? What sense do these improve?"

She almost blushed. "No. These help reduce stress and anxiety. I think it's important for you to keep a clear head."

He accepted the herbs, adding them to the others. "What do I owe you for them?"

Opening her mouth, Daciana nearly spoke before pausing. Yesterday, she would've been convinced Liviu was a potential murder suspect, but all at once she wasn't so sure. And she did regret the bilberry comment. "Nothing. They're my gift to you. On account of the bilberry barb."

"A gift?" His gaze flicked to the shelves. "But you were robbed. Surely, you can't just give herbs away."

"There's enough for us to get by," she said with a smile. "So it's fine."

They stared at each other for a long moment before he acquiesced and departed, leaving her wondering. She hadn't heard about anyone from the head family getting married recently, and Liviu didn't look as though he could be much older than Sorin. On top of that, he said no one besides Master Florin had known he was married or that his wife was expecting, and for some reason, she had a sneaking suspicion Elder Aurel wouldn't be interested in letting any of his family marry outside of the village.

All at once, she recalled the argument she'd interrupted between Liviu and his mother, and Andrei's comment about how Liviu had been making regular disappearances for some time. Had Liviu simply been married in secret this whole time? They hadn't been able to get a straight answer out of Liviu about where he'd been the night of the murder either, which was one of the prominent reasons for him being a suspect. Perhaps he'd been with a wife no one knew existed, one he couldn't reveal without inciting violent reactions from people in his family, which would explain his refusal to clear his own name.

She'd have to remember to ask Sorin when she saw him again.

The thought of seeing him made a thrill dance through her, which made her pause. She'd never been so excited to see someone before. It was different but...she had to admit it was nice.

Smiling a little, she pulled out the ledger to record the purchase. In the middle of writing, she paused, realizing that the page in the ledger was covered in indentations from the previous one—one of the missing pages. Her heart leapt, pulse accelerating.

Keeping the pressure on her charcoal stick light, she rubbed down the page, taking her time.

Ionel had come during the day while Liviu had come in the evening. That said, despite both Andrei and Sorin's warnings about him, Daciana was no longer suspicious of Liviu—he'd picked up chamomile on the night of Master Florin's murder, which was another herb given to pregnant women. Ecaterina's name was there as well, though. However, beneath the woman's name, hastily scribbled and not tucked neatly onto the next line was the name of an herb and nothing else: fireweed.

It wasn't a person's name. It wasn't one of the herbs that had been stolen. It wasn't even an item that was marked as being purchased; fireweed wasn't an herb they often used. She frowned at the page, trying to puzzle out what it could mean. Why had Master Florin written the name of an herb and nothing else here?

All at once, a cold realization swept over her, leaving emptiness in its wake. Had her master known his life had been in danger and tried to leave her a clue?

Once her thoughts latched onto the idea, she couldn't get her mind to move past it, horrible scenarios playing over and over again in her mind, ghastly apparitions of what her master's final moments must've been like waltzing before her eyes.

Daciana didn't realize how long she'd been sitting there, fighting against the urge to cry as she stared at the page of the ledger, until someone lightly touched her shoulder.

She jumped, turning to find Sorin. Her heart leapt, his presence almost chasing away the lingering gloom her thoughts had draped over her.

"Hi," she said, her relief and surprise leaving her a touch breathless.

"You don't sound happy," he observed.

"Rough day?" Calin asked.

Daciana turned, surprised to find him standing near the door. It almost looked like he was ready to run out at the drop of a hat.

"No," she managed, her gaze flicking to the ledger. "Not exactly."

Sorin leaned forward, studying the page she'd rubbed. "Is this...from the missing page?" He lightly touched his finger to the indents the rubbing had made stand out.

She nodded.

"Fireweed?" he muttered, glancing at her.

With a shrug, she finally admitted defeat. "I don't have a clue."

Sorin frowned, staring at the word.

Slowly, Daciana looked up at him, something about him being there making the tears she'd pushed away return. "Sorin?" she asked, her voice tight and quiet. "Do you think he knew he was going to die?"

Sorin's gaze snapped to her face, eyes wide. Immediately, his expression softened.

"I think he was trying to tell us something. I think this is supposed to mean something to me, but I've been staring at it forever and I can't—" she managed before her throat was so tight, she couldn't make a sound.

He wrapped an arm around her shoulders, pulling her close. She allowed her head to relax against the cool leather armor over his chest.

"I'm not going to lie to you," Sorin whispered. "Based on this, I think it's plausible he knew. At the very least, he suspected something bad would happen."

She wasn't sure what she expected, but she had not anticipated the mingled strands of dread and relief that twisted through her after his pronouncement. Dread at the realization of what Master Florin must've endured in his final moments. Relief that Sorin agreed with her and didn't try to coddle her.

"So, what is fireweed?" he asked gently.

"It's an herb," she explained, appreciating him turning her attention to something straightforward and simple. Pure fact. "It's almost a weed because of how well it grows, but it grows best in burnt ground."

"Hence the name, I take it," Calin interjected, reminding Daciana he was even there.

She nodded. "We don't stock much of it because there are other herbs that do the same things as it, but better. It's a pretty flower, though."

"Well, maybe it was symbolic," Calin suggested. "A plant that thrives in burnt ground—maybe he was referring to a person who's been burnt. Not literally, of course. Otherwise you'd have to consider everyone who'd gotten too close to a cooking fire."

"That hardly narrows it down. And we've already figured that out anyway," Sorin said. Still holding Daciana to him, he flipped through the ledger.

Ionel had bounced between coming at night and during the day, with no consistent pattern to the herbs he'd asked for. Ecaterina and Liviu both tended to come at night, but Liviu had only asked for herbs used during pregnancy while Ecaterina had often asked for herbs used in cooking or herbs used for blisters. That made Daciana pause. Why herbs for blisters? Considering the woman worked in a kitchen, she would've thought herbs for cuts or burns would've been of more use than ones for blisters.

"Once again, the three suspects," Sorin muttered, calling her back to the present. "And then that last entry that makes no sense."

Daciana didn't speak as she studied it more. "It must be referring to someone though, and any one of them could've come back despite being here earlier."

"Coming earlier would look less suspicious. So far, the ledger just confirms what Ecaterina and Liviu both told the watch."

Daciana noted he didn't accuse Ionel of anything. However, she supposed it must have been hard to imagine the man he loved so much could be a killer. It was easier to point the blame at people you weren't as close to.

"You don't think your uncle might've been the one?" she asked carefully.

Because she was pressed to his side, she felt him stiffen even though she couldn't see it. "Of these three, I think he's the least likely. I'm not saying he didn't, but I...I think him murdering his best friend, wanting to kill all of us, and abduct you is too big of a stretch to consider."

"But it's not for Ecaterina and Liviu?" she pressed.

The most conflicted emotion twisted his face, a mix of frustration and pain, and she was pretty sure he avoided her gaze on purpose. Her stomach clenched, and she regretted asking the question at all.

"I-I'm sorry," she said quickly, pulling out of his grip and getting to her feet. "I didn't mean to—"

She broke off when Sorin stepped after her, gently catching hold of one of her arms. Hesitantly, she turned back, scanning him for any hint of anger or resentment. Instead, a bit to her surprise, he just seemed...miserable.

"No," he breathed, "I'm sorry. I'm trying to be more objective, but..."

"I know you are," she said, taking his hands in hers. "And I'm not accusing any of them, but..." As she stared up into Sorin's face and the pain he trusted her enough to let show, a sliver of doubt wormed into her mind, making her look away.

Regardless of who the murderer turned out to be, it would be someone near Sorin, perhaps someone he was even close to and loved. Unless she held irrefutable proof one of those three had killed Master Florin before attempting to slaughter their own family, she couldn't accuse anyone.

Not because she thought Sorin wouldn't believe her, but because she knew it would be painful, regardless of who it was, and she didn't want to hurt him.

"Daciana," he said, but she couldn't bring herself to look at him with these awful thoughts revolving in her mind.

He released a bit of a sigh before gently cupping her cheeks with his warm hands and pressing a light kiss to her forehead. Her eyes widened, her heart racing like a horse in full gallop. It wasn't the kiss she'd expected, but it still made tingling warmth rush from her head all the way to her toes.

When he pulled back, it was a few moments before she found the courage to lift her head.

"We're going to figure out who did this," he whispered. "No matter who it turns out to be, because I want you to be safe."

Unable to speak, she nodded. Afraid he would try and genuinely kiss her while she had such wretched thoughts mucking up her brain, she hurried and hugged him before he got the chance. He held her tight, and for that moment, she could pretend everything was fine. So long as she was in his arms, the world was right, and no monsters lurked in the woods.

Then they parted, Sorin stepping back, and that moment came crashing to a halt. As Daciana met his gaze, his anguish no longer on his face but lingering in the depths of his eyes, she couldn't help but wonder if solving this murder was the right thing to do.

Lightly, Sorin ran a thumb over her cheek. "Let's go."

She allowed him to lead her from the workshop, and it was then she realized that at some point during their conversation, Calin had vanished outside. Even still, she sent one last look back at the logbook, just getting a glimpse of the enigmatic clue of fireweed. Taking a deep breath, she steeled herself. In order to figure out who her master had meant, she had to get better acquainted with the three suspects they had, despite the fact one of them was, without a doubt, a murderer.

23

The beginning of that opportunity came much sooner than she'd expected. The next day, Ionel dropped into the workshop to ask her to check on his bedridden wife.

Doing her best to keep her suspicions tucked as far away as possible, she followed him to the compound, both of her guards on her heels. Her heart thrummed at the idea Ionel might be the killer and what he might do if he got her alone, so she was especially grateful for the men who labored night and day to keep her safe. Then she blinked, surprised at herself. Once again, she found herself glad she wasn't alone, even though just a week ago, she'd been glad for her solitude. It was so strange.

Ionel led her to his small house and into the back bedroom where a painfully thin woman sat propped up by several pillows. Despite how thin and drawn her face was, she smiled as they entered.

"I'm sorry to be such a bother," she said, her voice as weak as the rest of her appeared. "I've never been well."

"But she's developed a nasty cough," Ionel murmured to Daciana. "Because she's so ill, that isn't unusual, but this time, it's been worse than usual."

His wife nodded. "We'd hoped it'd clear up after a few days, but I think it's gotten worse." Almost as if to prove her point, she had a brief coughing fit, a harsh almost hacking cough that left her frail frame trembling.

Daciana leapt forward to examine the woman, whittling down the list of potential causes until she was certain she had it. Ionel left and came back with tisane, the smell so intoxicating, it distracted Daciana from her examination. It was a peppermint tisane, and the drink was a lovely pale green color.

"She loves tisanes," Ionel explained before cocking an inquisitive eyebrow at her. "Would you like one as well?"

"I would love one," Daciana said without a thought. A second later, she realized that might've been dumb but was left with no choice but to return to her examination. So long as she didn't give herself away, she doubted he'd try something here. It would be rather idiotic.

At that moment, she recalled Sorin and several of his poisoned relatives mentioning trying a new tisane from Ionel. Surely that couldn't have been the fatal dose, right? After all, Ecaterina had made those herb scones—and they'd had a lot of herbs in them. Yet Daciana had eaten one and hadn't gotten ill.

Then again, she hadn't been slowly being poisoned, so it was questionable whether either the scones or the tisane would have done anything to her anyway.

Ionel's wife suddenly spoke, cutting through her thoughts. "You're Master Florin's apprentice, aren't you?"

"Yes, ma'am."

"I could tell. You have the same gentleness he did."

That made her pause, staring at the woman with wide eyes.

"See, my silly Ionel was hesitant to ask you to come when this cough first started because he didn't believe you were as skilled as our dear Master Florin, but I think he'll be able to rest easy now." The woman smiled, a quiet, gentle kind of smile. "You're remarkably skilled for your age. Clearly, our dear friend taught you well."

Despite herself, tears pricked at the corners of Daciana's eyes. "You're very kind."

Ionel returned with a peppermint tisane for Daciana, and it appeared and smelled identical to the one he'd given to his wife, which meant it was probably safe. Even then, she doubted there'd be enough in it to drug her the way Ionel could've drugged the rest of his family, if he was behind it at all.

She took a sip, savoring the minty flavor. That was a really good tisane.

"What do you think?" Ionel's wife asked, an eager light in her eyes.

"It's wonderful," she said.

"Ionel is so proud of his teas and tisanes—oh, Dear?" She turned to Ionel, making him lift a dark eyebrow in response. "You should show our new friend your herb collection. I know it pales in comparison to what the apothecaries keep on hand, but it still is a wonderful collection. And there are even a few foreign teas in there, aren't there?"

Ionel seemed to smile without realizing it. "Well, I have spent several years collecting them." He glanced at Daciana. "I'd be happy to show them to you, if you're not too busy."

Despite her reservations, she accepted his invitation with eagerness, practically leaping from her chair with excitement, and once they'd finished drinking their tisanes, she followed Ionel into the kitchen. On the wall opposite the hearth stood a massive shelf with dozens of glass jars, proud labels standing out on each.

"Wow," she breathed, her gaze roving over the shelves. "You have so many."

He laughed, ushering her forward and she all but ran across the room, bobbing up and down as she examined the shelves. Most of the herbs were familiar to her and were common ones she worked with on a daily basis, but there were a few rarer herbs that she and Master Florin had only been able to procure on rare occasions as they didn't grow here, no matter how they'd tried. Fortunately, they could do without them, but still, it would've been fun to be able to grow anything they wanted.

"You must really love tea," she said, only sparing him a brief glance before turning back to the shelves.

"Yes," he said. "Master Florin got me into them. They help Lucia."

"Your wife?" Daciana asked.

"Yes. Since her illness can't be cured, these...just make it better."

Her gaze roved over the jars one final time before she turned back to him. "Thank you for letting me see these."

He smiled, though she thought he seemed like he was trying hard not to laugh.

"Can I ask you a question, though?" she asked, wondering if it would be too much of a risk.

He raised an eyebrow, which she supposed meant she could.

"Given how Elder Aurel is...how did...how did you end up marrying your wife?" she asked, hoping she hadn't offended him.

He sighed, but he didn't seem unhappy. "The truth is, I didn't tell him when I got married."

Her eyes widened. "No?"

"Yep, I just went and did it. He found out eventually, but since I didn't have magic, he didn't...care much. And because Lucia's health is the way it is, I honestly think he might be pretending I never got married at all. After all, neither of my children had magic, and he chased them both out of the village, so it really is like..."

"I'm sorry," she said before she could think about it. "Nobody should have to go through that."

That seemed to catch him by surprise, but the emotion only lasted for a moment.

"Well, I should be going," she continued, adjusting her satchel over her shoulder.

He nodded, and she took her leave. As she left with her guards, she reviewed what she'd learned about Ionel, but she wasn't sure it helped her in light of Master Florin's clue.

Fireweed. Just what had he been trying to tell her?

As they neared the front gate of the compound, a sharp intake of breath distracted her from her thoughts, loud enough to get her to glance to the side. To her alarm, it was Elder Aurel, who'd been in the middle of speaking with Violeta, but now his gaze was fixed on her, his face rapidly reddening as he glared. Daciana only had a second to stare back before one of her guards fell back a step, planting himself right between her and the elder's glare, the tension in his stance making it clear that even though she couldn't see his face, he was giving the elder a warning. Possibly even a threat.

She stared at the man's back in shocked wonder, aware her mouth was ajar but too stunned to do anything about it.

However, she wanted neither to cause a scene nor be the reason for a fight, so she turned and kept walking, and her guard trailed after. She only glanced back once, and was startled even further when Violeta's face twisted with fury as she rounded on the elder.

Daciana could barely even think; she was stunned. No one in the village had ever stuck up for her before—even Master Florin, who wasn't a confrontational man as it was, had usually chosen to avoid bringing her to situations that would've sparked conflict unless it'd been a dire emergency. She didn't resent that, but it was still startling to have people standing boldly at her side, a place that until that moment she'd never realized had been so empty.

A bit hesitant, she slowly met the questioning gaze of the guard who'd placed himself in the perilous path between her and Elder Aurel, which got his attention. "Thank you," she managed.

He smiled, a real genuine smile. "Anytime."

They returned to the workshop, and enough people came it was almost as normal as it had been before Master Florin's murder, and she was busy enough she didn't have much time to think about the events of the day. When her guards switched out in the evening, instead of Sorin, they brought a message from him, saying Elder Aurel had called him away, but he would be a part of her morning watch.

She hid the disappointment behind a smile, an intense loneliness burbling up from the depths of her soul. She forced it down with the reassurance that soon she would be home with her family, where she wasn't alone.

She closed the workshop as the sun set, dusk casting a hazy purple across the sky, and hurried home, her distress pushing her to walk a bit faster than normal.

The smell of her mom's cooking brushed her senses and awoke her hunger before she was at the door, and when she stepped in, she couldn't help smiling at her family's greetings and the warmth of the fire washing over the room. As she'd told herself, the mantle of loneliness attempting to wrap itself around her was ripped free.

Her family greeted her guards, which made her smile. While the reason why wasn't ideal, it did amuse her that her guards were treated like friends when they came to her home, and there were always places at the table set for them.

They sat to dinner, a warm, hearty stew in a glimmering gravy that made Daciana and her guards drool just at the sight of it, but it didn't keep her from noticing an unusual air of energy buzzing over her family today.

She was only a couple bites into her delectable meal before she glanced at them all and said, "Okay, what's going on?"

Her dad hesitated before grinning. "I have some pretty big news today, Daci."

"Oh?"

"My friend has pulled a few strings, and he's offered me a job on his farm. A permanent one."

Her heart leapt. "Really?"

He and her mother both grinned, the years seeming to lift from their faces. "I start tomorrow, and what he can pay me will bolster what you bring us."

"That's amazing," she breathed, hardly able to believe it.

All her life, her father had never been allowed to have a permanent job; they'd always had to scrape by off any generosity someone risked showing them and Daciana's meager earnings, wages Master Florin should have kept but had chosen not to. She wasn't sure why the village's attitude had abruptly changed towards her father, but she was unfailingly grateful, a heavy weight she hadn't been aware of lifting from her shoulders.

"That's not all," her brother, Gavril, butt in, his dark eyes dancing with light. "The forest keeper, Master Silviu, offered me an apprenticeship."

Daciana nearly dropped her spoon. "He what?"

"Offered me an apprenticeship!" He grinned from ear to ear. "He said he'd seen me around playing in the village, and he thought my tracking skills were exceptional. Direct quote. He wants me to start tomorrow."

"Me too!" Mitica, the youngest of them, chirped, his eyes shining brighter than even Gavril's had.

"He did not offer you an apprenticeship," Gavril quipped.

Mitica blushed but pressed on. "Not Master Silviu. Master Dragos."

She stared at her youngest brother, thoughts coming to an abrupt halt. "The blacksmith offered you an apprenticeship?"

He nodded, beaming. "He said I'm crafty."

"Creative, is what he actually said," their father corrected, but he smiled, grinning from ear to ear like a school boy. Daciana almost didn't recognize him.

Her mother smiled too. "I'm not sure what's happened, but the boys will both begin their apprenticeships in the morning. Gavril will be a bit behind Master Silviu's other apprentices, but—"

"I'll catch up," her brother said. "I'm not wasting this chance, believe me."

Daciana's heart abruptly sank, dropping toward her toes at an alarming rate, but she fought with every fiber of her being not to let it show on her face. "Are you going to be alone all day, Mom?"

To her surprise, her mother smiled. "Actually, some of the other women have invited me to their houses. Something about a cooking party, I think?"

"Oh, that was me," one of Daciana's guards chimed in. "I mentioned to my wife how amazing your cooking is—"

"I did too," the other guard said between mouthfuls.

"—and my entire family wants to try some too. I'm hoping she gets a couple recipes, because I need more food like this."

Her mother laughed, and it struck Daciana she'd never heard her mother laugh that way before—the sound had never been so musical or so free. All at once, like a surge of spring runoff flooding a river, that sea of loneliness from earlier gushed forth, plunging her into its depths, so deep and poignant she hurriedly dropped her gaze to her food so no one would notice her eyes growing bright.

The conversation continued to swirl around her, the intense, happy energy almost foreign to her, and very acutely, Daciana felt like an outsider in her own family, like she peered in on them through a window instead of sharing the table with them. She'd never known Gavril had any interest in tracking or that Mitica was displaying creative skill with his hands. She'd never had a clue. For a moment, resentment towards her brothers for never telling her bit at her, but it was swallowed by the realization that it didn't matter whether or not she'd been told—she'd never been here to see it. She still wouldn't have known who her brothers were turning out to be.

Then, the reality her brothers were growing up hit her hard, like a horse striking out with a flash of solid hooves. They'd been growing up for some time, but she'd never noticed. Despite her efforts to fill a role her father had been unable to fill for all of them, she'd never been able to lift the stress from her parents' shoulders the way he had.

She lingered after the meal long enough to be polite before congratulating her father and her brothers and excusing herself. A part of her hoped one of them would notice her mood, but none of them did, simply bidding her goodnight before returning to their excited musings for the future.

Once Daciana reached the privacy of her room and the door was safely shut behind her, the weight of her emotions hit her full on. She'd told Master Florin over and over again she wasn't lonely, but now she was forced to admit the truth: she was lonely. Horribly lonely. Her one motivation for most of her life had been carrying for her family, even if it'd had to come at her expense. Even if it meant, in many ways, they were strangers.

She'd given up so much. She'd shoved so many wants and desires away from herself, not because she was content in her solitude, but because holding them close made it unbearable. And in that moment, the burdens she'd never let herself feel hit hard, knocking the wind right out of her.

For years, she'd masked the pain by convincing herself that she was happy. Or, that even if she wasn't truly happy now, she would be someday, and it would all be worth. However, if she truly was content to be alone and happy with her lot in life, then why had she jumped at the chance to pursue a relationship with Sorin?

All at once, she was like a solitary houseplant, abandoned and forgotten, and that warred with the choking guilt that came with knowing she should be happy for her brothers when she was anything but. She should be happy for her father, and most especially for her mother, but why did their happiness have to break her heart?

Her family was moving on without her; they were a complete unit while she was an attachment, and if she hadn't been an apprentice, she could've been here with them. She'd always loved being an apothecary, but all at once, she hated it and what it'd cost her. She loathed it so much, she wanted to be sick.

She fingered the metal of her silver leaf, the smooth surface warm from being near her skin, and for the first time in her life wondered why she wanted to be an apothecary so badly. She'd always striven for it because it'd been the path that would help her family. However, if they no longer needed that help, what was she supposed to do? Why was she doing all of this? Did this really make her happy, or had she just been pretending all this time?

Exhausted, she dragged herself over to her humble cot and curled up on it without bothering to change, but sleep didn't come, leaving her to her earth-shattering thoughts instead. After a while, the howling of the wolves touched her ears, and her soul howled back, crying out for a howl in return—just one—but she knew the howls of those wolves weren't for her. For her, there was nothing but silence.

24

The worst of her emotions passed with the night, but when she dragged herself out of bed with the sunrise the next morning, Daciana was still hollow, like those emotions had spent the better part of the night devouring her insides and leaving nothing more than a dry shell behind.

When she went downstairs, the emptiness intensified at the sight of a breakfast laid out for her and no sign of the rest of her family. They were already gone without having said a single word. An enormous cavern opened inside her, threatening to consume her whole. They'd never been awake and gone before her, not even her dad when he'd gotten spare jobs. It distracted her so much she didn't even realize Sorin and another guard waited in the front room for her. She barely registered the other watchman stepping outside as Sorin approached her either.

"Daciana?" he said, and she managed to pull her attention from the food. "Are you okay?"

Was it that obvious? Shaking her head, she managed, "I'm okay, I just didn't sleep well." Even still, her voice hovered somewhere between a whisper and a murmur, so faint, even she barely heard it.

Sorin remained silent for a heartbeat before gently taking her elbow.

"You should eat. Or try too, at least."

She allowed him to lead her to the table, but even with the toasted bread and cheese in front of her, she had no appetite. It was ridiculous; she acknowledged that. She had work to do—a shop to open, a murder to solve. Yet here she sat, a complete mess.

Sorin took the seat beside her, facing her with one arm resting on the table, but she kept her gaze lowered because she didn't want to see whatever emotions were on his face. If she did, she'd probably spill everything to him, and she didn't want him to see such horrible things.

Several minutes passed before he finally said, "Daciana, please tell me what's wrong. I can tell something is."

She risked a glance at him, and her tears from last night returned. Even though she'd cried a river, apparently, she wasn't through yet. Quickly, she looked away. "It's dumb," she managed.

"Is it?" he asked, not sounding convinced.

With just that, it all burst out of her. "For the first time in my life, my dad has been offered a permanent job, a real job. My brothers were both offered apprenticeships—both in positions they're interested in— and I should be happy. I should be overjoyed. Yet I—" Her voice broke, and frustration surged through her. She couldn't believe she could be so selfish. "I'm so dumb."

"No, you're not," Sorin said with a stern note in his voice. "Your life is changing; a lot of things are changing. That's always hard, Daciana."

"I know, but why can't I be happy for them? That shouldn't be so hard."

He smiled a little as he reached out and brushed some stray hair behind her ear. "Like I said, it's a change, and change is always hard. Especially given how close you and your family are to each other. And how much you love them."

She met his gaze, startled that he knew.

His smile softened. "It's pretty obvious."

Her gaze fell to her hands. "It's...it's always been us. Just us. And now, all of the sudden, it's just me. I'm alone all day, but I never noticed because when I came home, they were always here. And now they won't be, and that...that scares me. I'm so scared that from now on...everyday...it's just going to be me. On my own."

"No, you won't be alone," Sorin murmured, reaching out again, but this time, he cupped her cheek in his warm hand, getting her to lift her eyes once more. "It's you and me. I'm here, and I'm not going anywhere, even after we solve this murder."

She stared at him, all her thoughts and emotions teetering to an abrupt and unexpected standstill. Like a ray of pure sunlight breaking through the clouds of a tempest, Sorin's words shot right to her heart, filling it with the warmth that had been snatched from her last night. When she was with Sorin...

Yes, when she was with him, the loneliness disappeared. She hadn't noticed it before, but she did then.

All these years of pushing people away, of refusing to go with Master Florin to any party or celebration he'd been invited to, had not been because she was content in solitude, but because she feared the stinging lash of loneliness and the despair that flowed in the wake of true, brutal rejection. The pain that came from being forgotten and abandoned on purpose. That was what she was afraid of; that was what she'd always feared.

When she kept herself alone, it was harder to feel it, easier to ignore it like it was merely dust in a corner. However, it'd always been there, and after the murder investigation was over and the watch was no longer following her everywhere she went, she knew it would remain, stronger than it'd ever been before. Without her family, she would have to face it completely and utterly alone.

"Sorin," she began, her voice still little more than a whisper, but the emotions searing through her made her sound so desperate. "Do you promise?"

Even still, he smiled, a small but soft kind of smile. "I promise, Daciana."

She had only a second to register he was leaning towards her, a hint of his warm breath brushing her cheek, sending a flurry of tingles rushing through her chest, before, yet again, the door opened. Jerking back, Sorin dropped his hand as she turned towards the door, a blush rising to her cheeks when she discovered the intruder this time was her own mother. She nearly huffed with frustration but managed to catch herself and keep it quiet.

Her mother blinked, her gaze flicking between the two of them before she closed the door. And smiled. Adjusting her colorful, embroidered shawl around her shoulders, she came and took the seat across from Daciana.

"I was seeing your father and brothers off for their first days, but I wanted to make sure you had something to eat so you wouldn't feel forgotten. They wanted to wake you to say goodbye, but given how you were last night, I made them leave you to your rest. So, are you feeling better this morning?" she asked, her musical accent helping ease the pains splintering her heart even further.

Then she blinked, frowning at her mother.

That made her mother laugh, and she noted once again how free it sounded. "I could tell you were unhappy last night, dear, I just didn't want to say anything. After all, sometimes you just need a good night's sleep. So how are you now?"

"A little better," she confessed.

"But not completely," her mother finished, studying her with an assessing eye.

In an instant, Daciana found herself confessing the same woes she'd shared with Sorin to her mother, though with a little less detail, perhaps.

Reaching across the table, her mother pushed her breakfast out of the way and held out a hand. Daciana acquiesced and placed her hand in her mother's grip. "My dear, we're not leaving you. On the contrary, your brothers are simply growing up, something that was always bound to happen. Regardless, I'm sure they'll have plenty of woes to bring home to you and your experience. Do you not remember when you first began your apprenticeship?"

Daciana frowned, recalling the numerous times she'd come home crying for not remembering the right herb or not being able to make a salve correctly. She smiled a little at the memories even though they'd stung at the time.

"This is a big change, but your brothers will still need their older sister, Daci. For a little longer, I suppose. As for me and your father, we'll always need our daughter. It's just...a relief that the burden of caring for the family no longer rests on you. Just because you are no longer carrying the weight of this family doesn't mean we don't love you or need you."

"I wasn't complaining," Daciana said, though it sounded a bit petulant, even to her.

Her mother's lips quirked with a knowing smile. "Aye, you never uttered a word of complaint, but I certainly did and I wish you would have. What kind of parent would be happy having to deprive their child of a childhood in order to keep their family alive?"

She blinked. "I had a childhood."

Her mother shook her head. "No, you stopped being a child once you became an apprentice. You worked all day and came home only at night because you had to be the breadwinner for this family. That's not a childhood."

She frowned, but she had to agree with her mother. Most of her childhood memories that were genuinely child-like came from before her apprenticeship. Once she'd become an apprentice, however...

"You carried the weight of protecting our family for many years, Daci," her mother said, squeezing her hands, "and for that your father and I are profoundly grateful and proud of you. But that no longer needs to be your burden. Instead of living for everyone but you, we both want you to be able to live a little more for yourself—to do more than just work and sleep. Surely you weren't happy with the idea of carrying on exactly like this for the rest of your life?"

At that moment, Daciana realized she'd spent the last several years preparing to do exactly that. She'd never imagined the possibility of being married, not just because of her spurned heritage, but because doing so would've taken her out of the family that, until today, had so desperately needed her. She'd never pursued anything beyond becoming an apothecary because there'd never been the time or means for her to do so—she didn't have a single hobby. Until now.

Even though she'd spent so many years resigned to her fate, she never would've been happy forcing herself into that mold, regardless of what she'd been telling herself.

All at once, her mother stretched out her other hand, but instead of reaching for Daciana, she reached for Sorin. He blinked, hesitating before haltingly taking the woman's offered hand.

Surprising them both, the woman put their hands together before withdrawing her own. Daciana stared before blinking at her mother.

"Mom," she began before stopping, unsure what to say.

"I've been in your shoes before, Daci. Besides, it's hard not to notice the way you've come home glowing the last few days." Her brown eyes turned to Sorin, filling with warmth as she stared at him. "And I think that's because of you. Sorin, is it not?"

He stared before nodding and taking a firmer hold of Daciana's hand, which made her smile.

Her mother smiled too before placing a hand over their clasped ones. "Daci, it's okay to do something for yourself. In fact, I want you to do something for yourself for once. You're a gifted apothecary, and if that's what you want to do with the rest of your life, I'll be happy. However, regardless of what you decide, you don't need to do it alone. Especially since I like him."

Daciana blushed, but she couldn't help grinning as she met Sorin's gaze. "I like him too."

"But it's a secret," Sorin said quickly.

"Because of me?" her mother asked, lifting an eyebrow.

"Somewhat," he admitted, though he seemed abashed. "But also because the elder—my grandfather—is determined to choose who I marry, and he doesn't like Daciana enough as it is. I don't want to give him a reason to make things worse for her."

Making a noise of disgust, her mother rose and slid Daciana's breakfast back in front of her. "He's a such stubborn old thing. Sometimes I wanna—" She clenched a fist before cutting herself off and relaxing her hands. Almost as if embarrassed, she smoothed out her skirts before fetching a small basket and setting some of her spices inside.

Sorin watched her for a moment longer before turning back to Daciana, a smile dancing around his mouth. "I like her."

That made all three of them laugh.

Sorin and her mother settled into an easy conversation while Daciana ate her breakfast, her energy restored. If she was a little plant, then she was certain Sorin was her sunshine, his bright rays of kindness bringing her to life whenever she began to wilt. She wasn't sure how he managed it, but she knew she didn't ever want him to leave.

When she finished, Sorin rose with her. "Are you ready?" he asked.

She nodded, unable to keep a smile at bay. Now that she'd ripped herself out of the pain of last night, she knew without a doubt that being an apothecary was her dream, and she was eager to get back to it. "I am."

They bid farewell to her mother, who eyed the two of them with a smile, and left. Daciana was a bit surprised when Sorin and the other watchman led her all the way to the head family's compound.

"Sorin?" she asked, eyeing him.

When he glanced at her, he wasn't smiling, his stern watch leader persona out in full force, but there was warmth in his eyes that made her imagine he would've been smiling if they'd been alone. "We've narrowed it down to three suspects, so we need to investigate more in order to understand Master Florin's clue. Today, Elder Aurel insists the family has to eat together, which means Ecaterina should be hard at work."

Daciana perked up. A chance to witness the woman in that environment was exactly what she'd been hoping for.

Sorin had never been in the kitchens in the hours leading up to one of their large family dinners, and he confessed himself a little cowed by the noise and heat. Ecaterina was there, barking orders over the hiss of cooking food and the thunk of knives slicing through vegetables and fruits. The heat billowing through the room startled him, and he kept himself pressed against the wall near the doorway, Daciana following suit.

Ecaterina spotted him within a couple minutes, and she huffed, her cheeks red and her hair abnormally untidy. "What do you want?" she asked shortly before her attention was pulled away by Narcisa asking her a question.

He waited until the woman finished with her daughter before he said, "We're just observing." Then he couldn't think of another way to explain their presence, and Ecaterina raised an eyebrow, the sour expression on her face making it clear she intended to boot them back out the door.

Fortunately, Daciana's mind was a bit quicker than his. "We wanted to know more about how your kitchen worked. I've never seen cooking on such a large scale before. It's impressive."

That seemed to appease Ecaterina because she huffed and proceeded to ignore them. Sorin eyed his cousins working with his aunt in the lead, noting that few of them seemed to genuinely enjoy their work. One of his cousins, by the stoves, almost seemed bored using her fire magic to keep the food at the perfect temperature, her gaze whisking towards one of the windows, which brought Ecaterina down on her when the meat she cooked began to burn. He spied Narcisa cutting a mountain of vegetables with a face devoid of emotion.

For a while, as he watched, his thoughts kept circling back to the reality that none of his cousins who worked in the kitchens had asked to be here. While they were good cooks—especially Ecaterina—wouldn't they have been happier if they'd at least been able to choose to be here?

All at once, Daciana leaned a bit closer to him, speaking in a low voice he just managed to hear over the din of the kitchen. "You know, now that I've seen the kitchen in action, I'm not sure Ecaterina would've poisoned all of you."

He glanced at her. "No?"

Daciana indicated his cousin with fire magic and another cousin who was using air magic to work with raising bread. "There's a lot going on in the kitchen, and poisoning all of you would've taken out some important help. And clearly she's not happy in here, but she's resigned to it, so why would she do something that would make it worse for her?"

"It might have only been a temporary worsening of the situation," he pointed out.

She gave him a withering look, something about it amusing him despite the situation and topic. "You've never made bread before, have you?"

"No, I haven't," he admitted.

"What your cousin is doing with their magic is taking hours of work out of that bread."

Sorin eyed the process. His family's kitchen had always turned out incredible bread, but he'd never thought about the process of making it before. "Really?"

She nodded once, firmly. "Especially given how much bread is being made. Plus the ability to keep fire at the perfect temperature? My mother would kill for that."

Sorin frowned. He supposed Daciana had a point. While Ecaterina lashing out at her own family could have helped her escape from the kitchen, it also might not. If Elder Aurel had died, and then Sorin, his successor, had followed suit, eligibility to rule would not go to Ecaterina. She was Elder Aurel's youngest girl, and the position of head would default to the oldest child, which was one of Elder Aurel's sons. That son in particular enjoyed Ecaterina's cooking. As such, there was no guarantee it would grant Ecaterina a reprieve from the kitchens at all; on the contrary, the family would've kept everyone exactly where they were in order to survive such a massive shock and transition. She might've escaped someday, but her destroying the magical members of her family would've made her remaining time in the kitchens that much more miserable.

His ability to believe Ecaterina might have been the culprit shriveled to almost nothing. Though, of course, he supposed there was always the chance Ecaterina might be guilty anyway if she hadn't thought all that through, but to be frank, he had a hard time believing she was that dumb given the way she'd lived her life.

Liviu burst into the kitchens with a crate, not noticing him or Daciana as he stepped through the door.

Ecaterina turned, eyeing him and his crate without seeming the least bit interested. "What did they send me this time?"

"Honey," Liviu said, neither seeming annoyed nor pleased with that pronouncement. "Several different kinds of it: lavender, apple blossom, clover. Oh, this one's fireweed."

Sorin's gaze zipped to Daciana, but she frowned, a thoughtful kind of frown that gave him pause.

"Fireweed?" Ecaterina growled the word. "Why did you bring that here? You know Narcisa and I are allergic to it."

Liviu started, glancing into the crate. "Since when have you been allergic to fireweed?"

Narcisa shot him a scathing look without pausing in her vegetable cutting. "Since the day I was born, halfwit."

He stuck his tongue out at her, and she smirked at him, the exchange catching Sorin off-guard. He'd used to play like that with them too.

"Okay, I'll leave all the others here and take the fireweed ones to the grocer. They'll get rid of it soon enough." Liviu emptied most of his crate before hefting it and turning back towards the door, which was when he spotted Sorin and Daciana.

Sorin stiffened, staring back, but to his surprise, Daciana waved.

Liviu seemed startled by the sight of them, but even still, he returned Daciana's wave before eyeing Sorin with an expression that was neither warm nor cold.

"Oh, by the way, Liviu," Ecaterina said, getting the young man to turn back. "Dad told me to tell you the girl he's picked out for you will be here this afternoon and he expects you to be there." She ended that statement with a sigh, almost seeming annoyed about that fact.

"I'm busy," Liviu said, the words clipped.

Ecaterina sighed again, in exasperation this time. "Liviu, there's no point in fighting this. Just go get it over with."

He raised an eyebrow. "Because that made you so happy, didn't it?"

A flush burst over her cheeks.

With a storm brewing over his own features, Liviu turned and left without a glancing in anyone's direction.

After a few minutes more, Daciana nudged Sorin's arm, and they left the kitchens. They didn't speak until they'd left the compound and arrived in Daciana's workshop, and even then, Sorin stayed quiet for a few minutes, the frown on her face making it clear she was thinking hard.

Eventually, he ventured, "That fireweed was an interesting coincidence."

"It was," she said, a distracted note in her voice. Her forehead scrunched up and after a long moment, she huffed and sat on her stool, propping her chin in her hand. "I give up."

He raised an eyebrow. "Give up?"

"Fireweed honey," she said, her brow scrunching up again. "I'd forgotten it's used to make food a lot—not just honey, but butter and cheeses too. That said, I don't think Master Florin's clue was referencing Ecaterina."

"Because she's allergic to it?"

"It's something she wouldn't have anything to do with, so it makes no sense to me. If she was the guilty one, he could've written one of the herbs she frequently gets or something like that instead of an herb she isn't connected to. But the honey reminded me of something else about fireweed, something I'm forgetting. And the harder I try to remember it, the more it slips away from me."

"I'm sure you'll figure it out," he said as she rose and headed towards the door, almost seeming resigned at having to start her work day.

She met his gaze, and her expression relaxed. "I'll certainly try." Then she opened the workshop, and within a matter of minutes, her first customers arrived and Sorin had to settle into being her faithful watchman. Even still, his mind whirled. They'd quite possibly eliminated a suspect, but in truth, it didn't ease the discontent picking at him. It just made him even more anxious, the apprehension coiling inside him digging deeper.

25

Ionel called on Daciana to come check his wife the following day, and by the time Daciana finished her examination, she still couldn't free that niggling thought about fireweed. A glimmer of it kept flashing through the murky depths of her memories, but she couldn't seem to extract it, not even when she tried not to think about it.

Sighing, she shook her head, pausing where she stood on Ionel's porch. After yesterday, she found herself struggling to be convinced that either Liviu or Ecaterina could be the culprit, which left Ionel.

Yet she wrestled with the idea it could be him either; he didn't have the presence or manner of the killer she'd crafted in her mind. However, of the three likely candidates, he was the only one who still made sense. However, if it was Ionel, then she needed to have absolute proof of his treachery before she accused him, for Sorin's sake.

She didn't believe for a second she could ask the man and get straight answers if he was the guilty party, nor did she think it was wise. If he was the culprit, he'd threatened her once and hired the Thornwood Fell Bandits to abduct her. If he was guilty and caught on to her suspicions, she wasn't sure Sorin and his watchmen could prevent the man from getting his way.

Daciana wasn't afraid of dying or being taken captive; she was afraid of what that would do to her family and, most especially, to Sorin. She was well acquainted with loneliness, and she wouldn't wish it on anyone else.

What she needed was an opportunity, some way to check if he had the herbs or some contact with the bandits or something—anything. He collected herbs for tisanes—it wouldn't be difficult to hide the herbs among his stock, especially if he'd held on to them in an attempt to poison his family a second time. It wouldn't be smart as long as she was around, but if he was desperate enough...

She had to see if he had the herbs. They were the easiest thing to check for. Plus, it might be the only chance they had of catching the killer.

Repressing another sigh, she stepped off Ionel's porch, ignoring the questioning looks her watchmen gave her. As much as she wanted to rush back into the man's house to check, it was pointless to try it so long as he was there. Out of the corner of her eye, she spied Andrei working in his flower garden again, weeding this time.

After a moment's hesitation, she went over him. She convinced her guards to stay back a little before she approached.

"Hello, Andrei," she called.

He glanced up with wide eyes before a smile burst across his face. Standing, he brushed the dirt off his palms. "Daciana! What brings you back here already?" He eyed her up and down, and she could tell from the concern in his eyes he'd heard about the bandits.

"Ionel asked me to check on his wife. She's developed a bad cough."

"Ah. Auntie does get sick a lot," he said.

She leaned forward a little. "Your mom won't be mad if I ask you to take a break long enough to walk to the front gate with me, right?"

He raised an eyebrow. "You've got your guards, haven't you?"

She nodded before lowering her voice. "But I want to ask you something, and here seems like a bad spot."

Andrei stared before casting a glance at the half-weeded garden and relenting. "All right. If that's what you want."

They chatted about nothing in particular (though she did ask him in a roundabout way if he was interested in plants, and to her delight, he was) until they were at the gate of the compound, where it was easier to tell who was nearby and if they might be trying to listen.

Keeping her voice lowered, Daciana said, "You're outside a lot, aren't you?"

"Usually," he replied, hands tucked behind him and his shoulders shrugged up in a way that made him appear embarrassed. "Why?"

"Because, during the next couple days, I need you to keep track of Ionel and tell me if he leaves."

Andrei's brow furrowed and he regarded her for a long minute before he spoke. "Why do you...?" A flash of realization. "You don't think Io—"

"No," she said firmly even though the correct answer was yes. "I don't. However, there's something I need to check, and it'll be easier if he's not there. Do you think you could keep an eye on him for me?"

He eyed her for a long minute before relenting. "All right. He usually leaves in the afternoon, so if he does, I'll come get you then."

"Thank you," she whispered fervently. "And hey, one more thing. Don't tell anyone about this, okay? I've already been threatened twice, and if word gets out you helped me, I'm afraid they might retaliate against you. So don't say a word, all right?"

"Daciana—" he began, eyes going wide.

She shook her head. "I'm serious, Andrei. Whoever is behind this isn't going to hold back just because you're family. So promise me you'll be careful."

"Me? How about yourself?" he demanded, fists on his hips. "This isn't going to put you in danger, is it?"

"No," she lied. She smiled a little, hoping that would put him at ease. "I just don't want to upset anybody."

There was another long pause before he agreed and left.

Daciana stared after him for a moment before leaving the compound. If Ionel was the culprit, then the plan forming in her head *would* put her at risk of being in serious danger. She knew she'd promised both Sorin and Andrei she wouldn't do anything reckless—and they might not forgive her if this went awry—but she had to be certain whether or not Ionel was the culprit. Sorin's presence would be a dead giveaway, and Andrei shouldn't have to get involved more than he already was considering his age.

She couldn't, in good conscience, ask either of them to incriminate someone they loved without proof he'd betrayed them all.

The rest of the day passed with a couple house calls and no serious incidents. Ecaterina stopped by, acting like her usual self, though once again the woman asked for herbs commonly used for blisters. When Daciana peeked at the woman's hands, there were a couple blisters there, but only on her fingertips. Even still, given the weary, irritated mood overshadowing the woman, Daciana didn't say anything about it.

In the evening, Sorin and another guard came to take over the watch. Daciana did her best to smother a yawn as Sorin entered, though the other watchman remained outside the front door.

Had the watchmen caught on to her and Sorin? Whenever Sorin was around, they all seemed to disappear.

"Long day?" Sorin asked, calling her back to the present moment.

She shrugged. "No more than usual. What about you?"

He shook his head. "Not really. Some sheep have gone missing—though they just seem to have wandered off, thank goodness. And old Sebastian and Mihai are having their usual row over whose ancestors were more essential at the village's founding." A weary, though amused smile touched his mouth. "I'm surprised they still have things to argue about."

That made her smile, just a little, though it was strained. How could the world still be so decidedly normal?

"Are you heading home?" Sorin asked.

"No," she said, doing her best to come across as her usual, unstressed self. "I have a salve I'm running low on, and I need to get started on it before I get distracted and put it off any longer."

He accepted this and settled near the table, watching quietly as she gathered the ingredients she needed. They sat in silence for a while before Sorin broke it.

"You know," he began, getting her to glance his way, "the smell of the herbs you're using reminds me of something."

"Oh?"

"Yeah, of when I was little, and Liviu and me and a couple of my other cousins were playing near the river in the Howling Falls Ravine. I don't remember what we were doing, but we fell in. I think the herbs you're using grew on the riverbank."

She paused in her movements, blinking owlishly at the image that conjured in her mind. "That's a pretty dangerous river to fall into."

"Yeah, it wasn't our best idea. Thank goodness Ionel had come with us, and he hauled all of us out. I still remember standing on the rocky shore while he berated us for scaring years off his life." He smiled a bit. "I haven't thought about that in a long time."

A smile almost touched her mouth, but it faded like frost before the sun's mercy. She didn't want to imagine Ionel as the caring uncle Sorin knew him to be.

However, if Sorin noticed, he didn't point it out, instead continuing to regale her with stories of his youth and talking more than she'd ever heard him do before.

Despite the heaviness of her thoughts, Daciana couldn't help laughing at the antics of him and his cousins when they'd all been carefree children—tales of them climbing massive pine trees, games they'd invented, and a time when they'd tried to catch one of the wild ponies that roamed the nearby plains.

However, she couldn't help noting both Liviu and Ionel, in particular, were regular features in the tales of Sorin's past, and the unease and pain inside her burrowed deeper with every new tale she heard.

"What about you?" Sorin asked, eyeing her with an intensity that made her nervous.

"Me?" she asked, caught off guard.

"Surely you had some fun when you were a kid. Before you became an apprentice, I mean."

She frowned, doing her utmost to focus on his question rather than her gloomy thoughts. "Well, there was one time when my younger brother, Gavril, found an injured hawk and tried to keep it."

"He didn't," Sorin said, leaning forward.

She grinned. "Oh he did. He built it a nest and everything in his window. I remember we'd run out into the woods gathering everything we could think of to try and feed it, and we ended up plastered in mud from head to toe. Our room had feathers and bird poop everywhere, and when my parents found out, we were both grounded. But it was a cute bird."

For some reason, that made Sorin laugh, which made her pause. When he smiled—actually smiled—he appeared so much younger than usual, like he was truly just twenty years old, and that held her attention.

All at once, as the light of the setting sun touched the windows and painted them in golden light, it hit her how messed up his life had become because he'd woken up one day with magic, an ability he'd never asked for. In the blink of an eye, something completely beyond his control had drawn such divisive lines between him and people he'd cared about. It also struck her what it would do to him if Ionel turned out to be the murderer and had targeted him because of something that had never been Sorin's fault.

In an instant, all her mirth faded, and when she tried to check her salve, her vision blurred, making the task impossible. Once again, she couldn't help wondering if solving the murder was a good idea. Was it wise to chase the clues to their conclusion when it would hurt so many people?

However, at the same time, turning her back on it wouldn't resolve the pain that had already been inflicted; it wouldn't stitch a broken family back together. After all, the killer hadn't succeeded—it was only a matter of time before they struck again, undoubtedly causing more pain.

All at once, for the first time since the murder had taken place, she didn't want to know who had done this.

What if she proved Ionel was the killer, and Sorin hated her for it? They'd both be hurt, but for her, she would have to return to her unbearable isolation. The worst part was she wouldn't blame him for leaving, even when he'd promised not to; if Sorin ever accused a member of her family of the same thing, even if they were guilty, she would struggle with that. It would hurt.

Considering the idea alone was as painful as drawing blood.

"Daciana," Sorin said from her side, inciting a frantic attempt to hide her tears. How long had he been standing there? "I didn't want to mention it, but did something happen? You've been upset this whole time. It's not something with your family again, is it?"

She shook her head, but she didn't know what to say, torn between being pleased and dismayed that he'd noticed her despair.

Her hands shook as she worked to clean them, and no matter how hard she tried, she couldn't get them to stop. That made agitation build inside her, stupid frustration that made no sense, even to her. Even still, she couldn't get it to leave.

Rising, she gathered her tools and the salve and put everything away. Sorin followed, not speaking. He just watched her with the slightest bit of concern wrinkling his forehead.

She didn't dare tell him about her suspicions yet; she couldn't risk hurting him if it turned out to be false. Yet guilt seized her at the memory of promising him she wouldn't do anything stupid, and here she was, planning to do something arguably insane.

Would he be more hurt about Ionel turning out to be the murderer or more hurt that she'd suspected and hid it from him?

Daciana didn't know, but that thought made the tears burst free.

"What is it?" he asked gently, putting his hands on her arms.

The world began shrinking down to the two of them, but Daciana wrestled against the sensation, determined not to give in. There was a whole world out there, and she couldn't forget about it. There were people out there who needed answers, they needed closure.

"I—" she managed, her voice little more than a harsh whisper. She'd never wanted to tell someone something so badly before, and yet she couldn't say it. Not directly, at least. "I hate this case. It makes me suspicious and think the worst of people I don't want to think about that way. And what if the real killer is someone close to you? How can we—"

An actual sob cut her off, powerful like it held her lungs in a vice, squeezing hard enough she couldn't breathe. Yet that was enough for Sorin. He pulled her to him, holding her reassuringly tight.

A flicker of resistance flared to life in her mind, a fight to defy the pull, to battle against the desire to be held and comforted by him. She was lying to him; it may not have been a direct lie, but a lie of omission was still a lie. However that flicker of resistance died, and, at last, she surrendered, allowing her world to shrink and extend no further than Sorin. The worst sobs she'd ever experienced ripped through her, each one feeling like it would be the one that shattered her.

"I don't know how this is going to play out," Sorin whispered. "I don't know who did this, but regardless of whoever it is, it's going to be okay."

"No, it's not," she managed, her voice strangled and shaking. She couldn't bear to meet his gaze, so instead she spoke to his chest. It occurred to her this was the second time she'd cried in front of him, but this time, instead of being embarrassed, she was going to drown in guilt.

"The killer is someone in your family. When we accuse and punish them, what's that going to do to you?"

"Daciana, look at me."

She couldn't do it.

"Hey," he gently put his hand under her chin and lifted until their gazes met, the tenderness she found there making fresh tears spill down her cheeks. "Really, look at me."

She tried, but her vision kept blurring.

"It's okay. I already know whoever did this is someone close to me; I've accepted that. And finding the killer isn't about me; it's about Master Florin, his family, and you. It's so you can have closure and peace. It's so you can gather your herbs and do your job without having to look over your shoulder. It's so you don't have to be afraid to be alone anymore."

He brushed away the tears on her cheeks, no matter how many fell to take their place.

"It will be okay, Daciana. No matter who it turns out did it, I still have good people in my family." He paused, and the tenderness that had only been in his eyes blossomed over his entire face like a gentle sunrise. "And I have you."

"Me?" she asked, her voice small.

"Yes, you," he said, the most tender emotion she'd ever seen from him blossoming across his face. "Because I love you. So no matter what happens, everything will be okay."

He lightly kissed her forehead, his touch so gentle it was as if he was keeping the shattered bits of her from scattering. Maybe Daciana should have been embarrassed or something, but instead, all at once, she was safe. It was if he could extract all her fears with his touch alone.

She knew he'd meant what he'd said, and that both terrified her and made her feel like nothing could possibly happen to her—to them—so long as they were together.

Reaching up, she touched her fingers to the back of the hand cupping her face, closing her eyes. The emotion that passed between them was so special, so intimate, she never wanted the moment to end.

Sorin pulled back, neither moving the hand she held nor speaking. When she was brave enough to meet his gaze, there was a new warmth there, something different about the way he looked at her. She'd never seen him stare at anything else that way before. Then he pulled her back into his arms, holding her close, and for that moment, that was enough.

26

Sorin hadn't fully realized the depth of his feelings for Daciana until he'd said the words out loud, but the moment he said them he knew they were true. It'd been a slow, gradual thing, but it was real. He loved her.

Tears still ran down Daciana's cheeks, but she was no longer subjected to those gut-wrenching sobs from a couple minutes ago, so he felt it was safe to just hold her and let her get the pain out. He wished he had the ability to make her stop crying, to alleviate and fix whatever had broken her heart, but this was the best he could do.

They had a few minutes to spend like that, with just the two of them together while the rest of the world remained miles and miles away before someone pounded frantically on the workshop door. They jumped apart, and in only an instant, Sorin missed Daciana already.

She frantically swiped at her tears with her apron, so in order to give her time to compose herself, he went and opened the heavy door.

He stiffened, his eyes going wide. "Liviu?"

His cousin was pale, but even still, the guy stared at Sorin with his mouth wide open. After a moment, he stuttered out, "You're not the apothecary."

"N-no," Sorin managed, just as flustered. "She's over there." He gestured vaguely behind him.

Liviu stared a few moments longer before shaking himself and entering the workshop. "Miss Daciana, I think it's time."

Daciana stared at him for a second, seeming like she was thinking, but despite the fading, orange light from the setting sun, it was obvious she'd been crying. "Oh, you mean—"

"Yes," Liviu gasped, more desperate than Sorin had ever heard him. "My wife's having the baby now."

Sorin stared at the back of his cousin's head, shock rendering him mute. Liviu's *what* was *what*?

"She's been uncomfortable lately, but she had the...the..." Liviu gesticulated in an almost comical way. "The water thing."

"Her water broke?"

"Yes! That's what she said. She also says the contractions have been bad today. I-I think she's in labor."

"It seems that way," Daciana said, getting herself back together in an instant. "And if it isn't, you'd better get me there straight away."

"R-right," Liviu said as she gathered her things and headed for the door. "She's not alone—her little sister came—but even still—"

Sorin hurried outside and informed the other watchman to go to Daciana's home to inform her family where their daughter would be. Sorin didn't know much about the birthing process, but he did know it could take time.

Liviu's horse stood by the gate, and Sorin stared at it, his mind whirling. Its head hung low while its sides were damp with sweat. The poor thing needed a rest, which meant they'd need fresh horses.

Daciana and Liviu hurried out of the workshop, and Sorin glanced back. "We'll have to go to the compound for horses."

Liviu nodded, still pale as snow. "I know. That's... I'm afraid in this state I'll say something I shouldn't. If Elder Aurel found out..."

"I'll take care of it." Sorin took hold of the exhausted horse's reins and led it to the compound. He went straight to the stables, turned the animal over to the cousins of his who helped their parents manage the stable, and asked for three horses. His cousins leapt to it, even the little ones, something about their eagerness easing the tension coiling up his back.

Once the horses were ready, he thanked his cousins and led the horses out of the compound where Liviu and Daciana waited. Liviu mounted without hesitation, but Daciana hesitated.

She eyed the mare he'd led her to. "I've never ridden before," she whispered.

"It'll be okay," he murmured back. "This is Reanu, and she's quite calm. She'll be perfect for you, and I'll be next to you the whole time."

She nodded and let him help her into the saddle. She clutched the saddle horn for balance, but once he'd mounted his own horse, a massive stallion named Xandru, she seemed to relax a bit. He gave her a couple instructions, and once she'd obeyed, he turned to his antsy cousin.

"Lead the way, Liviu," Sorin said, his mind still reeling that Liviu was married. When had that happened? More importantly, how had he managed to keep it a complete secret from everyone, especially Elder Aurel?

They quickly set out, beginning at a walk until Daciana was more comfortable, and then they broke into a trot. Despite the fact she'd never done this before, Daciana was easy in the saddle, gentle on the reins, and whenever he glanced at her to make sure she was all right, she was beaming. Seeing her smile made him do the same, despite the situation.

Liviu led them along the northern road, towards Riverbend, a village a few miles away. Right after they passed through the village's dark gates, Liviu swerved, taking them to a little cottage set a bit apart from the rest of the houses. Faint light from inside flickered against the window, creating a yellowish glow.

Liviu leapt off his horse and all but sprinted inside. Sorin dismounted and helped Daciana down before he led the horses to the nearby paddock, where they all immediately dipped their mouths into the water. Daciana vanished inside the little house almost the second her feet touched the ground.

Since he was useless when it came to helping someone give birth, he decided it would be best if he stayed outside and tended to the horses, removing their tack and brushing them down. They would have enough time to rest before they could leave, so they might as well be comfortable. Once he was out of things to do, he sat on the paddock fence, gaze on the thick dusting of stars that had long since emerged in the inky expanse above.

A few minutes later, Liviu returned outside, staring around like a lost child before spotting Sorin and joining him on the fence. Sorin regarded him warily, but his cousin's gaze was fixed on the dirt, his shoulders sagging like he was exhausted.

"Why are you out here?" he asked.

Liviu seemed to startle, staring at Sorin for nearly a full minute before he found his voice. "I wanted to stay, but Miss Daciana said I was stressing Feli out, so she made me leave."

Sorin nodded, and silence draped itself over them, neither comfortable nor pleasant.

"So," he eventually said, making Liviu jump. "How...was it going?"

"It's okay, I think. Miss Daciana didn't seem worried." Liviu's grip on the fence tightened, his knuckles turning white. "But Feli is really in there giving birth."

"Daciana is incredible at what she does; I've seen that for myself. So long as it's in her power, she won't let anything disastrous happen to either of them."

The corner of Liviu's mouth twitched upwards. "That's high praise from you."

Sorin almost smiled, and they settled back into silence for a few minutes. This time, the silence was easier and lighter.

"So," Sorin eventually managed to say. "You're...married?"

Liviu flushed, but even still, he smiled. "It's been a little over a year—and no, we didn't rush into it because of something scandalous."

"I only briefly considered that reason," Sorin teased without a thought.

"It was legitimate, and I can prove it," Liviu said, sounding stern but he was grinning. "But Feli isn't the kind of woman the elder would let into our family—she's an orphan."

"Not to mention she's from a different village."

"Exactly." Liviu sighed. "It was easy to keep it secret at first. I'm always running errands between us and the other villages, so no one would think much of me being gone a lot, but then Feli got pregnant a lot sooner than either of us expected she would and keeping it a secret got harder. I wanted to be here, you understand?"

Sorin nodded.

"Not only did I want to be by her side, but this was something I wanted to share. It wasn't until I was about to start a family that I realized I wanted my kids to be able to grow up around my own family. But if the elder knew... Well, it wouldn't matter to him if the baby was mine."

Sorin understood what the elder would do all too well. One of their older cousins had eloped, and when the elder had discovered it—despite the fact they'd already had two children—his actions had almost shattered the marriage. Their cousin had promptly left the village, and they'd never seen her since.

"I want to do better for her than this pathetic shack, but my hands are tied."

"And the Elder is trying to force you to marry someone else."

Liviu shook his head, looking for all the world like the weight of the entire sky pressed on his shoulders. "There've been several close calls in trying to avoid that."

"So this is why you wouldn't tell anybody where you were the night of Master Florin's death?" Sorin ventured, finally fitting that piece of the puzzle into the picture.

Liviu glanced up, indignation flaring over his features. "Wait, did you really think I killed Master Florin before going after the lot of you?"

Sorin grimaced, searching for the most diplomatic answer he could manage. "Because of the nature of the whole thing, we...had to consider everyone in the family who didn't have magic."

His cousin froze before sighing. "Yeah, this is why. I was here that night. Feli can confirm it if you want. We were deciding on potential names for the baby. However, if I'd told you, Elder Aurel would've figured everything out."

Sorin frowned at the ground. That crossed Liviu off the list of suspects as well, leaving a grim reality in its wake he didn't want to think about.

However, Liviu provided a sufficient distraction when he abruptly asked, "Hey, do you hate me?"

Sorin's head whipped to the side so fast, he nearly tumbled off the fence. "Hate you? I thought you hated me."

"Of course you would think that," Liviu said with the barest hint of waspishness. "You pea brain; I've never hated you."

Sorin just stared.

"I was angry about Elder Aurel snatching you away and the way my mom treated me when I didn't get magic, and over the years, I was definitely taking all of that out on you. But I was...being stupid. There was no excuse for it. It's not like you asked to be born with magic or for the elder's undivided attention. I mean, it's not like he's letting you decide how to live your own life any more than he is me with mine."

"So you did overhear us that day," Sorin said with a hint of accusation.

"Accident, I swear!" Liviu held up his hands in mock surrender, and they both laughed. When it faded, they were serious again. "You were the special one who got all the attention while my mom didn't even seem to care about me or my siblings because we couldn't get her dad to acknowledge her. I've realized I was mad at the wrong people. Her and the elder are the ones I should've been mad at. They're the ones who decided whether or not I had magic dictated if I mattered."

"You know," Sorin began, Liviu's honesty and openness getting him to crack his own shell a bit, "I always thought if I just did what the elder wanted—if I didn't get to be happy—at least the rest of you would. I...I was scared and angry and alone, but I thought that maybe, for you, it wouldn't be..."

"I know that now," Liviu said with a huff. "I wish I hadn't been so obstinate. It would've been so much better if we'd stuck together."

He didn't disagree. Even though he didn't regret trying to protect his cousins, he did regret ostracizing them. What Daciana's mother had said to Daciana a few days ago struck him anew. Despite how their lives had unexpectedly diverged the day he'd woken up with magic surging through his veins, Sorin and his cousins still needed each other just as much as Daciana's brothers still needed her, and he regretted his choice to abandon them for the sake of their happiness. Never, even in the smallest moment, had it made a single one of them happy.

"And Sorin," Liviu continued, "it might be because I'm about to become a dad myself, but I want you to know I'm going to do everything in my power to ensure my children don't have to spend their childhoods the way you had to spend yours. I'm going to make sure they don't end up living like you did. No offense."

It almost sounded like an insult, but at the same time, it made Sorin smile. Liviu's children would be happy, for which—to his surprise—he was grateful. Nobody should have to grow up the way they all had.

"Also, even though it may be kind of weird, I wanted to tell you I'm proud of you."

Sorin raised an eyebrow. "Are you?"

"That day when I overheard the elder telling you about the marriage he's trying to arrange? You told him no. You've never stood up to him before."

Sorin almost laughed. "It...just kind of happened."

"The elder was furious, but it honestly serves him right to not get his way. He's so...so petulant!" He glanced at Sorin. "That's what Feli said."

"He's going to try and lash out at me somehow," Sorin said, a chill sweeping over him at the thought. He'd been doing his best to avoid the elder, but the man was always plotting something. "But I'm not getting married to someone he picks. I'm going to marry who I want, no matter how much of a fuss he makes. I've already done everything else he's ever wanted me to, and this is going to be my choice."

"Good for you," Liviu said with a real, genuine grin. "You officially have human emotions again."

"Oh thanks," Sorin snapped.

Liviu laughed, the years of tension that had spanned between the two of them seeming to dissolve and fade away like dirt caught in a river's flow.

Growing serious, his cousin considered him with a furrowed brow. "I've heard he's serious about this match he's making. Do you have someone special to you, or are you just fighting for the opportunity to choose?"

Daciana materialized in his mind, and Sorin couldn't help smiling. He hated how it had happened, but he was glad they'd grown close. She trusted him enough to let him see her both cry and smile; everything about her was so endearing.

"Oh yeah, you've definitely got someone. Who is it?" Liviu nudged his arm. "Who?"

Before Sorin could stop himself, he glanced towards Liviu's house. A woman cried out from inside, the sound making Liviu's head snap around, but the cries were quickly soothed.

Sorin could picture Daciana in there, calm and assured, that intense focus she always acquired when she worked undoubtedly keeping her from noticing the couple strands of hair that had most likely slipped out from beneath her headscarf.

Liviu's gaze returned to him, and then he glanced between him and the house. "No way. The apothecary?"

Not the least bit embarrassed, Sorin shrugged. "What can I say?"

"I'm not questioning your choice—she seems like an outstanding lady—but the elder might keel over on the spot if he so much as *heard*."

"I know. That's why we're keeping it quiet. You and Calin are the only ones who know. Oh, and Daciana's mother knows."

"On the contrary, I'm pretty sure all your watchmen know." Liviu grinned. "The one outside didn't want me to bug you two unless it was a genuine emergency."

That flooded Sorin with embarrassment. Of course they'd figured it out.

"What were you two doing anyway? Don't think I didn't notice you'd made her cry."

"I did *not* make her cry!" Sorin protested.

Liviu burst out laughing, and he realized his cousin was teasing him.

"Oh, har har, you're so funny."

The guy laughed harder, and after a second, he wobbled and fell right off the fence, landing flat on his back.

"Serves you right," Sorin said.

Once Liviu had his breath back, he scrambled back onto the fence. "Okay, but really. Why was she so upset? I mean, your front was soaked from all her crying."

"She's upset about the murder. She's already been threatened twice."

"No kidding," Liviu said. "Are you getting anywhere with it?"

Sorin hesitated, not wanting to follow the conclusion his thoughts led him to. "We have an idea of who it is, but there's no way we can prove it. Yet. But Daciana's afraid of who it'll turn out to be, in case

I'm...close to them. That's why she was crying."

It was nearly a full minute before Liviu spoke. "You'd better not let the elder sink his claws into her."

Sorin met his gaze, his resolve firming as the fiery determination inside him rose to meet the challenging spark in his cousin's eyes. "I won't."

No matter what it took.

27

They passed the next couple hours making idle chatter, the animosity between them melting quietly away like the morning frost in the warmth of the sunrise. Sorin couldn't help but wonder if this was because of Liviu's current stress or if it meant things between them were right again, but he hoped it would be the latter. He'd sorely missed his cousin's company, even if he hadn't realized it until right then.

When dawn was only a few hours away (and Sorin was struggling to stay awake), the first trembling note of a baby's cry split the early morning stillness. Liviu's head whipped in the direction of his house so fast, he fell off the fence for the second time, nearly landing on his face.

"That's no way to go about seeing your baby," Sorin remarked, hopping off the fence as Liviu rose, swiping at his dirty palms.

"I know, I know," his cousin said distractedly. In a bit of a daze, he wandered over to a nearby well and cleaned his hands.

A few minutes after he'd finished, the front door of the house opened, and a young girl, probably only a couple years younger than Daciana, peeked her pale blonde head around it. "Come on, Liviu! Hurry up already!"

Liviu sprinted inside, and Sorin hesitated before trailing after.

The house was warm, and by the time he arrived, Liviu was already at the side of a bed barely big enough for two people. A pretty but exhausted blonde woman was there, her face worn by fatigue though her eyes sparkled, and she grinned at her husband and the baby in her arms in turns. Then Sorin turned to Daciana. She seemed pretty tired and her hands and apron were smeared with blood, but even she smiled, which he took to mean things were all right.

She met his gaze, her smile growing and lighting up her eyes.

That made his heart flutter. Even still, he managed to whisper, "You did a good job."

"Felicia did most of the work," she corrected. "I just caught the baby, really."

"Sure," he said, trying not to laugh, "but I'm sure having you here helped her a lot. I doubt she panicked with you here."

For a moment, he thought she would protest, but she relented with a smile. "I suppose. That said, I need to clean myself off."

Happy as he was for his cousin, Sorin was content to stay by Daciana's side as she scrubbed at her arms. His gaze kept flicking around the tiny home, unease settling in his chest. It was one room, and between the tiny kitchen space, the almost too-small bed, and the little table with two chairs, it was pretty cramped. The compound had enough empty houses that Liviu and Felicia shouldn't have to raise their newborn in a place like this.

If only Sorin could do something about that, but Elder Aurel...

Sorin blinked, his mind whirling. Technically, when Sorin turned twenty-one in a few months, he could, according to the laws of their village, contest his grandpa for the position of elder. He was the next in line, and the position had already been promised to him, but if he claimed it on his twenty-first birthday and his claim was accepted, Liviu wouldn't have to raise his family in a shack. His younger cousins and siblings would get a freedom he'd never had. If he could fend off the elder long enough, Sorin would be free to be with Daciana; he'd be free to live his life how he wished at long last. He could change the village the way they needed to in order to protect and preserve it for the next generations. His family might even be happy. The elder would still be around, but he wouldn't have the power to do what he did to them now.

Sorin had never wished for the weight and responsibility of elder, but it appealed to him now more than it ever had before—and it was better than being stuck in a position where he was drowning. He'd grown up mistreated and abused because of prejudice that was perpetuated generation after generation in his family, and he hated it. His cousins hated it. However, for the first time in his life, it struck him that if he seized the mantle of elder, he could end it. Permanently.

Sorin and Daciana made ready to leave a couple hours later, once Daciana was certain Felicia and the baby were going to be all right. She'd gone and left a note with the village's apothecary—whom she knew, apparently—with firm instructions to take care of the two of them.

As for Sorin, he was honestly ready to pass out. Liviu had shown off his newborn daughter at least a dozen times, and as cute as the baby was, Sorin had had enough of that.

"I'll leave this horse with you," Sorin told Liviu as he saw them off, motioning towards the horse his cousin had rode. "You can bring it back and take yours with you next time you're in town."

"Thanks for coming, Sorin." His gaze flicked to Daciana. "And thank you again. It means the world to us."

Daciana smiled, and Sorin could tell she was exhausted. "I'm glad I could be of use."

"Good luck with the investigation," Liviu said as Sorin called Xandru over. "I'll be in town either today or tomorrow, even though I don't want to be."

Sorin almost laughed as he helped Daciana mount Reanu before using the fence to mount Xandru (he was far too tired to attempt to jump). He made sure Daciana was steady on her horse and ready for their long trek back home before turning back to his cousin.

Liviu grinned, his face as bright as a little kid's. "Take good care of my cousin for me, all right, Daciana?"

"Sure," she said, then her brow furrowed as Liviu's grin widened.

It took a lot of willpower for Sorin to suppress a smile. Right as he was about to encourage his horse forward, he remembered his earlier train of thought.

Glancing back at his cousin, he said, "Hey, if it was safe, would you be interested in moving your family into the compound?"

Apprehension swept over Liviu's face.

"Not now," Sorin added quickly as Xandru shifted restlessly beneath him, "but when..." He paused, shaking his head. "I want to change how the village is run—how our family works. And when I turn twenty-one, I can claim the title of elder. When I do, I can revolutionize things—so many things can change. If that happened, then would you be interested in coming?"

There was a thoughtful frown on his cousin's face. "Elder Aurel will still fight back—though I doubt there'd be much resistance from anyone else. You would have the real power."

"But he couldn't justify forcing you and Felicia apart, and if he tries, he'll have to deal with me."

"Oh, then your baby would be able to grow up surrounded by her family," Daciana chimed in. "She'd almost never be bored—and you and Felicia would have help."

"I do wish I could tell my siblings," Liviu said with a mournful expression. "Narcisa and Andrei would both be over the moon about the baby. And my dad has been wanting to be a grandpa for some time."

Sorin waited, not quite realizing he held his breath.

"We'll think about it, okay?" Liviu said. He flashed a grin at them, but exhaustion hunkered in his eyes. "If you can change the family and make it safe for us to live how we choose, I want to help you make it happen."

Sorin nodded, and then he and Daciana left. There was no sense in hurrying, so he didn't push Xandru faster than a walk, but even still, Xandru sped up to a trot on his own—coaxing Reanu to do the same. Silly horses. He kept an eye on Daciana, but she had taken to horse riding so well, he couldn't help grinning.

After they'd been traveling for only a couple minutes, Daciana's head drooped like she was on the verge of falling asleep. She jerked herself upright before promptly nodding off again.

Sorin reined in both of their mounts.

"Why are we...?" Daciana began in a sleepy murmur that made it difficult for him to remain focused.

"If we keep on like this, you'll fall asleep and fall off. So, here, I'll take Reanu's reins and keep an eye on her. You lay on her neck and I'll strap you to the saddle so you don't fall off."

She smiled a little despite looking ready to protest, but with a little push on her back, she complied, resting her head on Reanu's neck. Sorin tied her to the saddle with some rope—it was surprisingly difficult to stay focused being that close to her—and by the time he was finished, Daciana was fast asleep. The sight made a little smile tug at his mouth.

He gathered Reanu's reins before patting Xandru's neck. "Take it easy, boy. We don't want to wake her up."

The horse tossed its head with impatience, but even still, both the horses settled into an easy walk. With no company but his own thoughts, Sorin found himself reexamining the case.

Liviu had made a promising suspect for a while, but after last night, he was convinced his cousin had nothing to do with it; Liviu had only refused to give himself a way out of being a suspect because he would've had to expose a secret Elder Aurel would happily rip apart. Liviu had a home, a wife, and a baby—all things that would be in jeopardy if he'd decided to lash out against his family. He'd made a new life for himself, and he'd been willing to sacrifice himself in order to protect it. As such, he didn't have a motive to commit such heinous acts. Moreover, since he'd always been the ringleader of their cousins and their abuses, if Liviu hadn't taken part in the murder, then there was good chance the rest of his cousins were innocent too.

Ecaterina no longer made a convincing suspect in his mind either. While she arguably had motive, he wasn't sure she'd have the guts to go through with murder nor would the situation have given her a winning hand. On the contrary, it would've plunged her deeper into a position that already made her miserable.

Which left Ionel. Sorin knew he needed to remain impartial, but he couldn't bring himself to accept the idea that Ionel may have been the person who'd smashed the skull of his best friend or that he would've attempted to murder his father, siblings, nieces, and nephews. The uncle in Sorin's memories was kind and warm—how could he have done such cold and heartless acts?

A thought struck him light lightning: Daciana must suspect his uncle. Why else would she have sobbed over the idea of the killer being someone who's identity would wound Sorin? She'd known about the fractures between him and Liviu, and she'd witnessed Ecaterina's disdain for herself. She also knew how close he was to Ionel.

Closing his eyes, he couldn't help berating himself. He'd claimed he would be all right if Ionel was the killer, but even Daciana had known him better than that.

When they were halfway back to the village and the first rays of morning sunlight peeked over the trees, Daciana woke. He reined in the horses to unwind the rope from around her waist, and once he had, she sat up and stretched before glancing around.

"We've traveled a ways. I guess I really did fall asleep."

"Almost immediately," he said. "But you had a long night."

"Oh yes, I'm aware of that," She stretched again, and Sorin couldn't help wondering if it worked all that well when one was on horseback. Once the horses resumed walking, she said, "Hey, Sorin?"

He turned, a little surprised to find her watching him.

"After all of this, you don't think Liviu might be the killer still...do you?" The guarded tone of her voice confirmed in his mind who she thought the killer was.

"No, I don't," he confessed. "But you... You think it's Ionel, don't you?"

That sadness from the previous night touched her eyes. "I'm not going to accuse him unless we can prove he did it. I...I couldn't."

"If he is the one behind it, I'm not sure we'll find anything. He was in the watch; he trained most of the men there how to investigate."

"Maybe that's why there were so few clues," Daciana murmured.

He acknowledged her point even though it stung. Ionel would know what clues not to leave, unlike the rest.

As he returned his attention to Daciana, he spied that expression she got whenever she was considering saying something, one so subtle, he wasn't sure she knew she made the face. Even still, she stayed quiet long enough to make him uneasy.

"Sorin," she said, her voice hushed, "I'm going to search for something—some evidence. If Ionel is the one, then I'm sure it's gone, but I have to look anyway. I think it's the only way to prove whether or not he's innocent."

"I don't like that," he said. "At the very least, you're not planning on going alone, right?"

No answer.

"Daci, if he is guilty and catches you snooping around—"

"I know," she said, reaching across the space between them and squeezing his arm, making his chest tighten. "I do know what he could do. But I need to do this. I just... I couldn't do it without telling you just...just in case..."

Almost reflexively, he pulled his arm from her grasp and took hold of her hand with his own. "Let me go with you. Please."

To his dismay, she shook her head. "I can't."

"Daci—"

"It's not because I don't want you to!" she said, fixing him with a stern glare. "But Ionel's wife is sick. If I go in on a house call, I can poke around without raising any suspicion, but if you come with me, it'll be obvious what we're doing. The guards who follow me on my rounds never come in the house with me, which means you can't either. He'll know something's going on."

His mouth went dry.

"I've been able to so do little with this investigation, even though I promised to help solve it. At least let me do this one thing."

"Daci, you've helped plenty. I don't think we would be able to solve it without you," he protested. He didn't have an argument to present. She was right that when it came to searching Ionel's house for a clue that may or may not exist, stealth was the way to go. Sorin's presence would make it obvious they were up to something—to avoid arousing the elder's suspicion, he'd taken to only checking on her after letting at least one complete shift pass before he returned.

However, when he was honest with himself, the idea of potentially sending her into a wolf's den alone terrified him.

She squeezed his hand. "I will be careful, I promise. It's not like I want to die, you know. You'd miss me too much."

Her attempt at humor made a smile tug on his mouth, but it was short-lived. Torn between wanting to convince her to change her mind while knowing this plan of hers was the best chance they had—even if it was dangerous—Sorin pulled both of their horses up short and hugged Daciana tight to him. It was clever; so clever. Even if he hated it.

28

After pausing to speak with the watchmen at the front gate, Sorin took Daciana straight home, where her family would be able to protect her until he informed the watchmen she was back.

He dismounted before turning and helping her down, relishing being able to stand close with his hands on her waist. "You go straight to bed and get some rest, understand?"

For some reason, she didn't pull back but smiled instead. "I didn't think you'd be the type to worry about me so much."

He scowled at the teasing, but it was hard to keep the scowl when she smiled like that.

All at once, Daciana glanced up and down the street.

He half-glanced around as well. "What?"

"Normally, no one is awake, but I figured I should double check." She shot a furtive glance over her shoulder.

He cocked his head.

Before he could ask the question on his mind, Daciana rose onto her tiptoes and kissed him on the cheek. His heart stumbled. She quickly pulled back, leaving his heart reeling in dizzy circles. He wished she'd come back, but it was a bad idea to get carried away in the middle of the street—especially since several people had found them out already.

"By the way," she whispered while cleaning some dirt off his armor, which was very distracting. "I liked what you said earlier."

"What I said?"

She smiled at him, another one of those sweet smiles that made his thoughts turn to fuzz. "On our way back, you kept calling me 'Daci.' I really liked that." Then she turned and vanished inside her house.

Sorin stared at her closed door, no thoughts registering in his mind. It was nearly a full minute before he remembered Xandru and Reanu standing behind him, and, in a bit of a daze, he led them back to the compound stables. Even still, recalling what she'd said and her kiss had him fighting to keep a smile off his face—and he couldn't stop thinking about them. In truth, he hadn't realized he'd called her Daci, but if she liked it that much, then he would do it again.

He led the horses to the barn, and given the hour, already knew he'd have to take care of them by himself. He didn't mind beyond the fact he was exhausted.

As he led both the horses into the stable, he noticed the door to one of the empty stalls was cracked open. He peeked in as he passed, what he saw bringing him to halt. Curled up in the corner, fast asleep with a small harp in her hand, was Ecaterina. She must've snuck in to practice the music she loved without alerting anyone.

A spark of anger struck in his chest. The injustice of what the elder demanded of all of them seemed so foolish; why did they have to live in such a way that a grown woman would be reduced to sneaking around like a naughty child?

Exhausted by it all, Sorin walked on and tended to Reanu and Xandru.

Once the horses were settled, Sorin took himself home where he passed out the instant he reached his bed, not caring that he was fully clothed and coated in dirt and sweat from the night's adventures.

It seemed mere minutes later when his mom prodded him awake, but the amount of sunlight streaming through his window showed it'd been a few hours.

"Are you sick? You're never in bed this late."

"I'm fine," he mumbled, unable to convince his eyes to stay open.

"All right, that's a weight off my chest. Now what were you doing out so late?" Dropping her voice to a conspiratorial whisper, she said, "You weren't with Daciana, the lovely apothecary, all night long, were you?"

It sounded innocent, but even Sorin's sleep-fogged brain caught the implication. "Mom," he said shortly, pushing himself onto his side. "That's neither true nor funny."

"Of course," she said with a wink. "Only joking."

He scowled. "There was a medical emergency last night. I was the one on guard duty, so of course I went with her."

"And it lasted the whole night?"

Sorin hesitated. If he told his mother too much, it would expose Liviu and his family to real danger. However, if he worded it right, then he could explain. "A woman from Riverbend gave birth, and Daciana was asked to assist."

"Oh, that makes sense," his mom said before grinning. "But I'm sure you enjoyed being with her all night anyway."

"Mom," he protested—even though she was right—before dropping his face back into his quilt.

She laughed. "In all seriousness, though, Marian has already come by asking after you. Your watchmen are concerned about you, and even if they weren't, you've still got a job to do. There's no time for sleeping in."

Sorin groaned in response, making her laugh even more.

"Sorry, kiddo, but sometimes being an adult means you don't get to sleep. Come on." She ruffled his hair before leaving the room.

Against his will, Sorin got to his feet. His eyes were dry like he'd rubbed them full of sand, and every muscle in his body seemed to ache. Somehow, he managed to make himself presentable before stumbling down the stairs where his mom had cold toast and eggs waiting for him. He was hungry enough he didn't care.

Right as he sat to eat, the door opened. "Violeta?" came the elder's voice.

Sorin stiffened like cold water had been dumped over him. Since their fight, the tension between them cracked like lightning every time they met. Sorin had been doing his utmost to avoid the man ever since, and he wasn't in the mood to fight again. In a rush, he shoved all the eggs into his mouth and grabbed his toast. He'd have to get past the elder to escape, but if he made it seem like he was in a hurry, he might make it unscathed.

The elder stepped inside the house but remained in the doorway, glancing around before his gaze landed on Sorin. "Ah. I've been wanting to speak with you as well, but I thought you'd already be gone."

Sorin chewed and swallowed his eggs so fast, he was shocked he didn't choke. "Long night. But I have to get going." Mustering up all his courage, he tried to calmly walk past.

The elder held out an arm, barring the exit. "No, I need to speak to you, and I know you've been avoiding me. Your other duties can wait until we've had a chat. It is a matter of the utmost importance, and it needs to be resolved now, not later."

"Dad," Sorin's mom began as she entered the room. "Sorin's work—"

"Comes second to his marriage."

Sorin grit his teeth. If he had to wait until his twenty-first birthday to be with Daciana, he'd better get used to fighting back. "No, the safety of the village comes first. That's why you gave this job to *me* instead of Ionel, who we both know would've been a better fit for it." He couldn't keep the bite out of his voice.

Ducking under the elder's arm, he hurried down the front steps.

Some of his cousins milled around in the yard, not paying him any mind. However, as he left the porch, he heard the distinct sound of the elder following him. His stomach clenched.

"Sorin, you're acting like a child. Quit avoiding me," the elder barked, getting the attention of everyone in the yard.

"Watch me," Sorin snapped.

"I've made you a match! There's no escaping it, so get over here and face it like a man."

A thrill of terror shot through Sorin's chest. "I already told you I'm going to figure it out on my own. I'm not interested in your match."

"You will do your duty as the next leader of the family or—"

"Duty?" Sorin stopped, rounding on him. "This isn't about duty; it's about your ego and your obsession with magic."

"It's about taking care of this family and this village," the elder snapped, a red tinge appearing on his cheeks.

Sorin scoffed. "Taking care of the family? If you were interested in taking care of the family, you wouldn't be so eager to decide that our worth depends on whether or not we have magic. If you cared about protecting this village, you'd care about whether or not you're spreading us too thin. You'd care about whether or not anyone was happy!"

The elder glared, but for once, Sorin wasn't cowed. "Listen to me, young man. You will obey me and agree to this match—"

"I won't," Sorin snarled, almost having to shout.

"—because that's what's expected of you!" the elder shouted over him. "You have a responsibility to the village and the family to ensure there is magic to protect us, and you will do it if I say so. With that responsibility comes sacrifice—"

"I already am sacrificing!" Sorin snapped. "I've already given you and the village absolutely everything! I've let you dictate every single part of my life—my hobbies, my friends, my job—all in the name of you and your stupid magical obsession. With responsibility does come sacrifice, but what's the point if no one's happy? Do you not care how miserable everyone is? I've never done a thing I've ever wanted to do because I've spent my entire life living it the way you wanted me to!"

"What you choose to do with your life and who you marry are very different," the elder said coolly.

"Hardly," Sorin spat. Out of the corner of his eye, he noticed his cousins staring, but for some reason, it almost looked like they were cheering him on. Maybe he was more tired than he thought. "You have *never* given me the luxury of choosing what to do with my life. You decided everything. You, not me. So, who I choose to marry is not a decision you get to make. This is the one choice that is going to be mine. You can do what you like, but I will not change my mind."

"Sorin, marriage is a big decision someone as young as you can't be trusted to make wisely," the elder said, his tone reminding Sorin distinctly of the way one spoke to a child. "That's why you need to trust those older than you to make this decision for you."

"You don't trust my judgement? And yet you made me the head of the village watch."

The elder pinched the bridge of his nose.

Sorin huffed in response, turning to leave.

"She's already here in the house, waiting to meet you," the elder said, the finality with which he spoke making it clear he thought the matter settled.

"Then you can go apologize and send her home." He began to stalk off.

"Sorin," the elder snapped, the threat in his voice sending a chill down his spine. "This attitude of yours wouldn't happen to be due to your feelings for a certain...apothecary, would it?"

Despite himself, Sorin stopped, his heartbeat thrumming in his ears. He shouldn't have stopped; that was akin to admitting it outright.

"The seductress who has blinded you to your duty is this—this Daciana?" the elder spluttered, contempt dripping from every syllable of

Daciana's name.

Sorin's throat clenched tight, nearly rendering him unable to speak. This was the worst possible thing that could've happened. What lengths would the elder go to in an effort to force them apart? Would Sorin be able to protect Daciana until his twenty-first birthday arrived?

Slowly, he turned back to the elder, the anger flaring in his chest rising to match the rage on the elder's face. "You leave her out of this," he snarled, "or else."

"I'm ashamed of you," the elder said, venom dripping from every syllable. "How could you be so foolish as to fall in love with someone so far beneath us?"

"Beneath us?" Sorin said, his ears ringing from the elder's words. "She saved your life. If it wasn't for her, you'd be dead!"

"As she ought. It's the village's duty to serve and protect our family. She did her duty saving us; marrying her is a considerable misstep of yours."

Sorin stared, realizing that he was panting like he'd been running. All at once, he recalled the times he and Daciana had discussed the prejudice she'd faced because her mother was a foreigner and how it would taint the village's view of their relationship.

Thoughts racing, he narrowed his eyes. "Don't tell me that this attitude of yours is because of your hatred of her mother. You aren't that petty, are you?"

"That woman is an outsider who coerced one of our own into marriage. Her children carry her tainted blood, and if you were to wed that girl, your children would also be tainted. You would pollute our family."

Sorin nearly choked on his shock. "You hate her mother because she wasn't born here? That's a funny opinion coming from someone whose ancestors weren't born in this village either. They also came from 'outside.' I hope you realize that by your logic, Daciana and her brothers aren't foreigners—they were born in this village like the rest of us."

The elder's face was almost purple, a vein pulsing in his forehead. "Do not mock me, boy."

"I don't have to," Sorin snapped. "You do that all on your own."

"My word is law," the elder continued, raising his chin and taking a threatening step closer. "And if I say she's beneath you, then she is. You will have nothing to do with her from this moment onwards! Am I understood?"

Sorin stared at him, acutely aware of the rest of the family watching in total silence. His mother's proud smile then gave him the courage to say what he really thought. "Try and stop me."

That vein ticked again. "Sorin—"

"Know what else? In three months, I'll be twenty-one, and I hope you're looking forward to that day, because when it does, I'm taking your place." Ignoring the elder's protests, Sorin turned and stormed out of the compound.

29

Daciana hadn't gotten a chance to see Sorin again that day, something that made her a little sad when she glanced out the window at the mid-afternoon sky. Even still, she supposed that was to be expected when they'd been together all night. She was sore and tired—but the memory alone was enough to make her smile, and she couldn't help wondering if Sorin felt the same.

All at once, the door burst open, and she glanced up in surprise to find Andrei standing there, panting.

He glanced over his shoulder before padding up to her table and speaking in a low voice. "Ionel just left. He's only a few streets away, but he's going to the blacksmith. He's always gone for a while when he does."

"Perfect," she said, rushing to gather her things, her heart picking up its pace. She followed Andrei out of the workshop, her faithful watchmen only a few steps behind. However, as she headed towards the main thoroughfare, Andrei snagged her sleeve and pulled her onto a side street. "Where are we going?"

"The compound," he said before shooting her a look. "But we're going this way because it means you won't risk getting spotted by Elder Aurel."

That made her frown. "Why am I avoiding him?"

Andrei snorted, almost like he was trying not to laugh. "You should have seen it. Elder Aurel went to Sorin's house today—claiming he'd found him the 'perfect match' or whatever."

Daciana's heart fluttered weakly. Sorin had mentioned that, but what if he got roped into a marriage he didn't want and that forced them apart?

"But Sorin would have none of it; I've never seen him so mad. He and the old man were shouting—and then Sorin stormed off leaving the elder hollering and throwing a tantrum. It was awesome."

"Really?" she and the watchmen said at the same time. However, while she sounded more apprehensive, they seemed intrigued, maybe even excited.

"I mean, Sorin's never stuck up for himself before," Andrei explained as he motioned her through a little gate at the back of the compound, the place hidden by the trees standing behind the smaller family houses. "Normally the elder demands something stupid and Sorin just complies, but today he fought back."

A little flicker of pride bubbled in her chest. She only knew some of the details of Sorin and his family, but him fighting to live the life he wanted made her happy. He deserved to have that chance. When she saw him next, she'd have to let him know. "Okay, but what does that have to do with me hiding from the elder?"

"Oh that." Andrei sighed, stopping amongst the trees behind Ionel's house. "The elder's figured out Sorin's courting you, and he refuses to accept it. He...said some nasty things about you and your mother."

Her watchmen shared a look, but Daciana didn't react to the information. It was old news for her.

"And, in the past, he's done awful things to our other cousins who were in relationships with people he didn't approve of—he's made it so they couldn't buy anything in the village or made them lose their jobs.

It's always nasty. So be careful and avoid him as much as possible. I like you, and Sorin's happy. So." Andrei blushed.

Daciana couldn't help smiling a little. "Thank you for the warning, but how did he find out?"

"It was kind of obvious," one of her watchmen offered.

"If you know Sorin, anyway," the other said.

Andrei grimaced. "He's never paid anyone half as much attention as he pays to you, so it was pretty obvious, even to me."

Despite the situation, Daciana couldn't help smiling a little more. "It is what it is, I suppose. I'll just have to be careful." She turned in the direction of Ionel's house. "Thank you for helping me, Andrei."

"Are you sure this won't put you in danger?" he asked, eyeing her with disapproval, the expression almost making her laugh.

"I'll be fine. Really." She hoped.

"All right," he said slowly. "I have to go back to my chores, otherwise someone will eventually miss me and figure something out. But you make sure you go back the way you came in. The elder will be on the lookout for you."

She nodded, and Andrei hurried off in the direction of his house with only a few glances over his shoulder.

Once he was gone, she turned to her two guards, who watched her and their surroundings with a bit more worry than usual. "You two wait here. If the elder sees you, he'll know I'm here."

Their faces pinched with displeasure, but they both agreed. So, straightening the strap of her satchel, Daciana stepped onto Ionel's back porch and let herself in. Her mind screamed she was breaking in, but Ionel's wife was home alone, and it wasn't like she could answer the door.

So, as she stood in the kitchen, her gaze flicking to the shelves of herbs Ionel kept, she called out. "Hello? Is anyone home? It's me, Daciana."

"Oh, hello dear!" Ionel's wife called from the bedroom. "Come in. I've been waiting for you." Then she was seized by a coughing fit that spurred Daciana into action.

She hurried into the bedroom and set to work caring for the woman and assessing her condition. Ionel's wife's cough wasn't as severe as it'd been when she'd last checked on her, but even still, Daciana couldn't help noting how frail the woman appeared.

Ionel's wife must've noticed because she said, "Oh don't mind me and my poor health. It's always been like this for me, and it seems to be getting worse as I get older. A poor constitution has always been my lot."

Daciana smiled a little. "In that case, you must've taken good care of yourself."

The woman smiled. "That was more Ionel than me. We met when we were young, you see. Because of my health being the way it is, I wasn't ever planning on getting married—after all, how many men are interested in taking on such damaged goods?"

That expression made Daciana a little sad, but she kept quiet, allowing the woman to speak.

"But my sweet Ionel convinced me I wouldn't ever be a burden. He encouraged me to do my best, and even eventually asked me to marry him." The woman's smile broadened, and despite how frail she was, she shone like the sun. "We were only able to have a couple children but he's been very good to me all these years."

Daciana attempted a smile even though it felt like a knife had been rammed into her chest, driving all the air from her lungs. How could someone like Ionel really be the killer? If he was, what would happen to his wife? Sorin had insisted he had Daciana, so he'd be fine, but Ionel's wife only had Ionel. Their children had left the village some time ago.

All at once, Ionel's wife took her hand with her dainty, frail ones, and she was distracted enough it made her jump. "You seem a little down today, dear."

"Oh, I'm sorry," Daciana said, tucking a stray strand of hair out of her face. "I just..."

Ionel's wife patted her hand. "I understand. The elder found out about you and Sorin, right? It's hard for me to get much news being cooped up in here, but even I heard that argument."

That weighed on her some, so Daciana nodded. It was better than admitting what was truly on her mind.

"Look at me, dear." Ionel's wife lifted Daciana's chin. "The elder is a stubborn man. His childhood was difficult, and in many ways, that made him hard. However, if you genuinely love my nephew, then you shouldn't let his nearsightedness stop you. There are some things in life, no matter how frightening they may seem, that are worth fighting for. Love is one of those things."

Daciana hadn't known Sorin for long, and she couldn't quite say she loved him. However, she did know she cared about him deeply—more than she'd ever cared about anyone else, and she didn't want to lose that or see him hurt.

"I will," Daciana said, making the woman smile. "Sorin and I will fight through this together."

Before the woman could speak, she had another violent coughing fit.

Daciana patted her back; she'd already done most of what she could. All at once, like lightning, inspiration struck. "Would you like me to make you a tisane? I won't promise to be as good as your husband, but I'll do my best."

The woman smiled once more. "Oh, that would be lovely. And Ionel's so proud of his tisanes, I don't think he'd mind you making one for me and you. He loves to share with everyone."

"I'll be right back," Daciana said, quickly excusing herself.

Doing her best to ignore how hard her hands shook, she fetched the kettle and stoked the fire in the hearth back to life. While she waited for the water to boil, she steeled her courage and turned to the wall of shelves and foggy glass jars. It was difficult to see through the glass, but each jar was clearly labeled with its contents. After a few moments, she located the jar that contained bright sprigs of peppermint and took it from the shelf. Once she placed it on the table near the hearth and checked the kettle, she took another fortifying breath and turned back to the shelf.

Daciana wasn't an expert in the ways of dark thinking, but, if she had an herbal poison she wanted to hide, burying it amongst a sea of other herbs would be the first place she'd do it.

Doing her best to stay quiet and avoid disturbing the jars, Daciana inspected them one by one. Her heart hammered against her throat as she searched, hoping over and over she was wrong and someone else surely had to be the culprit.

Eventually, she had to kneel on the floor in order to inspect the final shelf. The kettle let out short bursts of steam and quiet hisses, meaning she was nearly out of time. She hurriedly searched through the jars, but in the end, none of them held the condemning concoction of herbs. She should feel relieved, but she didn't. If Ionel was the killer, he'd been smart enough not to keep such a condemning piece of evidence, and finding nothing here didn't clear his name. Scowling, she got back to her feet.

The kettle whistled, and she glanced its way, unable to deny the flood of disappointment and frustration rushing through her. Was it even possible to prove Ionel's guilt or would they never find the evidence they needed? The whistling of the kettle became more insistent, and Daciana threw one last scowl at the herb shelves. Her gaze landed on a jar she hadn't made note of during her frantic search, and she froze.

It didn't contain a mix of herbs. It only held one: fireweed.

Ignoring the kettle, she stepped back over to it, her eyes wide, her mind struggling to process her thoughts. Stopping right in front of it, she stared at the dried leaf, the label the only prominent indicator of what the jar contained.

That niggling, evasive thought from days earlier suddenly blossomed in her mind, unfurling in all its glory, making her insides go icy cold. While fireweed was used as a medicine and sometimes in specialty foods, its most common usage was in tea.

Tea.

No one in the head family loved tea as much as Ionel, something Master Florin had absolutely known.

"What are you doing?" Ionel suddenly asked from nearby, the deep tones of his voice startling her so bad, she jerked in surprise, smacking her hand against the shelf hard enough the jars rattled ominously.

Rubbing her knuckles, she turned around. "S-sorry," she managed, her thoughts spinning and billowing in frantic and erratic patterns that made it hard to think straight. "Your wife wanted a tisane, but I got distracted looking at all your herbs. I...I forgot how many you have."

To her relief, Ionel laughed. "And then I scared you bad enough for you to bang your hand. Come on—I'll make the tisane in reparation."

Hesitantly, she trotted over, not allowing herself to glance back at the jar of fireweed, the word seeming to blaze in front of her eyes. Had Master Florin been trying to warn them about Ionel?

Ionel took the kettle off the flames before fetching three cups and preparing the tisane. As he worked, her mind whirled, a plan falling into place. Ionel was too clever, so the chance of there being any physical evidence was next to none. However, there was a chance she could catch him in a lie, some verbal slip that would give him away. At the very least, she had to try.

"You know," she began, getting him to glance at her, "I was wondering about the tisane you gave everyone. That foreign one? I wondered if I could try it. For curiosity's sake."

He smiled, but it was a bit rueful. "It's all gone, I'm afraid. It was foreign, after all, and I didn't have much to begin with. I'm sorry to disappoint."

How convenient. "That's all right. But what kind of herb was it? Do you remember?"

He screwed up his face in thought, and she found herself holding her breath. "Ginseng, I believe."

He didn't have ginseng on his shelf, which is why she supposed he'd chosen it. However, this was her chance.

"Sorin said he didn't like it because it was too sweet," she said.

"Yes, it was such a shame it ended up being so sweet," Ionel said, handing one of the cups to her before picking up the other two. "I was shocked it turned out to be so startling, but it was fun to try something new."

Daciana's insides iced over, and she thought she would be sick. Ginseng wasn't sweet. Plus, Sorin had told her about that drink his uncle had given him. In actuality, the tisane had been too flavorful, a mix of competing tastes, something ginseng also was not.

Beyond that, Master Florin had kept her well-versed on teas and tisanes. She knew for a fact, since she'd had ginseng for herself, that it was bitter.

They joined his wife (whose face lit up at the sight of her husband), and Daciana drank her portion of the tisane without tasting it. After she'd listened to the couple talk for a bit, she gave Ionel's wife a few instructions, the herbs she would need, and left.

When she met up with her watchmen, they spoke to her, but she stared blankly back, not registering what they'd said.

The pinched look of worry returned. "Are you all right?" one asked.

She stared for another moment before nodding. It wasn't safe to talk about her discovery here, and she wasn't in the mood for conversation any longer. She turned, somehow making it out through the back gate and onto one of the side streets that led to the workshop.

She didn't remember most of the walk back; she didn't remember the faces of the people she'd passed on the street. Eventually, she simply found herself standing at the gate of the workshop.

It was Ionel. She didn't want to believe it, and yet she did. Despite his talents, his skills, and his nature, he'd been disregarded by his own father because of something he hadn't been born with. He'd had a brilliant career in the village watch, only to be denied the chance to be Head Watchman and watch his dream be passed on to an inexperienced Sorin, who hadn't wanted anything to do with the job. All because of magic.

Tears burned at her eyes, and she fought with all her strength to keep them from falling. She hadn't wanted it to be Ionel. However, now she had to tell Sorin, and she knew it would hurt him. It was going to hurt his whole family. What if the truth destroyed them? How would she face them—face Sorin? What if it broke Sorin enough it ended their relationship?

"Daci!" Sorin's voice broke her from her trance, and she turned to find him watching her with a bemused smile on his face. It vanished the instant their gazes met. "Your guards said you were acting strange. And you didn't hear me calling your name." It was at that moment she realized her two guards from earlier were gone, replaced with Sorin and Calin.

"Oh," she managed, her gaze dropping. "I'm sorry...I...I didn't notice."

His brow furrowed. "Is...everything okay?"

No, nothing was okay.

He eyed her. "You weren't threatened again, were you?"

She shook her head.

He stayed quiet for a moment before he began to gently lead her towards the workshop. Daciana halted when they were halfway up the path, her legs locking almost of their own volition. Ionel had killed Master Florin in there. Now that she knew who had done it, it was like her master had been taken away all over again, like he still lay in there, lifeless. Dead.

"What is wrong?" Sorin asked, his voice no louder than a whisper. "You..." He paused before setting both hands on her shoulders. "You went searching for evidence, didn't you?"

Slowly, she managed to nod.

"Did...did you find something?"

She forced herself to lift her head. When their gazes met, her vision blurred.

He remained silent, but he stiffened.

"I didn't find any herbs, but I finally remembered that thought that was bugging me. Fireweed is most commonly used for tea," she managed, her voice almost inaudible over the breeze stirring the plants in the garden.

His brow furrowed, but he remained silent still.

"And I asked Ionel about the tisane he gave you. I told him you said it was sweet."

"It wasn't sweet," he said slowly.

"I know, but he went with it—he agreed it'd been too sweet. He told me it'd been ginseng." She wrapped her arms around herself, the chill in her gut seeping through the rest of her, chasing away even the warmth of the late afternoon sun. "Sorin, ginseng is bitter."

Sorin stared, motionless, his face blank.

"If Ionel didn't use that tisane to poison you, then why would he lie about it?" Her tears nearly spilled down her cheeks. "It was him. He killed Master Florin, and he attempted to kill you too."

"Ionel?" was all the response Sorin gave.

It took all her strength not to cry. Daciana wanted to do nothing more than sit and bawl, her chest aching from the pent-up sobs, but she remained standing.

"But he... I..." Sorin said slowly, his voice unsteady. "A-are you sure? He's been helping me— Are you sure he was trying to kill me?"

"I'm sure he wanted you to think everything was normal between you," she said. "But he's angry, Sorin. Your grandfather denied him the job he worked so hard for just to give it to you, all because of your magic. You didn't even want it—but he did."

"No," Sorin said, struggling as much as she'd expected. "He...he wasn't mad at me..."

"His wife needs help, but Elder Aurel pretends she doesn't exist. Elder Aurel chased his children out of the village because they didn't have magic. And all his siblings with magic kept passing him by because of their magic, and their children get the elder's attention, while all he gets to do is buy stupid supplies—" Daciana choked on her tears again, and while she was fighting for her life not to lose to them, they were going to win. "And the fireweed. Master Florin's clue only fits him."

"Daci," Sorin said, almost sounding angry but there wasn't any fire behind it. "No one saw him here that night."

"No, we asked people if they saw anything strange. Ionel's always out here getting supplies. Nobody would've thought twice about him being here."

His mouth opened, but he didn't speak.

All at once, a guard cut through their conversation. "Sorin! The sheep are loose again!"

Sorin distractedly glanced over. "I— You guys will have to do it without me. I—"

"Cornel says something spooked 'em bad this time; they're running all over and it's getting dark fast. Please, Sorin. The sheep respond to you in a way they don't for the rest of us."

Sorin let out an almost growl, his gaze flicking between her and the guard, before his grip tightened on Daciana's arms. "You go into the workshop. I'll send guards over straight away, okay?"

She had just enough time to nod before he raced away. Daciana couldn't watch him go, still fighting for breath as she headed into the stillness of the workshop. Why did it have to be Ionel? She didn't want to believe it, but too many things made sense—like the lack of clues, something Ionel would know to do or using a tisane to attempt to murder his family.

As she reached the spot in the workshop where Master Florin had died, the door of the workshop slammed shut behind her.

She froze, her heart stopping as she slowly looked back.

Half-illuminated by the sunset, Ionel stood with his hand on the door, his expression blank, unreadable. The tilt to his chin and rigidity of his posture made him feel like an entirely different person than he'd been when they were at his house with his wife. Now, she could see the man who'd killed her master, his best friend.

And Sorin was gone.

Her vision blurred as she shook her head. "I didn't want it to be you."

With a somber expression, he locked the workshop door and stepped forward. "And you are far too clever for your own good."

30

Daciana took a step back for each one Ionel took forward until she bumped into the table. Her heart pounded in her ears, almost drowning out every other sound.

Was she about to die? Was Sorin going to come looking for her just to find her body?

Ionel stopped, sighing in a way that made him seem ancient. "Do you think I'm going to kill you?"

That seemed like a loaded, rhetorical question, so she didn't answer.

"A reasonable conclusion given the circumstances, I grant you, but the wrong one. Sit," he demanded, pointing at her stool.

Daciana hesitated before realizing she wasn't in a position to argue or put up a fight. If Ionel wanted to hurt or kill her, he could—easily. So she obeyed.

"How did you figure it out?" he asked, stalking towards the table. "I could see it in your eyes that you knew. So what gave it away?"

"Ginseng is bitter," she managed, not able to lift her gaze higher than his chest.

"I knew I shouldn't have said that. So, just how much do you know?" he asked, standing in front of her with one hand resting in a casual threat on the table. He was large enough and close enough she couldn't see anything past him.

"You killed Master Florin. You'd been gathering herbs before that—whether through legitimate means or theft, I don't know—and poisoning the magical members of your family by building up the herbs in their systems. In order to enact the final stage of your plan, you needed more herbs, and I imagine something happened the night you went for them. Either you were desperate and he refused, or he figured you out and was going to stop you."

"You are far more clever than he let on. All right, I won't mince words with you," Ionel said. "Your master figured me out, and he tried to reason with me. When that didn't work, he was going to tell the watch. I was on the verge of executing the last phase of a plan I'd been carrying out for months, and he was going to ruin it. That's why I killed him."

That made her shudder. "Once you had all the herbs, you made them into a tisane. That's what you gave to Sorin and the others, telling them it was something foreign and different. It was loaded with enough herbs to push their systems past their limits. I imagine your plan was to keep administering it or hope that me trying to save them by giving them more herbs would end up killing them."

"Yes. I admit I didn't think you'd figure it out. I was actively trying to find a way to incapacitate Master Florin—he'd have caught the poison in a heartbeat—but you'd spent all your days hiding in his shadow. I never imagined you'd be able to save anyone, let alone all of them."

Daciana kept her head lowered. Who knew her attempts to avoid harassment from the village would end up having been her saving grace? The irony nearly made her laugh.

"I've been planning this and working tirelessly for several months, and you were the one obstacle I didn't foresee. You ruined everything."

"So what are you doing to do?" she asked, wondering why the guards Sorin had promised hadn't arrived yet. Did it always take this long?

"I already said I don't plan on killing you," he said. "Given your abilities, I have something else in mind instead. A job, of sorts."

"A job?" She risked glancing at him, not liking the harshness in his face.

"I'm going to change Highfell—permanently. I imagine it will be violent; change is often that way. Afterwards, we'll need an apothecary to care for survivors and safeguard the village in the future, and you're the one I have in mind."

He wanted her to fix the town once he'd shattered it? "And if I refuse?"

A hint of a smile touched his mouth, but it was cold, chilling her to the bone. "I'd hoped we'd get to that."

She registered she shivered, but she didn't know if it was from the cold pouring off him or from her own fear.

"Here are the terms of this contract." He reached into his pocket and pulled out a vial of pale, semi-transparent liquid. "You recognize this, correct?"

Daciana studied it, struggling to puzzle it out based off sight alone. Herbs were much easier to distinguish in this form by smell.

Almost as if he could read her mind, Ionel pulled the stopper from the small bottle and held it under her nose.

She recoiled. "Valeria." Strong, concentrated valeria, which had to mean— Her eyes went wide.

"You reasoned it out as fast as I'd expected." Ionel returned the stopper to the bottle and set it on the table. "Now, you will take this of your own accord—it's a powerful dose of valerian root. It won't kill you, but it will render you unconscious within a matter of seconds. You will be my prisoner, where you will remain and prepare medicines and the like for after I've seized the village. Or—"

All the blood drained from her face as he produced a second vial, this one with the vivid green leaves of an herb she recognized on sight. "H-hemlock?"

He set it next to the vial of valeria. "Precisely. But it's not for you. If you refuse, you will be taken by force instead and the hemlock will be given to your family. And to Sorin. I swear they will all be dead before the sun rises tomorrow morning."

Her heart stopped, her gaze fixed on the hemlock. That little bit there was more than enough to carry out Ionel's threat. If she tried to escape, the only people she had left in this world would be gone and she would truly be alone. Yet, if she went with Ionel willingly, she would be surrendering herself into the hands of a murderer.

"Why are you doing this?" she whispered, her throat so tight she could hardly speak.

"I'm sure you've already deduced that," Ionel said. "Now make your decision."

She lowered her head. While she'd been investigating him, he'd clearly been investigating her in return. She sensed Ionel already knew what she would choose.

Tears stung her eyes, but Daciana ignored them and picked up the bottle of valeria. Sorin's face flashed in her mind, followed by those of her family.

"You promise you won't hurt anyone if I take this?" she breathed, staring at the cloudy liquid.

"I do." He nodded, his expression grave. "Your family and Sorin will live—I'll even be willing to spare most of the village for your sake. But if you don't, there will be nothing left for you, I promise."

For one second, she considered refusing. There was a chance she could warn everyone before Ionel could act, perhaps even escape. However, there was no guarantee she could prevent Ionel from making good on his threat, in which case, she would be utterly alone.

Forever.

She couldn't do that, not just because of herself, but because she couldn't willingly endanger the lives of people she held dear. They mattered too much for that.

As she uncorked the vial, she had one thought: she had to leave a clue for Sorin. It didn't matter if it was small—he and his watchmen would find it.

The powerful, wet horse stench of the valerian root washed over Daciana once the vial was open. Her heart shuddered with fear. Valerian root was a mild herb, so this much wouldn't kill her, but even still, her fear made her hands quiver so hard, the liquid in the vial trembled.

Ionel's gaze remained fixed on her face, watching with an almost disinterested curiosity as she lifted the vial to her mouth. As she took the first swallow, she tossed the vial's top as discreetly as she could. It landed on the rug—as she'd hoped—without a sound.

In seconds, the vial was empty, and she winced at the lingering, musty flavor. However, drowsiness hit her immediately, so intense her head swam. She lost feeling in her limbs; the vial slipped out of her grasp. She thought she heard it break, but she wasn't sure. For a second, she thought someone knocked at the door before her hearing fuzzed. As the darkness closed in, bleeding across her vision like ink spilled over paper, her heart cried out for Sorin, one moment of resistance and panic hitting her. Then everything went dark.

31

Sorin watched in exasperation as the sheep scattered before him yet again. They'd never been this jumpy; even the herding dogs couldn't get the sheep to fall in.

"Seriously? What is wrong with these sheep?!" Calin cursed as he stumbled and hit the ground. "We've already been at this for an hour already."

Cornel grew more and more worried as the sun began to be eaten by the dark horizon; the man kept casting glances at the sky.

Sorin huffed, his mind faltering like a ratty, fraying rag, before he forced himself to concentrate on the sheep and how they moved.

They were scared—terrified. Which was unusual. Even still, despite how skittish and agitated they were, they didn't wander from the fell or the safety of their shepherd or guard dogs. Every time the animals neared the fell's edge, they'd bleat in panic and scatter once more.

So what was at the fell's edge?

His gaze settled on the forest ringing the fell. The wolves had been quiet lately, but even still, it could be them.

"Stay here, Calin."

He walked towards the woods. It was difficult in the approaching dark, but Sorin studied the shadows of the trees as he walked. Perhaps it was paranoia from the murder and the ensuing attempts afterwards, but he suspected the sheep weren't acting out of rebellion or disobedience.

All at once, he spotted a massive shadow lurking in the bushes ahead and stiffened, stopping immediately. It looked eerily like a wolf. Sorin remained still, but it didn't move. He couldn't even hear it breathing. That made him frown.

"Sorin, what are you doing? The sheep are over here!" Marian called.

Sorin pulled his spear free and jabbed at the wolf-like shadow. The butt of his spear hit something solid, but even still, whatever it was, it didn't move.

Frowning, he stepped closer and touched it. Fur. But it was cold.

After another second, Sorin froze. This thing wasn't just wolf-like; it *was* a wolf. A dead one, carelessly strung across the bushes upwind from the sheep. All he needed to see was the gleam of dark puddled at the base of the bushes to know the wolf wasn't here by coincidence. Grabbing it by the scruff, Sorin hauled the massive beast out of the brush and back towards the others.

"What on earth..." Calin began as he neared.

Sorin tossed the wolf's body the last foot, putting it and its cause of death on full display. "Here's what's wrong with the sheep," he said.

With the wolf's body so near, the sheep let out high bleats of panic and streamed into their pen in a state of complete pandemonium. The watchmen closest helped as best they could, but Sorin's attention remained fixed on the wolf. It had been a beautiful creature, the gleam of its dappled gray fur like starlight, bordering on being majestic in the twilight. Yet someone had killed it without mercy.

"Someone scattered the sheep on purpose," he said.

"Why?" Calin said, an edge in his voice. "It's not like anyone was trying to steal them."

Marian frowned. "Unless it was a ruse to get the watch out of town. This happened the night of Master Florin's murder too."

"But it's happened several times, and nothing happened any of those times," Calin pointed out.

Sorin's pulse clipped along faster. "Unless those were just to make us relax and not think anything of them."

Calin stared at him, going ashen. "The sheep were a trap?"

All at once, Sorin's heart leapt into his throat. Daciana was back in town. This wasn't—the killer wasn't going after her, was he?

Unable to put his panic into words, Sorin turned to race back to town. He only made it two steps before he stopped, his heart nearly stopping as well. Nelu raced up the fell.

Nelu was one of the men he'd sent to guard Daciana when he'd left.

His worst nightmare was sketching itself in front of his eyes. "Oh no," he choked out before racing forward, meeting Nelu halfway. "What is it?"

Nelu was winded, but he gasped out, "We've been searching everywhere, but we can't find her."

Panic like Sorin had never suffered seized his chest, squeezing so hard spots of light flashed through his vision. His question came out in a near shout, echoing off the fell. "What do you mean you can't find her?"

The men behind him went silent.

"She's not in the workshop, the garden, the compound, or her house. She didn't get called out in an emergency. No one saw her leave the workshop. She's just gone." Nelu shook his head, a frantic panic in his eyes. "She couldn't have gone out to gather herbs or something, could she?"

"No," he said, shaking his head. "She said they can only gather them in the morning."

"Oh," Nelu's eyes widened and he pulled a wooden vial lid from his pocket and held it out to him, "we found this in the workshop. There was shattered glass on the floor, but it wasn't enough glass for a jar. Those are the only things we've been able to find, but I don't know if they mean anything."

Sorin took the lid and sniffed. The musty scent was almost familiar, but he couldn't place it.

Calin took it from him and sniffed. His eyes went wide. "My wife takes this, every night before she goes to bed."

"What?" Sorin demanded.

"She struggles to sleep, so the apothecaries give her a drink that smells like this, just not as strong. Within a couple hours, she's out."

Sorin stared, the pieces falling into place and paint a horrifying picture. "A sedative."

"You think Daciana was drugged?" Marian asked. He turned to Nelu. "We sent you straight to the workshop when we left."

"I know, but a horse got loose in the streets, and we paused to help catch it. It only took maybe ten minutes."

Light-headedness nearly overwhelmed Sorin.

"It was another diversion," Marian said, voice grim. "To keep us away."

A pained expression twisted Nelu's face as he ran a hand through his hair. "I'm so sorry, Sorin. We messed up. Because of that, I have to report that as of an hour ago, Daciana went missing."

One second Sorin stared Nelu in the face, and the next he sat on the ground, not sure how he'd gotten there.

"Sorin!" Calin said, hauling him to his feet. "I know how you feel, but you've got to keep it together."

For one second, Sorin was sure the person responsible had to be Elder Aurel. Then he recalled Daciana's distress about Ionel's lie. He'd refused to accept the idea before, but she'd gone there, had a confrontation with his uncle, and had vanished in less than an hour.

That couldn't possibly be a coincidence.

"Ionel," he barked, making the watchmen gathered around him freeze. "When you were searching for Daciana, did you see him?"

"Ionel?" Nelu paused, face scrunching in thought. "I think... When we arrived at the workshop, he was leaving town with his supply cart. I didn't think anything of it but... oh."

"What?"

"Ionel is always carting things off to other villages and such, so I thought nothing of him doing so today. But he's a day early. Why do you ask?"

Sorin almost couldn't breathe.

"We can't panic, Sorin," Marian said, clasping his shoulder in a firm, steadying grip.

Sorin's knees wobbled as he fought to stay upright. It made him sick, but Daciana was right. She'd figured it out, and because he'd been in denial, he hadn't put it together in time. "It's Ionel. He took her."

"What? That doesn't make sense."

"It does," Sorin said, staring at his watchmen. "Daciana went to his house earlier to search for clues. She suspected it was him but wanted to be sure. He lied about the tisane he gave me and the others, and she caught him."

Everyone stared at him with a mix of alarm and horror.

"I didn't believe her when she told me—I didn't want to." Sorin palmed his forehead, berating himself for doing that and proceeding to leave her unprotected. "I told her the tisane had too much flavor, but she told Ionel that it had been too sweet. He agreed with her, and when she asked him which kind of herb it'd been, he said it was ginseng."

Marian paled. "Ginseng is bitter."

"Yes." Sorin met his gaze, the pain ripping through his chest reflected in the man's expression. "And there's only one reason Ionel would've lied."

"The lack of clues," someone murmured, their shock apparent even in their voice.

"But if Daciana found out," Calin said, "why would he kidnap her? Wouldn't it make more sense for him to...you know?"

"Of course it does," Sorin said. "But when those bandits attacked, they weren't trying to kill her."

Marian's eyes widened. "Right. They wanted to abduct her."

"Which means there's something else going on, something bigger than just trying to murder his family," Sorin said, shuddering at the idea of Ionel—his uncle, of all people—doing any of the things it seemed that he had, in fact, done. He shook that away. Every second counted here. Pointing at a few of the watchmen, he said, "You four help Cornel search for and clear out any more dead wolves."

"What about Daciana?"

"I'm going to find her," he said, heading in the direction of the village. He beckoned to Marian. "You're the best tracker out of all of us, and I need your help."

Marian nodded, falling in step with him as he moved, setting off for the village at a rapid pace. "Absolutely, sir."

"The rest of you get back to the village. If Ionel returns before we do, you arrest him on the spot, understand?"

"Yes, sir!"

The conviction in their voices made him wince. Many of the watchmen were close to Ionel, so he was sure this was as painful for them as it was for him.

However, to his surprise, ensuring Daciana's safety mattered more than preserving his love for his uncle, and his watchmen seemed to agree. It made his stomach clench that this was what it had taken for him to accept the reality that his uncle was a killer and an abductor. It felt like a twisted nightmare, but this was real. All the signs had been there, and because he hadn't wanted to see them, someone he loved was in danger.

Sorin wanted to retch. He was numb. He felt puny and insignificant, too unremarkable to be squaring off against such an overwhelming challenge.

Even still, Sorin wasn't about to let Ionel go free after everything he'd done.

Sorin returned to the village at the same second Liviu did. His cousin stared at him in shock, but Sorin didn't have a second to waste.

Less than a minute later, Liviu caught up with him. "What's happened? You look like you've seen a ghost."

"It's pretty darn close," Sorin said, unsure whether he was angry or just exhausted. "Hey, I know this will be a chore, but come to the compound and help me get everyone together, all right?"

Liviu quirked an eyebrow. "Uh, okay?" Prodding his horse forward, he hurried for the stables.

"Sorin, time is of the essence," Marian warned.

"I know, but there's one thing I have to confirm before we go. You go to the stables and get the horses and anything else you think we'll need."

Marian nodded, and Sorin hurried to the compound. The others questioned him and Liviu as they rounded them all up, but he barely even noticed. When they had everyone, they joined them in the room where Daciana had saved all their lives. Most of the family was there with varying degrees of nerves or wariness on their faces. The elder already directed fiery glares his way, but Sorin ignored him.

"What is this about?" Ecaterina demanded.

His mom hushed her with a glare. "Sorin?"

For a long moment, Sorin couldn't speak. Then he took a deep breath and forced himself to. "Everyone who was poisoned, what did that tisane Ionel gave you taste like?"

His family shared a few baffled expressions, but his mom said, "Weird. It was like it had too much flavor."

"Yeah, that tisane was awful," one of his cousins said.

Aunt Raluca shuddered. "Yes, I've never had something that terrible before."

The others murmured in agreement, watching Sorin expectantly.

"And those of you without magic, did he ever give you that tisane?"

Slowly, Liviu and the others shook their heads. There was his proof; Daciana had been right.

"Why are you asking about tisane?" Liviu asked, his tone not scornful, something Sorin was still adjusting to.

"Because that tisane was supposed to be the lethal dose of poison that killed all of us who had magic."

Every head in the room snapped to him. Liviu and Andrei stared in shock. Ecaterina paled, speechless for once. Even Elder Aurel's glare lost its fire.

"It was Ionel," Sorin said, the words leaving a foul taste in his mouth like slugs leaving trails of slime. "Daciana discovered it, and she's the one who put the pieces together. She tricked him into lying, and the only reason Ionel would need to lie about the tisane was if he was guilty. However, Ionel realized she figured it out, and now both of them are missing."

Every face in the room was pale by the time he finished, even Elder Aurel's. Andrei in particular turned ashen, and Sorin hoped he wasn't about to pass out.

"My son...?" Elder Aurel murmured, swaying. One of Sorin's uncles, Bogdan, quickly fetched a chair and sat him in it before he could collapse.

Ecaterina gasped and clapped her hands over her mouth. "Wait, he was the one who— He gave me recipes to use for dinners with everyone— I couldn't figure out how everyone was being poisoned, but there were so many herbs in them and the apothecary said—" Her eyes went wide, her hands grabbing at her hair, and what she said next came out in a near whisper. "He used me?" A sob burst out of her, and her husband immediately pulled her to him.

"I just brought you together so you would finally know who did this," Sorin explained before heading for the doors. Now he could search for Daciana.

Andrei raced up, grabbing his hand and catching him by surprise. "Sorin, I'm so sorry. Daciana said helping her sneak into Ionel's house wouldn't be dangerous. I didn't really believe her, but I helped her anyway. If I'd known this would happen, I wouldn't have—" Emotion cut him off, but he wrestled against it, trying to force his tears away. "I'm so sorry."

Narcisa approached, her face pale, but she nudged Andrei. "No one blames you."

"It's not your fault," Sorin said firmly, clasping Andrei's hand. "Daciana's remarkably stubborn, so she would've found a way in, with or without your help. Plus, she already suspected Ionel but didn't want to accuse him because she knew it would do this—" He gestured to the room, where his family openly grieved. "And I'm sure she wanted to keep you away in case something did happen so Ionel wouldn't come after you too."

Andrei swallowed, still pale and grief-stricken. "You're going to find her, right?"

Even Narcisa turned to Sorin, the plea in her blue eyes startling.

Sorin nodded, his resolve firm. Nothing short of the world ending would stop him.

"Is there anything we can do?" Liviu asked, pale but more steady than most of his cousins.

Sorin almost said no, but he knew what he needed to ask. "There is one thing. If Ionel comes back before me, you make sure you stop him."

Without a moment's hesitation, Liviu nodded, one firm dip of his head.

"Go get her," his mom said, sorrow on her face but determined resolution burning in her eyes.

With a final nod, Sorin left, meeting Marian by the compound gates with two horses.

"Can you track in the dark?" Sorin asked after vaulting onto his horse's back.

"The moon will be out, so we'll be fine," the man replied.

They hurried out of town, Sorin's heart beating so hard, it hurt. If Ionel hurt Daciana in any way, he wouldn't let the man off unscathed. He didn't care if Ionel was family or not; what he'd done was wrong.

The tracks from Ionel's wagon were easy enough to follow out of town, even after they'd left the main road and dismounted from their horses while they walked through the brush. As they followed the trail, darkness fell, surrounding them on all sides, but the stars and moonlight broke through to light their way.

After nearly two miles, they were forced to stop. Even though they were in the woods, ahead of them lay a massive intersection of lines, wagon tracks weaving through each other in several different directions.

Marian huffed. "Great."

Sorin swallowed, heart pounding. There were easily a dozen sets of tracks, but only one of them led to Daciana. If they picked the wrong one or took too long, he might never see her again.

32

Daciana didn't have any idea what time it was when she came back around. The valerian root had been effective in knocking her out, but since she wasn't in the habit of taking it, it was only so effective at keeping her asleep. Even still, it left her in a kind of haze, a state of near blissful fogginess. However, she knew she was trapped somewhere dark, and she was quite uncomfortable, which made the fogginess a little less blissful. Things kept bumping and jostling around her, the jolts jostling the floor beneath her making her hips and shoulders ache. Perhaps she was in a wagon. She couldn't be sure, and her memories were too hazy for her to remember much past the valerian root.

As the valerian root wore off, more details returned—memories of her discovery, of Ionel, of the truth—and she was able to piece things back together.

She'd expected to find herself bound, but she was not. Rather, she'd been stashed amongst other cargo with a tarp thrown over the top, which explained the sounds and darkness. For half a second, she debated attempting to run; the cart was so weighed down her driver most likely wouldn't notice so long as she remained quiet. However, running would not guarantee the safety of those she held dear, so instead, she attempted to find a more comfortable position.

It occurred to her that Sorin would, without a doubt, be searching for her. She didn't know if she'd be able to escape later or not, but at the very least, she had information he needed: Ionel was plotting something, something big enough it would be possible to destroy Highfell entirely. Regardless of whether or not she could escape, Sorin needed that information.

Digging through her satchel, still anchored over her shoulder, she tugged a bundle of dried herbs free. Feverfew. It bit at her to do this, but it was the best clue she could leave. Staying quiet, she maneuvered herself closer to the wagon's edge, squirming a little and smacking her ankle against the corner of a crate. She winced but ignored the pain as she dropped the bundle of herbs over the side of the wagon.

Sorin grit his teeth as he and Marian backtracked for the third time. They'd had to resort to following each track one by one, and the two they'd followed so far had only been promising until Marian could isolate them.

Then, it immediately became apparent they were too old to have been Ionel.

"I know this isn't fun," Marian said, somehow picking up on Sorin's agitation despite being bent over with his eyes practically on the ground, "but if Ionel wanted her dead, he would've left you a body."

That chilled Sorin to the bone, but he knew his second-in-command was right. Ionel wouldn't have squirreled away a dead body, especially since he would've wanted to leave it as a warning.

Even still, the silence of the night and the monotony of Marian's work encouraged Sorin's thoughts to wander, and he kept imagining the horrible things Ionel could've done since snatching her.

As Marian identified the next set of wagon tracks, he briefly glanced at Sorin. "Don't worry, sir. Your Daciana is a tough lady. She'll be all right."

Sorin scanned the forest around them. "I know." He didn't even notice that his second-in-command had called Daciana 'your Daciana.'

By the time the wagon stopped and Ionel hauled Daciana out of it, the sunrise had just begun in the east, staining the sky with faint pinks and purples. Her legs were shaky from the drug, but Ionel dragged her into a hut that seemed to be carved into the grassy hillside itself without giving her much chance to use them.

Once they were inside, he dumped her onto a tiny cot in a damp corner.

"Here's where you'll be working for the next while," he said, waving a hand at the space. "Every tool you'll need is here, and you can work with the herbs I've acquired for you. There'll be more brought soon, so you'll have to work fast."

Daciana said nothing as she stared around at her meager conditions.

"And in case you think about escaping, remember..." Ionel produced the vial of hemlock once again. "You even try to leave, and I'll make good on my promise. Understand?"

She nodded, and he left without another word. Heavy locks clicked into place, the clacks seeming to echo.

Daciana allowed her gaze to drift across the room, and she actually studied her surroundings. The room was tiny, even smaller than Liviu and Felicia's hut. There was a ventilation hatch high on one side and a tiny sunroof of sorts in the ceiling, and that, besides the smoldering embers in the little hearth, was all the light she had. Apothecary tools were piled on a small, makeshift worktable, and there were rows of jars containing various herbs along the short wall between the hearth and bed. It was obvious Ionel must have been planning to abduct her for some time. This was too well-prepared to mean otherwise.

After a moment more, Daciana found the strength to get to her feet. If she had to work in order to keep Sorin and her family safe, then she'd better get started. Even still, as she began sorting through the herbs— some fresher than others—tears rained on her lap without her permission. She wiped them away, but they returned immediately, forcing her to acknowledge the pain lodged in her chest, sharp and ragged like she'd been stabbed and ripped open.

Her parents must be worried sick, and she dreaded the idea of what her younger brothers were going through. And Sorin— Her heart shuddered to imagine what he must be enduring. He'd said he'd be fine with Ionel being the killer because he had her, but at that moment, he'd lost them both. She missed him bitterly, but she was even more terrified of what would happen if she defied Ionel. After all, she was well acquainted with the deep, echoing pain of being lonely, and if she misstepped now, she would ensure either her or Sorin would carry that pain for the rest of their lives.

She didn't want to cry; she didn't have time to. However, once it'd begun, she couldn't make it stop.

All at once, she remembered what Sorin had said after their run-in with the bandits: 'Crying when you're scared isn't stupid; it's just a reaction. My mom says crying is like taking the lid off a boiling pot. It doesn't get rid of the heat, but it takes away the pressure so you can. So if you need to cry, you should.'

Hearing his voice in her head made her crumble, the pain and fear that surged at the idea she might never see him again flooding her and leaving her unable to think beyond those emotions.

However, once she surrendered and let herself cry, it was just like when Sorin had held her and given her the space to get her emotions out: eventually, the tears dried and her mind began to work, her thinking more clear. Now that the emotions were out of the way, she could think.

She studied her conditions again.

A chimney stood over the hearth, and the smoke would be a bit of a giveaway; it might even help Sorin find her. However, with the addition of the ventilation hatch, Sorin might be able to follow his nose. The steam had to get out somehow, so Ionel couldn't fault her for opening it. She couldn't leave, but if Sorin was able to find her, she could at least warn him, and with any luck Ionel wouldn't figure it out until it was too late. If she remained here, Ionel couldn't make good on his threat.

Scrubbing at her cheeks, she dragged her little stool beneath the little hatch. The rectangle was only slightly bigger than her hand, but she pushed it open. It gave gradually, grinding in protest as she forced it to move. It sent streams of dirt raining onto her boots in retaliation, but she barely noticed.

Once that was done, she hopped down and pulled the first batch of herbs that would need to be steamed towards the fire. It was time she made a trail for Sorin to follow. Somehow, they would stop Ionel for good.

Smiling a little to herself, Daciana studied the wood piled near the stove, the sheer amount a sure sign Ionel intended to work her like a slave. After a couple minutes, she found a few pieces that weren't as dried as the rest and added them to the fire. A smile touched her face as flames burst from the embers, enthusiastically biting at the green wood and sending up extra smoke.

By the time the sunrise began, Sorin's back was killing him. However, they'd reached the tenth trail; if this also ended up being a dud, there were only two more paths to follow, and one of them led to Daciana. Sorin was no longer riding his horse, both him and the mare too exhausted for that.

As they followed after Marian, Sorin absentmindedly rubbed her nose. "Just a little longer, all right? Then you can sleep and eat."

She nickered softly in response.

All at once, Marian straightened. "Sorin," he said, turning around.

Sorin stared at him, taking a minute to figure out what the man was doing. Marian held something in his palm, something he wanted Sorin to see. He walked closer, his breath hitching in his throat.

It was a little bundle of herbs, and after a moment, he recognized it as feverfew, an herb he'd watched Daciana collect before.

"What are the odds of finding something like this out in the wild, eh?" Marian said, depositing it into Sorin's palm. "And these tracks are fresh—the freshest ones yet."

"Daciana?"

Marian grinned. "I'm pretty sure."

Sorin's heart quivered with life for the first time since last night.

They followed it for a while longer before Marian turned and dropped a bundle of chamomile into Sorin's palm. This was followed by another little bundle of peculiar herbs he didn't recognize, most likely one of the uncommon ones Daciana cultivated in her master's garden.

Marian handed that to him with a triumphant smile. "See? I told you your Daciana is as clever as a fox."

Sorin carefully brushed the dirt and mud from each bundle of herbs before pocketing them to hide the pleasure that had surged through him at the compliment to Daciana. With any luck, she'd still be able to make use of the herbs.

Daciana had left them a couple more bundles, and after about an hour, Sorin spotted a hillside dead ahead. A thin curling tail of smoke rose above it, and if he squinted, the outline of a door could just be seen amongst the foliage. Plus, the faint smell of herbs lingered on the wind.

Daciana. Sorin was sure.

Handing Marian the reins of his horse, he instructed him to stay out of sight before stalking through the trees, keeping his eyes peeled and ears tuned for the slightest sign of another person—or worse, Ionel.

There was no one, and shortly, he arrived at the door held fast by heavy bolts. The scent of herbs was strong, powerful and clear.

Doing his utmost to keep his excitement at bay, Sorin unbolted the door, having to fight in order to get each of the rusted bolts to slide. There was nothing but silence from inside, but Sorin took a deep breath and cautiously opened the door.

The room inside was dark and dingy, but after a moment of scrutinizing the hovel, his gaze fell on the beautiful, pale-faced, dark-haired young woman kneeling in front of the hearth, frozen in the act of stoking a rather smoky fire. She stared with wide eyes, but when their gazes met, she smiled.

"Sorin," she cried, and he'd never been so relieved to hear his own name.

Sorin entered and instantly shut the door, just in case. Daciana crossed the room in four strides and threw herself into his arms.

33

Daciana closed her eyes, savoring the waves of safety that just came with Sorin whenever he was near. He'd found her much sooner than she'd expected, but she didn't care. She was so happy to see him, her heart was ready to burst with relief. Even though just the day before she'd been unsure of her feelings about him, in that instant she knew that she loved him.

"Thank you," she murmured. "Thank you."

"You made it easy to get here as fast as possible," he replied, holding her tight enough to confirm her worry that he'd been frantic.

She pulled back a little, just enough to see his face.

His gaze roved over her, and she knew he hunted for injuries. "He didn't hurt you, did he?"

"I'm fine in that regard," she said. "I'm so sorry, Sorin. I didn't want to go with Ionel, but if I hadn't, he said he would kill you and my family."

"Don't apologize. I would've done the same. But I wondered how he managed it." He checked her over one more time before relief touched his eyes. "The important thing is that you're safe."

She shook her head. "But you're not. Ionel said if I attempted to escape, he'd kill you and my family still. He'll poison you with hemlock, and I wouldn't be able to save you. There isn't an antidote. So I can't leave."

The relief vanished. "What?"

"He mentioned something when he threatened me, something about destroying the village. I don't know what he's planning on doing, but I think it's something big and drastic."

His brow furrowed.

"However, he said if I complied, he'd minimize the damage. So you have to let me do what I can, and leave me here so you can go stop whatever he's planning." It took all of her willpower not to look away from his eyes where the pain from earlier had returned. "Please, Sorin."

He closed his eyes, his brow scrunched up, the expression breaking her heart. "Daci, what if he lied?"

"And what if he didn't?" she said, her hands tightening on his arms. "We can't risk it. I want to go with you, but I don't want anyone to die either. So please, go stop him. I'll be okay."

Sorin met her gaze, and she hated that he was in so much pain. "All right. I'll stop him as soon as I can. So don't...do anything reckless, okay?"

She nodded.

He slowly let her go, stepping back and leaving cold air in his place.

Daciana dug her nails into her palms to keep herself still. She was sure if she changed her mind—if she raced after him—Sorin would take her with him in a heartbeat. Him leaving her in Ionel's hands was taking a lot of his strength, which meant she needed to be strong too.

Sorin made it to the door, his hand on the doorknob, before he stopped.

Daciana bit her lip to keep quiet.

All at once, Sorin turned and strode back with such a determined expression she thought he would take her by force.

"Sorin wait," she began.

The next second, he tenderly cupped her face and pressed his lips to hers. A pleasant kind of shock raced through her before the world shrank down to just him. It was a brief moment—a painfully brief few seconds—but for that moment, she was warm and safe. It felt like everything would turn out okay.

Sorin pulled back, touching his forehead to hers. His breaths were a bit ragged as his gaze intertwined with hers. "I wanted you to know how much I love you. No matter what happens."

She managed to nod, not trusting the tightness of her throat to allow her to speak without crying.

He brushed a thumb over her cheek before kissing her again. Then he stepped back.

Her heart shattered, but she did her best to hold back her tears. If she cried, he might feel the need to stay, and she couldn't risk that.

Yet, as he opened the door, she decided to take one risk. "Sorin?"

Immediately, he stopped and met her gaze.

"I-I love you," she managed, digging her nails deeper into her palms to keep herself in check. "I just... I just wanted you to know."

He smiled a little, but she could tell his heart was breaking. Finally, he turned and left, the thud of the door shutting behind him and the locks sliding back in place making the tears she'd held back spill down her cheeks.

The hardest choice Sorin had ever made was to walk out that door and leave Daciana in Ionel's hands. He'd come to save her; he'd come to take her to a place where she wouldn't have to be scared. And he couldn't do it.

As he made his way back to Marian and the horses in a daze, he questioned why Daciana had left him a trail to follow if she'd already known she would remain where she was. A flash of anger burned through his chest.

However, as fast as it had appeared, it was snuffed out. Daciana had, more than likely, led him to her for two reasons: so that Sorin would know she was safe and to warn him about Ionel. Even though he hated leaving her, he knew where she was and that she was as okay as she could be in her current situation. For the first time in hours, he could breathe again.

"Was she not there?" Marian asked, a hint of distress in his eyes.

Sorin couldn't keep himself from gazing back at the hovel where Daciana remained. "She is," he managed, his voice quiet. "But Ionel threatened to kill not only me but her family if she escaped, so she refuses to leave."

Marian was silent only for a moment. "Then we stop him."

Sorin nodded, doing his best to focus on that. Daciana was frightened; he'd seen it in her face and felt it in the tightness of her shoulders. Despite that, she chose to remain in a place of danger to protect the people she loved and give him a chance to stop his uncle for good. She was being strong—which meant he needed to do the same.

Shaking his head to get himself to focus, he said, "When Ionel abducted her, he let something slip. She said he's planning something— from the sound of it, I think he's going to attack the village."

Marian frowned. "We need to hurry."

Sorin nodded, but out of the corner of his eye, he spied faint smoke trails rising into the sky from the nearby woods. His eyes narrowed as he analyzed them. "Wait here for another minute."

Marian nodded, and Sorin crept in the direction of the smoke, moving slow and staying quiet.

After several minutes, he crouched and moved in closer. A few moments later, a sound touched his ears, making him pause, and it took him a second to identify it: snoring. Brow furrowing, Sorin followed the sound.

A short while later, he came across a swath of the forest that had been hastily cleared, the tree stumps cut in jagged patterns with some of them still weeping thin, glistening beads of sap. From behind the safety of his bush, Sorin stared, eyes wide. In the clearing were men, several men, settled around burnt-out campfires. It only took Sorin a second to recognize them as the Thornwood Fell bandits. The bandits didn't stay out in the open like this—the second unusual thing they'd done recently. If the bandits had made a habit of staying out in the open like this, they would've been rendered extinct a long time ago. The bandits being here like this meant they were on the hunt.

After a few more minutes of study, Sorin was about to creep away when two men unexpectedly emerged from the lone tent in the middle of the pack. One—massive and wearing the largest wolf pelt Sorin had ever beheld—he didn't recognize. The other Sorin did: Ionel.

Because of the early hour and the stillness of the woods, Sorin could just make out their conversation.

"You worry too much," the massive bandit said. "We haven't ever been able to get our hands into your village—of course we're going to be there."

Ionel didn't seem happy anyway. "Remember our deal, Boian. There can't be any mistakes, and you can't get carried away."

The bandit—Boian, Sorin supposed—waved a dismissive hand. "Don't worry about our part. Worry about yours. Otherwise tomorrow might end up going a bit differently than you've planned. If we don't get something there, we know where you've locked that girl up. Several of my tribe would enjoy a prize like that, you know, and not just because we need medicine. I myself am in need of a new mate—and I like spirited girls. Especially young ones."

Sorin nearly retched.

"Don't even think about it, Boian. She belongs to me."

Sorin didn't like that any better.

The bandit laughed, loud and carefree. "If you keep your end of the bargain, she will be. Otherwise, we'll take what you owe us—we've already paid for this deal with blood. Remember that, Ionel."

Sorin shuddered before creeping away. He couldn't risk staying and hearing anymore, but he had a disturbingly clear picture of his uncle's plan, and it was a matter of life and death he get back to the village. Immediately.

Ionel would use the bandits to seize the village—Sorin was sure they planned on doing some plundering, and what they couldn't find in money and food, they'd take in women and kids. More than likely, Ionel planned on killing most of his family too, though he couldn't safely say if it would be strictly magical or nonmagical.

Sorin didn't care either way—it was his job to stop his uncle. No matter how much that stung.

When he reached Marian, he explained the situation in as few words as possible, and the two of them promptly struck out for the village. There wasn't a moment to lose.

Daciana was in serious danger, worse than either of them had realized. If Sorin was too slow or failed to stop his uncle, then he was positive they would never see each other again.

Despite how long it'd taken to find Daciana, the return trip to the village was so short, it was almost laughable.

Ionel had her imprisoned closer to the village than he'd imagined, though he'd taken a long and twisted path to get there. Sorin and Marian sent their horses back to the stables before calling the entire watch together.

Calin, not seeming to care at all about manners, looked Sorin up and down with distaste. "Where is Daciana? You were gone all night and didn't find her?"

The exhaustion from being awake and stressed the entire night was sinking in, and Sorin couldn't hide his irritation. "Of course I found her."

Calin's eyes widened in exasperation. "Then where is she?"

Sorin huffed at him and waited until the entire watch was

assembled—a little more than fifty men all together—before he explained what had happened and what he'd learned because of Daciana's sacrifice.

Varying degrees of stress crossed most of the men's faces, and Sorin honestly couldn't say if it was because of Daciana's situation or Ionel's betrayal. Perhaps it was both.

"That said, Ionel is working with the Thornwood Fell bandits too, and he's going to bring them here. Tomorrow. I'm pretty sure they're planning to siege the village."

"What?" a few men hissed out, and Sorin saw that they too warred against the same pain jabbing his heart.

"I'm not exactly sure, but I imagine the goal is to get rid of—at the very least—the magical members of the head family. At worst, it's to destroy this place and turn it into some kind of stronghold with Ionel at its head."

"So what are we going to do?" Marian asked, already sharpening the edges of his lance.

Sorin glanced around at all of them. "We need every man who can fight to prepare to do so. If we want to protect our homes and our families, we're going to have to fight. This is war."

Marian nodded and issued orders. They didn't have much time, but they would have to make it work regardless. None of the villages had been able to defeat the Thornwood Fell bandits, but in order to protect Highfell, they would have to find a way to do exactly that. How would—

All at once, Sorin recalled when Daciana had reached out to other apothecaries for help with her herb stores, and how those apothecaries had rushed to her aid.

Their village as a whole wasn't as well connected with their neighbors, Riverbend and Stagwick, but even still, they weren't enemies either. All three of them held the bandits as a common enemy.

"Marian," he called, his mind racing with possibility. "I have another idea."

His second-in-command turned. "Yes?"

"Send messengers to the nearby villages. I'll write the missives, but we need to let them know our situation and ask for their help."

Marian drew up short. "But we've never— They'll want something in return."

"I know. However, if the three villages work together, then with our combined might, we might be able to stop the Thornwood Fell bandits for good—at the very least, we can deal them a serious blow. They'll think twice before ever coming back. Our villages have never aligned before, but this seems as good a time as any, and we can worry about the consequences after."

After another second's hesitation, Marian agreed.

As Sorin hastily scrawled the two notes, one for each watch leader of the villages, he didn't have a clue how either neighbor would respond, if they would at all. However, it was worth a shot. The Thornwood Fell bandits played dirty—but in a situation like this, Sorin did too. There was a lot he had to protect, and he would protect it, no matter what it took.

34

The village was a hive of activity before the sun had even fully risen. Because of the nature of the situation, and the fact the Thornwood Fell bandits were so nearby, no one was allowed in or out—the farmers with livestock had been ordered to bring all their animals within the safety of the walls, an order that hadn't been given out in some time, which had caused some protest. Sorin, however, didn't care. It was better to be alive than dead because he'd been afraid of what others would say about his choices. Even if that meant he had to weave through baffled sheep that kept trying to duck into people's houses.

Once the necessary tasks were delegated, Sorin hurried to his family's compound. In the past, the few times the village had been under attack, the magical members of the head family had spearheaded the fighting. While those whose magic was strong enough had joined the fight, most of its current bearers were children and under the age of fifteen, so Sorin wasn't allowing them to fight unless it became absolutely necessary. Besides, surviving this would take more than a handful of people who could manipulate the elements.

Today—probably because of the news—most of his family was in the main house. Sorin ducked past the elder (who let him know in no uncertain terms what he thought about that) and went straight to Liviu.

His cousin was paler than usual, and Sorin remembered with a pang that Felicia and his daughter were in Riverbend. Liviu had no way to get to them for the foreseeable future. However, there wasn't much he could do.

"You look awful," Liviu remarked, the corners of his mouth trying to rise.

Sorin waved away the attempt at humor. "It's been a while since I've slept, but that's not important. I need your help."

Liviu was on his feet in an instant, some life returning to his face. "Oh yeah?" As they walked out of the main house, he lowered his voice and said, "Thanks for getting me out of there. Elder Aurel has been going on and on about how the magic will save us all morning."

Sorin pulled a face.

Liviu made a knowing face in return. "So what is it about? It's not Daciana, is it?"

Sorin shook his head. "No. I wish it was, but it's something else. The last time the village was raided, our family fought it off with just our magic, but there's no way that's going to happen this time."

A guarded expression appeared on Liviu's face. "Don't tell me this is you asking me to watch over the village if something happens to you."

That drew Sorin up short, and the idea of making that request was so absurd, he smiled.

Then he shook his head again. "No. I'm not planning on dying. Not so long as Daci's out there."

That got his cousin to smile too.

"Do you remember when we were kids and how you and Andrei always made those contraptions that would get us into trouble?"

"Like the bug bomb?" An excited light danced in Liviu's eyes.

"Yeah, exactly like that," Sorin said, fighting against the pull of nostalgia. "Do you think we could make things like that to help us fight?"

Liviu paused, brow furrowed. "Sure, that's sounds manageable. But why?"

"The magic of our family has protected us for a long time, but there's no way we can do that how we used to. Most of the people in our family who can use it have too weak of an ability or are simply too young. We all know we need to figure out how to get by without depending on it so much, and we need to figure it out now. I can't take on all those bandits by myself, regardless of what the elder believes."

Liviu dipped his head, a thoughtful frown on his face. "You're right. Okay, tell me what you want, and I'll get the others to help me out."

Sorin smiled a little.

"Sorin!" Marian called, getting his attention.

"What is it?"

"The messengers just returned," the man said, holding up two letters.

Sorin took them, ripping them open without hesitation. They were brief and to the point. However, the responses made him grin.

"They agreed?" Marian asked, hope flickering to life in his eyes.

Sorin grinned. "They're preparing to come immediately."

"You asked the other villages for help?" Liviu asked, eyes wide.

He nodded. "Riverbend and Stagwick, the two closest, and the two that have also experienced a lot of trouble with those bandits. The apothecaries of those places and Daciana are close, and in times of crisis, they always jump to each other's aid, which has saved our skins more times than we probably even realize. I figured if the apothecaries could do that, then perhaps in a situation like this, so could we."

His cousin stared for a moment before smiling. "You know, I wasn't sure about your offer before, but I think I might take you up on it."

It took Sorin a second to realize he referred to moving his little family into the village.

"This place is already changing, and with you at its head, I think it will change for the better," Liviu said. "Anyway, I'll find you later when

I have something to show you."

Sorin nodded, and his cousin raced back into the compound. He glanced at the notes again. "They should be arriving within the next couple hours. Inform the watchmen at the gate."

Marian took off.

Sorin headed for the watchhouse. He was exhausted, but there wasn't time for him to rest yet. Soon, he hoped, but not yet.

After Sorin left, Daciana thought she would be taut as a rope until his eventual return, but the monotony of staying in one room with little to occupy her mind made it difficult to remain so tense. She wouldn't call herself relaxed—it was more that she was too exhausted to be stressed. She even managed to fall asleep for an hour or so. The anxiety in her chest still lingered, but it had eased some since she'd been able to warn Sorin about his uncle. While it wasn't at all exciting or dramatic, she was fighting in her own way instead of being dead weight. At the very least, she'd have extra medicine to help the village when all was said and done.

That said, when Ionel let himself into the miserable little shack around midday, Daciana's chest cinched tight.

"So, you are still here," he said, almost like he'd hoped she would run.

She didn't dignify his accusation with a response.

After a moment more, he came and inspected her work. With a frown, he said, "You haven't done much."

Doing her best not to let how that agitated her show, Daciana said, "Preparing herbs takes a while. I'm doing the best I can." It certainly took more than half a day, but she didn't think it was wise to say anything that would risk irritating him. As it was, she'd distilled a few batches of herbs and laid out several more to dry; she'd done a considerable amount of work and was tempted to inform him of that.

However, like it or not, Daciana wouldn't have been able to fight Ionel if he decided to seriously attack her. He was twice her size, nearly three times as broad, and he held nearly every card in this game of theirs. So, she decided it was in her best interest (and Sorin's and her family's) to be as demure as possible. That too, though not exhilarating or flashy, was still fighting.

"I see," Ionel grumbled. Even still, as he studied the herbs drying in the racks he'd provided, he said nothing more about it, so she supposed her answer was okay.

He stayed silent for so long, Daciana risked a glance at him. While he had the appearance of studying her drying herbs, there was a distance in his eyes, a far away look that told her his mind was elsewhere.

Not for the first time, she was struck with the painful thought that Ionel didn't seem like a murderer, despite the fact he'd confessed to being exactly that. He almost seemed....normal. A part of her mind still wanted to maintain the foolish belief he wasn't guilty, and this was just some bad dream. Yet she knew better.

Several minutes passed in tense silence before Ionel turned to face her, something in his eyes leaving her unsettled.

"I came to ask you a question," he said, a bite in his voice.

Her heart thrummed, chest cinching tighter. She didn't like the tone of his voice. It took a lot of control to remind herself to be demure instead of defending herself.

"The village seems to be preparing for war," he continued. "When they should know nothing about what's coming for them."

She froze, her hands hovering over the stalks she'd been preparing to distill. Would Ionel consider her informing the village resistance? Had she made a horrible mistake?

"I–is it?" she managed.

"You're still here, which means my nephew must've come here."

She didn't move.

"He did, didn't he?" he snapped, taking a step forward.

Daciana flinched, unintentionally, but maybe that was for the best. Perhaps he would calm if he believed he was in complete control.

He stalked closer, and Daciana shrank back. It also wasn't an intentional movement. As he continued to step towards her, she remembered with sharp poignancy that Ionel had smashed in Master Florin's skull. He'd killed his best friend and drugged his own family—his siblings and nieces and nephews—with the hope they would die. He was holding her here by threatening to kill more people, people she held dear. Was he angry enough he would kill her too?

In all the years she'd seen him around the village, she'd never once been scared of him. Yet as he cornered her, her back pressed as against the wall as it could be, she trembled; she couldn't even think.

"He came and found you, didn't he?" he asked again, this time his voice no more than a hiss. His eyes gleamed with the cruel intensity of a predator. "And you told him about my plans."

Daciana couldn't even move, let alone speak. She doubted anything she said would calm him anyway.

"Why do you keep ruining everything?" He grabbed her arms in an excruciatingly tight grip and shook her once, hard enough it made her dizzy. "If it hadn't been for you, everything would've been perfect. We would all be happy if not for you!"

Despite her fear, she'd been around his family enough for that to finally make her bite back. "No they wouldn't. They would never be happy with someone like you in charge. You may not be as deluded as your father, but you're just as cruel as he is."

He released her arms, but the reprieve lasted for only a second. He wrapped one of his large hands around her throat—not tight enough to choke her, but firm enough to render her immobile.

Her heart went still. She wasn't sure she was breathing.

Was he about to kill her? The malice smoldering in his eyes made it horrifyingly clear he wanted to. However, to her surprise, she wasn't afraid to die, even though this would be a miserable way to go—she was terrified of what it would do to Sorin to find her body.

"I'm not going to kill you," Ionel said, his voice a low growl. He shook her again, jarring her neck hard enough she winced. "But I want you to remember that your life is in my hands, and that all it will take to snuff it out is one, little—" For one, horrible, heart-rending second, he squeezed his fist, trapping her throat, cutting off her ability to breathe. Pain and panic flared bright. Then his grip slackened just enough for her to breathe. Her gasp of air was stuttery.

It was at that second she realized she'd grabbed his hand, her nails digging into his flesh.

"So," Ionel continued, the coldness of his tone more frightening than his hand around her neck. "I know you're clever. You're probably thinking you're brave too, but don't you dare forget—" another, breath-stopping squeeze, "—how easy it would be—" a crushing squeeze, "—for me to kill you." He squeezed her throat again, but this time, he added his other hand and lifted her so her toes barely scraped the ground. He maintained the pressure, his frigid glare boring into her as the most excruciating pain she'd ever felt racked through her. "Never compare me to that man again. Understand?"

She frantically clawed at him, her ears ringing and vision blurring.

Ionel released her, dumping her onto the ground at his feet. She coughed and gasped for air, her head pounding. Ionel spun on his heel and left, slamming the door so hard, a couple thin streams of dirt rained from the ceiling.

Her vision cleared, but her ears still rang, deafening like bells pealed over her head. Her throat burned; raw, vivid pain seared straight to her soul. Ionel hadn't killed her, but the realization that she'd hovered over the brink of death left her shivering and shaking uncontrollably. Even still, when she glanced at her quaking hands, there was some satisfaction at the sight of his blood smeared over her fingers. He'd not escaped unscathed either.

Forcing herself to move, she washed the memory of him off her hands before she cupped her hands to her raw throat, the chill of her skin and the water soothing against the burning pain. She didn't regret her decision to stay, but the reality that Ionel could very well ensure there was no happy future for her and Sorin was so real, it felt like she was choking all over again.

"Sorin," she managed through her throbbing throat. Every word that passed through her throat made it burn anew, and her voice was so raspy she could barely hear it. "Sorin, please help me."

Daciana knew he wasn't coming; he couldn't. However, saying his name helped her hold on to some of the fragments of safety he'd brought with him, cocooning them around her breaking heart. Hearing his name chased away some of her fear, even if it did sharpen the ache that came from missing him.

However, in the time they'd spent together, he hadn't let her down once. He'd risked his life to protect her from the bandits before—he'd been willing to fight the elder for her sake. So, despite the terror and pain battering her, she trusted without a doubt that the instant he could, Sorin would be there. After all, he'd sworn he wouldn't ever abandon her, no matter if it was to either physically or the dark depths of loneliness, and she believed him with every inch of her soul.

35

Sorin gazed over the forest from where he stood atop the village wall, his mind racing with all the preparations they'd done as well as the ones they still needed to do. Even though sunset drew near, there was still so much to be done.

However, as a lilting, accented voice brushed his ears, he glanced back at a group of women making arrows with Daciana's mom leading them. He knew now where Daciana's determination came from, and if they survived this, he didn't think Daciana and her family would remain outcasts any longer. As it turned out, growing up on the plains had made Daciana's mom a fount of information regarding warding off invaders.

Calin leaned against the wall next to him, squinting as he stared. "Hey there's the first of our neighbors." He pointed towards the group of men emerging from the trees, all of them clad in almost gleaming leather armor. "It's about time."

Sorin didn't say anything as he studied them. As the day had worn on, his weary thoughts had constantly returned to Daciana. Perhaps it was the exhaustion from having gotten next to no sleep over the last two days, but she was in every thought in his mind, and every time she resurfaced, he couldn't help but send up another prayer for her safety. If anything happened to her now, he wouldn't be able to forgive himself.

As it was, he'd been second-guessing his decision to leave her in Ionel's hands for the better part of the day. Since they'd been so on guard for Ionel, he doubted the man would've had a chance to make good on his threat to her; Sorin was sure he would've been able to keep her, her family, and himself safe. He should've just taken her with him.

However, it was too late, and he had no use for regret.

As he turned to leave the wall, he sent up what was no doubt his thousandth prayer. Then he descended to meet the new arrivals.

Sorin hadn't been sure what to expect from the other villages, but when the first man strode through the front gate—a large, burly man with a few scars across his nose and chin—and pinned him with an intense stare and a massive grin, for a second, Sorin questioned whether his idea was as sound as he'd believed.

"So, you must be the Sorin I keep hearing about," the man said, his effortlessly loud voice echoing off the wall. "I almost mistook you for a child!"

Sorin stared for a second before being snapped back to reality when the man clapped him on the back hard enough it stung, and he stumbled. "Y-you know about me?"

"'Course I do," the man said, the volume of his voice almost unbearable when one stood right next to him. "I make it my business to know things like that."

"Nicolae," one of his guards murmured, shooting him a pointed look. "You're being too loud already."

"Am I?" The man, Nicolae, frowned before shrugging and continuing to speak as he had before. "We're still outside. Anyway, Sorin, I take it you're in charge here?"

"For better or for worse," Sorin replied.

Nicolae let out a raucous laugh, but before he could say anything, a new, significantly quieter voice cut in:

"I thought it was you I heard, Nicolae. You're still only capable of being either loud or silent, eh?" The owner of the voice stepped around Nicolae, getting Sorin's attention in an instant.

This man was a shadow compared to Nicolae—both shorter and more slender—but there was still something about him that put Sorin on edge. He was significantly younger than Nicolae, but Sorin sensed the man was a bit older than him, though it was hard to pinpoint his age to what seemed like a safe range.

Plus, there was an assessing gleam in his eye that convinced Sorin in an instant the man already knew the entire layout of the village and everything there was to know about him, even though there was no way the man could have that information. At least, he thought there was no way the man could know any of that.

While Nicolae charged in like a boar, Razvan slithered in like a snake, and in truth, both of the men made Sorin a bit uneasy. However, he'd made his bed, and now he had to sleep in it.

Nicolae let out another one of those laughs and clapped the newcomer on the shoulder hard enough he had to take a step forward. "Razvan! I didn't know you were coming!"

Razvan looked askance at Nicolae while he adjusted his armor. "Of course we came. The Thornwood Fell bandits have been hazing my village for the last month. I'm not letting a chance to give it back to them slip past me."

Sorin realized after a second that Razvan had to be the other watch leader. "You both arrived quickly,"

Razvan shot Sorin an appreciative look. "And you catch on quickly."

Sorin waited for another comment about his age.

Fortunately, if Razvan had thought one, he had the tact not to say it. "You're in charge here, right? My men and I are the group from Stagwick. Where should I settle them?"

Sorin took a deep breath, studying the two men before him, both of them waiting with expectant expressions. Somehow, between the three of them, they would have to figure out how to stop Ionel and the bandits.

However, before he could say a word, a familiar but startlingly feminine voice from amongst the men caught Sorin's attention. Nicolae and Razvan glanced back as well.

Master Crina appeared from amongst the men, straightening her bag as she beelined it for Sorin. She smiled, the expression catching him off-guard.

"Y-you're back," he managed when she approached.

Master Crina put her hands on her hips, beaming. "Of course. We apothecaries stick together in a crisis like this."

Razvan lifted an eyebrow, that gleam reappearing in his eyes as he crossed his arms. "I didn't realize you'd tagged along, Master Crina. Your poor apprentices must have their hands full."

"They're fine. I'm more worried about Daci, so I came to help her out. Just take me to where she's setting up, Sorin, and I'll go right to her. I'm sure she'll need every set of hands she can get."

Sorin stared, a dozen emotions churning through him, each one making him sicker than the one before it.

Master Crina frowned. "What is it? Nothing...happened to her, did it?"

A heavy sigh slipped out of Sorin. "Calin, show their men where to go."

His friend nodded and stepped away.

Sorin beckoned Master Crina, Nicolae, and Razvan to follow. "It's a long story, so you'd better come with me."

After seeing the force of nature that Master Crina was, it was difficult for Sorin to witness her quiet, almost diminutive. It was obvious the knowledge of Daciana's ordeal ate at her like a disease, but less obvious was how he could ease her pain. With Daciana, when she was upset, comforting her was easy. With Master Crina, he was at a complete loss.

"Excuse me," came a soft, lilting voice, making Sorin turn.

Standing in the doorway of the guardhouse—where Sorin had led Master Crina, Razvan, and Nicolae—was Daciana's mother, one of her unique, colorful shawls wrapped around her thin shoulders. Compared to the last time he'd seen the woman, it was obvious to him she'd slept as little as he had since her daughter's abduction.

"Hello, ma'am," Razvan said with a dip of his head that bordered on being elegant. "Is there something we can help you with?"

"I came to tell you," her gaze on Sorin, "we've finished making the arrows out of all the supplies we have. We've decided to set up a clinic to be safe. That said, I heard Master Crina had arrived, and while we know a few things here and there, I'm sure we would benefit from having the guidance of an actual apothecary." Her gaze dropped, making her seem absolutely exhausted. "I just want to be busy until this is over."

Master Crina all but leapt to her feet. "You're right. So do I." The two women left the building, leaving Sorin with Nicolae and Razvan.

"Who was that?" Nicolae asked.

"Daciana's mother," Sorin explained.

"I can't say for sure since I haven't met this lady of yours," Razvan began, leaning back against the nearest desk, "but if she grew up surrounded by women like those, then I'm sure she's all right."

Nicolae clapped a hand on Sorin's shoulder, clearly trying to be gentle but somehow managing to buckle Sorin's knees regardless. "That's the truth. And women like them are always the ones worth fighting for. Don't worry kid, we're going to put an end to these bandits once and for all, and you'll be with your lady by sunset tomorrow. Bet on it."

Sorin did his best to put the emotions aside. There was a time and place, and now wasn't it. There was too much at stake for him to lose himself in the mists of his sorrows.

"So, what's your plan?" Razvan asked.

"We're going to stay inside the village walls unless we have to be out of them. We're in the process of digging ditches." And the couple magical family members with that power were making themselves useful.

"That'll give us an advantage," the man mused.

"Practically pick them off at our leisure," Nicolae said with a massive grin.

"And if they're prepared for an assault from above?" Razvan asked.

"My cousins are working on that," Sorin said. "I figured the bandits would have something up their sleeves, so we'll have a few tricks of our own. I just don't know what they are yet."

"You got any magic folk?"

"A handful, is all. Most of them are too young or too weak."

"Same for us," Nicolae said, his expression disturbingly serious.

"A few is better than none in a situation like this," Razvan said. "We'd better tour the battlements and make any last minute adjustments."

Sorin led the way.

The three of them talked in low murmurs as they moved along the wall, and even though Sorin knew there were multiple ditches dug around the village, they were so well concealed they were invisible in the twilight. Which, he supposed, was the point.

Once he'd finished showing the other two everything, they glanced at each other and nodded.

"You've done a good job kid," Nicolae barked. "Better than I thought someone your age would do!"

Razvan looked askance at the man. "There was a reason he was the one appointed. Don't you ever use your head?"

Sorin almost smiled at the two of them, but then Liviu shouted his name, getting him to turn.

"You've gotta come see what we cooked up," Liviu said, eyes bright. "It's some of our best stuff yet."

Sorin glanced at the two men with him, who followed with amused expressions. As they took in Liviu and Andrei's plans, the three of them shared a look, and though they'd only known each other for a few hours, Sorin felt like he stood next to the two older brothers he'd never had. They'd approved many of their plans and offered suggestions only when they deemed it necessary.

For the first time since he'd left Daciana in that little prison, hope gleamed on the horizon, as bright and welcome as the sun. Stopping Ionel for good might be possible after all.

As the thinnest trickles of morning sunlight made their way into Daciana's little prison, she roused herself from her restless sleep and did her best to shove off the sickening hunger pangs plaguing her. Since the day Ionel had attacked her, he hadn't returned, and there was no food in her hut. She'd munched on a couple of the plants that were safe to eat, but they only worked to keep the hunger at bay. However, she wasn't dead, which was a victory.

Her throat was still tender and throbbed when touched, and she was certain it was bruised. However, that was the extent of her injuries thus far.

Taking a deep breath, she put aside her aches and woes, brushed a spider off herself, and turned to her work. Despite the fact she'd been locked up for a couple days, it felt like she'd made barely any progress even though she knew she had. There were a few medicines and tonics ready for use.

As she stoked the fire, bringing the flames back to life, she was struck by a powerful impression something was about to happen, something enormous she couldn't see, and Sorin stood right in the middle of it. Despite the fact she couldn't see out of her prison, she stared eastward, in the direction she thought the village was based off the sunrise. Something colossal was about to happen—presumably whatever it was Ionel had planned.

The sensation was so powerful, it held Daciana fast, the scents of herbs and woodsmoke fading from her awareness. Something large enough to change the course of history was about to break loose—she could feel it like the tingles that came before a lightning strike.

Clasping her hands and lowering her head, she prayed like she'd never prayed before. It was okay if she was hurt and hungry and scared— so long as Sorin was okay, she didn't need anything else. So long as he was all right, that would be enough.

36

A young watchman roused Sorin at daybreak when the sun was just lighting the sky, little more than a band of pale light over the dark eastern mountains.

"They're coming, sir. The bandits have been spotted through the trees."

He was up in an instant, surprisingly alert and focused given how little he'd slept. However, as soon as they won here, he could finally save Daciana and this whole nightmare would end at last, and that gave him all the energy he needed.

He didn't bother to wait until he'd finished strapping his armor on before he was on the wall with Nicolae and Razvan. "Which direction?"

"East, mostly," Razvan said. "I imagine they want to wait until the sun clears the mountains so they can attack with the light in our eyes."

Sorin snapped the last buckle closed and secured his sword and spear. "It'll take more than that. Is everything ready?"

Nicolae grinned. "You bet. It's gonna take a miracle for those beasts to win."

He nodded, a grim kind of excitement taking hold of him. When he'd resigned himself to the position of watch leader, he'd never once imagined being at the head of a full-on war.

However, now that he was here, he wasn't about to lose.

After the three of them confirmed a few more things, they separated and took their places at three different spots along the wall. Sorin stood at the front with his men, watching the tree line that was just beginning to be dotted with thin rays of golden morning light. Nicolae and Razvan were both with their men on the sides, making their defenses complete.

"Ready for this?" Calin murmured from Sorin's left.

Sorin didn't answer that. Instead, he said, "Where were they spotted at?"

Calin pointed, and then Sorin was able to make out the bandits. They moved slowly, both because of the trees and because they carried large objects Sorin couldn't make out. "It seems they're prepared to be attacked from above. We figure those things they're carrying must be some kind of shield or something like it."

Sorin studied the bandits as they steadily drew near. Liviu's contraptions would come in handy sooner than he'd expected.

A few tense minutes later, Sorin spotted someone who made his stomach turn. As the first bandits cleared the trees, a massive man with a large wolf pelt draped across his shoulders stepped out, hanging back by the trees, just out of arrow range. With him, standing right at his side, was Ionel.

In seconds, dread swept through Sorin's men like an illness, a plague that sapped their resolve. He glanced sideways at them. "Don't lose heart. How we feel about him doesn't matter—if you let those feelings hold you back, he'll destroy our village, our families, and our freedom without hesitation."

He spied several glances thrown in his direction, but he kept his gaze on the bandits and Ionel. It was gradual, but the dread dissipated like the night's darkness before the brilliance of the morning sun. There wasn't room for Sorin to hold onto the love for his uncle pulsing through his heart. Ionel had cast his lot. If Sorin wanted to save both Daciana and his home, he had to cast his as well.

If Ionel believed Sorin would show him mercy after what he'd done, the man was dead wrong.

Rows of bandits marched from the trees, coming to a halt only a few paces from the tree line, surrounding the entire city. A shiver of fear zipped through his chest at the sheer number of them. Between them and the village stood the slight hill that sloped up to the village, where the concealed pit traps lurked, invisible even to Sorin's eyes. For the longest, most awful minutes of his life, they simply stood there, watching each other.

Ionel took a few steps ahead of his company. "Sorin," he shouted, his voice ringing over the hill and village, sweeping past Sorin like a frigid wind, "surrender the village, and no one will get hurt. I will lead the village and our family into a new age."

Sorin stepped closer to the wall's edge, keeping himself mostly behind the tall parapets, just in case. "You threw your family away the day you decided we were better off dead—and we've extended you that same courtesy. We aren't interested in an age brought about through bloodshed and subterfuge—that will only lead to more of the same. We will create a new age ourselves, and we will do it without you."

Ionel's face darkened. "I'm the one who taught you to think like that."

Sorin didn't dignify that with a response. He was bitterly aware of who'd taught it to him.

"This is your final warning!" Ionel called after a long pause. "If you don't surrender, we'll burn the entire village to the ground with everyone in it!"

"Go ahead and try!" Sorin snarled back.

Face twisting, Ionel turned on his heel and marched back to the bandit leader.

Sorin returned to his place as well.

"That was cold," Calin said with a bit of a laugh.

Marian was a bit pale, but he smiled. "But those were words to be proud of."

Despite the situation, a grim smile touched Sorin's mouth. "Well, he did try and kill me—and he abducted the woman I love. I'm not exactly happy with him."

A few of his men chuckled, but most just flashed grim smiles. In order to win, they would need to remember what lay at stake if they lost.

The bandits resumed their march.

"Here they come," Marian murmured, drawing an arrow from his quiver, getting the rest of the watchmen to follow suit. Yet he waited, watching the bandits' advance. It was good to be ready, but there was no sense in wasting arrows.

Almost as if to prove Sorin's point, one of the bandit groups stumbled into a pitfall, the entire group getting dragged inside, and their shield—which now that Sorin could see them better, appeared to be made from logs that had been halved and scraped out—trapped them below. A shudder raced down his spine at the sound of men suffering and dying, but he held firm. It was either that or listen to innocent women and children make those sounds instead.

Three more groups succumbed to the traps seconds after the first, and the rest began picking their way with greater care. The traps were strewn about haphazardly without rhyme or reason, making no clear pattern, and the ground erupted under the feet of a several groups, sucking them to their deaths.

The groups lucky enough not to fall prey to the pits made it in range.

"Give Liviu the signal," Sorin said.

One of the younger watchmen—a boy who wasn't yet seventeen—scampered to the lower level.

Sorin eyed the bandits' progress, waiting another second before calling out, "Ready your bows!"

His men all had an arrow in their hands, their bows ready.

Sorin caught a glimpse of Ionel smirking, something about his uncle's confidence making him smirk as well.

A second later, the first of the small barrels rolled down the hillside. The bandits didn't notice them at first, and only looked up when the little barrels reached them. One of the bandits kicked a barrel that rolled at him, and the little, shabby barrel burst open, throwing wet, sludge-like mud everywhere, making him laugh.

"That's it?" Calin asked, shooting Sorin a nervous glance.

"Wait for it," he replied.

Liviu's team had made hastily and poorly crafted barrels with one purpose in mind: that most of them would only last long enough to travel a brief distance before bursting open and throwing their contents—in this case, wet mud—everywhere. It was a ramped-up version of a trick they'd used to play as children on people they didn't like, though those barrels had contained bugs or spiders instead. Sorin almost smiled at the chaotic memories he wasn't entirely sure he was proud of, but he quickly shook them off. Now wasn't the time.

The barrels burst open within seconds of each other, splattering the hillside in thick patches of glistening mud. The bandits, undaunted, continued forward, some even laughing. Then the first one slipped on the mud, taking his entire group down with them, their tree shield spinning out of their hands.

"Release!" Sorin shouted.

The arrows zipped away, finding their targets only seconds later, and that group of bandits was finished in seconds. Sorin heard Razvan and Nicolae giving similar orders to their own men.

Calin whistled.

Ionel's face paled as another wave of mud-barrels tumbled down the hill.

Between the layer of slick mud coating the hillside and the hard ground beneath, the ground between the village and bandits was essentially a sheet of ice.

The bandits who'd made it past the traps slid everywhere, losing hold of their shields and exposing themselves to the sharp bite of arrows.

Sorin glanced at Ionel, who stared at the scene in shock. It struck him with the force of a burning whip that his uncle had expected Sorin to be an easy foe.

Sorin turned away, eyeing Razvan and Nicolae's progress with the bandits. The bandits who'd survived the assault scurried back down the hill, making frantic attempts to escape the arrows. In their panic, many fell prey to the pit traps that had been avoided the first time. Sorin's heart shuddered at the scene, but his village was unharmed.

That was what mattered.

From off to the left, Nicolae shouted, "Is that it?!" followed by a raucous roar of laughter.

Sorin shook his head. Perhaps it would've made for a grander story if the battle had been more intense, but, for him, if this was all it turned out to be, that was more than enough—

"Sorin!" Razvan shouted, startling him from his thoughts. "Ionel's on the run!"

Sorin raced to the wall's edge. The place where his uncle had been stood vacant. The leader of the bandits shouted at his men struggling down the hillside, oblivious to Ionel's desertion.

"Where'd he go?" Sorin demanded, scanning the trees.

"There!" one of his men shouted, pointing.

Sorin leaned over the wall, just managing to catch a glimpse of his uncle before he vanished amongst the trees. His heart stilled. The direction he was going led to— "Daciana."

"What?" Calin asked, brow furrowed.

His heart ignited, burning hot and furious as he glanced back. "Ionel's going after Daciana! Cover me!"

Without wasting a second, Sorin vaulted over the wall, reaching out to the mud below. It launched up, meeting him on his way down. He slid the rest of the way to the ground, hardly even noticing how fast he was going as he hit the ground and slid several feet, having to use his magic to whip himself away from a couple pitfalls.

Once he was on dry ground, he ran, racing faster than he'd ever run before. Ionel was on foot, and if Sorin was fast enough, he might be able to catch the man before he got to Daciana. His uncle had drilled into him that in a hostage situation like this, if things started to go south for the aggressor, there was always a chance of them turning on their hostage. Daciana was practically a sitting duck.

"Sorin! On your left!" Razvan shouted.

Sorin glanced left. The bandit chief raced for him, rage in his eyes. Sorin glowered. He didn't have time for this, but the bandit chief wasn't in arrow range.

Reaching out to the mud, Sorin jerked it forward like a whip, a rope-like strand of it striking the guy across the chest. The man staggered, narrowly avoiding stumbling into a pit, just managing to catch himself. Sorin turned to race on, but the bandit leader lunged, just managing to catch Sorin's leg with the flat of his axe. Sorin fell, half-sliding into one of the pits.

He scrambled to find a hold, just managing to keep the rest of him from sliding down. The bandit leader grinned. Scowling, Sorin flung mud into the man's face, using his magic to make it hold fast.

One of the other bandits spied his leader's trouble and raced their way with a spine-chilling war cry. Rushing, Sorin pulled himself out of the trap. The bandit leader ripped the mud off his face, gasping for air. Before he could recover, Sorin launched forward, plunging his spear through the man's unarmored chest.

There was a flash of light striking metal. He glanced up in time to spot an axe spinning for his face, thrown by the bandit sprinting for them. Sorin began to duck out of the way, but the dying bandit leader grabbed him, arresting his movement. The next second, an arrow rammed into the axe's blade, knocking it just off course. Instead of Sorin's head, it struck his shoulder, the weight making him stagger back. The bandit leader lost his grip and fell into the pit Sorin had narrowly escaped.

Sorin's smarting shoulder would bruise, but at least he wasn't dead.

"Don't worry about the rest of them!" Razvan shouted, making Sorin glance over. The man stood on one of the parapets, a massive bow in his hands. "Go!"

Sorin nodded, a hint of a smile touching his mouth. Jerking his spear free of the dying bandit leader, he raced off into the trees, mentally mapping out the quickest way to Daciana. If he didn't get there before Ionel, she might be dead before he even had a chance to save her.

37

Daciana nearly jumped out of her skin as the door of her prison slammed open, one of the rusted locks bursting free and skittering across the earthen floor. She whirled around, her heart leaping into her throat at the sight of Ionel, his hair askew and his chest heaving. There was a wild light in his eyes, one that made him look anything but human. For the second time since she'd been taken captive, fear exploded in her chest.

As he came at her, he muttered things she couldn't catch or understand, but she distinctly heard him say 'insurance.' Before she could puzzle that out, he approached and caught hold of her hair, grabbing right at the roots. She cried out in pain. He didn't seem to care. Her eyes watered, but he dragged her out the door before she could protest.

"You'll be my ticket," he hissed, shooting her a dark glare. "Sorin won't kill you."

She wanted to snap back at him, but her scalp screamed, the severity of the pain making it a struggle to breathe. It seemed whatever he'd cooked up hadn't gone well, and despite the tears of pain burning her eyes, it made her happy. At least he hadn't gotten his way.

"Ionel!" Sorin shouted, his voice ripping through the forest quiet.

Daciana's heart leapt in her chest.

She didn't even get a chance to glance back before Ionel took off, dragging her with him. She had no choice but to sprint alongside him, doing her utmost not to stumble or fall. Ionel's grip on her hair tightened, the pain so intense tears tracked down her cheeks.

Frantically, with the sound of Sorin racing after them filling her ears, Daciana swiped at her eyes with her free hand. Sorin was here, and she had to get away from Ionel. If she did, Sorin would be free to take care of him. She scanned the undergrowth flashing past. Because of the way Ionel held her, she was stooped over, which made everything ten times harder. All at once, she spotted something that would help. Stinging Nettle.

She reached out, braced for the pain, and jerked free a fistful of stalks. Immediately, sharp needlepoints of bright pain burst across her palm like a dozen bees had stung her all at once. It burned and itched, but she bit her lip and ignored it. Then slapped the nettle against Ionel's hand.

With a bellow of pain and surprise, he released her. Daciana stumbled and tumbled head over heels through the dirt. The pain of stinging nettles wasn't the worst, but its bite was immediate and surprising. The shock of it gave Sorin just enough time. He slid inbetween them, covered in mud and what looked suspiciously like blood, his bloodied spear ready as Ionel turned. There wasn't even a second of hesitation before Ionel lashed out with a weapon she hadn't realized he held.

Daciana furiously swiped at her eyes, clearing the tears so she could see. When she succeeded, she was in time to see Sorin jab at Ionel and the man dodge under his arm, landing a nasty hit to Sorin's ribs. Sorin hit the ground hard, making her wince, but he didn't lose hold of his spear.

Ionel must've been thinking something along those same lines because instead of pressing the attack on Sorin, he grabbed Daciana, hauling her to her feet. A second later, the cold blade of a knife touched her throat. She did her best not to give into the panic that came from him touching her sore neck.

"You stay where you are," Ionel demanded.

Sorin staggered to his feet, his eyes focused on Ionel. Even still, Daciana could tell he was in pain from that last blow. "Leave her out of this," he demanded, panting hard. "This is our fight."

"You have magic, Sorin," Ionel said, taking a slow step back, forcing Daciana to step with him. "You and I both know this is the only way I can win."

Sorin remained still, watching Ionel with a dark glare. "Leave Daciana out of this, and I won't use it. It'll be a fair fight."

"You are going to let me go, otherwise I will kill her," Ionel continued. "Understand? I'll do it."

Daciana met Sorin's gaze, and the fierce determination burning in his eyes strengthened her resolve. She had to get herself out of the way; Sorin wasn't going to make a move so long as she was trapped, and they all knew it.

Daciana tightened her grip on the stinging nettle, her hand so sore and stiff she couldn't make a fist. Even still, she wasn't going to be used as a bartering chip again; she was pretty fed up with that. She slipped her free hand between the knife's blade and her neck before twisting and shoving the stinging nettle into Ionel's face.

Sorin's eyes widened as Ionel released Daciana with a cry that bordered on being a scream, whatever plant she'd shoved into the man's face making his skin break out in an angry red rash. Daciana dove out of the way, and heart clenching, Sorin lunged. He managed to catch his uncle in the leg, biting deep.

He dodged as his uncle swung hard with his own spear, the air ripping past Sorin's skull. Out of the corner of his eye, he noted Daciana backing off, and hopefully she'd get far enough away that Ionel wouldn't try grabbing her again.

As Sorin jabbed and dodged, his mind kept going back to sunny afternoons when Ionel had trained him with the spear, when his uncle had taken Sorin under his wing and taught him how to be a strong fighter, a watchman who could truly protect his home and family. Anger burned through him at the twisted irony of his memories in juxtaposition to his current reality.

Even still, when he spotted an opening in his uncle's defenses, he stabbed, managing to slice through his uncle's unprotected side. Even though Sorin prepared to press the attack, he nearly vomited.

The sensation delayed him by the barest second, and Ionel capitalized on it, sweeping Sorin's feet out from under him. He fell, landing hard on the side Ionel had hit earlier and making nauseating pain spasm through his side.

There was a flash of light on metal in the corner of his vision. He looked up, heart stilling at the sight of Ionel, weapon raised, preparing to deliver what would undoubtedly be a death blow.

All at once, Daciana leapt back into the fray, latching onto Ionel's hair and yanking his head back. The man stumbled, arms flailing as he fought to regain his balance. Sorin tightened his grip on his spear and stabbed upwards. Ionel—presumably because he hadn't expected to do any fighting—didn't wear armor.

Sorin didn't move, almost unable to believe what he'd done until he caught sight of Daciana stepping away from Ionel and running towards him.

He yanked his spear free and backed up, ushering Daciana behind him.

Ionel seemed to have gone numb, the light in his eyes flickering as he stared at the wound in his chest, dark blood rapidly staining his front.

For half a second, Daciana trembled behind him, and Sorin was afraid she'd succumb to her apothecary instincts and try to save Ionel. If she did, he was positive Ionel would kill her instead, so he caught hold of her arm. However, she didn't try and break free. Instead, she hid her face against his back with a shuddering breath and remained safely behind him.

For a long moment, Ionel continued to stare at his wound in a shocked stupor before slowly lifting his head, taking in the two of them, eyeing the way they stood. For one second, the most intense, scalding anger Sorin had ever beheld swept over his face, all of it directed right at him. Without warning, the man turned and raced through the brush.

"No!" Sorin cried, lunging a step forward before Daciana grabbed his arm and dug in her heels, holding him fast. Which, while it hurt, he knew was wise.

The next second, Ionel, arms spread wide, vanished.

As Ionel disappeared as suddenly as if he'd been snatched out of thin air, Daciana realized where they were: the Howling Falls Ravine, a sheer drop off between the fells where more than one soul had plummeted to their demise.

Sorin and Daciana both flinched at the echo of the man hitting the bottom, the narrow ravine making it seem louder than it should have been. They glanced at each other, both pale, before Sorin ventured to the hidden edge of the ravine and stared over the edge. When he returned to her side, she didn't need to ask to know what he'd seen.

She'd never once seen Sorin cry, and he wasn't crying now. However, while his emotions had once been hard for her to read, now that she knew him better, she could see the depth of sorrow lurking beneath the surface. If he'd been any other person, he would've been sobbing.

Ignoring the mud and blood splattered across his front, she hugged him—not touching him with her burning hands—the relief that it was finally over bringing tears to her eyes. With a bit of morbid humor, she supposed she cried enough to cover both of them.

Sorin hugged her back without hesitation, how tightly he pulled her to him communicating far more than he could've with words.

After a few minutes, he pulled back, assessing her from head to toe. He tilted her chin up, and a glare snarled up his face. He must've found the bruises. "He did this to you?"

She nodded before nudging his hand away. "It doesn't matter now, Sorin. It's over, and I'm okay."

"Daci," he whispered, his gaze tracing the bruises on her neck, his voice hushed. "I'm so sorry. We all wanted the situation in my family to change, but I didn't realize Ionel was that desperate. I didn't mean for you to get dragged in either. I'm just so sorry, Daci."

She reached up, gently touching his cheek with the hand that hadn't held the stinging nettle. Even still, that hand had gotten sliced by Ionel's knife, so she had to be careful to avoid getting more blood on him. "Sorin, look at me."

He slowly did, meeting her gaze with eyes filled with such agony, it broke her heart. "It's not your fault. And bruises and cuts heal. Trust me. I really am okay."

He just stared at her, his eyes filled with so much sorrow but also the most tender expression, the intensity of both snatching her breath away a little. He didn't say anything else. Gently, sure he was more injured than he let on, Daciana rose onto her tiptoes and touched her forehead to his. He relaxed a little, lightly pressing back.

After a few moments, he leaned back and met her gaze. "I'm going to change how the village is run, Daci. I'm going to make it so Liviu and Felicia can live here and be safe and happy. I'll make it so Andrei can be your apprentice if he wants to— I'll even make it so Ecaterina can be happy—regardless of whether or not she deserves it."

Despite the situation, that almost made her laugh.

"I want to make sure no one goes through what Ionel did ever again; what happened to him will never happen to another person. My kids will never be treated the way my cousins and I were, regardless of whether or not they have magic. My family's horrible legacy is going to end with me. I swear it."

She smiled. "I know you can do it."

He smiled in return.

Moving fast, she stretched onto her toes once more and kissed him. It tasted like the mud they were both splattered with, but it got Sorin to smile even more.

"We should get back," he said. "Your family and Master Crina are waiting for you."

"Master Crina?" she asked. "What's she doing here?"

"Well, Ionel led the Thornwood Fell bandits against the village, and I—following your example—asked the other villages for help. She came with them, intending to help you."

"You asked the other villages for help? And they came?" she asked, eyes wide. While the apothecaries had been on friendly terms for a long time, the villages they served...hadn't been that way. For a long time.

He nodded, taking what seemed to be a reluctant step back. "I'm sure you'll hear all about it." He dropped his gaze before frowning, and for a second, she didn't get what he stared at. After a moment, she realized he stared at her hands.

"What?" she asked glancing at them.

He lifted an eyebrow. "How can I hold your hand when they're both like that?"

She laughed, and she accommodated him by slipping her arm through his. That seemed to be agreeable because he kissed her forehead. Then they began walking, the sun streaming through the green leaves around them. Despite how that day had gone, magic seemed to dance through the air like something out of a fairytale.

"What was that plant you grabbed?" he asked, eyeing her red and blistered palm.

"Stinging nettle," she said promptly. "It really hurts, but only for the first fifteen or so minutes. The rash will fade within a day or two. However, I figured the pain would be enough to distract him. It's like getting stung by bees when you touch it."

Sorin let out a huff, but it sounded suspiciously like a laugh. "You're a bit crazy, Daci. But that is part of the reason why I love you."

Smiling, she dropped her head on his shoulder for a few seconds. "And you came running after me when I was in trouble, despite the fact I'm a bit crazy. That's part of the reason why I love you."

He kissed her, full on the mouth, before glancing at the sky, a myriad of emotion shifting behind his face.

Her heart was lighter than it'd been in days—though it seemed like it had been years—and the warmth in her chest matched the brightness of the world around them. There was a lot to clean up and deal with, she was sure. There was a lot that would change in the village too, and some of those changes would undoubtedly be more difficult than others. However, with Sorin by her side, Daciana wasn't stressed about the future or being lonely, worries she'd once held tight. Regardless of what happened, she was sure they'd be all right.

38

By the time they returned to the village, the exhaustion from the last three long days and nights coupled with the battle left Sorin battered and aching; however, he was sure most of the exhaustion came from the relief that Daciana was safe. For good. He was drained enough that when Daciana slipped from his grasp and rushed into her parents' arms, he just stopped and watched, not even aware of the smile touching his mouth until Calin nudged him in the ribs.

"Good job, mate," his friend said. "Though if there was any doubt about the rumors of you two dating, it's gonna be gone real fast if you keep wearing that smile."

Sorin's smile disappeared as he whipped his head around. "What?"

To his annoyance, Calin laughed.

Sorin rolled his eyes, but as he returned his attention to Daciana—who was sandwiched between both her brothers now—that smile returned. "I think everybody already knows anyway."

"It was pretty obvious, not gonna lie."

"Lad!" Nicolae's booming voice cut through the noise of the village, nearly startling him out of his skin. The next second, the man clapped Sorin on the shoulder so hard, his knees buckled, making him stagger a couple steps in an attempt to stay upright. "You're still kicking!"

"He won't be for much longer if you knock him around like that," Razvan said with a world-weary sigh. His gaze flicked to the side. "So that's the lady Ionel abducted?"

They all stared in Daciana's direction as Master Crina grabbed both of the young woman's hands and lectured her furiously on the importance of caution and self-care. Daciana just laughed—until Master Crina poked her swollen hand.

"That's right," Sorin said.

Razvan huffed. "He sure didn't let her off easy."

Once again, Sorin's gaze took in the dark bruise on her throat and the cut across her palm from the knife, a spark of anger igniting in his chest at the sight. She'd told him not to worry, and he was trying, but it was difficult to see her blood, to hear the rasp in her voice whenever she spoke, to feel how weak her movements were and realize she probably hadn't eaten since she'd been captured days ago. The idea of anyone doing that to her made him furious, but the fact his own uncle was the guilty party left him livid.

However, Ionel was no longer a part of this world, and a part of Sorin was too miserable to stay angry.

"But she's a fighter," Razvan finished, glancing at Sorin with the hint of a smile tugging on his lips.

"That's true," Nicolae said with a broad grin and a laugh. Then he grew a bit more serious. "We've rounded up most of the bandits that were left. I doubt we got them all, but they should be battered enough we have a chance of stomping them out for good. Plus, there are no serious injuries to report on our side. That's a blessing."

"To be sure," Razvan said, his smile long gone. He seemed to be studying Sorin, and Sorin realized he was getting used to the man doing that. "And Ionel?"

The other two glanced at Sorin, serious expressions on their faces.

"He threw himself down the Howling Falls Ravine," Sorin said, the memory running through his head again and taking another piece of his heart with it.

The others cringed, but it was Razvan who asked, "And you're sure he's dead?"

"Yeah. He was kind of..." Sorin trailed off as he fanned his hands in front of him.

Calin shuddered.

"I suppose it's best to let nature reclaim him," Nicolae said, a serious expression on his face.

Sorin nodded. "We don't bury traitors in the village, so the ravine is the best place for him, I think."

The three of them nodded as well, and Sorin turned his attention back to Daciana. A lot had happened in the last few weeks, but he supposed not all of it had been bad. As he thought that, Liviu entered his field of vision, and he couldn't help noticing his cousin was the happiest Sorin had ever seen him, despite the situation.

Ionel had been the catalyst for changing the village, in a sense, but Sorin desperately wished he'd gone about it in a different way. After all, more people than Ionel had wanted things to change; Sorin and his cousins did too, and if Ionel had taken his stance differently, they all would've stood with him.

They would've still been a family.

However, that wasn't what had happened, and Sorin had to accept what had.

Even still, as Daciana glanced over and caught his eye, both of them smiling in response, he believed things would get better. In time.

Still smiling, Daciana extracted herself from her family and trotted over to him, and the three men with him stepped back. "You're coming with me."

He raised an eyebrow, doing his best to ignore Calin's teasing snicker. "Why?"

With the hand that was smeared with blood from her knife wound, Daciana jabbed him in the side, right between the seams of his armor.

The pain made him double over with a wheeze.

"That's why," she said, still smiling. "And we don't ignore anyone's wounds here, so come on."

Nicolae and Calin laughed, and even Razvan cracked a smile.

Nudging him, Razvan said, "Don't worry; we'll get everything cleaned up. Just be sure to invite us to the wedding, eh? You do owe us, after all, and friendship with someone of such high standing in your village might be satisfactory."

Sorin scowled, his cheeks getting warm, but Daciana distracted him by tugging on his arm, careful of both his side and her own hands. When he caught up with her, she threaded her arm through his again.

"No!" Elder Aurel's voice cut through the din, making the entire square go quiet as he rushed towards him and Daciana. "Sorin, don't you dare take another step."

Sorin instinctively moved so he was between the elder and Daciana.

Even still, Daciana wasn't intimidated. "He needs treatment, Elder Aurel. He may seem all right, but he's not."

The elder barely spared her a glance as he pointed an accusing finger at their linked arms. "But you don't need to behave like this in order to get treated! Our family's legacy is at stake; our reputation!"

Sorin stared, wondering how he'd been cowed into obedience before. At the current second, the elder seemed more petulant than intimidating.

"Why not? This is the woman I'm planning on marrying, after all." He turned to Daciana, whose mouth fell open. "That is all right with you, isn't it? We don't have to get married right away—I'm content to take our time. But you're the person I want to spend the rest of my life with, and I won't be moved on that point."

Tears shone in her eyes, but a grin burst across her face, the tears making her eyes sparkle and his heart melt. "That's absolutely all right!"

"Sorin," the elder snarled.

Sorin shot the elder a glare before he turned and kissed Daciana. On the mouth. In front of what was probably the entire village. And Daciana responded eagerly.

There was some shouting from the elder, some arguing from his family in Sorin and Daciana's favor, and some cheers from his friends—both old and new—but Sorin hardly noticed.

He was satisfied with keeping his attention on Daciana. She was the first thing in his life he'd gotten to choose, and he wouldn't ever let her go.

Epilogue

A light spring breeze blew past, tugging on the flowy skirts of Daciana's new, though borrowed dress. She held it carefully so the hem wouldn't drag through the mud as she approached Master Florin's grave. It was hard to believe it'd been almost an entire year since her master had passed; some days, she woke up expecting him to still be there, waiting for her in the workshop.

However, now that it was spring, two of his greatest wishes had come true: he was survived by the Lady's Bedstraw he'd wanted planted over him, and as of today, Daciana would officially begin walking the rest of her life with someone by her side. While she hadn't done it for her master, she did hope he would be able to rest easy now that she was no longer alone.

With a bit of a smile, she picked a couple sprigs of the bright yellow flowers decorating his grave and added them to her bouquet with great care. Her master would've been overjoyed.

"Did you get them?" Sorin called from behind her.

Turning, she smiled and showed him the bouquet with its new additions.

A smile illuminated his face, bright as the sun, making Daciana's breath catch in her chest. The days of his dimmed light were far in the past.

Sorin caught hold of her hand as she drew close, and he helped her avoid stepping in a particularly deep patch of mud. Before they left the cemetery, they both paused in front of one of the newer graves: Elder Aurel's.

"Do you really think he would've accepted us?" she asked, glancing at Sorin.

He had a thoughtful frown on his face, a trace of sadness visible behind it. "He was coming around towards the end."

She gave him a little smile before they both continued on, leaving the cemetery. As she departed, her gaze passed over another grave, one only a few months older than Elder Aurel's—Ionel's wife's, Lucia. Not even Daciana had been able to bring herself to tell the woman about what Ionel had done or the true nature of his death. Even still, the woman had seemed to know, though they'd never spoken of it. In a way, it was a mercy she hadn't had to linger long with the knowledge or the pain from her never-ending illness.

However, today, of all days, wasn't when Daciana wanted to dwell on such gloomy thoughts.

Turning her attention back to Sorin, they continued on to the hubbub of the village preparing for what was shaping up to be one of the biggest and most festive weddings they'd had in a long time. Sorin, the instant he'd turned twenty-one, had petitioned for the right to be made elder, and had been unanimously voted in by the senior members of the family. Since then, the village had become even more smitten with him. Though they had warmed up to Daciana too. Eventually. They'd even taken it upon themselves to ensure their wedding was a celebration that wouldn't be forgotten for years to come.

After a moment, Daciana realized Sorin was watching her.

"What?" she asked.

He stared for only a second before his smile returned. "Your mother's dress is beautiful on you, you know."

That made her blush, and she nudged him with her elbow. "And you look handsome as well, Elder. Very dapper in your regalia."

He laughed. He wore one of the traditional, embroidered tunics specific to their village—and she'd gone through the pains of making sure it'd been made with the finest wool. He wore first-rate trousers and boots, and the blue sash that would be part of the ceremony was fastened around his waist. Even though he was no longer part of the watch and no longer wore his flattering leather armor, Daciana thought he was handsome no matter what he wore. That said, he was particularly handsome today. Blue complimented his eyes very well.

Which was why she appreciated that her mother's wedding dress was a striking combination of a beautiful sky blue and a gentle white.

They walked in companionable silence down the hill and into the village. Nicolae could be heard a mile away, and Razvan seemed to be keeping his distance from the man. Even still, Daciana was ecstatic to see both of them and their families again—since the war against Ionel and the Thornwood Fell bandits, they'd all become good friends.

As they neared the center of town where the ceremony would be taking place, she spotted Liviu and his wife, Felicia, animatedly talking with Sorin's parents. Daciana's brothers were with some of Sorin's cousins while Calin fretted over his own pregnant wife, who seemed both amused and annoyed by his excessive attention. Ecaterina was one of the handful of musicians, and Daciana frankly had never even imagined the woman could be so happy. Andrei was near Daciana's parents, where he seemed to be in a losing battle to prevent Liviu and Felicia's baby from throwing fistfuls of dirt everywhere.

Sorin nudged her. "Your apprentice does realize he doesn't need to wear his satchel all the time, right?"

Daciana grinned, glancing at Andrei again, who was indeed wearing his newly acquired satchel and bronze leaf—the mark of a young apprentice—with obvious pride. "The novelty will fade in time."

As she said it, her hand went to her throat, where her own novelty hung—her golden apothecary leaf. She'd traded the mark of a senior apprentice—a silver leaf—for that of a master's some time ago, but it was still surreal. Though it still made her smile when she recalled that one of Sorin's first acts as village elder had been to award it to her, as Elder Aurel had refused.

"There you two are!" Calin said, racing up to the two of them. "We were starting to think you wouldn't make it in time. To your own wedding, even!"

Sorin sighed, but he seemed in good humor. "We had to pay a final visit." He indicated the special flowers in Daciana's bouquet.

Calin's eyes lit up with mischievous humor. "You know, those flowers are supposed to mean—"

"Enough out of you," Sorin said, clamping a hand over his mouth. He glanced at Daciana with a smile. "I'm going to get rid of him, so I'll meet you there. All right?"

She nodded, unable to resist smiling as Sorin hauled his errant friend away.

Her mom noticed her seconds later and hauled her away to be fussed over by her, Sorin's mother, and Master Crina until it was time for the wedding to begin.

Once everyone had gathered, Daciana's dad took her arms, tears in his eyes.

"I couldn't have born seeing you with anyone less worthy than Sorin," he whispered before kissing her forehead.

That made her smile.

Accompanied by the musicians' soft music, he walked her through the crowd to where Sorin waited, his smile softening when he met her gaze. When they reached him, Daciana hugged her dad. Then her dad turned and embraced Sorin, and Daciana couldn't help but be pleased that the two of them got on as well as they did. Especially since her dad had not been amused with the nature of Sorin's proposal.

"You protect her," her dad murmured, looking Sorin in the eye. "Understand?"

Sorin smiled. "I do. And I will."

Daciana grinned.

The ceremony seemed to pass in a complete blur; in truth Daciana hardly remembered most of it. Yet she did remember how she felt. That she would never forget. From this day forward, she would never truly be alone again, no matter what happened.

Nor would she forget how it felt afterwards when she and Sorin smiled at each other and, accompanied by the cheers of those they loved, stepped into their new life together, arm in arm.

The series continues in…

THE WITCH'S DAUGHTER

Coming Soon

Thanks for Reading!

Thank you for picking up this book and tagging along on Sorin and Daciana's adventure! I enjoyed writing it, and I hope you enjoyed reading it. If you did, please consider leaving a review (or even just giving it a rating) on Goodreads or wherever you purchased your copy. It makes all the difference in the world for both me and this book if you do.

And, if you enjoyed the book, please keep an eye out for the next installment! The best way to stay abreast of all my upcoming releases, see behind the scenes, and receive little short stories is to subscribe to my newsletter, which you can find on any of my socials.

Instagram: @bookdragonsnest.com
Facebook: C. S. Doraga

Once again, thank you!

Acknowledgements

Writing out the acknowledgments for a book is a definite sign that my time working with it has come to an end, which always makes me a little bit sad. However, I genuinely loved telling this story and being able to work with new characters and genres. As such, there are several rounds of thanks that must be given.

The first, as always, go to my sisters, Shaylee and Rachel, for their invaluable advice on the book and putting up with me as I crafted the story from beginning to end. They've had a lot more patience with me and my ramblings than I do, I think. The next round of thanks goes to my editor, Kenneth, for his insights and help shaping this story into something truly amazing. The next bit of thanks goes to my team at 100 Covers for gracing this story with its wonderful cover.

The next, and most important, round of thanks goes to God, my Lord and Savior, for continually helping and pushing me on this path, and for the opportunity I have to be able to tell and share my stories. I wouldn't be able to do this without Him.

And lastly, thank you! (That gave me the vibes of those PBS commercials...) Without you, lovely reader, I wouldn't have anybody to tell stories to, so it means all the world to me that you're here with me, and the characters, etc, etc. I hope to see you again soon!

About the Author

    C. S. Doraga is the author of the *Rise of the Empress* series. She grew up in the shadows of the Rocky Mountains with her nose stuck in any book within reach and imagination constantly running wild (to her parents' chagrin, at times). Her favorite author is the amazing Mangaka, Hiromu Arakawa, the author of *Fullmetal Alchemist* and *Silver Spoon*. What little free time she has, she spends playing the *Fire Emblem* video game series and a few, choice others. She has a deep love for the fantastic but also loves mystery and those characters that sit with you long after the story is over.

    She has a bachelor's degree in creative writing from Weber State University and lives in beautiful Northern Utah with her family and two, crazy cats.

Discover the *Rise of the Empress* Series

The first Dragon Kin was supposed to save the world. They failed.

Now the frightened and unsure Imperial Princess has been called to find the second. If she fails, the world is out of chances.

www.ingramcontent.com/pod-product-compliance
Lightning Source LLC
Chambersburg PA
CBHW021454110726
47899CB00001BA/161